The Emperor's Due

Volume One

Fate, Chance, Kings and Desperate Men

Chase

Rika

The mouse darts through a thickly wooded forest, jumping over fallen branches and dodging between stones and roots, almost there... Taking the road would have been faster, but that path lies littered with spying eyes.

Constantly alert, not intending on becoming a meal for a passing hawk or cat, the mouse scurries through a hollow log. Coming out the opposite side it finds a stream blocking its way, trickling around a shady bend.

The mouse looks upriver, eyeing a group of children playing and splashing in the water. It scurries up the bank of the stream towards their shouts and laughter, stopping when it reaches the shore across from them. Quickly peaking around, the mouse takes a step back before sprinting forward and lunging into the moving water.

A few strokes ahead she surfaces, an eleven-year-old girl gasping for air. Deep brown eyes and a button nose are centered between freckled cheeks, and her light brown hair is tightly pulled back exposing mousey ears.

She swims through the other children, no one giving her a second look. Approaching the opposite shore, the girl slips out of the river and sneaks into the trees. Once the shadows conceal her from view, the mouse scampers off again.

Reaching the town's outer wall, it stops to look for something. A few yards away it sees a crack in the base of the wall, barely large enough for a mouse. The stone sides scratch its fur as it scurries through the opening. On the other side the mouse pauses in the shadows, searching the skyline for the castle keep.

Locating the tower looming over the rooftops in the distance, the mouse darts down a back alley towards it.

Abruptly stopping in its tracks, the mouse notices a tomcat slowly inching forward on the wall above. In a flash, the cat pounces, its claws extended and hungry jaws open.

Suddenly, the feline finds itself on the shoulder of a little girl, her eyes pinched into a menacing glare. It leaps off the girl's shoulder and sprints away down the alley, clearly startled by the encounter.

Turning back towards the tower, the mouse takes off again. It enters the courtyard through the front gate of the keep, easily slipping between the steel bars of the lowered portcullis. Ahead, it sees a wooden door with a small gap between the bottom and floor. The mouse exhales, trying to flatten itself as it squeezes through the tight opening.

Dashing down a cold stone hall, the mouse searches for the passage leading to the dungeon. Around a corner and up a corridor it runs, until reaching a descent of stairs. It makes its way down, each step requiring a leap of faith and a hard fall.

A cell lined room waits at the bottom of the stairwell. Wooden doors reinforced with steel frames keep the prisoners securely confined. A passageway lays open on the far end of the room, leading to the dungeon. The mouse hugs the wall, running through the shadows towards the opening.

Entering the dungeon, the mouse sees torture devices hanging along the wall and suspended from the ceiling. A gaoler stands before a bloody man, grinning as his prisoner desperately pleads and begs.

Taking one of the man's fingers in his hand, the gaoler snaps it backwards, laughing maniacally before screaming into the man's face.

"Tell me what you know!"

"I swear… I swear…. I know nothing…" The prisoner begs. "Please, please, please… I swear it…"

"LIAR!" The gaoler yells, taking a finger from the man's other hand and bending it back until it cracks.

"Why…? Why…? Why…?" The prisoner cries.

"You want to tell me what you know… You want to tell me while you still have the ability to do so…" The gaoler turns, walking to a table at the back of the room. Inspecting a pair of pliers, he sadistically begins explaining to the man, "First, I am going to remove each of your teeth. Then, if you still don't want to talk, I am going to rip out your tongue."

"What do you want to know? Please, please don't. I swear… I'll tell you anything you want!"

Smiling, as he turns around with pliers in hand, the gaoler takes a step towards the man. But something makes him suddenly stop, a sharp pinch just below the ribs. Looking down, he finds the little girl staring up at him, then notices the hilt of her dagger buried deep in his torso.

He swings wildly as he falls to the floor, but the dying gaoler only strikes air, and the girl quickly darts out of the room.

"You can't leave me!" The prisoner cries after her. "Come back!"

She ducks around the top of the staircase, ignoring the man's pleas. Then the mouse scampers back to the courtyard, sneaking through the front gate and taking off sprinting towards the town docks.

As it scurries along the shadowed edge of an alley, the mouse hears a group of guards running towards it, making their way to the keep. It ducks out of sight, watching the men stumbling over each other and shouting to hurry as they rush past.

Reaching the docks, the mouse surveys the ships at port, looking for the right one. Spotting the light elven schooner anchored at the end of the dock, the mouse runs up just as the last of its cargo is being loaded. Jumping quickly, it hops onto the edge of a wooden crate being carried onto the boat and rides it to the cargo hold.

Below the deck, the mouse looks around, searching for the correct box. It finds a crate in the far corner of the room, a black X burned onto the side. Darting towards the box, the mouse sees a tiny hole cut into the base, just big enough for it to squeeze through.

Once inside, the little girl feels around and gets accustomed to her surroundings. She finds a few flasks of water and a stash of honey cakes that had been hidden for her long trip home.

She takes a sip of water, then enjoys an entire cake. Its sweetness courses through her, as she revels at the success of her first assignment.

Jia

Jia walks alone, sauntering through the moonless night. Unafraid...

To be afraid, what a foreign concept... She thinks, as she continues along the path. *What could hurt me?*

The warmth of the day fades fast as she strolls along the curving road, a coal black cloak covering her face. Jia thinks back to the inn she had passed at sunset, and to the innkeeper imploring her to stay.

For him to tell me not to leave, that the road isn't safe... Laughable. If he only knew... What do I have to fear?

Lately, there had been reports of a gang patrolling the lonely road at night, robbing and killing everyone they come across. But the city watch had been unwilling to aid in stopping them, claiming it lies outside their responsibility.

The innkeeper had looked her over as she sat and enjoyed a drink, no doubt assuming she would make an easy target for the brigands. A pretty young girl wandering unarmed and alone on the road at night.

Jia had stayed long enough to have a glass of wine. But now, as the temperature continues to drop and the darkness deepens, she finds herself wishing she had lingered for another.

Opening the delicate hinged door of her lantern, she blows towards the flame inside. The gentle breeze coaxes it to dance, twirling and swirling and licking the air. The fire grows larger, radiating more warmth from behind its beautiful stained glass encasing.

Father would not approve... She thinks, a slight grin slipping across her face. *Walking all alone, along the road at night... Inviting trouble... But it is the incompetence of his patrols that allows these atrocities to happen! He is the Lord of the City of Light, Warlord of the Firelands! Every attack on his people, every theft in his domain, every crime committed with impunity, makes him look pitiful and powerless.*

She would never allow herself to look so weak…

Jia hears a cry, piercing through the darkness. She picks up her pace, moving quickly down the road. Light begins to come into view ahead, torches and lamps swaying and swinging in the night. A tattered gang circles an ornate wooden carriage, tied behind two black steeds.

A well-dressed man lies dead on the ground. Another traveler kneels next to him, fat and wrapped in fine silk, displaying the desperate gestures of someone entreating for his life.

An especially large and rough member of the bandits steps forward, slicing the begging man's head off with a powerful swing. Drops of crimson drip from the edge of his long curved sword.

He reaches inside the cabin door and pulls out a young maid. Laughing, he throws her towards his men. The brigands begin ripping at her clothes and jeering at her screams.

As the men shout and grab at the girl, Jia steps into the light. The men don't acknowledge her presence at first, too busy fighting over their prize.

The large bandit, who appears to be the leader, notices her first.

"What do we have here, another treat?" He asks, sniffing the air with a flourish. "A young girl shouldn't be walking alone at night…" Shooting a look at a few of the men, they begin to move around her.

So this ugly oaf is in charge? Jia thinks, surveying the advancing gang.

Setting her lantern gently on the ground, she stands up straight and lowers her hood. The men's eyes widen as they see the striking features of her face. Her tan skin and delicate smile, accentuated by fiery eyes, whose amber color reflects the flames as if smoldering with some untold energy.

Her dark black hair is held back by a thick golden band, a large ruby shining at its center. The firelight plays across the planes of the gem, catching the leader's eye.

"This one is mine!" He yells, handing his sword to one of the men, before rushing quickly towards her with his fists clenched.

As the grunt approaches, Jia gently gestures to the lantern. Sensing her movement, the flame inside suddenly leaps out, landing on the ground before springing up to her palm.

Jia raises her hand, smiling at the dancing flame. It jumps from her hand to shoulder, somehow leaving her hair and cloak unburnt.

The leader halts, and the men step back, bewildered by the animated fire. Their fear humors Jia, making her sweetly laugh. She notices the mesmerized men are too distracted to see the maid crawling away to safety in a nearby bush, making Jia giggle even louder.

"Witch…" A man stammers.

"Kill this demon!" The leader yells out, "Slit her throat!"

The group advances with their weapons raised. But Jia continues laughing, each breath she takes causing the flame on her shoulder to grow taller.

One of the men springs forward with a dagger in hand, aiming for Jia's heart. But a blast of flame bursts from her shoulder, generated by the blazing figure now dancing wildly in the night.

Fire starts flowing with the wind as the air around Jia ignites, engulfing her in a raging firestorm. Quickly expanding, the flames circle the men around her, jets reaching out and devouring all who try to flee.

The leader is the last left standing, dumbfounded and dazed by the spectacle before him. The brigands who had once been his cohorts, now lay strewn about, burning and writhing on the ground. All the while Jia smiles, staring into his eyes.

When the blaze around her subsides, she holds a hand out, inviting the flame to return. It leaps forward to her palm and gleefully spins, reveling in the destruction.

The leader falls to his knees, vacantly staring at her and unable to say a word, the dancing flame reflecting in his eyes.

Her smile fades for a moment, as Jia brings the fire to her lips and gently blows towards the man. The flame extends from her outreached hand, carried by her breath, lighting up the night as it consumes the man in fiery despair.

His screams ring out between the trees, echoing into the darkness.

The flame retracts, then spins in her hand, performing a victory dance of sorts. Jia watches as it becomes a miniature version of herself, leaping across her palm and grinning up at her as it twirls.

Jia smiles back, then reaches down, letting the flame jump into its lantern. The glowing colors emanating from behind the stained glass cast eerie designs on the dead men around her.

As the bushes behind the carriage begin rustling, Jia remembers the girl. Moving towards the trees, she pushes aside some brush, exposing her hiding place.

"It's okay," Jia says. "I'm not going to hurt you. Come out."

The girl hesitantly approaches, tears streaming from her eyes. Bowing at Jia's feet, she begins speaking in a hushed tone. "You saved me, my lady. I will follow you anywhere, my life is yours."

Jia smirks, looking at the dead man dressed in silk. "Who was he to you?" She asks.

"He was my master." The girl answers.

"Your master?" Jia replies, indignantly. "Slavery is illegal in the Firelands."

"We are from the River Realm, my lady. My master was coming to the City of Light for business. Then we were to travel to the Great City, for the prince's tourney"

"Well, you are free now. No more talk of masters or their plans." Jia reaches into her cloak, taking out a leather coin pouch. She removes a small fistful of rubies and gold from the purse, handing them to the girl.

"My lady, I cannot accept this." The girl says, trying to push the currency back to Jia.

"You are going to take it, and you are going to keep it. Use the gold for travel expenses. Hold the rubies close, use them to start a new life, one of your choosing…" Jia says, before turning and pointing to the southern sky. "I want you to take one of these horses and ride south to the next town, Xaolov. The Flying City is harbored above there now. I want you to board first thing tomorrow morning and ride to the next stop, the Pillar. You can easily find a place to live there. Those gems will keep a roof over your head and food in your belly for years."

"You are too generous, my lady!" The girl cries, kissing Jia's hand. "What have I done to deserve such kindness?"

"You will do me a favor, and I need you to do it well." Jia says, patting the girl's shoulder.

"Anything, my lady."

"When you arrive at the Pillar, I want you to go to the Emperor's Tower. Tell anyone and everyone who will listen what you saw here tonight." Jia puffs her chest out and raises her chin. "Tell them Huo Jia, daughter of Huo Jain, saved you. Leave out no detail."

"I do not understand, my lady. But I will do it. I swear to you."

"Good. Now go." Jia takes her cloak off and gives it to the girl, revealing the orange and magenta silk of her expensive clothing.

As the girl rides away, Jia mounts the remaining horse, then trots off in the opposite direction towards home. The City of Light.

It is far past her curfew, and she knows her father will be angry if he realizes she is not at home in bed.

Chion

Chion walks along the causeway. Gazing off the side of the Flying City, he sees the volcano in the distance, and the magnificent capital of the Firelands surrounding it.

The magma oozing from the open crater at the mountain's peak is diverted through metal channels and reservoirs, weaving through the city, giving off light and heat. Aqueducts run parallel to the magma channels, delivering hot water to the homes of the wealthier citizens.

The Flying City floats above the Firelands, harbored over the small trading town of Xaolov, outside the City of Light.

Even though the City of Light is the capital of the Firelands, the captain of the Flying City will not approach too close as a precaution. The Flying City is suspended from a giant balloon, a mile long from front to back. Centuries of wear have been repaired with layers of improvised patchwork, giving the balloon a multicolored piebald appearance, and even a small burst of heat from the volcano could send the ancient airship crashing to the ground.

Giant steel chains connect the balloon to the foundation suspended below, a circular platform two miles across, upon which the Flying City is built. Rudders and propellers on the back of the massive structure enable it to fly between cities, allowing its citizens to trade for what they need, and providing an easy way for people in the realms below to travel. Those who can afford the fare...

It is a breathtaking sight... Chion thinks to himself, as he looks off the edge towards the orange glow of lava, contrasting against the lush green landscape of the surrounding jungle.

Since moving aboard the Flying City, Chion had seen the capitals of almost every realm, but in his opinion, the City of Light was by far the most beautiful.

He notices a brightly colored hot air balloon rising towards the Flying City's landing dock, bringing people and supplies up from the town below. The balloons run a few times a day, for the three days the Flying City spends harbored over each location on its route. Today is the last they will spend in the Firelands, departing in a few short hours for the Pillar.

He likes the journey between the Firelands and the Pillar most of all, as it is always the most profitable leg of the endless route the Flying City makes around the realms. The Firelands are a rich producer of fine goods such as silk, masterfully crafted weapons, and exotic fruits and spices, while the Pillar is home to many of the richest families in the Empire. It is an equation that always equaled profit for Chion.

He feels the winds carrying the hot air balloon up to the landing dock. He knows there is business arriving for him. Traders with goods to sell at the Pillar, but without coin to pay the fare for the trip upfront.

Chion is the proprietor of the Bank of the Flying City, a branch of his family's bank, the oldest and wealthiest in the Empire. His location is the newest, the only one that had been opened during his lifetime. His family members run branches in many other cities throughout the realms, all divisions of the flagship bank in the Plateau, operated by his father, Lord Chancellor Clion Antissi.

Even though Chion's branch is the youngest, it has quickly become the most profitable aside from his father's. Merchants and artisans who are looking to trade their goods in other cities, but who can't afford the fare, come to Chion for an advance. The passage fare of two gold pieces is far more than most common folk can afford, so Chion developed a loan system, where his bank would pay the travel fee and then the trader repays him after reaching the next destination and selling their wares. Chion had never made a bad investment, and he always kept plenty of his debtors' wares in his vault as collateral.

The clock tower, reaching high above the city square, begins to chime. *Only a few hours to finish work, before the city sets sail.* The hot air balloons will soon be making their last round trips to the town below, ejecting all non-citizens who haven't paid their fare, and returning with the stragglers below, running last minute errands and gathering supplies.

Chion walks into the heart of the Flying City, making his way towards his business in the center of town. He likes it there, much less windy than the areas around the edge of the city, quieter.

He opens the front door of his bank. Aline looks up from behind the counter, a pretty girl with long blonde hair. She had come to the Flying City many years ago, while it was harbored above the Frozen City, the capital of the Southern Realm.

He can remember the day she had walked into the bank, looking to finance her trip away from the south. Chion had been looking for help with his growing business, and Aline was looking for work, she had been with him ever since.

She had never told him what is was that made her want to leave the Southern Realm, and he liked letting those close to him keep their secrets, so he never searched for the answers.

"How are we doing today?" He asks.

"Better than usual." She says, cheerfully. "Deposits are up, all loans have been collected from the last leg, and the vacant rooms upstairs have been booked through to the Pillar."

"That is good news." He says, grinning. Everyone having paid back their loans meant his associate Yaaln wouldn't have to go out and collect last minute debts, and the rooms above are expensive for travelers to rent, a good source of side income for him.

He had been trying to buy up any available real-estate around his shop, to expand as much as possible. Chion now owned the building above his bank, a ten room hotel, as well as the tavern next door, which has another fifteen rooms for rent above it, one of which Chion had fashioned into a home for himself.

"You have one more appointment left today." She tells him.

"Whom with?"

"A farmer from Xaolov. He wants to trade for passage to the Pillar, I believe."

A gentle breeze blows through the open window, he catches the scent of dragonfruit, subtly sweet. Lifting his ear, listening, he hears nothing.

Silence is strange, he thinks. The district around the shop is densely populated, buildings growing taller with each generation, and the sounds of the city are usually audible.

Aside from those paying for quick travel between realms, most of the people who live in the Flying City were born there. Working for family run businesses that had catered to travelers for generations. Others are employed in upkeep of the city, maintaining the balloon and propulsion systems, navigating and piloting, and operating the hot air balloons to transport people and supplies to and from the city while it is harbored. The Flying City's markets have the widest selection of goods in the Empire, shop owners having the ability to select the freshest local supplies from each stop they make.

He thanks Aline, as he steps into his office. Closing the door behind him, he takes a seat at his desk. Yaaln looks up from his post at the edge of the room, in front of the large iron vault door. He is Chion's head of security, as he had been his father's once before. Chion knew Yaaln was sent to keep him safe, as much as the vault.

Aline shows a man into the office. He is a peasant, a farmer from the Firelands below. Chion looks him up and down, noting his tattered clothes and matted hair.

How can he possibly afford the fare? Chion thinks, as he stands and opens the window behind his desk. "That's better…" He says, before returning to his seat.

The man starts speaking, standing before the desk. "Many thanks for seeing me, sir. See, I cannot afford the trip to the Pillar. I was told to find you, that you could help."

"Then you have come to the right place. Our dealings are honest, and interest rates fair. You will find none better."

"I've never been here before. I don't know how it works… I heard stories from a farmer in town. We both sell dragonfruit, you see. Well, he said the prices was better at the Pillar. That he flew there with his stock and made a decent price. The damned things grow everywhere here, but I guess they don't have them around the Pillar."

"All passengers must pay the Captain's Collectors two gold pieces, plus room and board, if you can find anywhere with vacancy." Chion says, from behind his desk. "If not, the traveler's bunks are located near the loading docks. You can keep your goods with us here during transit, we have extra storage room."

"What debt comes with it?"

"Ah yes, the bank's due is twenty-five percent, being in this case half a gold piece, or fifty silver."

"Sir, that is three months' food for my family…"

Chion smiles as a breeze carries fresh air through the window, swirling through the office. He listens to the wind for a moment, before responding. "Dragonfruit sells in the Firelands for ten silver pieces per crate. The Pillar must import dragonfruit, driving the price up. There, it sells for one gold piece per crate. Tell me, how many crates do you have?"

Nonplussed by Chion's depth of crop knowledge, the man stutters a reply, "Th…Th…Th…Thirty sir."

"Thirty crates. In the Firelands, at ten silver per, they are worth three gold at most. At the Pillar, they could fetch you thirty gold. Now with those types of profits you will have no problem repaying our small fee." Chion laughs, quietly to himself.

"I… I suppose you're right… You sure do know a lot about dragonfruit."

"No more than you do." Chion replies, grinning.

"Could I give you three crates now, that would be three gold worth, you would make even more money that way." The man volunteers, grasping to avoid the large debt.

"I will gladly accept payment in the form of goods, and no extra incentive required, an even exchange. Twenty crates, and we will call it square."

"Sir!" The man exclaims. "That's twenty gold worth!"

"It's twenty gold in the Pillar, but today we are in the Firelands. It seems unwise to pay Pillar markups, when I am not even there." Chion stands and places his palms on the desk, leaning toward the man. "Our prices are fair, shall we start the process or no?"

"Very well..." The man stammers, signing the document Chion pushes before him.

"It is ten days' travel to reach the Pillar. Your goods will be safe here until then. Repayment is due within twenty-four hours of arrival. If you don't come to me, Yaaln will come to you." Chion glances to the man in the corner, picking at his fingernails with a dagger.

"Yes, of course." The man replies.

"Aline out front will get you your gold and arrange for your goods to be picked up. It has been a pleasure doing business with you." Chion turns to face out the window, bringing the dialogue to an end.

The man exits the office, closing the door behind him.

"Boons from above!" Yaaln shouts, "Who would have known you could make that kind of money off of fruit?"

"I had no idea..." Chion says, thinking quickly. "Send someone down on the last balloon, fast, it's probably leaving soon. Have them buy every crate of dragonfruit they can find. We are going to make a quick investment."

"Always the opportunist..." Yaaln smirks, before leaving the room.

Relorn

Reza, Andrew and Matio sit around him, trying to pay attention as their teacher speaks. Almost an entire day spent seated on the hard marble benches of the lecture hall has put Relorn's legs to sleep, sending a prickling sensation down to his feet.

Their teacher, Eristoclese, paces at the head of the class. His presentation today is on the many forms of government throughout the realms. While it isn't a boring lecture, the swelling heat of the quickly approaching summer is enough to distract even the most studious students.

"The Empire is broken into many realms." Eristoclese pontificates, surveying the class. "While each is left to choose its own form of local government, all of them are ruled over by the Emperor."

Relorn looks over and notices Reza pull an arrowhead from his pocket, toying the piece pf metal and trying to balance it on his fingertip.

"Does anyone know what the capital of the Empire is?" Eristoclese asks, looking around the audience.

A young lady on the far side of the room throws her hand in the air. As the teacher averts his eyes and moves towards the raised hand, Reza quickly pokes Matio in the leg with the arrowhead.

"Ouch!" Matio cries out. "What was that for?"

Reza cackles in reply, drawing Eristoclese's attention back towards them, the teacher's kind old eyes sharpening into a glare.

"Does my question amuse you, Te Reza?" Eristoclese asks, calmly. "Please, let us hear your answer."

"The Pillar is the capital of the Empire, it's where the Emperor lives." Reza answers, with confidence.

"Incorrect," Eristoclese replies. "Prince Relorn, do you know?"

"The Great City." Relorn answers, softly.

"Very good, and who moved the Emperor's court to the Pillar?"

What will make them laugh more? Relorn thinks, as his face begins to turn red. *If I say 'my grandfather' or if I just say his name?*

"It was Emperor Johaner." He answers, meekly.

Relorn likes Eristoclese, but the teacher's constant reminders to everyone that the Emperor's son was among them had always made him uncomfortable.

"Also correct." Eristoclese says, turning his attention away from Relorn. "Te Reza, what is the capital of the River Realm?"

"A'Tannia." Reza answers, without hesitation. "It is quite an exciting city, as long as you're not too afraid of those monsters of theirs."

"And how do the River People choose to govern?" The teacher asks.

"When someone breaks the law, the people throw them into that giant reservoir in the middle of the city, to let the water monsters eat them. I don't know what you call that form of government, but it is really fun to watch..." Reza's reply elicits laughter from the students in the auditorium.

"The A'Tannians do have some interesting ways of dealing with their criminals, but that does not answer the question. Matio Nodovin, perhaps you know?"

Matio looks at the faces around the room, everyone staring back at him. The boy tries to stammer out a shy reply, but Andrew answers for him.

"It's a republic, they elect senators to rule."

Eristoclese raises an eyebrow. "Very good, though I do not recall your name being Matio. Perhaps you can educate the class on some of the Empire's other governments too."

"Perhaps I can..." Andrew says, looking up at the brilliantly frescoed ceiling, trying to find clues in the pictures. "Well... I am from the Southern Realm. The capital is the Frozen City, and our government is a monarchy."

"A very unique form of monarchy too. So many kings. Do you know why the south has over a dozen kings?"

"From what I understand..." Andrew begins to explain, "A few hundred years ago there was only one king in the Southern Realm. But when he died without children or naming someone to succeed him, all the southern lords each declared themselves king and rose up to take his place. A brutal civil war broke out. It seemed like they would all kill each other off. But, the Emperor of the time intervened, telling the lords of the south that moving forward they would all be king of their own castles and lands, but that they were to elect a grand marshal to act as a representative of the Southern Realm. The lords consented, and elected Kent Barren, the King of Barrenport, as their representative. King Barren's heirs have continued serving as grand marshal ever since."

Eristoclese smiles, pleased by the reply. "It was a very effective move on the part of the Emperor. Nothing changed at all, save for the self-important titles the lords used. Lords became kings, and the king became grand marshal... Are you paying attention, Relorn? You will be Emperor one day, and situations like these will be yours to resolve."

"Yes, teacher..." *Why does he always single me out? I don't act out as much as Reza or Andrew, but he always comes back to me. Just a few more days...*

He will be turning sixteen soon, and that is when his real education will begin. His father, Emperor Jero, will select a council from around the Empire. A person near the prince's age from each realm. Typically, the one deemed to have the most powerful or useful gift.

Then, his father's council will teach and guide Relorn and his new council. Educating the prince on how to rule, and the young selectees on how to assist him, just as his grandfather's council had taught his father's, as far back as could be remembered.

As long as father picks Reza to represent the Firelands, Andrew the South, and Matio the Plateau. Relorn thinks, looking around at his friends. *Then let him choose whoever he wants to from the other realms, I couldn't care less...*

When Relorn was a child, his father explained that the members of the council were selected this way as an ancient punishment towards the other realms, in retribution for an uprising against the Empire that had occurred centuries before.

After defeating the rebelling realms, the ruling Emperor proclaimed that once a generation they would be required to pledge fealty, by sending the strongest and most promising of their gifted youths. This served to weaken the individual realms, while strengthening the Emperor's own forces. Yet, in peaceful and prosperous times like these, being selected to the council was seen as an honor instead of a punishment, and the councilors are treated as trusted friends, not hostages.

A bell begins to chime from the top of a nearby building, signaling the end of class. The friends grab their belongings, rushing out of the auditorium.

Four burly bodyguards wait at the rear of the room for them. As the young men pass, the guards begin to follow, staying close behind Relorn. Another man walks slightly behind the entourage, his face all but covered by a long gravel colored cloak, his electric blue eyes constantly scanning their surroundings.

A breeze envelops the group as soon as they step outside, carrying the sweet summer scents of honeysuckle and citrus across the Plateau, invigorating them from the staleness of the lecture hall.

"Race you to the melon patch!" Reza yells, taking off at a sprint.

The others follow him, down the road and up a nearby hill, on top of which Matio's family home is built. Matio's father, Atasio Nodovin, is serving as the boys' steward while they attend the Academy. He is one of the richest men in Triali. And, as a member of the Oligarchy of Twenty, he is also one of the rulers of the Plateau. A good friend of Relorn's father, the wealthy merchant is the only person in the Plateau that the Emperor would consider entrusting his son to.

The boys stop when they reach the base of the hill, on the side facing the western ocean.

Relorn is out of breath. The last to arrive, but the first to speak. "No fair, I wasn't ready…" He huffs.

"Maybe next time." Reza grins, as he walks towards the guards who are just now catching up with the boys. "Bow!" He shouts at the closest.

The bodyguard sets a large bundle of leather on the ground, rolling it out to reveal four elaborate wooden bows. He tosses one to Reza, and then begins to gather melons atop a nearby incline.

As they string their bows, Andrew starts proposing a bet. "We each take turns calling a shot, and the rest have to match it. If you miss twice, you're out. Last man standing gets a gold piece from each loser."

"Deal!" Reza says, excitedly. Looking up the hill at the guard collecting melons, he yells, "THROW!" Notching an arrow and drawing the string tightly, Reza watches as the guard heaves a large ripe round fruit off of the hill, sending it sailing out towards the sea.

The head of Reza's arrow begins to glow, getting brighter and brighter each second he holds the string taught. As the flying melon reaches the peak of its arc and starts to fall, Reza calmly looks away from his target and towards his friends.

"No eyes!" He says, releasing the arrow. The tip bursts into flame as it sails through the air, leaving a faint trail of cinders and smoke behind. Just before the melon hits the ground, Reza's arrow makes contact, creating a small explosion and vaporizing its target. The light sea breeze sends notes of baked fruit drifting up the hill, which Reza dramatically wafts towards his nose with smug satisfaction.

"Easy…" Relorn steps forward, dropping to one knee. He pinches the dirt beneath him and pulls up with his fingers. As he does, the ground gently flows up in the form of a stone arrow, made of the very earth below. He notches the newly created arrow and glances to his friends, before shouting, "Throw!" His bow is made of the hardest yew wood in the Empire, releasing it causes a shockwave to chase his arrow through the air. The prince's aim isn't far off, but his shot just misses the flying melon. "Damn…"

Matio steps up to shoot next. He releases three arrows in rapid succession. The first splits his melon in two, while the second and third impale the remaining falling halves. A look of pride swells on his face, as he steps aside with a wide grin.

Andrew is the last to try, his arrow flying straight through the center of its target. As it passes through, the fruit seems to freeze. Streaks of frost creep throughout the melon, making it glisten like fresh rime, before it comes crashing down, breaking into a burst of ice and frozen fruit flesh.

A few shots later, they are all tied with one miss, and it is Relorn's turn to call.

Hmmm… He thinks to himself. *What won't they be able to do? They are all more accurate than me, but I am stronger…*

Pointing down to a cluster of boulders built up against the shore, he pulls a quartz arrow from the dirt, drawing with all his might. When he sets the arrow loose, a sharp whistle screams out, as it rips and tears through the air. It strikes the rock, reducing it to rubble.

A cloud of dust floats across the beach, as he looks at his friends and laughs. "Who can match that?"

Reza jumps up, taking aim at the boulders. Drawing the bow as hard as he can, the tip of the arrow begins glowing with fiery energy.

Relorn backs away as the arrowhead starts to radiate with an overwhelming fervor, but Reza seems unfazed by the heat. The arrow roars as he releases it, shooting through the sky like a comet in the night. It hits its target and bursts into flame, billowing smoke and ash. The scorched rock becomes visible as the haze clears, charred and scarred, but relatively intact.

"Shit… How am I the first one out?" Reza whines.

"Because, you're far too cocky." Matio says, taking aim towards a large stone in the distance. He sends an arrow loose, and then another, and another, and another. His arm moving so fast it becomes a blur, not stopping until his quiver is empty. All the arrows find their target, each chipping off more stone than the last, but not enough to do any serious damage. Matio stares at the stone, dejectedly. "I suppose that's it for me."

Andrew walks to the front of the group. He draws and fires, his arrow stabbing into the side of a boulder, sinking straight into the rock's surface. Then he lets loose a second shot, the striking force of which shatters the stone, sending pieces of rock and ice bursting into the air.

Relorn shakes his head, laughing. "Still tied then…"

"Well, I am getting hungry, time to end this." Andrew says, pointing in the distance. "You see that ship, harbored in the bay?"

Relorn looks over the water, shielding his eyes from the sun. "Yeah, I see it."

Andrew nods, then sets an arrow free, high in the air, before turning and starting to walk up to the house.

It seems to take an eternity to make its way to the bay. Just as the arrow disappears from sight, a poof of feathers erupts from atop the ship's mast, and a dead seagull falls to the deck.

The boys burst into laughter, listening to the confused yells of the sailors carry across the water, before turning and following after Andrew, marching off to their waiting dinner.

Ral

Ral walks through the Slave Quarter, along the north side of A'Tannia. The streets around him are home to the basest of shops. Open air stalls sell vegetables, fruits and bread, while blacksmiths beat against anvils and carpenters beat upon nails.

For each merchant peddling some form of food or sundry, there are three more selling slaves. Tents, shops and auction blocks, all filled with people in chains, waiting to be sold. A look of defeat and despair is beaten onto the face of each man, woman and child.

Would Bentino ever sell me? Ral ponders, passing a loud auction in progress. *No, I make him too much money. Maybe when I am old, no longer useful. Assuming I live that long...*

Bentino is his master. Not an unfair man, as far as slavers come. He specializes in fighters, gladiators for the arena.

The man has a standing deal with his slaves, if any of them is able to make him one thousand gold pieces, they will be set free. Each fight one of his men wins nets Bentino about ten gold, but he loses just as much if his fighter is defeated. He keeps a running total of each of his men's earnings, freeing them once their profits hit the one thousand mark. In his years serving Bentino, Ral had seen only a small handful of men set free.

As Ral makes his way out of the Slave Quarter, nicer establishments begin to appear. Leather and fabric shops, vendors selling snacks and hot meals. The smell of hot fruit pies, laden in honey glazed crusts, wafts sweetly through the air.

Running up a set of stairs to get a better view of the city, Ral looks out over A'Tannia and the Great River enveloping it. The city is built upon a giant circular foundation, lain in the middle of the river, protecting it from attack by land. Across the city, over the reservoir at its center, and past the temples on the western edge, Ral can see the ocean. The sun slowly chases the horizon, sending bright beams of light reflecting over the water, stinging his eyes.

The reservoir at the heart of the city contains creatures not known to exist anywhere else in the Empire. Serpents, carnivorous fish, reptilian beasts, and hundreds of slimy things even more unimaginable. No one knows where the creatures in the reservoir came from. Even the earliest histories of A'Tannia make mention of them, but give no hint as to their origins.

Prisoners too weak to be a good fight for the gladiators, often find themselves being thrown into the reservoir for the amusement of the citizens. The spectacle brings out the entire city, people crowding around the reservoir to get a view of the creatures as they surface to devour their victims.

Ral stops at a well-stocked fruit stand. The many brilliant colors of exotic produce shine beautifully in the sun. Apples from the Orchard line the stall, coming in every shade of red, orange, yellow, pink and green, accented with bright crimson dragon fruit and blueish-purple water berries. Sweetlimes and tangerines are interspersed amongst the bulkier items, surrounding the stall with the refreshing smell of citrus.

A'Tannia's location at the mouth of the Great River means that any ships coming to and from the ocean have to pass by, providing plenty of foreign delicacies to the merchants in the city.

Ral picks up a purple and orange melon, small enough to fit in his palm. Holding it up to the sun, he calls over the proprietor. "Where is this from?" He asks, curiously.

"Ah, you have a good eye." The fruit peddler replies, picking up another melon from the cart. "A Triali melon, they only grow on the westernmost edge of the Plateau, where the sea meets the cliffs. It's said they get their sweetness and color from bathing in the glow of the sunset."

Ral nods his head in approval, and tosses the man a few copper pieces. The explanation was not needed, but he respects showmanship, often trying to bring the same flourish to his fights.

If the people like you, you get more offers, more business. Fighter, merchant, or beggar, it is hard to make money when people don't like you.

If Ral hurriedly killed his opponent every fight, the people would quickly lose interest in him.

Best to wear them out, make them surrender. And then... Show mercy.

That was Ral's strategy, and it had been working well for him. The citizens of A'Tannia had come to love Ral. At only sixteen, he is one of the youngest fighters, yet he is undefeated, with a longer record than the most seasoned gladiators.

Even though he has never lost a fight, his kill count is relatively low. Ral only kills his opponents when forced to. Sometimes the other fighter is so intent on killing him, there is no other choice then to beat him to it. At the other extreme, if the opponent doesn't put up enough of a fight, their own master will give him the nod. If it was up to him, Ral would refuse, but Bentino always seconds the nod.

Can't go against Bentino...

Ral enjoys many liberties that a lot of other slaves do not. He is allowed to walk about the city without chains, he has a nicer room than most gladiators, and he is even given a little spending money. All it would take is one disagreement with Bentino, and everything would be taken away.

He stops in front of a large marble building near the fighting pits, operated by the Collectors of Debt. Looking inside, Ral sees lines of employees behind counters, taking bets on any events occurring throughout the Empire.

As a slave, Ral is not allowed to place wagers. Yet he had worked out a system with a friend in the city, where she would place bets on him, using his money, and they would split the profits. Once he gained his freedom, he hoped to have enough money saved up to find a place to live, somewhere outside of the Slave Quarter.

Can't imagine I would stop fighting though... Just start making money for myself, instead of Bentino.

He finishes the melon, and spits a bit of rind off the inner railing, sending it sailing down into the reservoir below. Peering over the edge, he looks to see if any shapes move beneath the surface.

Do the creatures eat fruit?

When criminals are thrown into the reservoir, the school of darters is usually what kills them. The carnivorous fish swarm their prey, consuming a man whole in seconds, leaving behind nothing but a glistening skeleton sinking into the depths. But looking over the edge, Ral doesn't see anything moving, save for the rind drifting out of sight.

Stepping back from the railing, he continues along the edge towards the Grand Quarter. He can hear the clash of steel ahead, as the familiar metallic stench of blood floods his nose.

A fight is taking place in the arena closest to him, one of the outer pits meant for lesser events. Untested fighters and criminals, facing punishment from experienced opponents.

The center pit is reserved for the best fighters, the ones whose names the people shout and cheer.

Tonight, I'll be right there. Maybe for the last time...

This is the first time he can remember being worried before a fight. Looking away from the pit, he turns to the Grand Quarter, rising up from the causeway, fifty stories high at its peak. The side facing towards the center has a greater slope then the other quarters, providing large terraces and patios for the expensive businesses, restaurants and apartments above. Only the senators and richest of families are able to afford to live in the Grand Quarter, its hotels catering exclusively to the wealthiest visitors coming to A'Tannia.

Continuing on his way, Ral moves past the pits, past the Senate Hall and the large marble Antissi Bank, down towards the Southern Quarter. Home to the less prosperous of A'Tannia's citizens. Low level merchants and slavers, mercenaries, gamblers and night workers. Even most of the city watch lives there, unable to afford the extravagant prices of residences elsewhere in the densely populated city.

The apartments in the Southern Quarter are not like the palaces above the Senate Hall. These shacks have been built one on top of another, for years and years. The lower levels are crafted of stone and brick, the higher levels of wood and scrap metal. Independent sections rise up from the city like mountain peaks, connected by rope bridges and filled with cave-like passages and alleys.

Ral starts running up a set of stone steps. The stairs in the Southern Quarter twist and turn in random directions, built more as an afterthought when more and more levels were added to the structures. Like a winding maze, it is easy to get helplessly lost if not intimately familiar with the layout.

Climbing up a few more flights of stairs, and crossing a narrow bridge swaying in the wind, Ral steps into a dark doorway. Inside, the barkeep, a barrel chested man missing two front teeth, looks up at him and flashes a goofy smile.

Ral waves to the man, as he walks to the iron spiral staircase in the back of the room. The tavern is seven stories tall, eight if you include the owner's apartment on top. He runs up the first few levels, passing the patrons. The bar caters to many tastes, and is always busy. Some play games and toast each other, while others sit looking out the open front wall, trying to see the action of the fights below.

The upper floors are filled with people relaxing on large lounging pillows, smoking leaf. Lazily gazing out at the city and water. Clouds of smoke hang thick in the air, as Ral steps out of the stairwell on the top level of the tavern. He walks through the plumes of pungent haze being exhaled by the giggling patrons, drifting towards the open wall. He steps out onto the porch, overlooking the city below.

You can see everything from here... He thinks, stopping for a moment to take the view in.

Making his way around the corner of the patio and up a short set of steps, he approaches the owner's apartment. He slowly walks up, reaching out to knock, but the door opens before he has a chance. A pretty girl grins and grabs him by the shirt.

"About time!" She exclaims, pulling him inside.

The girl's apartment is filled with a perfumed haze, drifting from a stick of incense burning on the table by the door. Ral smiles at her, moving towards her porch. As he parts the curtains to step outside, she jumps onto his back, giggling in his ear and wrapping her arms and legs around him. He stands strong, not stumbling beneath her weight.

"You'd have us both killed, it's a hundred feet to the ground below!" He shouts.

She repeatedly kisses him on the neck and cheek, then playfully asks, "Did I scare you?"

He tosses her onto a lounging pillow, propped against the side of the patio, then walks to the railing.

"I always forget you're so young." She coos, patronizingly. "Come to me, let me hold you."

He scoffs at her, then smiles. "I suppose being twenty makes you an old maid?"

She laughs and stretches, arms over her head and feet towards him, as if pulling life back into her limbs after a deep sleep. Her brown hair is braided, exposing her lightly tanned face and sharp features. Hazel eyes look up at him with affection, their warmth drawing him to her.

She relaxes, resting her chin on a small fist and laying out across the pillow. Lifting a leg up, she gently runs her toe down Ral's thigh.

"Come here…" She whispers, coaxingly.

"I fight in an hour… You know I can't." Ral says, tickling her foot before turning away.

"To save your energy?"

"To save my energy." He replies, nodding his head.

"Then why have you come?" She pouts. "To rile me up then leave me alone, so you can go play with some man?" Her frown quickly turns to a smile, as Ràl shoots her a glare. "Fine… I understand, I suppose…"

He tosses her a bag of coins. "The odds are against me tonight, bet it all."

"What is this?" She asks, looking at the bag.

"My life's savings, all the money we… You… Made betting on me."

"It's your money…" She says, quietly.

"The man I am fighting tonight, he… He is favored to win. They say he is a barbarian, captured in the wastelands. I've heard he is the size of two men, and stronger than three. Barbarians don't grant mercy. If I lose, I die… Money is no good to a dead man, so bet it all."

She stands up, slowly, putting the bag on a side table, then pushes him down on the pillow. He looks up her with a half grin, as she straddles his lap.

"Save your energy…" She whispers, kissing him passionately, before gently sliding her hips forward.

Tiaries

Tiaries meanders along the river's edge, her bare feet splashing in and out of the water with each step. The cuffs of her tan pants are rolled up to her knees, keeping them dry. Tulips lie tucked behind her pointed elven ears, and the morning's bounty of fresh picked flowers sticks out from the many pockets sewn into her clothes, covering her in the beautiful colors of spring.

The streaming trickle of the water is calming, momentarily distracting her from tonight's performance. Tiaries is one of the few women in the troupe, and the only elven girl. As such, she typically has very little selection over her roles. Any role requiring an elf immediately goes to her, the elf-less plays being the only performances where she is allowed to hide her telltale ears.

Reaching into one of her endless pockets, Tiaries pulls out that night's script. Only a few pages long, *The Fall of Tritan* is her least favorite of the plays in their repertoire. It is the story of the last King of Elves, and the birth of the Empire.

Her eyes dart across the smudged text, quickly glancing through the pages, barely paying attention. She has very few lines, and already knows each by heart. She is playing Tritan's consort, Yella, the Queen of Elves.

The Fall of Tritan

Characters:

Emperor Harlorn – Leader of men
Te Rexow – King Harlorn's advisor and friend
Lord Aaron – King of the South
Tritan – The King of Elves
Yella – The Queen of Elves
Elven Guard – Tritan's bodyguard
Emissary – Tritan's messenger
Senator Lycis – Senator
Senator Dukas – Senator
Additional actors – placed in audience to play senators

ACT I

Scene one – The Great City – Tritan and Yella at a table, Elven Guard posted at the door

Tritan: The men grow fat on our lands. We must remind them who serves who.

Yella: What would you do, my lord?

Tritan: I will increase their taxes and push them back from the fertile lands. These stupid men do not know how to properly use the land, why should they have it?

Yella: You are wise, my lord. Push them back to the sea.

Tritan: Guard, send word to the council, have them dispatch an emissary to the kings of men. Taxes are doubled, effective now.

Elven Guard: Yes, my lord.

LIGHTS

Scene two – The Pillar – King Harlorn, Te Rexow, and Lord Aaron stand around a table

Emissary: I bring word from Tritan, King of the trees and streams, of Elves and Men. His greatness proclaims, from this day forward, taxes are hereby doubled. You are to abandon all lands you have

taken beyond the coasts. The lands of
trees and forests are not for you or yours.

Harlorn: Is that what Tritan proclaims?
Well, please tell Tritan - I will burn his
trees, I will poison his waters and I will
kill any Elf that is stupid enough to try to
stop me!

*The Emissary exits stage right, with
Harlorn chasing him and kicking his rear.*

Harlorn: Well, it would seem we must
prepare for war. Aaron, will you rally the
men of the south?

Aaron: It would be an honor. I will set sail
tonight.

Harlorn: Be weary on the river, it runs the
edge of the elven lands. You don't want
to catch one of their arrows. When it flies
from the trees, you'll never even see who
loosed it. Sneaky elves...

Aaron: Aye, and their ships are faster than
ours. Fear not though, my men are brave
and we will sail with vigilance. I will send
word as we move north, though I am sure
you shall feel the land quake as we ride.

*Aaron exits stage left, Harlorn
approaches Rexow.*

Rexow: Shall I ride north my liege, rally
the Firelanders?

Harlorn: Send a carrier pigeon to your
brother, have him lead his troops south, to

the Great City. You and I shall sail for A'Tannia, to rally the River People.

Rexow: Do you think they will help, my lord?

Harlorn: I expect they will, when I give them our terms.

Rexow: It's impossible to get the River People to agree on anything, and they won't march to war without a consensus.

Harlorn: Well then, let us convince them all.

CURTAIN

ACT II

Scene One - A'Tannia - Senate hall - Harlorn and Rexow meet with Senator Lycis and Senator Dukas

Lycis: You mean to send our soldiers to their deaths, why should we agree?

Rexow: The King of Elves grows more unstable with each passing day. It is only a matter of time before he aims to eradicate us all.

Lycis: He has raised taxes and halted progression into his lands, what should we care of this? We have plenty of lands of our own, and more than enough abundance to pay the taxes.

Harlorn: Are you men? You would just… Bow to the will of some elf? What about when they take your lands from you, and starve your people with their taxes. They will not be content with what they take now, he means to push us back and let the sea wash us from this land.

Dukas: We cannot decide without the consent of all the senators. We will bring your case before them and take it to a vote, there must be a consensus. We shall send for you when we reach a verdict.

Harlorn and Rexow exit stage left

Dukas: Lycis, if these men fail we will most assuredly feel the wrath of the elves tenfold. Their ships are faster than ours, and our lands border theirs. Might it not be wise to join the men now? If they lose and the elves advance on us, we will be unable to defend ourselves. But if we combine forces with them now, we may have enough strength to prevail.

Lycis: Let us convene then.

Dukas - (addressing audience): Esteemed senators, we must decide. War is brewing to the north. The kings of the realms would have us march on the Great City. Many of our soldiers would be lost. But how many countless more will be lost if the elves push into our lands? Shall we fight for what is ours? Or do we hide behind our walls, and hope the elves do not look our way?

Actors in Audience: TO WAR! TO WAR!

LIGHTS

Scene Two – Harlorn and Rexow stand waiting, Lycis and Dukas enter stage right.

Harlorn: And?

Dukas: To war is the verdict, so to war it is. We will supply twenty thousand spearmen and two thousand javelin throwers, with the ships needed to carry them.

Harlorn: The elves will stand no chance. The troops of Lord Aaron will come from the south, thirty thousand swordsmen strong. Rexow's brother rides from the north with a legion of mounted swords and a thousand archers of the flame. Once the elven ships come to shore to engage us, your people shall sail in through the river, attacking from within. Destroy their ships first, and then move on the Grand Hall.

LIGHTS

Scene Three – Tritan sits on his throne. Yella stands beside him. Elven Guard enters from stage left

Elven Guard: The battle is lost, my lord. Our remaining soldiers are retreating. We must leave now, before they come and take you prisoner.

Yella: Yes, we should go, my love. Slip out of the city before they reach the Grand Hall.

Tritan: Never... I will never leave! Let them come. I will slay every last one of them.

Yella: My love, my king, please...

Harlorn, Rexow and Lord Aaron enter stage left. Harlorn walks towards the throne, the elven guard rushes at him, Harlorn slays him with his sword.

Harlorn: Kneel before me, or stand and fight!

Tritan: You... You, insolent man. You will be the one to kneel!

Tritan lunges forward with his short sword aimed at Harlorn, Harlorn deflects and they begin to battle. Rexow and Aaron move forward to assist, but Harlorn orders them back.

Harlorn: Do you give up, elf? Ask my mercy, and you might receive it.

Tritan: You come to my palace, to my city, and offer me mercy?

Tritan lunges forward with all his might.
Harlorn side steps and decapitates him.
Harlorn walks to the throne and sits, as
Yella runs to her husband and sobs over
his body. She takes his head in her hands
and kisses his lips.

Harlorn: From this day forward, I
proclaim these the realms of man.

Rexow and Aaron: Long live the
Emperor!

CURTAIN

The kiss… She knows it has to be timed perfectly. More
important than any of her lines.

Focus, count the seconds.

She sees the ships ahead, harbored next to each other on the
dock, the wood of their hulls stained green and their sails dyed
purple. Four identically colored vessels that the traveling
carnival her troupe performs with uses to move their show
between cities.

Inland from the docks, stands the entrance to the carnival
grounds. A large clearing filled with tents and booths, dancers
and jugglers, drumbeaters and fire-eaters. *The Deepriver
Carnival* is written in gold lettering upon a purple and green
banner, waving in the breeze above the entrance.

Her brother, Jaties, stands inside the grounds. The rich green of his shirt brings out the even darker green of his eyes. People say her eyes look like a spring meadow, interspersed with golden flowers, while his resemble the canopy of a forest, letting beams of moonlight shine through the leaves. Their hair is an identical shade of auburn, shining crimson in the sunlight.

As she walks towards him, his gaze rises to meet hers. "Ready for tonight?" He asks, "You're not going to let me die, I hope…?"

He grins as she swings at him, her fist landing hard on his shoulder.

"Have I ever let you die before?" She asks, her nerves beginning to get the best of her.

"I don't think so, but my memory isn't what it used to be." Jaties says, beginning to walk in a circle, looking at the sky in bewilderment. "Wait… Who are you again…?"

"That's not funny, Jaties!" She shouts, "You know how scared I get… Why do you torment me? Is it silly to be worried for my brother?"

"Ah, you know I trust you." He answers, smiling. "It will be the same as every other night. What are you worried for? You've never messed up before. No reason tonight would be different."

"This play worries me the most, why do we do it?" She cries, "I'm not going to do it again after tonight, it's too dangerous."

"Ask Mr. Deepriver, you know he picks them all. I'm sure he would change it if you asked him to. People come to the carnival from miles around to see you… When audiences are screaming your name… Tiaries! Tiaries!" He stops, trying to remember what he was talking about. "All I'm saying is, if you don't want to do this play, just tell him."

She nods, "You're right. I'm going to say something, not tonight though… It's too late for tonight's show. The bills are already posted all over the city."

"I hear the mayor is coming." He says, looking up at the brightly colored buildings above.

The Painted City had always been her brother's favorite stop among the many the carnival made along the river route they traveled. The city has only one road, a great winding switchback that runs up the side of a gorge, which the river had long ago cut into the landscape. It was a thousand feet from top to bottom, each level populated with beautifully colored homes and shops, each a different shade of the spectrum.

The decorations and landscapes coordinate with each structure. Near the shore, a deep blue house sits facing the water, mirrors on the façade reflect the waves, giving the home a fluid appearance. Nestled on the level above is a bright green building, with vines creeping up to the roof, and a yellow bakery, surrounded by sunflowers and emitting from its chimney a sweet smell of freshly baked bread and warm cinnamon.

The mayor's home is in the center of the city, about halfway up the incline. Its face is covered in red stained glass, giving the owner a rose tinted view of the city below.

Long way to walk for such a chubby man. Tiaries giggles, as she pictures him waddling along the winding road, trying to keep his belly from pulling him down the incline.

"He brought us chocolate covered cherries last time, he's nice." She tells her brother, laughing and taking his arm in hers.

They begin walking through the carnival, moving between the booths and attractions. Next to a large purple tent, a blindfolded man stands with a bull's-eye painted on a large wooden board behind him, an apple placed on his head.

Cooper, one of the carnival workers, waves to the gathering crowd, a large knife in his hand. As the mob moves in to witness the spectacle, Coop seizes the moment, throwing his dagger at the blindfolded man.

The apple flies off his head, impaled into the center of the bull's-eye by the knife. As the crowd erupts in cheers, the man removes his blindfold. Grabbing the apple, he takes a bite, throwing half to Cooper. The knife still wobbling in the center of the target.

"He didn't bring *us* chocolate…" Jaties softly corrects, a look of worry on his face. "I think he fancies you."

"He's old enough to be our father." She says, aghast. "He was just being nice."

"I'm sure that age difference doesn't bother him, and I'm sure he wasn't *just being nice.*"

"Well, we are only here for a couple nights, then the carnival leaves for Tarin and Naries. So let us take his chocolate, smile, and be on our way." She gently pats his arm, walking towards the main tent.

It's time to head backstage and change into her costume. The sun is setting, and the show will start soon. Streaks of purple, pink and orange paint the sky above the city, accentuating the warm colored structures below, while bathing the blue buildings in a glow of royal purple and giving the greens an amber glow.

It almost looks as if the buildings are projecting colored beams of light into the sky. It would be worth learning to paint, just to be able to capture this...

For a moment, Tiaries is filled with glee. But as she approaches the main tent, pied with purple and green fabric, her heart begins to sink again.

As the sun finishes setting, Tolaf the Tall Man walks by on stilted legs, lighting the inside of the purple and green lamps, strung throughout the carnival.

She walks backstage, ducking into her dressing area. It isn't a room, as much as three sheets hung around an interior wall, hidden behind the stage. Her emerald green dress is thrown over the top of one of the sheets, causing it to droop down lower than the others.

Removing the clothing she had worn to the river, Tiaries approaches a mirror propped against the side of the tent. She examines her naked body, a light shade of pink covering her face and arms.

Too much time in the sun today...

She pulls the dress over her head, and shimmies the ruffles below her waist. The red on her face is made even more noticeable by the brightly contrasting green of her dress.

No one will notice, not with Jaties' head flying through the air. What if I can't get to it in time...?

Standing and parting the sheets, Tiaries exits her dressing area, moving towards the side curtain and preparing to walk onstage. Jaties approaches her, silently nodding.

They enter the stage, and walk towards a table at the center. The curtain is down, but she can hear a full crowd behind it. The thought of the plump mayor sitting in the audience, plopping chocolate cherries into his mouth, makes her smile.

Don't smile. She reminders herself, forcing a straight face just in time, as the curtain starts to rise.

The audience stares up from the stands.

Don't look at them, look at Jaties. She focuses on his eyes, waiting for her cue.

"What would you do, my lord?" She says.

Jaties replies, but she doesn't even listen to his words. Only waiting for him to finish his lines.

"You are wise, my lord." She elocutes, "Push them back to the sea."

That's all for this scene... Just look at him until the lights go out.

Acrobats suspended from the wooden framework of the tent lower metal cylinders over the torches that illuminate the stage. After the lights fade, she and Jaties run backstage. The crew moves the backdrops and changes out the furniture, preparing for the next scene.

"They don't need us for a bit, not until the end." She looks at Jaties' hands, as they nervously shake. Taking them in hers, she asks, "Are you ok?"

"You know how it is… While you spend the whole day worrying, I get it all out of the way ten minutes beforehand."

"It'll be fine, just remember to fall on your back when he swings for your neck, we don't want me having to try to roll you over like last time." She smiles and laughs, "Or accidentally put your head on backwards."

They stand in the wing, watching the action on stage. The part of King Harlorn is being played by Cooper. She had never known anyone better with a blade. He always plays the hero, killing Jaties, who, with his elven ears, invariably plays the villainous roles.

That's what it means to be an elf and an actor... Always playing the villain. It's good that he's fighting Coop though, Coop doesn't ever miss. One slip and... She didn't want to think about it.

"Destroy their ships first, and then move on the Grand Hall." She hears Coop bellow onstage.

Then the lights go out.

Tiaries hears props moving and people shuffling, as she feels her way towards the throne that has been placed at the center of the stage. She can feel Jaties walk past her, and hears him sit on the throne.

The lights return, as the metal cylinders used to blot them out are slowly lifted. She hears her cue, then says her lines.

"Yes, we should go now, slip out of the city before they reach the Grand Hall." She feels the words leave her mouth, and she means them. An overwhelming feeling to leave the stage comes over her, to run away and bring Jaties along.

Stop, just think about your lines. Remember to count... Fifteen seconds.

Jaties and Cooper fight, moving around the stage, their swords glancing off one another's. Jaties clumsily lunges forward, over extending his body. The crowd bursts into laughter. He blocks Cooper's next swing, and then lunges again, with even more flair than before. The audience roars.

They love Jaties, even as the villain.

Be ready, here it comes… Almost over.

Cooper swings, and sparks fly as metal slides across the top of Jaties' sword. Cooper's blade comes up, finding Jaties' neck.

A lady in the audience screams, fainting in her chair. The crowd gasps, and then quickly falls silent, as Jaties' head slides off of his neck and drops to the floor.

One, Tiaries chokes, as she tries to scream

Two, she runs forward, fumbling to grab his head

Three, almost there…

Four, she brushes his forehead with her finger

Five, she takes his head in her hands

Six, she moves it towards his body

Seven, she places his head in position

Eight, she hears Cooper speaking to the crowd

Nine, she leans forward

Ten, the crowd cheers

Eleven, she kisses his lips, waiting for a response

Twelve, the theatre pulses with tension

Thirteen, she begins to sob. *Please, please, open your eyes…*

Fourteen, the curtain drops

Fifteen, the lights go out…

The crowd falls silent, save for muffled breathing. A child in the front tugs at his mother's sleeve.

"Is the elf dead?"

His mother gives no indication of having heard the question, as she stares at the purple and green stripped curtain draped from the framework above.

As the curtain begins to rise, the torchlight spills across the stage, staining it a deep shade of orange shellac. The actors stand along the front, all except Jaties. They somberly join hands and bow towards the stands.

The audience claps lightly, still in disbelief, when a trumpet begins to ring out. Whispers and gasps begin flying, as Jaties walks onto the stage, taking his place at the center between Tiaries and Cooper.

Joining hands, the performers all bow again. As they rise, Jaties cranes his neck for the crowd, grinning and showing off the ring of blood caked to him.

Cheers and applause boom, threatening to bring the high-top crashing down around them. Tiaries looks at her brother and smiles, as the curtain drops.

Kzhee

The wind blows about his face as he rides over the hilly plains, surrounded by innumerous mounds of earth painted green and gold by a sea of waving grass, tickling his horse's hocks as they sail above.

Kzhee's riding skills are already legendary among the Hill People, though he is not yet seventeen years. He learned to ride at the turn of his fourth. Most of the boys don't learn until after six, but his father insisted he accompany him on all excursions that required the Hill-Chief's attendance.

The day Kzhee's legs could straddle the smallest horse in the herd, his father had him on it. They would ride for hours each day, across the plains and hills. He learned much on these trips, his yearling dancing beneath him as his father recited stories of wisdom, caution, bravery, and family. Tales of the old chiefs, and the Lightningbird.

The horizon he rides towards is painted lavender, contrasting against the viridescent glow of the grass, reaching towards the sky. Dark clouds swirl ahead in the distance, threatening to pour rain across the Plains. But the sun still shines strong on his back, as it floats west, descending towards the sea.

The smell of warm wet dirt drifts upon the breeze. His horse seems to notice it to, extending her nostrils in the air, trying to catch the wind as she runs. The horse's name is Sparks. A sandy tan mare, with a cream colored mane and fetlocks, she had been a gift from his father at the turn of his fourteenth year. She was young, but already the fastest horse in the Plains. The Hill children race their mounts often, and Kzhee can't remember the last time he had lost.

Slowly at first, the tops of trees begin to come into view ahead, a canopy of leaves resting on huge trunks, breaking above the horizon like a giant ship barreling towards them. Suddenly, the edge of the Forest Realm dominates the landscape, extending as far as he can see in either direction. Kzhee had only ventured into the forest once before. There are things lurking in those trees, that frighten even the most hardened warriors.

The Tree People seem to get by just fine in there though... The thought of living in the trees, amidst the things that creep in the shadows, gives him goosebumps.

His father travels into the woods on occasion, to visit the Tree People, his mother's people. The one time Kzhee had joined him didn't go well. He was lucky to be alive. Their trip to the Twin Trees had been largely uneventful. It was very nice to see his Uncle Sy, the Apex of the Twin Trees, and the lunch table in his uncle's tree home had been laid with fruits and delicacies that Kzhee had never seen before.

The visit was pleasant, and the feast left him feeling lazy and relaxed. His father kept them along the trail, as they returned to the Hills.

'Always stay on the trail.' His father's words had seemed to have just left his mouth, when a screech rang out from behind them. Kzhee would never forget the terror he felt, as a gigantic bat grabbed his shoulders, and began to lift him from his horse.

His father had leapt from the back of his own mount, rolling through the dirt, before coming up on his feet. As the bats flew over the Hill-Chief's head, he swung his mace, striking one of them on the wing. A blast of blue lightning erupted from his father's arm, running the length of the mace, then crawling over the bat like a creeping web and spreading to those around it, stretching and arcing between their wings.

Several of the bats fell screeching to the ground. Throwing his mace aside, his father swung his bow forward, notching an arrow and sending it at the bat carrying Kzhee away. The fall had hurt, and Kzhee had had trouble breathing for weeks after, but he'd survived.

Broken ribs are better than whatever grisly end the bat was flying you to... Kzhee had thought.

He came out relatively unscathed, but had not been asked to accompany his father on those particular trips since.

Kzhee's daydreaming comes to an end, as he approaches the outskirts of the woods.

Why did I ride all the way out here?

It was a long trip to have made for nothing. With a click of his tongue, Kzhee sends the horse racing along the edge of the trees. He looks into the woods as they ride, occasional sights making his head quickly turn as he tries to focus his eyes on movements in the shadows.

A long way off, he sees the trees begin to change from the overgrown ancient giants of the forest, to the uniform rows of the Orchard, its beautifully manicured trees spotted with red, gold and green apples, stretching as far as Kzhee can see.

A sweet Orchard red... Probably more refreshing than filling. The thought makes his mouth water.

The Orchard is about a half mile ahead. He squeezes his legs, urging Sparks to run faster. "Don't worry girl, there's an apple or two in it for you."

As they gallop, he notices a figure appear behind the shadows of the trees, hidden amongst the foliage. When they ride past, Kzhee turns his head to try to make out the shape.

It can't be...

Through the trees, just for a moment, he thinks he sees his mother's face, partially hidden by a patch of moss dangling from a branch above.

What is this? It isn't possible...

He veers Sparks sharply into the woods, riding hard towards where he thought she had been. The brush and bramble ahead of him shakes, as something scurries away. Kzhee rides harder, but the apparition quickly gains distance on him.

What could be running faster than Sparks?

The wind whistles past his ears, cutting and biting into his flesh as they sprint through the trees. Sparks darts left and then right, narrowly skimming past massive trunks, then jumping high to clear a cluster of roots grasping up from the forest floor.

Kzhee hears a voice, crying on the wind.

Is that a call for help?

He can't make out the words, but he keeps pushing forward. Suddenly his pursuit ends, as whatever he was chasing vanishes. Kzhee rides on, confused, looking around for any signs of movement. But the woods around him are silent. He realizes the edge of the Plains is out of sight.

It must have just been my imagination... He thinks, taking a look around. *I'd better head back, if the sun sets I won't be able to find my way out.*

He glances around, starting to turn Sparks back the way they had come, when a rustle from the leaves above grabs his attention. Looking up, Kzhee notices something beginning to descend from the forest roof, repelling down from a nearly invisible thread of silk.

Kzhee sees the shape becoming clearer, shining, black as pitch, reflecting the tiny beams of light managing to find their way through the dense leaves. The lower it sinks, the easier it becomes to see. As it nears him, the creature's descent stops.

Gazing upon its gleaming carapace, Kzhee realizes instantly.

It's a spider...

Larger than any he has ever seen. The spider begins to extend its body, uncurling and stretching its foul limbs, while keeping hold on the silk thread with its hind legs. From the front of the beast grows a torso and head, resembling a man's.

Dropping to the ground, it lands on all eight limbs, continuing to move each of them as it stands, alternatively clicking and tapping the ground, as if trying to keep off a burning surface.

The sight of the creature makes Kzhee's heart sink and his head begin to spin. He knows he must ride away, flee as fast as he can.

Where do I ride? Which way did I come from?

He sends Sparks into a sprint, directly way from the creature.

Faster, get away. Before those legs...

He hears the clicking of the spider's limbs, scrambling behind him in close pursuit. The moment he looks back to see if it's still chasing them, the earth in front of him and Sparks gives way. Kzhee and the horse fall together, but they do not hit the ground.

He feels his body suspended in the air. Struggling to move, he realizes that they are stuck in place. Looking about he sees the ground below, hidden beneath layer after layer of spider's silk, spun between the sides of the pit to catch anything foolish enough to walk over the covering of leaves and brush that Kzhee and Sparks had fallen through.

The creature peers over the edge of the pit, smiling an unnatural smile, sickeningly sweet and seemingly stuck in place. Its unblinking eyes are locked on Kzhee, frozen open, just like its grinning mouth.

Slowly, it moves towards him, stretching each leg delicately and deliberately, taking its time. The creature stops at Kzhee's side, bringing its smiling face right in front of his. He can smell each breath it takes, putridly leaking from its gaping smile.

Will it swallow me whole, or will it have to take bites? The thought horrifies him.

He struggles desperately, trying to turn and twist his body, anything to get his head away from the creature's face. As Kzhee squirms, the spider lifts one of its many limbs, slowly bringing it forward and stabbing into his leg. Kzhee feels his body start to go limp, as the warmth from the wound begins spreading to his extremities.

After poking him a few more times to ensure he's incapacitated, the creature moves towards Sparks. Kzhee's limbs no longer respond to his mind's commands. From the corner of his eye, he can see the creature reaching a limb towards Sparks. Heart racing and blood rushing to his head, Kzhee begins to panic.

Do something... Now! It'll kill Sparks if you don't.

He tries to scream for help, but can't even move his lips.

He knows he needs to free himself, but his body won't budge. Glancing back at Sparks, Kzhee can see the creature's mouth getting larger, unhinging and opening, impossibly wide. Yet somehow, still smiling.

Kzhee summons all the strength he can, pulling and twisting in an attempt to maneuver a limb free.

Pull hard! Get one arm loose and maybe you can cut yourself down.

Suddenly, Kzhee feels the webbing around his arm break, leaving residue and wisps hanging from his sleeve. He reaches towards Sparks, but his body is still stuck in place.

Think... What do I do?

He screams at the creature, hoping to distract it from Sparks. Undeterred, it moves its head closer to the horse's face. As the creature's teeth brush against Sparks' neck, it turns its head to face Kzhee, rubbing cheeks with the horse, taunting his inability to move. Sparks struggles desperately, letting out a frightened neigh, but the webbing holds her firmly in place.

The creature's head is above Sparks now, its mouth beginning to widen, becoming more warped and grotesque as it grows in size. When its mouth reaches out towards the horse, Kzhee screams. As he does, a sharp flash of light erupts and a deafening crack rings out, its resonance amplified by the walls of the pit.

Kzhee tries to look around, to grasp what has happened, but his sight fails him. The flash leaves his field of vision snowy white. He attempts to blink life back into his eyes, but the smell of smoke reaches his nostrils, its salty burn blurring his sight even more.

As Kzhee's vision slowly begins to return, all he can see are flames, bright and hot. The web around him begins to burn away at an alarming pace. He falls to the ground when the last of the webbing suspending him melts and recoils, landing hard on his side and knocking the wind out of him.

The shape of the horse, still struggling above him, begins to come back into focus. But only briefly, before the final strands supporting her give way. The last thing Kzhee sees, before the world goes black, is Sparks' head crashing towards his own.

Rosemary

"Matron Holly?" Rosemary begins to ask, looking up from the hearth in her room. "How do you think they'll arrive?"

"I'm not sure, my dear." The matron answers. "Maybe the rail sleigh, maybe the sea."

"Do you think Prince Bastion will remember me?"

"Of course he will, little princess. Who could forget a face so sweet?"

"I'm nervous… I wish they would arrive. Are you sure this dress isn't too white? I'm scared I'll look like a floating head out in the snow."

"You look very nice, my dear." Matron Holly says, smiling at her.

Rosemary's sky blue eyes are brightened by streaks of baby blue dye running through her light blonde hair. Matron makes the dyes for her, from dewberries that grow around Castle Blackburn.

The dress is sleeveless, with a snow white fur wrapped around Rosemary's shoulders for warmth. But, even with the shawl, her lips are almost as blue as the streaks in her hair.

"Are you cold?" Matron asks, stoking the fire.

"If I say yes, may I change dresses?"

"Prince Bastion's family sent it, they had tailors craft it special, just for you. It is made out of some rare sort of goat's wool, it is supposed to be the softest material in the Empire."

"Softer than silk from the Purple Coast?" Rosemary asks, skeptically raising an eyebrow.

"Well, you're wearing it, you tell me."

"Would you grab my silk dress from the wardrobe, please?" Rosemary asks. "The one from my sister's wedding."

Matron Holly walks to the large dresser and removes a long purple dress, the shimmering fabric decorated with orange and red jewels.

Feeling both garments at the same time, Rosemary furrows her brow. "The silk feels cold, like water running through my fingers. The wool is a lot warmer… I'm not sure about softer though."

"The silk is from the Firelands, they must make their clothing to be cool, otherwise they would burn up!" Matron replies, laughing heartily.

Outside, the sound of clapping hooves comes rising. Shortly after, the ground begins to rumble. Rosemary steps out through her balcony door. Peering into the distance, she sees snow being thrown into the air by some unseen force. The billowing column of powder flies towards the castle, gliding along a set of twin metal tracks leading into the town below her family's castle.

I wonder if they have their own sleigh car... She thinks to herself, doubting that the Grand Marshal of the Southern Realm would ride in the same transport as everyone else.

Rosemary's father is the King of Blackburn and its surrounding lands, one of the many southern kings. But Prince Bastion's father is the Grand Marshal of the Southern Realm, and King of the Frozen Palace. As the ruler of the Southern Realm, he is one of the most powerful men in the Empire.

They must have their own car... She continues thinking. *Painted in their colors and luxuriously furnished inside.*

She can't remember Prince Bastion and his father having come to visit her family's castle before. The only times she had ever seen him were at the few tournaments they had both attended, and most recently at his mother's funeral.

He had been crying... She can picture his steel grey-blue eyes, bloodshot from tears.

"Come back inside, it's time to go." Matron says, sticking her head of out the door.

Rosemary steps back inside, the warmth bringing color back to her cheeks. "Wish me luck!" She chirps, trying not to sound nervous.

"You don't need luck, my dear." Matron Holly hollers after her, as Rosemary excitedly takes off down the corridor.

Her mother and father are waiting in the grand hall. Hazel and Birch, Queen and King of Castle Blackburn. They smile widely, beaming as Rosemary enters the large stone room.

"She's so beautiful." Her mother says. "Do you remember when you proposed to me, my love?"

"Of course I do." The king replies, putting his arm around his wife. "And yes, you look very lovely, Rosemary. Let's not speak of nuptials yet though. The grand marshal hasn't said anything. We don't know if that is even what brings them."

"What else would they be coming here for?" Her mother asks, looking up at him. "The marshal sent her this dress, and he is bringing his son. It seems fair to assume."

"We shall see soon enough." He replies, "They should be arriving any minute."

"Let us go out front to meet them." The queen says, pulling her husband's arm. "Come, Rosemary."

She follows her parents outside, carefully holding up the trail of her dress, trying to keep it out of the snow. Looking down at the town below, Rosemary sees the sleigh cars pulling to a stop at a building outside the edge of the city. Her father had sent carriages and a handful of knights to escort the party from the sleigh station.

As the carriages move up the hill, a harbinger rides into the courtyard ahead of the procession. "All hail, Grand Marshal Barren! King of the Frozen Palace!" He shouts.

Rosemary's breathing is strained, made worse by the cold. She is struggling to remember her manners. Matron had taught her to always be polite, curtsey when introduced, smile, stand straight… But when the carriage door swings open, Rosemary begins to sulk and shyly stare at the ground.

Stop it! She thinks, scolding herself. *Look at them, smile.*

The grand marshal steps out of the coach, his portly girth making it difficult to squeeze through the small door. He is tall and square, with shoulders wider than his belly. His hair has retired to the sides of his head, leaving a ring of bare skin between the few remaining wisps and the base of his large gold crown.

Prince Bastion steps out after his father, much leaner than the old man, and still in possession of all his hair. Even though he is young, the prince's shadow of a beard and strong shoulders project a regal presence.

She feels her stomach twisting. *He's staring right at me. Do I say something? Do I move? No, just keep smiling...* It feels like hours since the last breath she took. Her head begins to spin.

"George!" Rosemary's father cheers, as he moves forward and clasps the marshal's hands. "How was your trip? Smooth I hope."

"The ice on the tracks makes for a rough ride, and those sleigh cars are dreadfully cold. I don't see how people travel like that." The marshal says, chuckling, "I was told the southern sea is too icy to sail. I'd have preferred to take my ship."

"Of course, the rail is best suited for cargo. It's no way to travel comfortably." Her father says, gesturing for the door. "Please, let us go inside. Sit by the fire and shake the cold. You remember my wife, and our daughter, Rosemary?"

"Yes, yes, of course. So nice to see you again, Hazel, you look beautiful." The marshal says, kissing the queen's hand. "And you… Rosemary, such a doll. How old are you now?"

"Fifteen, your grace." Rosemary answers, softly.

The marshal looks at his son. "Why don't you two become better acquainted while the adults speak."

"Yes, father." The prince replies, extending his elbow for Rosemary.

She wraps her arm through his, and they walk out of the courtyard, heading towards the sea behind the castle. As they walk away, Rosemary can hear the prince's father booming behind them, "*A fine match indeed!*" The smile on her face spills wide, and her cheeks grow pinker than the cold has already made them.

Each breath they take hangs in the air, rising like smoke signals. She leads him to a trail near the castle, winding through the pines and down to the ocean. The smell of the trees is strong. Rosemary loves the woods, and the prince seems to notice the change in her stride as they enter. He moves his hand down her arm, wrapping his fingers through hers.

"Would you like to walk through the trees?" He asks.

"Yes..." Rosemary replies, squeezing his hand as they step off the trail.

Walking through the pine grove, she sees strips of sun burst through the trees. Catching on the snowy mist, the beams of light seem to have a solid appearance. Looking back, she can see their dreary shadows, following like specters in the fog.

As she and the prince reach a small clearing, he stops and turns to face her, taking each of her hands in his.

"We have huge pine forests around the Frozen Palace. Would you like to see them sometime?"

She nods her head, smiling, trying to avoid his piercing gaze.

"My father intends for us to wed." He continues, "Would that make you happy?"

"It would make me very happy, your grace."

"Please, call me Bastian."

"Bastian…" She looks up, meeting his stare. His eyes have a kindness and warmth that seems to radiate in spite of their steely color.

"Rosemary?" He asks, softly. "Will you be my wife?"

She feels a warm tear welling on her smiling face. "Yes, of course I will!"

He runs his thumb across her cheek, brushing the tear away. She gazes into his eyes, smiling as he leans forward, his head moving towards hers.

Rosemary closes her eyes, waiting for the moment, extending her face ever so slightly up to meet his. Her whole body is tense with anticipation, waiting for his lips, her first kiss...

As their lips meet, she feels his warmth, feels him exhale. His breath tickles her nose, eliciting a gently giggle. She feels her muscles relax as the cold flows from her limbs, replaced by the soft heat of his body.

As the kiss goes on, she feels his lips begin to cool, and she notices him stop moving. Taking a step back, she looks at her betrothed.

Rosemary screams, as she sees his cold blue eyes staring back at her, unmoving, unblinking.

She grabs his arm and screams, "BASTIAN!"

He doesn't move.

She shakes him, yelling again. "BASTIAN! BASTIAN!"

No response.

Rosemary begins to back away, unable to avert her eyes. She wants to run, but her legs won't move. The trees and sky being to spin. Everything looks like it's moving, drifting farther and farther away. The whiteness of the snow begins to expand, overtaking her field of vision.

She wants to cry out for help, but is unable to breathe, her lips stuck in a silent scream. Then, as she gasps for air, everything goes black.

The Assassin

The room is damp and dreary, and an earthy scent fills the air. Uneven stone blocks make up the floors, walls and ceilings. Moss and lichens growing in the cracks between them. The only source of light and heat is a small fire, burning in a hearth along the main wall.

The assassin sits on a hard wood stool, one arm resting on a stone table piled high with books and scrolls. On the far side of the room is a large cabinet. Behind its thick glass door are stocks of variously sized bottles, housing a variety of strange liquids, pastes and gels. Green poisons, purple potions, and various other agents of death.

A door opens, and the guild master enters. Moving swiftly for an old man, he quickly takes a seat across the stone table.

"It is done?" The master asks.

"It is."

The master smiles. "Chase us, the light of dawn."

"For I am the shadow." He replies.

The master sets a jingling leather purse on the table, pushing it towards him. "Are you ready for another assignment?"

"There is to be a tournament in the Great City, I'd love to get out of town before the throngs arrive."

"What if the job is here?" The old man asks, shuffling through a stack of parchment.

"At least that will give me something to take my mind off the tourists and peddlers." The assassin says, grinning.

The master selects a piece of parchment, and hands it to him.

He takes the paper, looks it over, then nods. "Before I leave… I spoke with my friend on the Emperor's Council."

"Yes?"

"The councilor tells me that the Forest Realm has no gifted child to send for the Emperor's Due. Warden Tane has reported that none have been found. He fears for his head of course, being the closest thing the Forest Realm has to a leader."

"How many people live in that realm?" The master asks, curiously.

"Fifty thousand live in the Orchard under Warden Tane, maybe twenty thousand more from the smaller towns and the Vintners. No one knows how many live in the forest itself, the people in there can only be found if they want you to find them."

"The Tree People still have plenty of children born with the gifts."

"True, but the Tree People refuse to participate in the Emperor's Due."

"What does any of this have to do with us?" The master asks.

"That little mouse of yours… She is from the forest, no?

"The Emperor wants children near his son's age." The master replies, a look of concern flashing across his face. "She is too young..."

"They are willing to take her." The assassin presses, "Think master… We would have ears on the new council. When Relorn becomes Emperor…"

The master stares at the ground, pondering the proposal. "Presuming she stays loyal to us… It could prove advantageous. Arrange it. I will speak with the girl."

"Consider it done." He says, standing and walking towards the door.

Stopping at the cabinet against the wall, the assassin grabs a vial of green-grey liquid and removes a dagger from his waistband. Dripping the fluid onto the base of the blade's edge, he lets it run to the tip, before replacing the poison and ducking out of the room.

Seaborne

Gulls cry overhead and men yell around him, as Captain Seaborne sprints across the deck. Suddenly, the drawn cord of a scorpion next to him snaps, firing a barbed harpoon through the air with a deafening *crack*. The enormous projectile broadsides the trading vessel attempting to flee, smashing through the wooden ship just above the waterline and embedding into the hull.

After the sharp sound of the scorpion, all Seaborne can hear is a loud ringing in his ear. He can see men around him shouting silent orders to each other, pirates waving their arms, calling men for the fight.

As his hearing begins to return, Seaborne slaps the pirate who fired the scorpion, hitting him hard on the back of his head. "We want that vessel, ya son of a sea cow! Don't sink it…" Moving to the head of the ship, he hollers, "Bring us about!"

The helmsman begins to spin the ship's wheel, turning the boat in pursuit. Seaborne bites down upon the blade of his cutlass, grabs a rope, and swings from the ship's upper deck. He sails across the narrow gap of water, landing aboard the trading vessel. Most of the sailors lay on the deck cowering, as a boarding party of pirates follows him onto the ship.

"Throw down ya arms, and lay on the deck!" Seaborne shouts. "Unless ya have a death wish…"

The sailors on the trading vessel all lay face down, the few armed men throw their weapons aside and follow suit. The pirates restrain the captured sailors, tying them to the mast.

One of the pirates approaches Seaborne. "Captain, we believe all the men are accounted for. Twenty-two slave sailors, two mercenaries serving as guards, plus the cook, first mate and captain."

"Bring me the captain." Seaborne replies, turning to face out over the ocean.

The ship's captain is rotund, short, and completely bald. Clean shaven, save for a single patch of hair beneath his lower lip. The man stares down, as he is pushed on deck by a large pirate.

"Take me to my chambers, sir." Seaborne commands.

The terrified man leads him beneath the quarter deck, to the captain's cabin.

Grabbing a sweetlime from a pile stacked inside a cherry wood bowl, Seaborne takes a bite from the top. Rind and all.

"Tell me all about my new ship." Seaborne says, his mouth full of half-chewed fruit. "Its cargo, its crew, its intended destination."

"We were heading south, sir, to Seacliff. Our hold is filled with trade goods from A'Tannia and the Orchard. Apples, cider, olive oil, garlic, sweetlimes. A few barrels each of rum and fish sauce. Most of the sailors aboard are slaves, meant to be sold to the Southern Trading Company. We intended to return with less than ten men."

"I appreciate ya being forthcoming, and I'm sorry to spoil those well laid plans." Seaborne says, taking another bite of sweetlime. "Do ya wish to live?"

A light of hope bursts through the man's eyes. "I do, yes! I will never speak of word of this, I swear to you."

"PARROT!" Seaborne yells, sticking his head from the cabin.

A well-muscled man in his early twenties runs in. Upon his bare shoulder sits a red, gold and green macaw.

"Aye, cap'n." The man named Parrot replies.

"Escort our prisoner to the deck."

"Aye, cap'n." Parrot nods, grabbing the man and dragging him from the cabin.

Seaborne finishes the sweetlime, then grabs another. Slowly consuming it as he looks around the room. Some books are stacked upon a shelf, held in place by large orange and amber stones wedged at either end. A circular feather bed stands in the center of the room, covered in luxurious furs and silks, and draped in curtains of satin.

I'll have the bed moved to my own cabin. He thinks, sitting on the edge to test its softness.

This is the second ship Seaborne has captured since being promoted to captain. He would probably have Grimy Waters prize command it for their return trip. Grimy and Parrot had been among the first volunteers to join Seaborne's crew when Captain Noft had promoted him a month past, giving him a ship of his own.

Seaborne had named his new ship, *The Masthead,* after the piece of wood he had been found upon years ago at sea. He had hardly been more than a boy when Captain Noft found him floating in the water. No recollection of who he was, or where he came from. Now, all these years later, he was a captain himself. Captain Seaborne, born upon the turbid sea.

He exits the cabin, returning to the deck and whistling loudly. "Men, anyone who joins my crew will be a free man from this day forward, with an equal share of plunder. Rest assured, no harm will come to ya should ya decline. I'll set ya free with the captain here, and wish ya the best of luck."

All the sailors begin to shout, volunteering to join him. The bald captain looks sick, as Parrot loads him onto a small raft and lowers it into the water.

My fleet is forming nicely. Seaborne thinks, looking at the vessels around him. *Almost time I presented to the admiral...*

"Avast, ya dogs!" He shouts, to the crew. "Prepare to disembark."

Relorn 2

The boys finish eating dinner, seated in the dining hall of Atasio Nodovin's home. Remnants of the feast lay around them. Roasted pheasant and herb crusted fish, sweet corn from the plains slathered with butter, green beans drowned in roasted garlic, and rolls of bread glazed with syrup and honey.

Atasio allows the servants to pour wine for the boys, an early celebration for their upcoming graduation. He had already drunk far too much himself, and was now stumbling about the room, the blood colored contents of his cup splashing onto the iridescent marble floor. Putting his hand on his son's shoulder, the intoxicated man begins slurring.

"I am proud of... *Hic*... Of you, boy." He says, hitting the rim of Matio's goblet with his own, in a clumsy attempt at a toast. Walking around the table, the old man takes a seat next to Relorn. "You won't forget old Atasio when you become Emperor, will you? I've been kind to you, have I not?"

"Yes, most kind." Relorn answers, "I will surely tell my father of the generosity and hospitality you have shown me these past years."

"Thank you, your grace. Thank you..." The old man replies, a strange look of relief on his face.

Standing behind Atasio, Reza puts his hands together in a mock pleading gesture. Andrew laughs, drawing the old man's attention.

"Ah, Andrew." Atasio says, his eyes beginning to water. "Of course, I am proud of all of you. It will be quite lonely around here once you boys leave. I don't know what I..." He trails off, shaking his head. "Sorry boys… It seems I've enjoyed a bit too much wine. I shall excuse myself for the night, have a good evening."

Reza yells, "Goodnight!" Watching the old man leave, before grabbing the nearest bottle of wine and beginning to chug, shooing off a servant who politely offers him a glass.

Andrew gives a dramatic yawn, stretching his arms above his head. "Well, I don't know about you people, but I am ready for bed." He stands, starting for the stairs, the rest of them in close pursuit. As they exit the dining hall, four bodyguards and the man in the gravel cloak turn and follow closely behind.

The boy's rooms are upstairs, in a separate wing of the mansion. As they depart for their individual chambers, the guards take their posts in the hall.

Relorn walks around his room, changing into a warm set of clothes. Their sleeping chambers are connected by doors, Matio's to his left and Reza's to the right. After a few minutes, Reza and Andrew enter his room.

"Matio here yet?" Andrew asks, looking around.

"No." Relorn replies, as he finishes preparing.

Reza walks to opposite wall, trying to open the door to Matio's room. "Little twit barred his door…" He hisses, tapping gently on the wood.

The door cracks open, and Matio sticks his head through. "What do you want?"

"We're going out, get dressed." Reza whispers.

"It's always something…" Matio sighs, "Can't I get some sleep for tomorrow?"

"No, put your clothes on." Andrew chimes in, before stepping out onto the balcony.

Relorn finishes getting dressed and joins Andrew on the patio, overlooking the city of Triali. Fires burn in large pyres from the front of grand temples and sprawling palaces, projecting eerie glows and casting shadows of large marble statues across the city plaza.

Pinching the hard granite railing, Relorn pulls a large stone arrow from it. He ties a rope to the back, looks for the correct tree below, then shoots the arrow towards it. The projectile finds its mark, splintering into the tree and sinking deep.

He pulls on the rope, laughing and congratulating himself on the shot, while they tie the other end to the railing. Using their bows as handles, the boys slide down the line and drop to the ground beneath the tree.

They run through the willows that decorate the front of the mansion, ducking and weaving in an attempt to keep the trees' thin arms from whipping their faces. The evening breeze blows intently, causing the billowing branches to dance and wave, reaching towards the lights of the city.

Approaching the white stone wall that surrounds the palace, Relorn sees sentries posted at all the gates. Throwing their bows over first, the boys scramble up the side of the barrier. Spikes line the top, but the boys carefully slip past and jump down to the other side. All except Matio, whose tunic gets caught on a spike, leaving him dangling from the side of the wall.

"C'mon clumsy, what are you doing?" Reza growls, through clenched teeth. "He's going to get us caught. We should have left him in bed."

Andrew joins Relorn in pulling their friend down. Matio's clothes rip as he falls hard to the dirt. Reza laughs, then helps him up.

"So where are we going?" Relorn asks, as they lightly jog away from the house, down the hill towards Triali.

"I heard about a tavern in the city from some of the attendants at the Academy. It's supposed to be the best in Triali, if not the whole Plateau." Reza answers, as soon as they are out of earshot of the sentries.

"A bar? We've been drinking already… We could just have more wine inside." Matio complains. "What do we need to go to a bar for?"

"Girls dance on the tables at this place." Reza replies, proudly. "We're celebrating graduation, don't ruin the occasion!"

The boys slow down to a walk as they enter the city. Large marble buildings line the streets, held up by giant carved columns. Ornate designs cut into the marble, make each building unique. Large statues stand in front of the various temples, tributes to whichever deity they worship inside.

"What are you shivering for, Matio?" Andrew asks.

"We're heading to the docks… Cutthroats, mercenaries and pirates hang around there. We shouldn't go, not without guards. If the Emperor finds out…" Matio trails off, not finish his thought.

"What does it matter to you?" Relorn asks, defensively. *What is he talking about, what does he care if I get in trouble?*

"What do you think your father will do if you get hurt on my father's watch?" Matio blurts out.

"I don't know… What are you saying?" He asks, hurt by the insinuation.

"Forget it…" Matio whispers, looking at the ground. "I shouldn't have said anything. Let's just not draw any attention, hopefully no one will recognize you."

Relorn glares at him, but quickly puts it out of his mind as they reach the noisy building. A large man stands at the door, so wide he completely eclipses the entrance, blocking their way. Reza pulls a few pieces of silver from a silk sack, and hands them to the man.

With a laugh, the door man steps aside, letting the boys enter.

Torches line the walls and braziers burn, bathing the bodies of the belly dancers in flickering light as they contort upon the tables. A cheerful girl with rosy cheeks sings from the stage, surrounded by a band of instrumentalists, the pulse of their song setting a rhythm for the dancers. A beautiful girl approaches, guiding them to a table near the stage.

"A round of drinks!" Reza yells, flicking a silver piece to the girl, who walks off with a grin. He holds his arms out, gesturing around the room. "What do you guys think?"

Relorn's jaw hangs low, as a girl climbs onto their table and starts swaying her hips and gyrating her torso, dancing to the beat of the drums. "I've never been anywhere like this before…" He stammers.

Matio ducks his head, as a loud crash interrupts the music and two men near the bar start to fight. Another picks up his chair and breaks it over one of their heads, dropping him to the floor. As the fight begins to spread through the room, the girl on stage raises her voice, sharply projecting her singing over the sounds of the brawl. The song hits a high note, causing the patrons to stop fighting in unison, enchanted by her voice. Guards run in from outside, but shortly depart with confused expressions when they find nothing amiss.

Their server returns with four tankards of beer, setting them down on the table before walking away. Patrons around the bar yell and cheer, toasting one another. Sailors take turns singing songs from their home lands. Silk dresses of pink and green and teal and gold flutter through the air as the dancing girls spin. Relorn finds his eyes wandering from table to table, looking at the dancers and at the men staring as if entranced.

Andrew is the first to break the silence that has fallen over their table. "A toast my friends, health, happiness and graduation."

"Hear! Hear!" They cheer together, turning up their drinks. One round of libations goes by, then another, their conversation rising in volume until the tables next to them start glaring over, clearly annoyed.

"Server! Server! I said I need service!" Reza yells, as their serving girl makes her way through the crowd. "What took you so long? We require another round." He shouts, reaching into his pocket and taking out a gold piece, gently placing it in the girl's hand.

She takes it, holding it up to the light in clear disbelief. "What'm I spose a do wit dis?" She asks, biting the coin.

"It's yours, see to it that our glasses don't go empty again." Reza says, waving her away.

She excitedly hurries off to refill their cups, clutching the gold close.

The hours seem like minutes, when the barkeep starts closing up. Patrons loudly and begrudgingly make for the door, shouting at the dancers, inviting them to join.

The boys stumble out together, Matio suspended between Relorn and Andrew, too drunk to support himself. Reza leaps and dances ahead of the group, belligerently singing off-key.

"Stop messing about, Reza. Help us with him…" Andrew shouts.

That fool is going to rouse the guards, then we'll be in it… Relorn thinks, looking around the quiet city streets.

"I love you… *Hic*… You guys." Matio mutters, "You're gonna… *Hic*… Bring us to the Pillar with you, right Rel…?"

"Of course, pal." Relorn says, grinning. "Wouldn't leave you behind for anything. You'll be my councilors, and we'll rule the Empire together!"

The boys break into laughter, stumbling through the street. Relorn smiles, enjoying the walk.

I hardly want to leave… He thinks, a sudden pang of sadness coursing through him. *Once school is over, wouldn't it be nice to find a place here? Sail and drink and explore… Not worry about the pressure? My dad would never…*

His thought is cut short by a sound ahead. Two men appear, whispering and peering from around the corner.

"Stop, stop…" Relorn hisses, "Look."

Reza draws his bow from his shoulder, notching an arrow. "Come out from there!" He yells.

The two men walk out, followed closely by three more. From an alley next to the boys, another group approaches.

Relorn looks back, trying to find some direction to escape, but his heart drops as a large gang shuffles up the street behind them. He quickly tries to count how many. *Fifteen, maybe twenty...*

One of the men behind them begins to shout, his words barely intelligible. "A gold piece, a buy sum beer, never seen 'at b'fore. Who is ya twits, a be spendin a year a pay on a night a booze?"

"We're nobody." Andrew calls, as the men begin approaching from all sides. "Just let us go, and we'll give you what coin we have."

"Oh, e'll 'ave ya coin, might a be we take ya eyes too, and ya tong. Keep ya from squealin." The man growls, as the mob advances.

"Can you take them?" Relorn whispers, to Reza.

"Yeah, sure... Let me shoot all thirty of them." He answers, sarcastically through clenched teeth.

Andrew and Relorn both let go of Matio and grab for their bows, their friend crumpling to the ground with a groan.

"Ya gonna shoot all us?" The man asks, laughing at the boys and looking around. "Hows a many arrows ya got?"

Damn... Relorn thinks, looking at Matio slumped over, drunk and moaning on the city street. *He probably could shoot them all before they even knew what happened...*

The boys stand back to back with their bows drawn, as the mob converges. Out of the corner of his eye, Relorn can see one of the thugs dive towards him, a large knife gleaming as it flies at his neck.

Senator McKenna

He looks down on the city of A'Tannia, from the balcony of the Senate Hall. Throngs of people gather around the fighting pits, celebrating the week's end festivities. Vendors holler from their carts, peddling snacks and libations, sending the savory smell of grilled meats, roasted corn and fried bread wafting through the late afternoon air.

Babies cry in their mothers' arms, while children laugh and hang from the railing that surrounds the reservoir, spitting and throwing scraps of food to try and catch a glimpse of the creatures lurking beneath the surface. A group of boys jump back from the edge and scream, then begin rolling with laughter.

I wonder what they saw… He thinks to himself, excitedly. *Wouldn't that be something if it was a serpent rising from the depths?*

"Senator McKenna?"

Damn, what do these fools want now…? I am so sick of listening to old blowhards endlessly pontificate about nothing.

"Yes, Senator Nassius?" McKenna replies, sweetly addressing the eldest of the senators assembled in the hall.

"There is the matter of selecting a gifted child for the Due."

"What of it?" McKenna snaps, "We elected you to the task. Have you not found someone?"

"There are a few candidates." Nassius says, meekly. "No one spectacular, to say the least..."

"Have the Emperor's people sent a request?"

"No word from the Emperor." Nassius answers.

"Tell us of the candidates then."

"There is a girl from a fishing village on the river." The old man replies. "She can produce bubbles, I am told."

"Bubbles!? Bubbles!? You would have us offer a girl who blows bubbles!?" McKenna shouts, trying to stifle his laughter. "Do you value your head? Because I have grown accustomed to mine where it is, and Jero will have all of ours on spikes if we send him a girl who blows bubbles."

"Of course, of course..." Nassius says, nodding. "I said they were not spectacular."

"If that is who you lead with, I fear to hear the rest." McKenna rolls his eyes and walks towards the back of the hall. "I think we can adjourn for the evening, concurred?"

"Aye!" The senators cry.

Bubbles... He thinks, waiting for the lift to arrive. Shaking his head and chuckling to himself.

Looking from an opening in the exterior wall, he can see men adjusting doors and levers hundreds of feet below, allowing water to flow in from the river and raise the lift. He steps on as the platform comes to a stop in front of him, riding it down to street level.

The fights are visible from the patio of his apartment, but he prefers to see them up close, to feel the energy of the crowd. Near the center pit a gargantuan man shakes his cage, a few of the bars already bent from where he has been attempting to pull them apart.

That man's arms are the size a normal man's legs, and his torso is the size of a tree! Damn barbarians, they're hardly human...

A crowd starts to gather near the reservoir, jeering and shouting at two men as they are led out in chains.

Good riddance, rapists and murderers... Such types have no place in A'Tannia.

The men are being shoved towards the reservoir, their screams for mercy answered with an onslaught of rotten produce. Tomatoes and cabbages fly at their heads, while children throw stale bread in the water, trying to entice the creatures to the surface.

McKenna diverts his attention from the spectacle long enough to procure a goblet of wine from a nearby vendor, then makes his way to an open section of railing surrounding the water.

The city crier steps up onto a stool, calling out over the audience. "Hear ye, hear ye. Good citizens of A'Tannia. These men before you have been sentenced to death. May they go swiftly."

"Slowly!" The crowd chants. "Slowly! Slowly!"

Most of the garbage being thrown at the convicts is missing, sailing off the edge and splashing into the water behind them, causing the surface to ripple and churn. A burly guard removes the first man's shackles. Then with a heave, he throws him over the railing, sending him screaming and tumbling through the air, splashing into the murky water below. The prisoner submerges, sinking out of sight. The crowd waits silently, wondering whether he will surface or if he has already met his fate beneath the turbid waves.

Suddenly the water breaks, as the man comes up gasping desperately for air. The crowd cheers, relieved that the show will go on. The man fights and slips, futilely trying to climb the reservoir's slippery stone wall. But the moss covered stones are slick, and there is nowhere to grab ahold.

As the first man struggles below, the second criminal is shoved over the railing. The crowd pushing with such force that he is sent spinning and somersaulting through the air as he falls.

Just before splashing into the water, the surface beneath him erupts, and an enormous set of jaws surges into the air, hundreds of shining teeth rising from the depths. Snapping closed around the man, the scaly creature bites off all but his shoulders and head, before sinking back into the bloodstained water.

Screams of excitement ring through the crowd. The deafening roar of conversation echoes, as people shout above one another, reveling in the rare sight of one of the larger creatures.

I've never seen that one before... The senator thinks, still in awe. *What else is hiding beneath the surface...?*

Looking down, he sees a frenzied school of fish start swarming the remnants of the creature's meal, quickly picking the bones clean. Once they finish, they divert their attention to the man vainly attempting to hang onto the wall. He screams, as dozens of long fanged fish jump into the air around him, snapping barbed jaws that seem to make up half the length of their bodies.

One bites into the man's leg, holding tightly. More begin to latch on, easily pulling him from the shallow crack his fingers had found. Seconds later, the man is gone, consumed by the ravenous school.

The senator snickers, as he turns away from the execution and heads back towards the pits, unable to stop thinking about the barbarian he had seen caged earlier.

The main event will start soon, and I really want to see what that man can do…

Ral 2

The cage violently rattles as the barbarian shakes the bars of his prison, pulling and prying in a vain attempt to escape.

Stupid brute. Ral thinks, snickering to himself. *Where are you going to go when you break out of those chains? Not the brightest bunch, barbarians… But I guess they make up for it with all that muscle.*

Ral looks up at the sky, deep blue and purple, just a twinkle past twilight. Looking back across the ring, he realizes the giant is staring right at him as he fights to get free.

He doesn't want to escape. He wants to get at me…. I wonder what his master offered him if he manages to win.

With each fight that Ral is victorious, the masters of the fighting pits like him less and less. His success infuriates them, just as much as it pleases his own master.

Ral scans the area, trying to locate Bentino. Finally, he spots him standing in front of a meat vendor, grabbing two large salmon skewers from a greasy looking man in stained rags.

He's cockier than I am, the thought of me losing hasn't even crossed his mind... Stuffing his face and smiling like the prize gold is already in his pocket.

A group of slaves begin to push the barbarian's cage towards the pit, hanging it just far enough over that he has have no place to go but into the ring. The spectators start to cheer, the noise growing deafeningly loud.

Ral looks around and sees the enormous crowd swelling, moving towards him, crushing each other as they push for the stands. More than thirty thousand people watching, most from apartments and patios, high above the action. Others from taverns and food halls with a decent view. The rest surround the ring, circling the arena and squeezing into the seats of the huge stadium that surrounds the pits.

He hears the crowd chanting, "Ral! Ral! Ral! Ral! Ral! Ral!" And his stoic expression slips into a smile.

Ral turns to the stands behind him, looking for her face. Satia had left him alone in her apartment earlier to go and place money on the fight with the collectors of debt, but she should have arrived by now.

The odds are against me, but if I win... If...

He sees her walking between the stands, exiting the market. She looks towards him, catching his glance, then waves while ascending the stairs to find a seat.

Focus...

Ral stands on the edge of the pit, taking deep rhythmic breaths and stretching the muscles in his arms. He stares at his opponent. The giant stares back at him.

I liked him more when he was fighting and beating on the bars, wasting his energy...

The barbarian's sudden calmness sends chills down Ral's spine.

You've won dozens of fights. He reminds himself. *This is just another night. It will be fine... Fine...*

He tries to stay relaxed, but the man's eyes won't break their stare.

Silence befalls the onlookers as the master of games walks to his appointed seat, nestled on a dais between the pit and reservoir. He struggles to climb the rungs of the elevated chair. Upon reaching the top he settles in, brushing the wrinkles from his shirt. Then he begins to address the hushed audience. For such a small man, his voice projects deceivingly loud across the silent city, echoing from the stone and marble buildings.

"Ladies and lords! If it please you, introducing... The dread of the waste... HORAM THE BARBARIAN!"

Some in the crowd begin to cheer, but most boo and hiss.

"And of course, his challenger... The son of the city. The pride of A'Tannia... RRRRAAAAAAAAALLLLLLL!"

The city erupts with applause and cheers, the ground shaking beneath thousands of stamping feet. A shrill screech rings from the reservoir, causing a few bystanders to jump back scared. Eliciting a wave of laughter from those around them.

I'll take it as a good sign... Even the creatures sound like they're on my side.

Ral makes the most of the moment, jumping down into the pit and landing in a somersault, before rolling to his feet. He throws his arms in the air, bringing about another roar of applause.

The attendants working Horam's cage move quickly to unlock the door. As soon as the padlock is removed, the barbarian kicks the bars, causing the gate to swing open, nearly taking the head off of one of the workers.

The walls of the pit are lined with all manner of shields and weapons. Swords, spears, axes, maces, javelins, hammers, even a triple headed flail. The barbarian jumps into the arena, joining Ral, who now paces the perimeter, eyeing the selection of weapons.

"BEGIN!" The master of games shouts.

Without even picking up a weapon, the barbarian charges at him, screaming a curse Ral can't understand. A giant fist plunges towards his face, narrowly missing as he sidesteps the blow.

Grabbing a spear from the wall, Ral lunges at the man. Stabbing at him with the metal blade on the end of the pole, alternating repeatedly from right to left, forcing the barbarian to take small steps back each time, until his back presses against the edge of the pit.

The giant man grabs a great axe leaning against the wall next to him, and begins deflecting Ral's lunges, diverting the strikes while trying to get a clean swing at his torso. Ral begins to retreat, using the spear to block and parry the mighty sweeps of the axe.

Again and again the barbarian swings, slicing through the air as his target ducks and spins. Ral dances to the side, avoiding a crashing blow, then strikes forward with the spear, its blade digging into Horam's shoulder.

Letting loose a mighty roar, the barbarian grabs the end of the spear and pulls it from his shoulder, yanking with such force that Ral that is thrown to the ground. Lifting him from the dirt, the barbarian brings Ral over his head, then throws him across the ring.

He lands hard on his side, rolling twice before coming to a facedown stop. Shaking his head and gathering his strength, he tries to rise, but Horam is on him like lightning, his axe flying down in a swinging arc towards Ral's head.

Rolling aside at the last second, he narrowly avoids the crashing blade. Out of the corner of his eye, Ral sees the head of the axe break apart from the wooden handle, as the hilt splinters beneath the force of the strike. The audience gasps with delight.

Ral can feel Satia staring from the stands.

Will she cry for me?

He struggles to regain his feet, while the barbarian grabs a great sword off of the wall and beings to advance again.

Stumbling to a weapon rack on the side of the ring, Ral grabs a javelin, throwing it hard at his advancing opponent. Horam dodges the full force of the blow, but the javelin manages to take a hunk of flesh from his left arm. Ral hurls a second, which lands square in the giant's shoulder, enraging him. Horam's two handed great sword slashes to and fro, whistling through the air as Ral ducks and dodges the unwieldy swings.

Grabbing a spear, Ral deflects a particularly nasty slice, then returns the blow, cutting the side of the barbarian's leg.

Screaming with a bestial rage, Horam charges, driving Ral into an empty weapon rack. Narrowly avoiding his swings, Ral jumps up against the side of the pit and pushes back off, sailing over the barbarian and landing behind him. Ral stabs the spear into the giant's back, then quickly pulls it out.

Horam roars as he turns to face Ral, seemingly unaware of the blood freely streaming from his wounds. Swinging hard, the barbarian goes berserk, advancing relentlessly and no longer attempting to divert blows. Ral tries to retreat, but his back hits the wall.

The cold metal of the sword stings as it strikes him in the side. Ral tries to gasp, but is unable. He can feel the blade splitting through his insides, cutting him in half at the waist.

Is this it? He thinks to himself, as the world begins to spiral around him.

He hears the crowd gasp and some people scream. Finding Satia's eyes in the stands, he looks for a tear. Instead he finds them open wide, staring at him in disbelief.

Looking down, Ral expects to find guts and organs, sinew and viscera and blood. Instead, he sees his skin give a gentle ripple, like the wind blowing across a pond. The blade passes through him and out the other side, as if the sword had been swung through water. Waves of azure tinted flesh splash and flood in on themselves, closing the wound in their wake.

The crowd falls silent. Even the barbarian stares at him, unblinking, not knowing how to proceed. Without waiting or warning, Ral seizes the opportunity, plunging his spear into Horam chest with such force that the point exits through his back.

As the barbarian stumbles to the ground, coughing and dying, Ral turns to face the city full of people staring down at him. There is no applause, no cheers. Only a sea of dumbfounded faces, mouths gaping open in silent disbelief.

Then one man stands up from a luxury seat in the senator's box. He slowly begins to clap, breaking the silence, a smile sliding across his face.

Tiaries 2

Jaties raises his glass, toasting the troupe as they congregate backstage. "Here's to another brilliant performance! I would like to thank Coop, and of course my lovely sister. Without the two of you I would surely be dead!"

Tiaries hears the cheering of her friends and feels their pats on her back. She nods and thanks them, trying to get to her dressing room. As she breaks away from the crowd, three men step through the curtain, blocking her path.

"Hello Tiaries, so splendid to see you. You're as gorgeous as I remember." The portly mayor tells her, smiling sweetly as he reaches into a fold of his robe, removing a slender box wrapped in gold and silver foil and topped with a green ribbon. "I have something for you, a present."

She takes the gift and peels away the wrappings, carefully opening the box. It is filled to the brim with an assortment of different colored leaves, shimmering like gems in the torch light. She looks at the mayor, giving him a grin. "These are wonderfully pretty, thank you."

"They are indeed, and quite delicious." He says, taking a magenta leaf from the box and biting the end off, exposing the chocolate hidden beneath the spun sugar coating. Sticky purple filling spills out, leaving a trail dripping down the front of his bright white robes. He tries to wipe it away, but ends up smearing it across the front of himself. "Dear me! I seem to have soiled my shirt..."

Her employer, Mr. Deepriver, laughs at the Mayor, but the third man remains silent, his face hidden beneath the shadow of a gravel colored cloak.

"Where are my manners?" Mr. Deepriver asks, gesturing to the silent man. "Tiaries, this is Councilor Lingonberry, he has come on behalf of the Emperor himself."

"How do you do, my lord?" Tiaries asks, as she curtsies politely.

The councilor silently nods from under his cloak. His bright green eyes fixated on Tiaries.

Mr. Deepriver breaks the silence, "The Emperor's Theatre Company is interested in bringing you on as a performer, Tiaries. The pay is very generous, and you would be entertaining some of the most prominent people in the Empire. It is a great honor to receive an offer to join…"

"A great honor indeed!" The mayor seconds, picking a teal leaf from the box in her hand and beginning to nibble on it.

Tiaries sees the smile on Mr. Deepriver's face and the gleam in his eyes.

What is he getting out of this?

"Jaties too?" She asks, nervously.

Mr. Deepriver looks at the cloaked man, who gives half a nod in approval.

"Of course he can come too, the company is always looking for bright young performers. Jaties is the best we have, after you of course. The carnival will surely be in dire times after you leave." Mr. Deepriver replies, shooting the cloaked man a grin. "What ever will we do…?"

"Wonderful to see you as always, Tiaries." The mayor coos, kissing her hand and turning to escort the councilor out of the tent.

She looks at Mr. Deepriver and asks him, "Do I have some time to think about this? I will need to speak with Jaties, and I'm not sure if…"

Her employer cuts her off sharply, glaring at her with a golden fire in his eyes. "Get your brother and your things, now… You are going with them. It is not up for discussion."

Sneaking past the household guards, Jia creeps into her room scarcely an hour before sunrise. Her face and clothes still covered in a thick layer of ash and soot.

She sets her burning lantern on a jeweled pedestal, before sauntering between black granite arches into her bathing room. Removing her riding clothes and throwing them aside, she steps naked into a shallow circular pool.

Pulling a lever sends a stream of hot water showering onto her head, pouring from an opening above.

Looking out an orange stained glass window, Jia can see the channels winding through the city below. Streams of water and magma glow brightly as they meander next to one another, running along the tops of homes and shops, cascading from the corners of buildings as they make their way down the many levels built around the volcano.

Steam fills the room, as she washes beneath the pouring water. The runoff from her body is blackened by the ash stuck to her sun kissed skin. She turns the lever further, increasing the flow, then plunges her head into the steaming stream, letting the hot water run through her long black hair.

"Jia! JIA!" She hears a voice, calling from her room. "Get in here, now!"

She turns off the water and steps out of the pool, making her way to a robe of magenta silk hanging from a rack across the bathing room. She slides into the smooth garment, before stepping into her bedchamber. "Hello father, how are you this morning?"

"Oh, is it morning...? Have you just woken...?" He shouts, condescendingly.

"What do you mean?" She asks, taking a seat on the edge of her bed.

"The guards tell me you never returned from your practices yesterday. I came to your room after midnight, just to find it empty. Now I have received word of men slaughtered and burned on the southern road. What do you know of this? Where were you?"

"I was in the jungle practicing and lost track of time... I'm sorry, father."

"And of the burned men?"

"What would I know of burned men?"

"Don't toy with me, Jia! Don't think I have forgotten finding you that day. We both know what you are capable of... I told you not to take matters like these into your own hands!"

"I have explained *that day*! He was beating a little girl!" Jia hisses, anger flaring in her voice. "She would have died if not for me!"

"Who are you to decide who deserves to live or die? Who appointed you judge?"

She sits in silence, staring at the ground to avoid his eyes.

"You are my daughter, a lady of the City of Light, you cannot burn men to death on the street." He looks away, sighing. "Now tell me... Did you attack the men on the road last night?"

"I did what you and your guards refused to do." She shouts, jumping to her feet. "I made our lands safe."

"So it was you?" Anger burns like an inferno in his eyes. "Jia!"

"Will I be the offering from the Firelands? For the Emperor's Due?" She asks, interrupting him.

He looks at her with a dumbfounded expression. "Of course not, Jia. The other warlords and I have selected Te Reza. We will present him at the tourney…"

"I figured as much…" She snarls, looking out the window.

"Don't try to change the subject! You need to move past this childish rebellion…" He pauses, then adds quickly, "I have been speaking with Che Haros, Lord of Panascus. We will be announcing your betrothal to his son, Che Hoondo."

"What…?" She stammers, blindsided. "When?"

"After the Emperor's tourney. We will announce it to all the nobles of the Empire, and host a feast in your honor. Put the Emperor's Due out of your mind, girl… You shall be a lady of Panascus before the year is up." He turns and exits the room without saying another word, his pomegranate dyed cape whipping around the corner to punctuate his departure.

The Emperor will never choose Reza over me, not if that girl keeps her word… If he knows what I can do…

She smiles confidently, sitting on the stool next to the jeweled pedestal that supports her shining lantern. The flame still dances behind the colored glass designs. Sticking her hand through the opening, she plays with the fire, letting it swirl and burn, licking the skin between her fingers.

"Goodnight," Jia whispers.

The burning doppelganger spins and waves, blowing her a fiery kiss from its miniature hand.

Kzhee 2

Beams of moonlight peek through the dark foliage above, like stars scattered through the night sky. Kzhee drifts in and out of sleep, riding through fields and over the hills of his dreams, Sparks running beneath him, gliding atop the tall grass.

He feels the horse lick his face, slowly bringing him back to reality. Stirring from his slumber, Kzhee sees Sparks moving away to graze on the few tufts of grass growing in the pit. Across the way he sees the creature that attacked him lying dead on the ground, a hole burnt clean through its carapace.

"What happened?" He turns and asks the horse.

She looks up at him with soulful eyes and shakes her head, letting out a snort.

Kzhee slowly climbs to his feet, looking around the hole for a way out. "What are we going to do?" He asks aloud. But the horse ignores him, continuing to search the small pit for grass to chew on.

At their lowest point, the walls of the hole are twice as tall as Kzhee. He looks for anything to grab ahold of, noticing only a few roots and some remnants of the creature's web. Whistling to get the horse's attention, he climbs up on her back and tries to balance as she sways from side to side.

He jumps and grabs a root protruding out of the dirt. Once his feet find some footing in the earthen wall, he pulls up hard and grabs some webs of spider silk hanging above. Struggling, he gets one hand over the ledge, trying to get a grip on the damp forest floor.

Cautiously, he lets go of the web to try and grab the edge with his other hand. The loose dirt of the pit's rim gives way, sending him tumbling down and slamming hard into the ground. He gasps for air, unable to breathe.

Sparks whinnies in concern and starts pacing the circle, growing upset as she begins to realize there is no way out.

I'm going to die here... Kzhee thinks, fear gripping his chest.

The frustration sets in and he begins to yell. "Help! Help! Help! Someone, HELP ME!"

No one can hear me. Only the beasts of the woods...

Looking around the pit, he realizes that anything that stumbles by will have no trouble cornering him.

I'd better shut up, if I don't want to become something's next meal...

Climbing on Sparks' back again, he jumps once more for the ledge. His fingers clench tightly as his feet scramble for any form of footing. Grasping and squirming, he tries to get an arm over the edge, but his hand slips on a clump of leaves. He falls on his rear, hitting his tailbone hard.

"AHHH!" Kzhee screams, and a flash of lightning erupts, sending dirt exploding in every direction. Shards of rock and clay cut his face, filling his mouth with debris.

"What was that?" He tries to choke out, coughing up dirt.

Looking around, he sees Sparks running away, disappearing through the haze of smoke and dust. "Where are you going!?" He calls after her.

Stumbling to his feet, Kzhee moves through the smothering cloud of dirt and dust, trying to figure out what happened. As the smoke settles, he sees a wall of the pit collapsed in front of him, providing a way out. He climbs up, then carefully looks around.

Sparks is long gone and out of sight as Kzhee pulls himself up and starts walking through the forest, hiding beneath trees and darting between them, trying to avoid detection.

I think the edge of the forest is this way... If not, I'm never going to get out of this place.

The tiny bit of light that peeks through the foliage is barely enough to keep him from walking into tree trunks. The forest is quiet and still, but he knows better than to believe he's alone. A slight breeze begins to whistle through the branches, causing him to pick up his pace.

Running now, dodging through the trees, the once gentle breeze behind him begins to grow louder and louder. Over the mounting roar of the wind, he can scarcely make out the distant flutter of wings. Images of bats fly through Kzhee's mind, sending a chill down his spine.

Finding a fallen log, not quite as long as he is tall, Kzhee wiggles inside its hollow core. His head sticks out just far enough to spy a living cloud begin to pass over. He closes his eyes tight and tries to pull into the log as far as possible, hoping the swarm will pass without noticing him. But a chirp above draws his attention.

That doesn't sound like a bat...

He gathers his courage and looks up out of the log. The creatures flying above him aren't bats, but birds. A giant flock of blackbirds, flying close together, darting between trees and catching bugs dangling from branches and fluttering from the floor.

I've seen this flock before... He thinks. *They come pouring from the trees during the night to sleep on the Plains. What if I follow them? What time is it? If it is evening they should lead me out, but if its morning they will lead me deeper into the forest.*

Kzhee climbs out of the fallen tree and starts running after the flock, letting their wings mask the sound of his footsteps, praying that they are leading him out of the woods to safety. He is a fast runner, but it is still hard to keep up with the flock as they glide, quickly beginning to pull out of sight.

I don't remember riding this far in... But I was on horseback before...

He keeps running, following the now distant birds. His legs begin to burn, as the flapping of their wings fades into the darkness, taking his last bits of hope with them.

An exposed root sticks out, grabbing his foot as he runs over it, bringing the ground rushing quickly towards his face. He slams into the dirt, then tumbles down the hill before him, smacking his bruised head and limbs against rocks and trunks and stumps. The trees begin to part as Kzhee rolls past the base of the hill, and he realizes the forest is behind him.

The sweeping savannah before him is a beautiful sight. Struggling to his knees, Kzhee raises his hands and head to the sky in a triumphant gesture. Looking around, he doesn't recognize where he is, and Sparks is nowhere to be seen.

Better to be lost out here, than lost in the woods... He thinks, grinning widely.

Moving away from the forest, he heads in what he imagines to be the direction of his home, drudging through the tall grass. His thirst is intense, and it has been a while since he last ate.

How far from home did I ride?

The fastest route to the Forest Realm from his village is a three hour ride by horse.

What is that by foot?

The stars above provide ample light, and Kzhee covers ground quickly. The rugged terrain begins to give way to gentle hills, sprawling and lying like so many stones on a shore.

I'm going the right way!

He begins whistling a tune, excited by the familiar sight of the hills, but stops as he feels the ground beginning to shake. He runs up a small mound, keeping low to the ground. His father has many friends among the neighboring tribes, but a kidnapping and ransom wasn't unheard of between villages.

Better to be safe and make it home...

Across the horizon, he sees a group of riders heading in his direction. Squinting his eyes, Kzhee tries to make out the faces in the distance. In the early morning light, it looks like the head rider could be his father, but Kzhee stays ducked down behind a rock, waiting to be sure it is them.

Peaking around as they draw closer, he sees Sparks at the back of the group, galloping without a rider. Kzhee's father is mounted at the head of the entourage, his warriors behind him. Standing up, he waves his arms as they begin to ride past the hill.

One of the riders sounds a horn, echoing between the grassy slopes.

There must be other groups looking for me.

His father approaches, towering over Kzhee. "Your horse returned home without you. I feared the worst. Where have you been?"

"I went into the forest…" Kzhee begins, "I was attacked."

"What were you thinking? You know not to go in there! I have told you. Do you not remember the last time?"

"I'm sorry…" Kzhee says, gazing back at the forest as the group begins to ride away. It looks peaceful from outside. The only sound emanating from within the trees, is the sweet song of birds.

Councilor Quezada

"Can I get you another drink?" His server asks, an air of annoyance in her voice.

"No." He answers, pulling a piece of silver from his gravel colored cloak and tossing it to her, then looking back out the door. "Close my tab." His electric blue eyes are fixated on the entrance of the tavern across the street, on a table with four boys sitting at it.

The waitress smiles at the silver coin in her hand. "Do you need change, or…?"

"Keep it, I'd like to be left in peace though."

"Of course, thank you." She says, cheerily slipping the silver into her blouse, before leaving to help the patrons at the next table.

The same glass of cider has been sitting in front of him for the entire evening, having long since gone flat. He finishes the last of the drink, trying to ignore two drunken sailors loudly proposition the server, ignoring her protests.

Stupid sailor pigs… He takes his eyes off of the door to look at them. *Nasty shits look like they're one missed meal away from being pirates. How did I get stuck in this damned stinking hell hole? Jero never should have sent his son here…*

"Let go of me!" The serving girl cries, while the men at the next table start grabbing at her as she tries to pull away.

Quezada stands, calmly walking to their table. "Take your hands off her." He tells the drunks. "And leave, now."

"Piss off!" The closer man shouts, pushing the woman to the ground as he gets out of the booth. His friend stands up behind him, removing a dagger from his belt.

"Last chance…" Quezada replies, nothing but a grin visible beneath the hood of his cloak.

The man in front of him grabs a knife from the table and lunges forward, slashing wildly. But he isn't fast enough.

Quezada sidesteps the attack, sliding a concealed blade from his robe and dragging it across the side of the man's neck as he moves past. Before the second man can react, his throat is cut as well, and he crumples to the floor.

The waitress screams, as Quezada walks away. Turning back, he throws her another silver piece, then puts a finger to his lips in a silencing gesture.

Looking out the door, he sees a large group of men leaving the tavern across the street, and an empty table where the boys had been sitting.

"Damn!" He hisses, before vanishing into thin air, leaving the barmaid in a state of shock.

Materializing outside, he looks up and down the street, then vanishes again. Reappearing on the corner at the end of the block. He checks the side alleys and back streets, then he begins to work his way towards Nodovin's home, hoping to find the boys before anything happens.

At the end of a road he comes across a mob forming a circle, blocking the street. Moving closer, he sees the prince and his friends at the center of the crowd, their bows drawn in self-defense.

What are you stupid shits planning to do, shoot all of them? He thinks, while looking for his opening. *Last thing I need is for one of you boys to stick me with an arrow while I'm trying to save you.*

The leader of the gang yells something, and a man lunges for the prince, a dagger aimed at his throat.

Quezada suddenly appears between Relorn and his attacker, sticking a blade into the man's stomach. As he slumps over, the man's cohorts begin to charge from all sides.

"Don't move!" Quezada shouts at the boys, before vanishing.

As each man moves forward to attack, Quezada appears behind them, slicing their throats. He vanishes whenever an attack comes his way, reappearing next to his attacker and driving his blade into them before disappearing again.

The boys watch, dumbfounded, as men drop helplessly around them. Ten lay dead, then fifteen. Quezada laughs heartily, as more rush forward.

Idiots… Ha, keep trying!

When he sees the gang leader make a move, Quezada appears behind him, putting his dagger to the man's neck and whispering in his ear. "Bite off more than you could chew?"

"Demon…" The man gasps, as the blade digs into his flesh.

"STOP THIS AT ONCE!" A voice booms, echoing between the buildings.

The gang immediately stops moving. Most throw down their weapons and scamper off, those who remain hide their faces and look away from the old man slowly approaching. But Quezada keeps his blade at the leader's throat.

It's that old bat Eristoclese… Even these stupid goons love him. Look at how they cower.

"You can let him go, councilor." Eristoclese shouts.

Stupid old man, who are you to tell me what to do?

Quezada pulls his blade across the gang leader's throat, then lets him drop dead to the ground.

"What was that!?" Eristoclese cries, "They stopped fighting!"

"Watch your tongue, old man." Quezada says, as the last of the gang runs off, leaving him alone with the boys and their teacher. "It's convenient of you to show up now and preach. Where were you when those men were about to kill the Emperor's son?"

"The commotion roused me... I came to see if I could help. I had no idea they would be here, and I am very curious as to why the prince is out so late." Eristoclese says, eyeing the boys.

"We were just trying to celebrate," Reza volunteers. "We didn't try to start anything, those men wanted to rob us, kill us!"

"You're lucky not to be dead!" The old man shouts. "Your last class is in less than five hours. I recommend getting some rest." Looking at Quezada, he asks, "You'll get them home safely?"

"Indeed, let's go... Pick up Matio if he can't walk."

The boys pull their passed out friend to his feet and drag him down the street. When they are a way off, Quezada turns to the old man and snarls, "The Emperor will be hearing about this..."

Then he vanishes, reappearing next to the boys as they make their way back to the house.

Chion 2

Stale beer on the table makes Chion's arms stick to the wood as he sits and eats. Salted beef with grilled onion is piled on his plate, a beer stein and basket of toasted bread sit to the side. The barkeep meanders over after finishing a conversation with a patron sitting a few seats away.

"Can I top off ya drink?" He asks, an unabashed smile painted across his pink face.

"One more, yes." Chion replies, between bites of beef.

It is the end of their first day of travel, on the route towards the Pillar, and the usual boredom is setting in.

I see why there are so many habitual drinkers around here, it gets terribly boring...

He had taken to drinking when he moved to the Flying City. The days spent harbored were exciting enough, dealing with clients and visiting the cities below. But the time spent in the air was always the same, tedious... When he was new to the city, he loved to look over the side rails at the moving landscape below. But after making the trip around the Empire a few times, the excitement had vanished, replaced by cool indifference.

"Put it on ya tab, sir? "The barkeep asks, as Chion finishes the last bits of food on his plate.

"Yes Jay, thank you." He replies.

Chion hates when the old man calls him sir, but no matter how many times he asks, the barkeep always replies, *'As long as ya paying me, ya name is sir.'*

He stands and walks to the back of the room. His apartment is above, and the stairway inside the bar leads there, albeit with some twists and turns. As he approaches the stairs, a cloaked man sitting at a nearby table tugs on Chion's shirt.

"Do I know you?" Chion asks, curtly pulling away.

"Not yet, Chion. Not yet..."

"How do you know my name?" He asks.

"I know that, and more. Sit with me?"

He doesn't want to sit with the man, and the stairs to his apartment are so close… "What can I do for you?" He asks, begrudgingly taking a seat.

Always someone looking for a loan or investment…

"I came a long way to see you. How is the trip so far?"

"Just as well as always." Chion answers, annoyed. "I don't mean to be impolite, but do we know each other?"

"I know much of you, but no, we have yet to be introduced."

"Well then, what can I do for you?"

"Straight to business." The cloaked man chuckles. "Just like your father."

What is this guy getting at…?

"Are you a friend of his?" Chion asks.

"An acquaintance." The man nods, staring at a mural painted across the wall. "It has been a while since I've seen him though. I do however, consider your uncle to be a good friend of mine. We often walk through the Emperor's gardens together, talking of birds and watching the sun set between the mountains."

It's time to get some answers. Chion thinks, focusing on the man and listening intently. But try as he might, the room remains silent and still.

"What are you hoping to hear?" The man asks, smirking.

"I'm not sure I know what you mean…"

"You are trying to listen to my thoughts. What is it that you hope to hear?"

He knows...

Chion's eyes dart around the room, trying to find the best means of escape. Unable to see the door through a crowd of people accumulating in the tavern, his gaze falls to the knife next to the man's empty dinner plate.

"Whoa..." The cloaked man says, placing his hand on Chion's arm. "No need to panic, I mean you no harm."

"Who are you?" He replies, sharply pulling away from the man's touch. Keeping the knife in the edge of his field of vision. "Tell me straight."

"I am Sage Coda Sa, councilor to his imperial majesty, Emperor Jero." He answers, swelling with pride. "And the Emperor wishes to see you."

Senator McKenna

"Tell me about yourself, Ral."

"I am a fighting slave. My master is Bentino."

Might as well take care of that now...

The senator raises a hand, signaling to one of his men-at-arms. "Go to this man, Bentino. Inform him that due to an important matter of state, Ral is no longer his slave."

"What shall we do if he refuses?" The man asks, placing a hand on his sword.

"Bring some gold." The senator answers, nonchalantly. "Hopefully he shall understand the importance his noble charity will have for our realm, and consent of his own best judgment."

"Aye, senator." The man-at-arms replies, walking away with a small entourage marching at his heels, leaving him and Ral alone in the Senate Hall.

"You are no longer a slave. You no longer have a master. Now, tell me about yourself."

A dumb look of disbelief freezes upon the boy's face. He doesn't even attempt to stammer a reply.

"Are you slow, boy?" The senator asks, waving a hand in front of his eyes.

"No, sir. I just don't know what to say. Thank you…"

"For what?"

"For freeing me, my lord." Ral replies.

"Ah, well, for that you are welcome I suppose. I am sure you know though… Nothing comes without cost."

"Yes, my lord." Ral answers, staring at the ground. "I have some gold, if you…"

"I don't need your gold, boy. And you need not be frightened, not of me." He can see the apprehension on the kid's face. "I mean you no harm. Where were you born? In the city? Do you know your parents, or where they are?"

"I don't know, my lord."

It's going to be a long night if he doesn't start talking. He says he isn't slow, but he has yet to show otherwise…

McKenna picks up a small bronze bell, ringing it twice. A girl enters the room.

"What can I get for you, senator?" She asks.

"A bottle of white and two glasses, if you would be so kind."

She nods and runs out, then immediately returns with the order, as if it had been waiting ready outside.

"Here you are, senator." She smiles meekly and curtsies, before running back out of the room and closing the doors behind her.

The senator pours a glass for each of them. *A little extra for the lad, speed this along.*

"Drink boy, deep."

Ral sets the glass down, empty. "I was sold three times before Bentino bought me, but I can't remember the first couple of owners. I do remember the man before Bentino though. He was tall and sharp, and would cane us if we cried or tried to steal food. But when we fought each other he would laugh and cheer and smile, and give the winner extra dinner. So we got mean... I fought hard. I can't remember the man's name now, but I remember how much he liked to watch me fight. When I got old enough he sold me to Bentino, so I could start fighting in the pits."

"Did you know you could...?" He looks at the boy's torso.

"No, my lord. Tonight was the first time." Ral shrugs, "I don't know what happened. To be honest, I am not even sure that this isn't death right now."

Haha, the boy thinks that he's dead. What would that make me?

"I am not the ferryman, coming to take you home. No, boy. You are very much alive, and you must get your wits about you. Do you think you could do it again?"

"I don't know, my lord. I can try…" He holds out his hand and squints, turning his head to the side. He flexes and focuses, shaking with stress and exertion.

"Here…" McKenna says, handing the boy a blade.

Ral takes the knife and drags it across his palm. He winces slightly, as the skin breaks, expecting blood. But no blood comes. Instead, a gentle ripple. A skin hued shimmer. As the knife passes through, a wave of flesh closes the wound behind it.

"Consistency is a thing of beauty." McKenna says, smiling, "Do you know what the Emperor's Due is?"

"No, my lord."

"When the Emperor's son comes of age, each realm must send one of their own youths, someone with a gift… A gift like yours. Those selected become the prince's councilors, and help rule the Empire when he becomes Emperor." McKenna stands up, pausing his speech and walking down the steps to the floor of the Senate Hall. "We have been having… Trouble. Trouble finding someone to bestow this incredible honor upon. Someone just like you." He stands, silently looking at Ral, letting his words take root.

"I am a slave, my lord. I cannot help rule the Empire. They wouldn't have me…"

The thought had crept into the senator's mind, but he'd quickly quelled his doubts. "No, they care not for where you come from. You bring a unique perspective, and a very unique gift. You will be welcomed with open arms."

"If you say so, my lord."

"Are you hungry?" He asks, "Shall I send for food?"

"No, my lord. My stomach…" The boy trails off, looking at his torso where the blade had cut through him only hours earlier.

"I understand. You should get some rest. We leave tomorrow morning. There is to be a great tourney for the prince's birthday, and that is where the Emperor will have his due." McKenna rings the bronze bell once, calling in a man-at-arms. "Take Ral to a guest suite, make certain he has all he needs. We sail for the Great City on the morrow. Be sure he is ready to embark at daybreak."

The Glorious Knights and Illuminated Priests of the Order of Justice, Honor, and Chivalry

"Wake up! Wake up!" An armor clad knight yells, banging a pot with an iron ladle. "We have work to do!"

A sleepy man stirs, rubbing his eyes. "What do you mean, work?"

"King Birch has summoned us. Get dressed, I'll debrief you on the way."

The disheveled and groggy group of men assemble in front of the small stone tower that the Order uses for a base in the town of Blackburn. The group's leader, Sir Simon, sits atop his mount. His shining armor is the standard of the Order, gold plate ornamented with brightly colored calligraphy, bearing the arms and mottos of the knights and the priests and the Order.

His men mount their horses, preparing to ride. The morning is cold, and the foggy breath of man and horse hangs in the air. The wind whips past them as they ride, whistling through the cracks in their armor.

"King Birch has sent word, pleading that we come to the castle. Yesterday, Grand Marshal Barren and his son arrived, intending on pledging marriage between Prince Bastion and Princess Rosemary. It would seem the two youths entered the woods together. When they didn't return, a search party was sent to find them." Sir Simon sighs, spurring his horse along. "They found them in the trees. The girl was unconscious, and the boy... Well, they say he was frozen solid. The grand marshal seems to have decided the girl is to blame, and he is demanding her head. The king has closed up his castle, and refuses to release his daughter to the marshal, he hopes we can come to investigate and clear her name."

"Sounds like a clear cut case of witchery to me." Sir Marcus retorts.

"No, no, no. It is the Lord above punishing the grand marshal for some offense. Why else would his son be taken so?" Friar Philip replies.

"Obviously it is an attempt of King Birch to seize the Southern Realm for himself, kill the marshal's heir, then the marshal." Sir Joel chimes in.

"That is dumb..." Sir Kevin interjects. "There must be a monster or beast in the woods. Something wicked, capable of freezing the boy."

Sir Simon shakes his head, "Where do you witless loons come up with these theories? Just keep riding, and let me do the talking."

As they approach the castle, the grand marshal and his men prevent the knights from nearing the front gates.

"Who approaches?" The marshal's herald calls.

"Sir Simon and the Glorious Knights and Illuminated Priests of Justice, Honor, and Chivalry, at your service, my lord."

"What are you doing here!?" The marshal yells, "This is no concern of yours!"

"King Birch has requested we investigate the occurrences surrounding…"

"I am the ruler of the Southern Realm! I am the grand marshal! I do not need your assistance here. I will punish the girl as I see fit. It is my right as ruler… She has killed my only child, and she will pay in kind."

"My lord, I understand your frustration and anger. But what proof is there that it was the girl who killed your son?"

"You dare to question me?" The marshal snarls, "This is my realm!"

"The Order is not bound by the laws of individual realms or whoever happens to rule them, my lord. We are slaves of truth, and champions of the innocent. Let us by, or we will report your hindrance of our investigation to the High Priest, I am sure he will share our displeasure with the Emperor…" Sir Simon dismounts after his speech, walking towards the gates. He steps past the grand marshal and through his men, the knights of the

Order following. As they enter beneath the portcullis, the gate slams shut behind.

King Birch meets the knights in the grand hall of the castle. The roaring fire at the end of the room warms them from the bitter cold outside, and the pungent smell of pinewood smoke fills the air.

"Thank you for arriving so fast." The king says, bowing his head.

"Of course, my lord." Sir Simon replies, "Tell us of what has happened."

"The two of them went into the woods, my daughter and the marshal's son. When they didn't come back by evening fall, we went looking after them...." The king trails off for a moment. "She... She was laying on the ground. Her lips blue from the cold. The prince was leaning forward with his eyes closed, like he was trying to kiss the air. The marshal was livid, he blamed my daughter! I told him there was no way, she wouldn't even if she could. She was excited to marry the boy. His father is one of my dearest friends, though I fear not anymore..."

"Where is the boy?" Sir Simon asks.

"His father has the body. I presume it has been sent back to the Frozen Palace."

"Where is your daughter? Has she woken?"

"No, but she speaks in her sleep, pleading for help and fighting the sheets."

"May we see her?"

"Of course, this way." Birch Blackburn leads them through his castle, up a tower to Rosemary's chambers. An elderly matron sits on the bed with the girl, while a small white dog lays next to her neck, its tail tucked beneath its chin.

"She still hasn't woken, but the color has finally come back to her." The matron says, rubbing a warm cloth across the girl's cheeks and mouth.

The dog darts up quickly, licking at the water on her lips. Its tongue begins to freeze as it makes contact, followed by its head and body. The ice continues to spread until the dog is left frozen solid, a coating of hoarfrost clinging to its fur.

"Oh mercy!" The matron screams, pushing the dog off of the bed.

It hits the ground, shattering to pieces at the feet of the knights. They stare at each other, then at King Birch.

"Did you know she could do this?" Friar Philip asks, avoiding a glare from Sir Simon.

The shock is painted across King Birch's face. He tries to stammer out a reply, but is unable to respond.

"I'll take that as a no." Sir Simon says, letting out a tragic sigh. "This appears to have been an unfortunate accident, but one that we can hardly hold the poor girl accountable for. However, I recommend you send her to the Order's Grand Temple, in the Great City. She will not be able to wed or bear children, and the sisters of the Order are always in need of new devotees."

"No, never! I won't send her away! Especially not there, to spend the rest of her days in servitude..." The king protests.

"Serving the Order is a great privilege, my lord. It is a very fulfilling life…"

"Maybe for you it is, able to roam about and live. But she would be locked in some temple, hidden away from the world."

"If you change your mind, my lord, you know where to reach us." Sir Simon replies, nodding his head solemnly. "Let's go, knights."

The men turn to leave, winding their way through the castle towards the exit. Their metal armor clanging on the stone floors and stairs as they move.

Outside, after having left the fires of the castle, the air seems colder than before. Sir Simon cups his hands and blows in them for warmth, as he approaches the grand marshal and his men.

"So, what did your investigation reveal, knight?" The marshal inquires, in a sarcastic voice.

"The girl appears to have a gift that no one was aware of. It is most unfortunate, what happened to your son… But we cannot punish the girl for something beyond her control. I am sure this event will haunt her for life, which is a far worse penance than any sentence we could impose."

"She killed my son, and you propose to let her live on with impunity!?"

"You are letting your emotions cloud your vision." Sir Simon says, turning to leave. "Return home, mourn your son, let this pass."

"Let this pass?" The marshal spits, as the knights ride away. "I will destroy the whole lot of them, I will dismantle this castle… I will burn this city to the ground!"

As they ride down the hill from the castle, Sir Marcus laughs and jokes to the group. "Do you think they could just dangle him over a fire, bring the boy back to life?"

"The Lord above works in his own way," Friar Philip retorts. "There's a reason the boy was killed. No fire will bring him back."

"Shut up, both of you. This is bigger than the boy now." Sir Simon hisses, through clenched teeth. "This could lead to war."

"If so, what do we do?" Sir Joel asks.

Sir Simon stares intently, plotting their course of action. "Send a carrier pigeon to the Grand Temple. Report on what has happened, and ask for direction. Then send word to the outpost at the Frozen Palace, let them know what has transpired here."

"I will, at once." Friar Philip replies.

"Good. Sir Marcus, I leave you in charge in my stead."

"Of course." Sir Marcus says, nodding.

"Sir Kevin, pack your things..." Their leader adds, as they arrive back at the outpost. "We are leaving early for the tournament, to speak with the High Priest. We shall charter passage on the next ship leaving for the Great City."

Relorn 3

"Rise and shine!" Reza yells, jumping onto Relorn's oversized bed. "Get up, we don't want to be late for our last day."

Relorn groans and rolls away. *I'm never drinking again...* He thinks, clutching his head in pain.

"Come on, let's go!" Reza exclaims, pulling off the blankets.

"How are you so cheery?" Relorn asks, sourly.

"I come from a long line of heavy drinkers... Must have inherited a tolerance."

"Does Matio's father know about last night?" His voice is laced with concern.

"Not sure..." Reza answers, absently looking around the room. "It's not like he can get mad at *you*."

"Still..." He says, pushing himself out of bed. "I don't want everyone finding out about it."

Last thing I need is more bodyguards...

They leave the room and walk through the foyer. Two guards fall in line behind them as they exit the living area and make their way to the lower levels.

The palace baths are in a large marble room. Huge pools sunken into the ground, scented by exotic oils and perfumes, filling the chamber with aromatic steam. Andrew and Matio sit in a large tub, positioned at the center of the room.

Andrew nods as they enter the water, but Matio refuses to lift his head from its resting position on the edge of the pool.

Poor guy looks like he's ready to vomit... Relorn notices.

Reza laughs and reclines. "How's everyone feeling?"

"It feels like I fell on my face." Matio answers, meekly, cradling his head in his arms.

"You didn't fall, your pals here dropped you!" Reza shouts, splashing a wave of water at Andrew.

"If you hadn't been acting like a fool, Reza, we wouldn't have even been in the situation." Relorn mutters, sinking into the warm water.

"Speaking of which..." Reza says, scrubbing himself with a pumice stone. "Are we going to talk about how your crazy bodyguard killed twenty people in the blink of an eye last night?"

"Yeah, how did he even know we were there?" Andrew asks.

"I don't know what happened." Matio squeaks, "The last thing I remember is Reza ordering drinks, and a pretty girl dancing."

He has no idea we almost died...

"Reza got flashy at the bar," Andrew begins to explain. "So, of course, a bunch of thieves followed us out of the place. A gang of about thirty of them tried to rob us, probably would have too, but Councilor Quezada appeared out of nowhere. He would have killed them all if Eristoclese hadn't of shown up and stopped it."

"Oh shit..." Matio whines, "If my dad finds out about this I think he might go insane. He and Eristoclese are both members the Twenty, they talk all the time..."

"I'm more worried about class today." Relorn says, exiting the water. "Eristoclese knows we were drunk, and he saw Quezada kill all those men. What do you think he's going to say?"

"Only one way to find out!" Reza exclaims, leading the way back to their rooms.

After getting dressed, they meet in the foyer and leave for the Academy. The air outside is crisp and fresh as they exit the palace. Clouds block the sun, and a cool wind blows in from the sea.

The walk to the Academy doesn't take long. After a few minutes, they approach the meadow that extends in front of the grand marble building. The smell of wet grass wafts through the air, and bees dance between the petals of teal colored tulips that peek up from the untrimmed lawn.

As they walk into the lecture hall, Relorn notices the room is much more full than usual, hardly any seats remain open.

"Who are all these people?" Matio asks.

"The usual, plus all those who never come to class." Andrew answers, "Can't miss the last day..."

The only group of seats big enough for the four of them are in the front row. As they make their way down, Relorn expects Eristoclese to say something. But the teacher looks away as they pass, turning to speak quietly with a group of students across the room.

He continues to ignore them for the rest of the lecture. Luckily it is much shorter than usual, and Eristoclese begins to wrap up before midday.

"To surmise…" The teacher articulates. "History always repeats itself. But if you learn from it, you are not doomed to repeat the mistakes of the past."

Eristoclese calls the class to a close, ushering a stampede of youths to rush for the door. But as Relorn stands up, the teacher approaches, taking him aside.

"I presume you made it home safely last night?" The teacher says, watching the room begin to empty out.

"Yes, with the councilor with us…"

"Of course…" Eristoclese says, absently staring at the beautiful paintings on the ceiling of the auditorium. "Relorn, do you know what I mean when I speak of learning from the past?"

"I think so."

"It's more than just reading history books. It's being able to learn from experience. Not only your experience, though that is a large part of it, but the experience of those around you and those who came before you. If you can learn from your own mistakes, as well as the mistakes of others, there will be no telling what you can achieve. But…" He pauses for a moment, "If you follow others into their follies and make their mistakes your own, then you will equally suffer in the consequences of their actions."

Unsure of what to say, Relorn just nods, waiting for the teacher to finish.

"This may very well be the last time I ever see you, so listen to my words. Remember them…" Eristoclese puts his hand on Relorn's shoulder. "One day, you are going to be Emperor, the ruler of us all. What kind of leader will you be? A strong man, who thinks for himself. Or one who lets himself be ruled by others? Be the change the Empire needs. If you do not… Then may the Lord above help us all, for we are surely doomed."

Seaborne 2

The night rests heavy on silent spring waves. Blackness engulfs the pirates as they paddle aboard a small pinnacle, its oars cutting through the open ocean, pulling them towards the merchant vessel drifting in the darkness.

Curse this idea… Seaborne thinks, rubbing his hands together for warmth. *We should have just pulled alongside with the warships and boarded as usual.*

He had wanted to try a stealthier approach with their next attack. But now, amidst freezing water and icy fog, he finds himself regretting the decision.

"G-g-g-gr-grab on." Seaborne stutters, through chattering teeth, as their small boat bumps into the side of the large merchant ship.

Grabbing ahold of a rope hanging from the side, Seaborne begins to ascend the slippery hull. At the top, he peeks over the rail, surveying for any guards on night watch.

A man walks down from the upper deck, coming towards the side of the ship. Seaborne ducks, holding a finger up to his lips to keep the pirates below him quiet.

As the sailor approaches the rail, a hand shoots up and grabs him by the shirt, pulling him over the edge. Splashing into the water below, the man comes up to find a pirate holding a knife at his neck.

"Go, now!" Seaborne hisses, waving his men over the railing.

Pirates scamper across the deck, kicking open cabin doors and rousing the sailors, threatening them with swords and knives and clubs.

Seaborne throws open the door to the captain's chambers. "Rise and shine!"

"Wh-wh…" The sleepy man stammers, startling awake from his slumber. "What do you want? Who are you?"

Seaborne chuckles at the man lying before him, then begins moving about the cabin, rifling through drawers and dressers. "I will answer ya questions in the order which they were asked. Firstly, I want ya ship. That particular want has been satiated, as I am now the commander of this vessel. Secondly…" He takes off his hat and places it over his chest, before giving a dramatic bow. "Captain Seaborne, at ya service."

"You… you can't. Where are the guards?" The man asks, frantically.

"*Haha!* Don't make me laugh, captain… What's ya name?"

"Guards! Guards!" He yells, ignoring the question and trying to stumble out of the bed. But the blankets trip him up, sending the man falling to the floor.

Seaborne shakes his head and roars with laughter, before yelling out the door. "Parrot! Come get the former captain out of my chambers."

Instead of an answer, he hears a yelp from across the ship, followed by men starting to shout excitedly. Leaving the man lying on the floor, Seaborne runs out to the deck to find a knight wildly swinging a sword, a dozen pirates surrounding him.

Clad in full plate armor, the man is an intimidating sight, and none of the pirates seem too keen on being the first to come at him. Seaborne notices one of his men lying dead on the deck, done in by a wide slash across the waist.

He killed one of my men...

"Take him! Tie him up!" Seaborne shouts. "He can't cut all of ya!"

Parrot grabs the man from behind, tangling up his arms as the other men grab his blade and knock it to the deck.

"He kil'd Squid, cap'n!" Parrot yells, "'He cut 'is belly!"

The macaw on Parrot's shoulder jumps into the air, fluttering onto the knight's head, pecking his helm and cawing, "Murder! Murder!"

A group of pirates come on deck, throwing another armored man next to the first. He falls to his knees, putting up none of his cohort's fight.

"Who are the two of ya?" Seaborne snarls.

As the pirates remove his visor, the struggling man spits at him. Parrot drops an elbow into the back of the knight's neck, sending him to the ground with a painful sounding grunt.

Seaborne wipes the spittle off of his cheek. Turning towards the calmer man, he asks again, "Who are the two of ya?"

"My name is Sir Kevin." The resigned man states, "And that is Sir Simon. We are knights of the Order, bound for the Great City."

"Did ya murder this man?" Seaborne asks, pointing to the dead pirate.

"Not I, captain." Sir Kevin replies.

"Captain, is it?" Seaborne asks, laughing to his men. "Looks like this one actually values his life."

Sir Simon begins to struggle again, head-butting one of the men standing above him. Parrot kicks the knight in the jaw, sending him falling forward and screaming in agony.

With painful exertion, Sir Simon looks up and declares defiantly, "I was defending the ship... Defending myself... I have done no murder."

"Defense... Murder..." Seaborne spits the second word out. "Call it whatever ya wish, it makes no difference to me. Someone must answer for this... But ya soul shan't be on my chest. The Scales will decide what happens to ya..."

A pirate walks out of the front cabin, checking off a ledger in his hand. "All have come to our side, captain. Apart from these two soldiers, the coxswain and the merchant captain."

"Thank ya, Bradley. Put them on one of the ship's boats and send it off towards shore. Except this one... This, Simon..." Seaborne hisses the name. "He comes with us."

"Nooo!" Sir Simon screams, driving up to his feet. He knocks back the men trying to hold him down, and lunges for the ship's rail. Before anyone can grab him, the knight tumbles off the edge and splashes into the sea.

The pirate waiting in the pinnacle below yells up, "Do I go af'r 'em, cap'n?"

"His hands are bound and he's wearing metal armor... He's already dead!" Seaborne shouts, off the side of the vessel. "Is there a ship's boat ready to set these men adrift?"

"Der ain' seem a be no li' boat, cap'n!" One of the pirates yells from across the deck.

Looking at the merchant captain, Seaborne shakes his head. "How do ya not have any ship's boats? What would ya do if she sank?"

"I've been meaning to..." The man begins.

"Shut up! It doesn't matter..." Seaborne shouts, cutting him off. "Parrot, take these prisoners below deck and tie them up."

"Aye, cap'n."

"One-leg Oleg, I name ya prize captain of this vessel."

"Aye. Thank you, cap'n."

"Men, to ya stations! Make ready to depart!" Seaborne shouts, before looking off the side of the deck and calling to the man waiting below. "Take me to *The Masthead*, we set course for home."

Sir Simon

The turbulent tides pull him beneath the waves, the sunlight slowly fading away.

Think fast, this can't be the end. Lord see me through...

Sir Simon sinks deeper into the sea, struggling against his restraints. Reaching down with his bound hands, he fumbles with the plate boots concealing his dagger. He grasps and grabs, trying to get it loose. As he pulls the blade from its leather strap, it slips through his fingers and starts drifting down into the depths.

Desperately lunging and stretching, he is barely able to catch the knife as it starts to sink. A few quick slices and his hands are free. Looking up towards the fading light, despair sets in. For a moment he almost succumbs to fate, almost stops fighting.

But then, from above, the light grows brighter. Blinding, burning his eyes. His limbs go numb, his vision blurs, then his ears ring loud with a tumultuous roar. Diverting his gaze from the bright light above, he can see his armor sinking away. The shape of a dying man fading to the darkness.

A sudden lightness overcomes him, and he begins to swim. Rising higher with each stroke, as if flying through the sea. The burning in his lungs is unbearable. His lips open to draw in air, but cold stinging water floods into his mouth instead.

Don't breathe, you are almost there...

Then, as his head starts to spin and the light begins to fade, his arms break through the surface.

Air!

Sweet breaths fill his lungs as he gasps and chokes. Salty morsels of seawater hit the back of his throat, making him cough. He looks at the sky, the white sun cutting though a soft blue backdrop.

"Boons from above! Thank you, my Lord!" He screams, fists raised to soft golden clouds.

Sweet tears flow down his cheeks, as the pain in his chest subsides. In the distance he can see four ships sailing away, their black flags waving in the wind.

"Good riddance!" He shouts, "Scum and filth!"

Surveying his surroundings proves to be a dismal exertion. The morning sun is blinding, reflecting brilliantly from the ocean that extends endlessly around him.

The rising sun! Can't you see? The Lord is calling... Beckoning with his divine beacon... East, to the shore.

He begins to swim, gliding along as if carried by the sea itself.

Rosemary 2

Beams of sunlight burst between the half-drawn curtains, blinding her as she opens her eyes. Rosemary tries to hide from the glare, before awkwardly attempting to climb out of bed.

What is going on...? Why do I feel like this...? She asks herself, trying to ignore the pain that shoots through her head and reverberates between her eyes.

Taking a step towards the balcony, to try and draw the blinds, a stinging numbness in her legs causes her to fall forward and land flat on her face.

What is happening...?

"Help..." She tries to choke out, but the dryness in her throat catches the word.

Each breath becomes more strained than the last. She tries again to speak, but only gasps come out. The room begins to spin around her, sending the feeling of needing to vomit gripping at her stomach. Somewhere in the distance she hears a door open, and a woman shouting faintly.

Blackness falls. Then it starts to fade, giving way to bright white light. Towering pines surround her. She runs through the woods, snow falling on her bare arms. Her sleeping gown clings to her skin, pasted on by tingling sweat, freezing against her body like a layer of rime.

Rosemary stops, unsure of where she is running to.

Am I being chased? Am I looking for something?

Stumbling through the trees, pine needles scratch her face. Her feet begin to turn blue, as they disappear in and out of the freezing snow. She sees something shining ahead, between the deep green branches.

There it is! Keep going... Be strong...

Trees part in her path, making room as she approaches a clearing. A wave of excitement crashes over her.

I'm here!

She smiles when the sun hits her face. But as her eyes become accustomed to the morning light, the object before her comes into focus. A statue carved in ice, shaped like a young man.

As she approaches it, the face becomes visible, its features twisted and locked in a look of terror. Prince Bastion stares at her, accusation burning in his frozen eyes.

No! No! I didn't mean to… It wasn't my fault. Forgive me…

She beats her fists on his icy chest. "Wake up! Wake up! Wake up!"

The snow falls harder and the sky grows darker, while her screams rise higher and higher.

"Wake up… Wake up, my dear." The sound of her mother's sweet voice lulls her screams to sleep. "Wake up, my love."

A cold wet feeling slides uncomfortably across her face. She twists to get away. Looking up, Rosemary sees her mother holding a moist cloth, reaching to wipe her forehead.

"No…" Rosemary tries to say, weakly lifting her hand to her mother's. "What is happening to me?"

"My dear, my darling… Are you ok? I was so scared. We didn't know if you would ever wake."

"Tell me what happened," Rosemary coughs. "How long have I been asleep?"

"You have been sleeping almost a week. We feared…"

"A week!" She nearly screams. "The prince… I remember something about Bastion. Where is he? Is he well? Will he see me?"

"Rosemary, I don't know. Your father should explain…" She looks nervously around the room, as if searching for something else to speak of. Tears well in her eyes.

Rosemary sees the tears start falling. *Why won't she tell me what happened, and why does she cry?*

"It's okay, mother… It's all going to be alright." She smiles up at her mom, hoping to see the smile returned. But the only emotion Rosemary can see is fear.

Her father comes crashing into the room, breaking the tension.

"Rosemary!" He shouts, throwing his arms around her, brushing her hair and taking her hand in his. He almost kisses her hand, but at the last second decides against it.

No matter how he tries to hide it, she can see the fear in his eyes as well.

"Will you tell me what has happened, father?" She begs.

His eyes turn red as he tries to avoid her stare. "Your… You… You couldn't have known."

"Known what?" She asks, desperation rising in her voice. "Just tell me, please!"

"You have a power inside you. You are one of the gifted. When you…" He looks around, uncomfortably. "It appears you froze the prince with a kiss."

Her nightmare suddenly comes to life, leaving her fighting for every breath.

"Is he... Is he ok? Will he be ok? Will he see me? I am so sorry... You must know I didn't mean to..."

"Of course, dear... You couldn't have known." He chokes on the next words, "H-h-he... The boy is dead. His father took his body home to the Frozen Palace. The knights of the Order absolved you of wrongdoing, proclaiming it the accident that it most certainly was. But the grand marshal... He left very upset."

Rosemary begins to sob. "Can I talk to him, tell him what happened? I have never been sorrier about anything, he must know. I want to... Wanted to marry the Prince. I would never, I couldn't!"

"Dear, don't fret. Dry your eyes." He puts on the best smile he can muster and pinches her cheek gently. "The knights of the Order recommended that you become a sister of the Order. I told them to shove off. That you are my daughter and..."

"Maybe I should..." Rosemary whispers.

"What!?" Both her parents exclaim.

"I'm scared... I killed him. What if I..." A sudden fear grips her heart. "It could happen again. I need to get away from everything, everyone..."

Her mother and father reach out to hold her.

"NO!" She cries.

Don't touch me. Don't touch me. Don't touch me.

Pulling away from her parents, Rosemary wraps the sheets around herself tightly and screams. "DON'T TOUCH ME!"

Rika 2

Her stomach rumbles loudly, as she sits cramped in the shipping crate.

It's getting too loud. Rika thinks, rubbing her belly. *Someone is going to hear...*

The small wooden box had been her home for over a week. There'd been supplies waiting for her, but she finished them too fast. They were supposed to last until she and the crate had been shipped home, but she didn't know when that would be.

I have to eat something...

The master had said the trip was ten days. But without the sun, she could not tell how long it had been.

Once the cakes ran out, she had turned into the mouse and scavenged every last crumb off of the floor of her container. Then, as the hunger continued to grow, she attempted to venture out as the mouse, searching through the ship's hull for a crate of food to rummage through.

She had found a wheel of cheese, loosely boarded up. But only managed to eat a few salty morsels before a gang of rats crept out from the stack of crates around her. Being a little mouse, the rats' teeth seemed larger than a snarling wolf's to her. They surrounded the mouse, snapping and hissing, their fiery eyes burning with feral hatred.

The largest sprang forward first, biting at her arm. She darted away, narrowly avoiding its jaws. Quickly, she scurried back, dropping between two boards, wood splinters catching her fur as she fell through the slight opening.

Two of the rats dove headfirst after her. Their heads were able to fit through the opening, but their large bodies became stuck.

She darted through the boxes, searching for her own. The one with the X burned into the side.

Barely having made it back to her crate, teeth grazed her tail as she leapt through the hole. The rats were too large to fit their heads in after her, but she could hear their jaws snapping in the darkness. Quickly turning back into the girl, Rika had stuffed the hole full of straw to make sure none of the rats could find a way in.

Since then she had remained in her box, her hunger growing. The mouse's little stomach is easier to keep full. But the thought of sleeping so small and defenseless with the rats outside terrified her too much.

I won't tell the master about the rats... Won't let him know I was scared...

She feels extremely tired, but the hunger and fear had been keeping her awake.

How long has it been since I slept...? She thinks, curling up in a ball. *If I don't fall a....*

Her sister's soft giggles carry through the air, filling the room with joy. Jas, always happy, always smiling.

The small wooden treehouse is gently lit, illuminated by a fire burning in a little clay bowl. Their father, Boro, grins widely as he holds up a bone. Her sister's fox dances on the floor of their home. Balancing and spinning, the fox begs for the treat, while the girls smile and clap.

As her father throws him the bone, the fox leaps in the air, snatching his prize before it lands, then scampering off to enjoy it in peace.

Their mother, Dee, climbs in through the door, a basket of berries tucked over her shoulder. Smiling and kissing their father, she sets the basket down on the table before taking Rika and Jas into her arms.

Outside the sun settles beneath the trees, leaving nothing but torches and braziers to light the Grove. Music begins playing and mirth abounds, the woods are alive with sweet songs and sounds. The girls hang their legs from the sill of the window, listening to the musical instruments around. In treehouses built high off the ground, the happy Forest people dance and eat with their families and friends.

Then shouts ring out from the overgrowth, interrupting the cheer. Soldiers start to yell and scream. Fires begin burning among the trees, glimmering and reflecting off of the shining scales of the soldiers' armor.

"FLEE IN FEAR, FOR WE ARE HERE!"

"FLEE IN FEAR, FOR WE ARE HERE!"

The screams of the soldiers disorient the residents of the Grove, sending them from their homes and into the fires creeping up through the trees. On the ground, soldiers wait with heavy chains and pointed spears, grabbing people as they attempt to flee.

"Run!" Rika's father yells, pushing her and Jas onto a branch. "Now!"

Their mother jumps from the treehouse, towards the forest floor. While in the air, her body begins to elongate, and spots begin to cover her skin. A leopard lands smoothly on the ground, before leaping at the throat of one of the soldiers.

Their father follows quickly. He is the Apex of the Grove, the leader. "To me!" He screams, jumping to the ground and roaring, as he doubles in height. Fur sprouts from his back and chest, and his hands grow into clawed paws. A swipe of his mighty arm sends three soldiers flying through the air, but many more begin to close in around him, swinging ropes and jabbing their spears.

"Let's go…" Her sister whispers, grabbing the collar of Rika's shirt and pulling.

"We have to go help them!" She hears herself scream, but before she knows what is happening they are sprinting along the tree branches. They dart around trunks, gracefully leaping the gaps between trees, jumping through the air like squirrels.

Jas's fox scampers behind them, giving sharp barks and whines every so often to let his displeasure be known. Running above a roaring river, the girls jump to a branch hanging over the edge of the water. The fox jumps after them, but its landing is off. It slips from the branch and splashes in the river beneath, giving a pitiful yelp.

"Bear!" Her sister screams, as she spins around and jumps, disappearing with a splash into the water below.

"Jas!" Rika cries, staring into the darkness.

Please, please, please…

Her legs begin to shake, as fear overcomes her. Suddenly, she slips, screaming as she falls.

"Wake up, little mouse…"

Darkness, darkness, everywhere. Then sparks! A sharp sound rings out as a flint strikes, and a glow begins to radiate, casting shadows around the darkened room.

"Is it done?"

Get your wits about you. She thinks, trying to regain her composure

"It is done." The words escape her dry mouth, hoarse as a croak.

An old man reaches his hand into the crate, helping her out. She almost falls over when trying to put her full weight on her legs. The old man grabs her, setting her down gently on a table.

"Thank you, master."

"Your first assignment done." He says reflectively, a gleam of curiosity in his eye. "How did it go?"

"It went well, master. All according to plan." In the faint torchlight, Rika thinks she can see a smile forming on his wrinkled face. She hears a coin purse rustling, and a cold piece of metal is pressed into her hand.

"A piece of gold, for you."

"Thank you, master."

What else do I say?

"Come," The old man says. "Let's head upstairs, you must be starving."

A grin leaps across her face. "Yes, I could eat…" She says, trying to sound indifferent. But her stomach betrays her as she thinks of food, letting out a clearly audible groan that echoes off the walls.

The old man laughs sharply, almost a cackle. "Do we need to leave more cakes for you next time?"

The light begins to brighten as they climb the stairs. The catacombs are far underground, as is most the Guild Hall. The chambers above hold stores of books, weapons, food and supplies, rooms used for training and meetings, and quarters for the members who choose to live in the hall.

Above the Guild Hall lies the Shady Tavern, an ill reputable establishment in the most notorious area of the Great City. Their meat pies are delicious though.

Aside from the better than average pastries, the only reason to ever brave entering the Shady Tavern is if you are looking to have someone's life extinguished.

As they step into the light, the old man looks down at her. "Tsst…" He hisses, pointing at her back.

A large mouse tail sticks out from beneath the hem of her shirt, whipping back and forth as they walk. Rika squints her eyes tightly and scrunches up her cheeks, and the tail quickly disappears.

They walk through a secret door, hidden behind a bookshelf, and step into the dimly lit tavern. As they take a seat in a booth in the shadows, a boy quickly runs over to serve them.

"Hello, sir." He says, politely bowing to the guild master. "What can I get for you?"

"I will have a glass of red. From Vala, if you have it." He says, before gesturing to Rika.

"Can I have two meat pies?" She squeaks, excitedly. "One with beef and beans, and one with chicken and onion. And a *big* glass of water!"

"Bring out a pitcher of water." The master remarks, with a grin. "I think she's thirsty."

Rika tries to hide her excitement, but her smile grows wide at the thought of chicken pie, smothered in caramelized onions and gravy.

After the server drops off their drinks, the old man holds his glass out to Rika for a toast. "Chase us, the light of dawn."

"For I am the shadow." She replies, hitting her glass against his.

The food is delicious. The pies seem even bigger than she had remembered. She finishes the chicken pie in moments, then dives straight into the beef.

The master watches her eat, quietly explaining the differences between wine from Vala and wine from Viali's Vineyards. After half the beef pie is consumed she becomes incredibly full, but still shovels the remaining bites into her mouth. When she finishes, Rika lets out a little hiccup and lies out across the bench, her stomach sticking out to twice its normal size.

"Satiated?" The old man asks.

She nods her head happily. "Thank you, master."

"Good, good." He pauses, collecting his thoughts. "You are young, Rika. I do not doubt you could become one of the best of us, if you so desire. I was much older then you when I began my training, and more than twice your age before I made my first piece of gold. When I found you on that river bank, a mouse's tail hanging off your back, I thought you were dead. But as I picked you up, you stirred, burying your head in my shirt. I heard your tears, felt their warmth on my chest." His old eyes grow misty, glistening in the dim candlelight. "I have come to think of you as a daughter, so it is natural that I only want the best for you. A selfish part of me wants to keep you here, close by… But an opportunity has arisen, one that would provide you with all the comfort in the world."

Thoughts of fear begin to race through her mind. *What? Is he going to make me leave? I won't go! I'll hide in the walls as the mouse, they can't make me leave…*

"You wouldn't send me away would you?" She cries. "Did I do something wrong?"

"Of course not, little mouse." He says, taking her by the hand. "Just listen… What was it you told me you want more than anything?"

Staring deep into the master's eyes, she can hear her sister's laughter echoing, louder than a river's roar.

Ral 3

The sweet chirping of birds floats in from outside, rousing Ral from his slumber. He had dreamt of some barbarian cutting him in two. Quickly, he pulls up the sheets to check his midsection, making sure it had in fact been a dream.

It felt so real…

Satia lies next to him, her warm naked back lightly pressed against his side. He begins to rise, trying to get his bearings, but a splitting ache runs through his head.

"Ahh!" He exclaims, grabbing his temples. Trying to dull the pain.

"Are you okay?" Satia asks, rolling towards him. Gently caressing the back of his neck.

"My head, why does it hurt so much?" He winces, stumbling to get out of bed.

"You were very drunk when the senator was done speaking with you. I waited outside, afterwards the guards brought us here."

He looks around the room, realizing he has never been there before. It isn't Satia's chamber as he had thought. "Where are we? What happened?"

Before she can speak, a knock echoes from the door and a voice he doesn't recognize calls out. "Get ready, we leave for the docks in half an hour!"

"It is nice of the senator to allow me to come to the Great City with you for the tournament. But how I will miss you when it's over." She kisses him, softly. "You won't forget me, will you? When you're big and important...?"

The memories begin flooding back... The fighting pit, the sting of the blade across his stomach, the look of disbelief from the silent crowd.

It wasn't a dream...

He turns and vomits on the floor, the sour taste of wine and bile filling his mouth.

"Is that a no?" Satia asks, laughing as she rubs his back.

"If you are coming, why would I forget you?"

"I'm only coming for the tourney… After, you will leave with the Emperor and his son. They live at the Pillar, on the other side of the Empire."

"You won't come with me?"

"Ral…" She pauses, wiping away a tear, "My life is here. The tavern is all my mother left me, as my grandfather left it to her. I can't abandon it to move a world away."

He sits in silence, thinking. *This can't be happening… I woke a slave yesterday. I can't… I don't want…* "I don't want to leave you." He says, suddenly. "I won't!"

"What will you say?" She asks, with a sigh. "They may have freed you last night, but that doesn't mean they don't still own you… You just have a new master."

"We could run!" He exclaims. "We could move to some other realm, far away from here."

"Ral, I can't… Please, put on some clothes. We have to go." She approaches him, long hair flowing about her breasts. Lovingly taking him in her arms, she whispers in his ear. "It's going to be alright, my champion. You're the strongest man I know. You will be so great one day, one day soon…"

"But…"

"*Shhhh,*" She places a finger on his lips. "If life ever starts getting to you, if you lose your way. You know where I'll be. Come to me. I will be waiting for you, ready for you to lay me down." She pulls him onto the bed on top of her, kissing him with fervency and passion. Her silky skin is warm and inviting, the smell of vanilla and oranges hangs in her hair. Pinning his arms back, she whispers in his ear. "I will always be yours..."

The senator's ship pulls out of A'Tannia's docks within the hour. Ral notices the boat has no mast or sails. Instead, three men sit on platforms at the rear of the vessel, jets of water, steam and air coming from their hands propels the ship forward.

He and Satia are escorted along with the other passengers to a stately dining hall, where Senator McKenna is waiting for their arrival.

"Welcome, guests, senators. I hope you will find my ship to be a suitable means of transport. All the comforts one could desire are available. I insist that you make yourselves feel at home..." Senator McKenna says, grinning for the crowd.

Thanks are exchanged, and the guests begin grabbing bits of chocolate, caramel, strawberries and candied cherries from a banquet table set out.

"We have a special guest joining us for our voyage." The senator adds, "Please join me in welcoming, Sir Simon. A knight of the Order."

Ral looks at the gruff man, whose unkempt beard and sun-blistered face clash with the newly made snow white dress robes that hang loosely from his gaunt frame. The knight steps forward, silently bowing.

"The good knight has had quite an adventure, it would seem." The senator says, with a grin, "On his way north to the Great City, his ship was commandeered by pirates."

Gasps escape from the mouths of the senators and guests.

"He alone managed to escape after the ship was boarded," McKenna continues. "Her crew turned on the poor captain, joining the pirates. Sir Simon was able to jump overboard and swim to safety. He was found floating on his back, after days at sea. If the fisherman who rescued him had not happened by, I fear the Order would have one less man."

"The Lord above guides his flock, even those who run astray." Sir Simon croaks, his hoarse and gravelly voice hardly louder than a whisper.

Tiaries 3

Purple clouds hang low, suffocating the pale grey night. Thunder clashes and lightning flashes. Blinding streaks light up the sky, illuminating the ship's small cabin and casting wicked shadows upon the wall. Each booming blast shakes and reverberates through her bones.

The storm has been raging for the past two days, ever since they had left the Painted City.

Was that a bad omen? Did it mean something?

Their goodbyes were quick, having left that night. The councilor's ship had been waiting prepared, ready to depart immediately.

Why was it so important that we had to leave immediately? I didn't even get to see everyone. The thought turns her stomach. *Will I ever see Coop again? Tolaf the Tall Man? Ruby and her snake?*

Lightning flashes again. She tenses, waiting for the thunder. It comes quickly with a *BANG!* She flinches, curling deeper into the blankets, covering her head with a pillow.

Where is Jaties, is he crazy?

Her brother had been on the deck last she had seen, helping the men with the sails and ropes. He laughed at the lightning, and told her to go back into the cabin.

She had asked him why they didn't find an inlet somewhere and dock, but he had dismissed the idea, '*There are only steep cliffs on either side of the river for miles ahead and behind,*' He told her, "*We can either run upstream with the wind, or let the current do what it will.*' He laughed and went back to work, as Tiaries retreated inside.

What if someone gets struck by lightning? The idea startles her. *They would die!*

Tiaries gasps and crawls out of bed, creeping to the door. She holds onto the bedpost, and then the table, trying to keep her balance as the floor sways recklessly beneath her. Through the door she climbs, letting it slam behind her. There is nothing to hang onto in the hallway, so she crawls along the grainy wood floor.

Her palms and knees are red and aching by the time she reaches the door. Her hand flails up to grab ahold of the frame. Pulling herself up, she peers through the rain soaked window.

If someone is stuck by lighting or if some tragedy befalls, I will be ready... I will save them...

Radiant beams of sunlight burst through the cabin window, waking her from a deep sleep. She had stayed up until the storm subsided, watching over the workers on the deck. As the tempest began to fade, and the turbulent shaking of the ship gave way to a gentle rocking, Tiaries had drifted to sleep. Laying in the hall between the cabins, refusing to abandon her post.

Someone must have carried me to bed...

She begins to rise, stretching her arms and legs. Changing out of her still damp sleeping gown into a dry set of clothes, she walks out to the deck. The sound of birds fills the air, as a pandemonium of parrots erupts from a sweetlime tree near the edge of the shore, their bright green wings flapping on orange-yellow bodies. Tiaries smiles as they circle over the ship, before departing for some unseen destination beyond the far side of the river.

"You're awake! How did you sleep?" The councilor asks, calmly, as if the stormy night had been like any other.

"I was terrified! I thought we would sink for sure." She replies.

"Do not be weary, dear. These are some of the finest sailors in the Empire, you are in good hands."

Tiaries looks around as the councilor removes his hood, taking a long drink from the gourd he keeps on his side. He offers her some, before replacing the cork and relaxing against some furs piled against the wall. His hair falls as he leans back, exposing the long telltale ears of an elf.

"Your ears!" She almost squeaks.

"Don't tell anyone my secret..." He smiles and laughs, not moving from his reclined position.

"But you are one of the Emperor's councilors. Can they be elves?"

"One can, yes. A person from each realm is chosen, and the Elven States are a realm..." He gestures to himself with a dramatic flourish.

"I never knew…" She remarks, almost apologetically. "Excuse me, my lord."

She scampers across the deck looking for Jaties, finding him at the front of the ship. He leans from the rail with one arm around the figurehead, the other outstretched, catching the air with a cupped palm.

"Look at how fast we're sailing!" He says, a smile stretching from ear to ear.

She looks off the edge with him. Water sprays out as the ship cuts through it, flying across the surface. Looking to the shore, she can see how quickly they are moving. "How are we sailing so fast against the river's current?"

"Good winds and a very fast ship." He laughs, "I have never seen a ship move like this, and the way the sailors are trained is unbelievable. We never came close to hitting any of the rocks in the river, they sailed around obstacles effortlessly, I have no idea how. By all means we should have sunk during that storm. But somehow we survived!"

"Boons from above!" She exclaims. "Do you know how much longer until we arrive? How much of the river did we cover?"

"Tarin and Naries should be just ahead, then with luck we will be in the Great City within a few days."

"Good, I don't like being on boats this long…"

"Look!" Her brother shouts, pointing upriver.

Tiaries can see it too, something rising over the horizon. She smiles and shakes his shoulders, as two huge statues become visible in the distance. On the left riverbank lies Tarin, of the River Realm. On the right shore lies Naries, of the Elven States.

From the Port of Tarin, a monumental bronze statue of a man reaches into the sky, holding its hand outstretched to the opposite shore. From the Cove of Naries, a huge wooden woman stands as tall her metal suitor, carved of a single colossal tree, casting her hand to meet Tarin's over the river. The ship passes beneath the statues, as it pulls towards port.

"They make you feel small, don't they?" She says, looking up in wonder.

The councilor approaches behind them. "Do you know the story of Tarin and Naries?" He asks.

"Yes, of course!" She answers, cheerily. "Tarin was an adventurer, during the early days of man. He travelled further into the Great Forest than any man had been before. One day he was attacked by a tiger. While he was somehow able to defend himself against the first attack, his leg was badly wounded. He lay against a stump listening to the tiger rustle in the brush, expecting that any moment would be his last. When suddenly, a beautiful elf came down from the trees. She defeated the tiger, then bandaged Tarin's leg, bringing him to a hidden grotto. She helped him to heal, and the two fell in love."

"Sounds about right." The councilor replies, nodding. "And the twin cities here?"

She gives an unknowing shrug.

"After Emperor Harlorn defeated King Tritan, and the elves fell back behind the river, there was a law passed that elves were not allowed to leave the Elven States. So the people here built Tarin and Naries across the shore from each other. There were so many people that had family on both sides of the river." He smiles, looking out as they pull into the Port of Tarin. "You know, almost all the citizens of Tarin have some elven blood and the same for Naries. They built the statues above us to symbolize love and unity, in open defiance of the Emperor's law. Even back during the years when consorting with elves was punishable by death, the people of Tarin and Naries freely travelled between the two shores."

"Good." Jaties says, "Those laws were stupid."

"They were, yes." The councilor replies. "It was a long time ago. Things have come far since then."

After re-supplying, the ship returns to the river. The next two days bring smooth sailing, relatively uneventful. Tiaries takes the time to read through her stack of scripts.

I wonder what plays the Emperor's Company performs...
Hopefully we won't have to learn all new productions.

She sets down the script she was leafing through, and dances across the cabin. She spins, then stops, freezing in an open pose with her arms stretched over her head.

Jaties opens the door abruptly, shouting. "The locks are up ahead, come see!" He is gone before she can reply, dashing back to the deck.

Tiaries follows him out of the cabin, into the bright sunlight. She sees a huge waterfall coming up, rising from the river before them. Its roar is deafening. To the side of the falls, maneuvering around them, are the locks. Interlocking channels with large wooden doors, separating multiple levels of water between them. One above the other, climbing from the lower river up to above the waterfall.

As the ship gently glides into the lowest lock, a man on a small boat rows up, knocking on the ship's hull with a metal staff. "Toll! Toll!" He calls, from below.

One of the men, she presumes to be the ship's captain, walks to the edge and throws a piece of silver down. Without a word, the toll man pushes off and rows up to another ship. A few minutes later, after more ships file into the enclosure of water, the gate is lowered behind them and the lock ahead is opened. The ships all rise as the water begins to rush in.

Oars hit the surface and they maneuver with the vessels around them, all moving to the front of the next lock. When all the ships have made it in, the next wooden door drops behind them, raising the ships another level.

After repeating the process for what seems like hours, they reached the top section. The door ahead opens and they are off again, leaving the falls behind amidst a procession of ships.

The next morning, Tiaries wakes early. She looks at the bed across the room, with Jaties still sound asleep, then walks alone to the deck. Fog hangs heavily on the river, hiding their path. The cold morning air is crisp, fresh and sweet. She walks to the aft of the ship, sitting with her legs sticking between the rails, hanging out over the water.

She imagines the Great City, its beauty. They had been once before, but only to the outskirts. They hadn't been allowed to perform in the city proper. She had seen the buildings in the distance though, some so large they seemed to reach the clouds.

I wonder what the troupe will be like… Will we live in the Great City?

She hadn't thought of that yet.

Does the Emperor live in the Great City? I thought he lived in a tower somewhere. Will we live there too?

She had been so worried about leaving the carnival that she hadn't taken the time to think about what was coming.

The councilor will tell me... I'll go find him and ask.

She gets up and meanders to the front of the ship, looking for Councilor Lingonberry. The men run about the deck, adjusting sails and riggings. She finds him in his favorite spot, reclining outside the door to the cabins.

"Good morning, Tiaries." He nods to her. "We should be arriving in the Great City any time now. Have you been before?"

"Never to the city itself, no. Will that be where we live now? In the Great City?"

"We are just staying there for a few weeks, preparing for the festivities. The whole Empire will be coming for the birthday of the Emperor's son. He will be sixteen. How old are you again?"

"I am fifteen, my lord."

"You don't need to call me lord, my dear. Feel free to call me Lanties, unless the Emperor is within earshot."

"Lanties..." She repeats. "Your first name?"

He nods, "The one my mother gave me. Anyway, after the tournament and feasts are over, we will return with the Emperor to the Pillar.

BOOM BUM BUM BUM BUM BOOM BUM BUM BUM BUM BOOM

Drums erupt from below the deck, and oars emerge from the ship's sides, beginning to rhythmically sway to the beats. Sailors lower the sails, as the ship pulls into the busy waters of the Great City.

Tiaries sees the city's core ahead, its enormous buildings rising along the water's edge. It is built at a point where three rivers meet and converge into the one they currently sail upon.

Temples and palaces line the banks, their facades facing the water. Hundreds of pyres and braziers burn in front of the structures, some of the fires rising taller than the buildings themselves. Marble walls and pillars support gilded roofs, shining bright and gold in the morning sun. Statues of gods and men stand above the buildings, as if guarding over the followers singing and praying below.

"We've arrived!" The councilor says, rising from his seat. "The Great City…"

Jia 3

Hints of lemongrass waft amid a sea of lavender as she strolls through the atrium, a gentle warmth filling the air with their aroma.

Her father's throne room lies across the courtyard, the beauty of the atrium set as a backdrop to his large black marble seat. It had been more than a week since she spoke to him last. He had avoided her for days, letting his disappointment be known.

Yesterday he had broken his silence, but only to ask her about the impending engagement.

That old fool. We shall see...

She had only smiled at his questions, and silently excused herself from the room. But today was different, today she needed something.

"Father, you look well." Jia says, approaching his throne and giving the slightest of a bow.

"Ah, I thought you had forgotten how to speak." He replies, reproachfully.

"Of course not, my lord. I had merely forgotten my place. If you wish me to wed, then I shall." She smiles up at him, a daughter's love lightly painted on her face. "We will announce it to the world. After the prince's tourney has finished, of course. It would look most rude to try to upstage the Emperor or his son."

"Of course, of course." He replies, waving his hand. "I am glad to see you have come to understand."

"I have, father."

"You have no idea how important this marriage is. There are th…"

"I understand well enough, father. There is no need to elaborate. I will do my duty." Jia interrupts, before turning to leave him. Pausing at the door, she faces him once more to add, "I am going to leave for the Great City today. A group of friends are tying their pleasure barges together and riding down the river."

"Floating pleasure barges down the river would take weeks."

"We know, but it will be most relaxing. The water between here and the Great City is so very gentle. And it is as warm as a hot spring this time of year. It is slow, yes. Your ship will most likely overtake us on the trip. I can always join you then, if I am growing bored."

"Whose barges are you taking?" He asks, with a hint of suspicion in his voice.

"Sandy's father is letting us use his. We are tying it up with Lee Ryan's barge, Jo Var's, Ka Ammi's, and I think Jorrun Frostburn's. But obviously there are a bunch of people staying on each."

"I am not sure if I want you travelling with the Frostburn boy." He replies, coldly.

"Why not?" She asks, with genuine surprise.

I've never heard him speak against the Frostburns before. Why now?

"Things have been tense between Lord Frostburn and myself, ever since his last visit from up north. He mentioned in passing that his troops have begun to outnumber mine own. He jested that as such, he should be the warlord of the Firelands. Since then he has been absent from court. I worry his jests might have gone to his head."

Yes, father. I sure they are just jests, nothing more... Jia ponders her reply silently for a moment.

"I know nothing of that, father. But I do know Jorrun could not care less about his father's feuds, nor I of mine..." With that, she leaves the room.

Early in the evening, Jia sits aboard a pleasure barge. A large flat-bottomed boat, tied between half a dozen similarly designed vessels. All topped with elaborately decorated buildings, gardens and pools fed by the river below.

The ship Jia lounges on with her friends is built to look like one of the great temples of the Plateau. Large columns support an upper story of rooms, casting shade on the patio below where they sit and dine. The building material has the look of marble, but she can easily tell that it's wood, painted to give the impression of stone.

They dine on fish that Ryan had caught earlier in the lake, while he waited for everyone to arrive. Roasted bluegill and rainbow trout line the table, surrounded by bowls of buttered potatoes, covered in diced garlic and parsley. Fresh berries, mangos and dragonfruit are beautifully displayed, chilling atop blocks of ice carved into the shape of flowers and leaves. Smaller pieces of ice shaped into bees and raspberries decorate the sculptures and lie interspersed with the frosted fruit.

Jo Vali laughs loudly, as her brother Var recounts the time one of their footmen was bitten on the rear by a stray dog whilst he was trying to get another scavenging mutt out of the household pantry. The farce had played out as comically as possible. If Var's retelling was to be believed, the footman had run crying halfway across town before he could be consoled.

After dinner, Ryan pulls a harp from under his seat. He starts to strum, sending a sublime melody rising into the sunset. The gentle notes calm the clamor of the party, bringing the guests to silent reflection.

As the noise subsides, he begins to sing.

Cry beauty when you see our sky

Blue newly summer stings the eye

Across our mountains, rainbows lie

Our fire burns

Waves ebb upon our purple shore

And warm winds sweep as come before

The flame has fought since years of lore

Our fire burns

In emerald fields, maidens pray

Come day from day does beauty stay

Until night falls, but as we say

Our fire burns

The flames, they keep our fear at bay

When darkened night does fall from gray

We'll show no fright, and join the fray

Our fire burns

Jia gets up from her chair and moves to the edge of the barge. Kneeling, she lets her hand dip into the water dragging her fingers across the surface as the ship drifts along, leaving behind a serpentine wake.

A cough from behind grabs her attention. She turns to see Jorrun standing above her, smiling in the twilight. The sapphire sky lies saturated with billows of purple clouds, softly illuminated by the last remnants of the setting sun.

"Lovely night for a trip down the stream." She says, with an overdrawn yawn. "Wouldn't you agree?"

"Gorgeous, indeed." He remarks, grinning as he stares at her. "But beauty isn't always as it appears. You never know what lies beneath the surface..."

Jia hears a disturbance in the water. Looking around, she sees two reflective yellow slits gliding forward, moving quickly towards their boat.

What in curses is that?

Taking a step back, Jia sees the creature in full, an enormous wraith sliding beneath the water. Twenty feet long, maybe more. She moves away from the edge of the ship, distancing herself from the beast under the surface.

The boat lurches as the thing bumps against the side. Huge jaws burst open, erupting from the water and latching onto the edge of the barge, jolting the ship's deck and sending plates flying from the table.

"What the… What happened? What is that?" Ka Ammi shrieks, grabbing a column for stability as the barge lurches sharply forward.

"It's a crocodile!" Jorrun answers. "A big one, by the looks of it."

Ryan grabs a spear from a rack near the building in the center of the barge, and rushes towards the beast, but Jorrun grabs him before he can attack.

"I can handle it… No need to risk getting pulled in." Jorrun smiles, as he approaches the edge and removes his shirt. The crocodile still gnaws and lashes at the side of the vessel, causing the ship to tilt towards the water.

Jia looks for her lantern on the table, before quickly remembering she had left it on Sandy's barge with the rest of their things.

Damn…

She looks back to the scene, just as Jorrun makes his move. A blaze of bright blue flames erupts from the small of his back, arching over his head like the tail of a scorpion. At the end of the fiery jet, the flames take the form of a snake, snapping at the night air and projecting an eerie azure glow across the rippling river.

The crocodile releases his grip on the boat and submerges, but the flood of light keeps its body clearly visible beneath the turbulent aquamarine water. Jorrun's flaming appendage whips about, coiling above him, stalking its prey.

Leathery ridges break through the water, as jaws snap onto the back of the ship. A flash of blue light sweeps through the night, snapping around the crocodile's neck and pulling the beast into the air with such force that a large mouth shaped section of the ship is ripped away with it.

Jorrun draws a sword from his waistband, its hilt crusted in sapphires and gold, the bright blue firelight reflecting across the surface of the blade. Bending his knees and bracing for impact, Jorrun holds the sword out as the burning serpent snaps back, yanking the beast through the air with the ease of a child swinging a doll.

Terrible noises escape its burning throat as the flailing crocodile flies down toward the ship, its head meeting Jorrun's outstretched sword with a sickening thud.

Kzhee 3

A twisting baobab stands tall and sturdy among the sea of grass, a lone soldier waving in the wind.

"AHHH!" Kzhee screams, throwing his arms forward, palms facing towards the tree.

Silence.

"Baaahhhmmmm..." He hums, deep and drawn out. His fists shaking in the sky, before drawing them towards the ground with all his strength.

Nothing.

Kzhee arches his back, breathing deeply. Staring at the baobab with focused concentration. Then he closes his eyes and exhales, willing with all his heart for a flash of lightning to strike the tree.

But not even a spark falls.

It couldn't have been me... If it was, would I not be able to do it again? It was the Lightningbird, its blessing. It has to have been... That makes no less sense than the bolt somehow coming from me.

'Don't think about it.' His father's voice runs through his mind. *'You were blessed, you were saved. Do not dwell on that which has passed. Do not waste the life that was almost robbed from you.'*

A gentle mist rose in the mighty hill-chief's eyes.

'And please, please... Do not try to make it happen again. The Emperor's Due will be behind us soon, no one can think you are one of the gifted. Not until it is over. You cannot be selected.'

Kzhee did not understand his father's fear. Other children constantly competed with each other, trying to prove who deserved to be offered for the Due, who would bring the most honor to the Lightning Plains.

Why should I be scared of an honor that other people fight over?

He mounts his horse and turns towards home. A warm westward breeze drifts against his face, mingling through the crisp spring air as it makes its way across the prairie, searching for the freedom of the sea. Kzhee squeezes his legs urging Sparks to sprint, trying to race the wind.

'You cannot be selected...'

But why father?

Silence.

The smell of burning mesquite floats from the fires of the feast, letting him know he is almost home. Mool Moolson, the island-chief, and Kaav Braalson, the rock-chief, had been spotted that morning by outriders, traveling east to the village amongst a vast entourage. Moving slowly, no doubt hindered by the troves of gifts the chiefs had gathered for the Emperor and his son.

Kzhee rides on, not wanting to be late for their arrival, or for the feast being prepared in their honor.

The festivities have already begun when he pulls his horse into the village, nestled between the grassy hills. Laughter fills the night, and clangs ring out as cider mugs are brought together in cheers and toasts to good health. The scent of roast rhino and grilled bison wafts in the air, riding on clouds of salty smoke.

His father sits at the head of the great table, beneath the moonlit sky. Chiefs Mool and Kaav sit on either side of him, in the highest places of honor. The three laugh loudly, clapping each other's backs, as if they are the greatest of friends just arriving home from some lively sport.

Chief Mool is older that Kzhee's father. A wise man, with white hair and large protruding ears. Surrounded by his numerous children and grandchildren, all adorned with the same light hair and rich tan skin of those who populate the ocean's beaches.

Chief Kaav is very young, for a chief at least. A strong man of twenty, with a warm smile that somehow shows all his teeth, even the grinders in back. He is broad of chest and shoulder, with long black hair reaching to his waist. He has been chief of the Great Rock for less than a year, since his own father's heart had failed. But already the people of the Rock loved and accepted him as they had his father before, some even saying his abilities as a leader surpass those of his predecessor.

Kzhee approaches the great table. "Father, chiefs." He says, bowing politely. One hand at his waist and the other on his heart.

"Kzhee!" Chief Mool exclaims. "How long has it been? I swear, you were knee high to a runt last I saw you."

"He grows tall indeed." His father agrees. "He will surely make the Hills proud in time."

"Does he show any of his father's gifts?" Kaav asks, with a sly grin.

"No, neither him nor my daughter." His father answers, flatly. "My wife never showed any, the children must have taken after her."

"May she rest in peace…" Chief Mool says, lowering his head in respect.

Later on, the clamor of the feast begins to wane, giving rise to sweet music, emanating from all around. Reed flutes whistle and drums boom, while crickets play along in the night, chirping their songs to the beat of the instruments.

Kzhee excuses himself from the feast, and walks back to his family's home. The cool night air sobering him from the cider he had drank. The opening in the exterior of his family's hill leads to the chambers inside.

In the night, the dwelling's only light is cast by candles and fires, dying in their hearths. He throws more wood in the fireplace of his room, swirling the glowing coals with an iron rod and sending up a billow of smoldering embers and warm smoke.

He begins throwing some spare clothes into his riding sack, as well as a formal tunic. They would be leaving before sunrise the following morning, to join with the other chiefs on the trip to the

Great City. All the leaders of the realms were expected to attend the prince's tourney, and to present their selections for the Emperor's Due.

"How long is the ride grampapa?" One of Moolson's grandchildren asks the next morning, bouncing on the back of a piebald pony, struggling desperately to keep up with the riders at the head of the traveling party.

"Ehh, we'll meet Herd-Chief Ruul by weeks' end. From there it is another ten… Maybe eleven days to the Cliffs to meet Chief Talii. Then yet another couple weeks to the Great City."

"It will be months, if we continue ride at this pace…" Kzhee's father retorts, looking over his shoulder at the massive procession following behind. Wagons and carriages drawn by teams of buffalo crawl along, interspersed among the droves of men and women on horseback.

"Are you in a hurry, Chief Rhee?" Mool asks passively, taking a deep breath of dusty air. "I would rather not show up a day before we must. The Great City is filthy, it is crowded, it reeks of piss and shit, and best of all, our majestic Emperor will be there… Jero the Magnificent."

Kzhee sees the old man wrinkle up his nose, like he had just caught scent of a pile of rhino dung.

Haha, the Chief of Otter Island looks just like one of the water rodents that swarm about his isles.

"Why doesn't he like the Emperor?" Kzhee whispers, to his father.

"Taxes," Rhee Leeson responds, with a grin. "Moolson is a rich man. His island and the channel it harbors are the only protection for ships passing through Pirate Bay on the trip south to A'Tannia. If you don't pay his fee, his great harbor chain stays taught, blocking off the straight, and you must sail around the ocean side of the island. Not many ships that venture that course ever arrive at their destination."

"What does that have to do with the Emperor?"

"The Emperor feels that since he is lord of all the oceans and seas, the fee should go entirely to the Imperial Treasury. But he claims that to be fair, he will only take half."

"Is that not fair?"

"The tax on Mool's family had been a tenth under Emperor Jero's father, Emperor Johaner. I am not one to say whether the increase is fair or not, but it is certainly why Mool holds a grudge against the Emperor."

A fortnight later the procession arrives at the cliffs, the end of the Lightning Plains and the edge of their realm. Above the towering cliffs is the southern end of the Windswept Plateau, stretching hundreds of miles north to the Firelands.

A thundering waterfall cascades from the cliff's rim, falling over the buildings and residences carved along its face. Cliff City, hanging high above the Plains, separated from below by a single stairwell, heavily guarded day and night. Protecting the gem mines above, excavated deep into the rock.

Herd-Chief Ruul and his family had joined them a week past. The drove of a procession had doubled in size with their arrival. Thousands of Rhino, Bison and Buffalo were being driven north with them, to supply meat for the great feasts to come. Ruul's gift to the Emperor and his son. Cliff City would be their last stop, before pushing on to the Great City.

Cliff-Chief Talii is waiting at the base of the towering stairs that lead up to his city, his entourage ready to depart. No feast prepared, or hospitalities arranged.

"Welcome, you are late!" The cliff-chief shouts to the arriving horde. Gesturing to the rippling lake beneath the waterfall, he adds, "Let the beasts have their fill before we ride. It is many days before the next stream northward."

Rhee Leeson approaches Talii, opening his arms for an embrace. "Old friend, it has been too long."

"Too long indeed, are those whiskers of yours graying?"

"With wisdom comes gray whiskers." His father chuckles. "You remember my boy, Kzhee?"

"Of course, last I saw you I believe you were playing naked in this very lake with my son and daughter. Lord, how time flows like water. Is your sister here as well?"

"No, sir. She stayed in the village with the midwives, the ride is long and…"

"We hope she will be able to make the next trip." His father interjects. "She is such a frail thing…"

"We must come to you then, one day. I recall when we would visit as children, the summer breeze rolling through the hills. There is never any wind here, did you know that?" He asks, looking up at the cliffs towering behind him.

"Kzhee, go and take Sparks to drink before we leave."

"Yes, father." He says, turning towards the lake, trying to steer through the throngs of people and beasts amassed around the pond. The shore is packed with animals squeezed side by side, growing tighter as they lap up gallons of cool water.

The far side of the lake appears relatively empty, so he gives Sparks a nudge and gallops around the crowds, splashing through a stream as he rides to the opposite shore.

He dismounts and leads the horse to the edge of the lake, kneeling and taking a deep drink himself. The warm sun stings his sunburnt face, so Kzhee curls up in the shade of a lime tree, drifting off as he waits for his horse to have her fill.

"Are you asleep?" A sweet voice asks, gently coaxing him from his slumber.

He looks around, startled, forgetting where he is for a moment. His horse lays lazily in the cool shade next to him, unalarmed. Above them stands a figure, the bright sun behind blocking her face from view.

"It has been a while, Kzhee." The girl kneels next to him, smiling in the shade. Her round cheekbones give her grin the illusion of stretching from ear to ear. Her kind hazel eyes shimmer with blue waves, reflections of the lake. "Don't tell me you don't remember me... My first kiss, my only love. How you hurt me so. My heart... She bleeds."

"Rilii, is that you?" He stammers, struggling to find the words. "I had... I'm so sorry, I didn't realize."

"*Hehe,* I am just teasing, my sweet boy." She says, laying down in the shade, her face resting before him, staring into his eyes intently. Gently, she touches her mouth to his, softly kissing him.

Her lips are moist and sweet, almost cool compared to the heat of the blazing sun. A flood of memories fills his mind as she pulls away. Playing in the waterfall and swimming through the lake, pushing one another beneath the surface and darting away before the other could launch a retaliatory splash. Laughing... Smiling... Happy...

"It's good to see you, Rilii. I've missed you so." He puts his arms around her, pulling her close and losing himself in the smell of honeysuckles on her skin.

She hugs him back, so tightly that her arms shake with glee, rubbing her cheek against his in an intimate embrace. Loosening her grip, she begins crawling over him. "What is this here?!" She asks.

Oh lord! Kzhee thinks, rolling onto his stomach quickly. Embarrassed. Assuming she must have noticed his excitement.

"Would you look at this?" She chirps, climbing off him and brushing aside the grass and weeds growing from the roots of the lime tree.

"What is it?" He asks, waiting an extra moment before standing up.

"It looks like a little statue." She says, holding up a small brown figurine, no larger than a finger. Depicting a bird with its wings outstretched, as if soaring through the air. "Here you are," She places it in his hand. "A gift for you, my love."

He runs his thumb along the statue, its surface left warm by the sun.

"You have been riding with the other chiefs for days now, right?" Rilii asks, coyly. "Have you heard anything about the Emperor's Due? Who they are offering...?"

"I only heard them say that all the chiefs needed to be present to discuss it. They were waiting for your father. What have you heard?"

"Father thinks it should be my brother Drii, but I was under the impression that you had to be intelligent to be on the Emperor's Council." She snickers at her joke. "If not him, then me."

"You? I didn't know you... Wha..."

"What can I do?" She finishes.

Crossing her legs and closing her eyes, Rilii takes his hands in hers, breathing deeply. For minutes she sits in silence. Her touch, soft and soothing.

Kzhee feels the world around him start to melt away, the only thing he can see is her beautiful face, glowing in the sunlight. His muscles relax, and he begins to think of what life would be like if they were always together.

Then suddenly, she shrieks, startling him from his daydreams. "I hate spiders! Did that really happen to you?"

"What!?"

"Were you and your horse really attacked in the woods by a giant spider creature thing?"

"How do you...?"

"I see things when I touch people." She says, with a grin. "Though, sometimes it is hard to tell the difference between reality and inventions of the mind. It is almost like seeing people's memories, played through a dream."

"That is incredible!"

"More so than being able to make lightning strike?" She asks, dramatically. "I've seen people be able to cast sparks, throw little jolts, even cause other's bodies to seize up just by touching them. But to bring a bolt of lightning from the sky… It's been centuries since there was someone that powerful. Does anyone else know?"

"I don't even know if it's real. I haven't been able to do it again. My father said not to tell anyone, to forget about it until after the Due."

"Being selected is the greatest honor you could ever have bestowed! If I was you, I would never stop talking about it, practicing. Kzhee…"

"Like I said, I haven't been able to do it again. I don't even know..."

"AHHHH!" She screams loudly, pointing near the base of the tree. "Snake!"

Kzhee jumps back, away from the tree. As he does, a jolting crack explodes, ripping through the cloudless sky above. The bolt of lightning splinters the lime tree, throwing him and Rilii to the ground. The smell of burnt citrus and smoke drifts through the air, as his horse jumps to her feet, rearing and whinnying with distress.

"Ohh…" Rilii says, with demure innocence, as she picks a smoldering stick up from the ground. "My mistake. It wasn't a snake, just a root…" She laughs, stroking his arm. "But, at least now you know."

The propellers rumble and knock as they begin to slow to a stop. Wooden flap brakes extend from the city's foundation, bringing its speed down slowly to a halt, just before bumping into the edge of the landing deck.

A wooden gangplank drops with a thud. Attendants run down, wrapping huge iron chains from the deck of the Flying City to stone bollards lining the edge of the dock.

Chion and Councilor Sage stroll down the gangplank, past the stalls and carts of the open air market, thousands of feet above the ground. The landing dock surrounds the top level of the Tower of Trade, one of the immense towers that rise from atop the Pillar.

"Have you been in the Emperor's Tower before?" The councilor asks.

"Once for a feast, when I was young. My father brought me." Chion answers. "Nowadays, when the Flying City makes its stops here, I usually keep to the Tower of Trade. Sometimes I visit my uncle, when he is not busy…"

"Ah yes, Lord Antissi is a busy man. An important man. Chancellor of the Bank of the Pillar, Vice-Chancellor of the Antissi Bank, and his imperial majesty's own Lord Treasurer. A very important man, indeed." Councilor Sage smiles, "Let's go bother him!"

They step onto a stone platform, set in a granite lift-shaft. Once the lift fills, two men at the rear standing on marble pedestals raise their hands in unison. As they do, the stone lift starts to lower.

Beginning to drop, the platform moves slowly at first, then faster and faster. Floor after floor flies by, each drawing Chion's eyes up as he tries to focus on the myriad of sights. Theatres, taverns, fighting cages, food carts and fine restaurants. Each floor with its own theme, catering to every possible type of consumer.

The lift begins to slow as the men lower their arms. One of them announces, "The Pillar Square, Antissi Bank."

They exit the stone lift and walk into his uncle's establishment. Compared to Chion's humble setup in the Flying City, this bank is a palace. It occupies the first three floors of the Tower of Trade. Everything is made of white marble, speckled with veins of pink and gold. Brightly lit and sparklingly immaculate.

Councilor Sage approaches a teller, standing on the ground floor behind a large marble counter.

"Wondrous day to you, sir. How may I help you?" She asks, cheerily.

"My good lady, I must speak with Lord Antissi at once." The councilor states, matter-of-factly.

"I am quite sure that I do not know where the Lord Treasurer is at this moment." The teller says, a look of confusion on her face. "I can take a message to one of his officers. They can relay it to him."

"Inform him the Emperor wishes to see him at once. We will be in the Grand Hall." He turns to leave briskly. "Oh, and tell him his nephew is here..."

The councilor places his arm on Chion's shoulder as they turn and leave. The sun outside is bright, blinding him as they walk across the top of the Pillar, through the square, past the amphitheater, approaching the Emperor's Tower. It is the tallest of the towers, rising hundreds of feet above the top of the Pillar.

The guards standing erect at the gates to the tower fall back as he and the councilor approach. "Good day, Lord Sage. Welcome home."

"Thank you, it is good to be back." Sage replies, politely. "Is the Emperor at court?"

"Indeed, my lord."

Chion can hear the guard thinking. *'Who is the boy? What's this man got him for? Arrogant up-jump shits looking down on us.'* The wind atop the Pillar is strong, whipping past them and carrying the man's thoughts as if he was screaming. *'Good day to you too, ass.'*

Councilor Sage nods his head, leading Chion past the silent guards into the gargantuan tower. The doors open into an enormous lobby, black and green granite lining the walls. Plants hang from notches in the stone, giving Chion the feeling of walking through a dense forest.

Rainbow finches and parakeets chirp and sing, hopping between plants, sending flashes of color flittering through the room. There is a stone lift in the center of the building, stretching up through the tower. Much smaller than the lift in the Tower of Trade, but more ornate. Decorated in tessellating tiles and golden leaf.

"To the throne room, Loak." Councilor Sage says, to the lift attendant. "Thank you."

"Of course, councilor." The young lift operator replies, raising his hands and looking up at the shaft above them. The lift shoots upward, almost knocking Chion off his feet.

"This one is really fast." He remarks, trying to keep his balance.

"Yes, indeed. Loak here is the strongest Earthmover I have ever had the pleasure of meeting."

"Thank you, my lord." The operator replies.

"Do you think you could raise the great lift on your own?" The councilor asks.

"My lord… The great lift must be a hundred times the size of this one. I would be too terrified to even try." The smile on Loak's face lies in juxtaposition to his humble words.

Chion listens intently as the air in the shaft rushes past them, trying to investigate the operator's knowing grin.

Silence…

What is happening, why doesn't it work here?

The lift grinds to a halt as they reach a large hall. Attendants run from one antechamber to another, while supplicants wait for an audience with one of the various lords, masters, and chancellors of the court. The councilor leads Chion to a cavernous chamber off of the main hall.

"Wait here, I will let you know when the Emperor is ready to see you." The councilor walks into the throne room, closing the double doors behind himself.

Chion looks around the empty chamber, his stomach beginning to turn with anticipation. *What am I doing here?* He feels a burning feeling, rising in his throat.

The edge of the room is lined with towering stained glass windows, depicting a battle between elves and men. He finds a clear section of glass and peers outside, trying to clear his mind.

The tower overlooks the range of peaks that make up the Mountain Realm, standing tall over an expansive valley, reaching above the surrounding summits. The view is breathtaking, but falls quickly out of sight as a cloud drifts past the window, engulfing the Emperor's Tower in a veil of fog-white mist.

Chion paces back to the bench. As he sits, a door on the far end of the chamber opens, causing a burst of air to escape beneath the double doors of the throne room. The wind carries voices that only Chion can hear, barely audible even to him.

'We gain nothing from Matio. This one is stronger, more useful. And his father...' Chion can tell it is Councilor Sage speaking.

'What does he do?' Asks an unknown voice, raspy and cold.

'A wind-whisperer, I believe.' The first voice answers.

'Can he hear us now?' A new voice asks, a lady.

'No, he has much to learn before his gifts will work on any of us. He tried listening to my thoughts when I met him on the Flying City, but wasn't able to. One day though, I see him...'

The main doors to the chamber swing open, slamming against the walls with a thud. A procession enters with his uncle at the head, followed by countless attendants, accountants, managers, and men-at-arms. All seem to be speaking at once, and all are addressing his uncle. A large man, taller than most. His elegant clothes and ornate jewelry opulently showcase his unlimited means.

"Chion!" He booms, ignoring the swarm of people buzzing about him like flies. "How great to see you."

He approaches swiftly, throwing his large arms around his nephew.

"It is good to see you too, uncle. Though I wish it was under different circumstances. Do you know why I am here?"

His uncle's kind eyes glisten for a moment, before he blinks the emotion away. Chion can feel his stare, penetrating.

'Can you hear me?'

His uncle's voice runs through his head, but his lips stay pursed.

'Yes, uncle.' He finds himself thinking.

'That is why you are here. I assume they are thinking of selecting you for the Emperor's Due.' A look of fear crosses his uncle's face. He winces, almost as if he hears something unsettling uttered in the distance. *'They're going to get me to agree to it now, so your father won't have time to protest. They know he would never consent to this. But as the Lord Treasurer, I cannot decline a request from the Emperor.'*

Quickly his uncle grabs one of his attendants by the arm, whispering in his ear. The man turns and runs from the room, without saying a word.

As a door slams shut behind the attendant, the doors of the throne room open. Councilor Sage enters the chamber first, quickly followed by a woman draped in a gown of purple silk and magenta satin. Her dark golden skin glows, like honey and sugar caramelizing in the sun.

Then comes the Emperor, his elegant blue and crimson robes gently dragging on the floor behind him. A white haired man follows in the Emperor's shadow, casting suspicious glances in every direction.

Emperor Jero's voice echoes across the granite chamber. "So glad the two of you could join us. I would like to invite you to accompany me and the council on my personal ship, for the trip to the Great City. You are planning on attending the tourney, I presume?"

Loak

"Loak! You are relieved. Fall in line." Overlord Erop says, quickly, not breaking his stride.

The young Earthmover exits the lift and joins the trail of men following the overlord, like ducklings following their mother. Another Earthmover leaves the ranks, hurriedly taking over Loak's post.

"There you are!" Herny exclaims, clapping Loak on the back as he falls in pace next to him. "Have you heard?"

"Have I heard what?"

"There is a new wife being brought in. Maybe she'll be the one!" He says, excitedly elbowing Loak in the side.

"Oh, you mean maybe she will be wife number five for you?" Loak asks, with a smirk.

"Of course!" The brawny man says, jokingly punching him in the arm. "No, you fool, I mean the one for you. It is beyond comprehension how you haven't been able to find a girl to your liking. They're practically bringing in one a week. I don't know how many more wives I can handle."

"Then quit picking more." Loak says, with a roll of his eyes.

"Ah, alas, they are all so beautiful… What am I to do?"

The procession exits the Emperor's Tower, walking through the square, past the library and training grounds. Dense evening fog lies thick over the top of the Pillar, causing groups of people to fade in and out of sight as they pass through the crowd.

"Guro! You are relieved. Fall in line." The overlord shouts, as they enter the Dawn Tower and pass its central lift.

The short man steps in next to Herny and Loak, scurrying to keep up. "Hey, did you guys hear that there's a new girl tonight?" Guro asks.

"Yeah, I was just asking Loak if it is going to be wife number one for him."

"This guy," Guro says, laughing. "No one will ever be good enough for the mighty Loak."

"You better not like her Guro, I'll pick her just to spite you." Loak jabs back.

"What makes you think I won't challenge you? I could win!"

The three break into laughter.

Dinner and drinks are laid out in the dining hall of the Earth Tower, waiting for them when they arrive. Dancers twist on ropes hanging from the ceiling, while minstrels pick at citterns, singing songs of strength and honor and duty.

"Try some of this dragonfruit." Herny says, handing half of one to Loak.

"Not bad, it's real sweet."

"Just came in today, I saw them getting loaded out of the Flying City."

The music falls silent, as Overlord Erop walks onto the dining hall's stage. He claps his hands, and a girl walks out from behind a side curtain. Her red hair hangs almost to her knees, a lifetime of growth. Her skin is milky white, with just the faintest of freckles upon her cheeks. Her shy eyes stare at the floor, but her lips are drawn back in a smile of joy.

"Let me introduce a wondrous beauty from the faraway Southern Realm, certainly worthy of being a mother of earth. Myrrh!" The overlord proclaims. "After tonight, Myrrh Earthmover!"

The girl steps forward to the edge of the stage, still looking at the ground. She takes a deep breath, holding it in. Her body begins to shake and her face flushes red. Then, just as it appears she'll faint from the strain, her face relaxes and her lungs exhale, and the girl begins to glow. Bright white luminescence radiates from her skin, while swirls of copper and gold glide and circulate through her coruscating hair.

The men in the room stare, gawking at the beauty before them. All except Loak, who seems far more interested in the spice crusted beef ribs on his plate.

"Loak!" The overlord exclaims, a condescending tone in his voice. "Is Myrrh here enough to move you to finally take a wife? You do know your duty as an Earthmover, no?"

"Of course, sir. However, I fear that I don't like redheads, too bold and fiery for my taste. Perhaps the next one will be more to my liking."

Erop scoffs and storms off the stage.

"I'm taking her if Loak isn't." Herny states bluntly to the congregation, his eyes locked on the young woman.

She looks up at the charming, well-built man, and her face turns bright pink. The girlish smile widening, unable to conceal her happiness.

"No!" Sounds a shout from across the hall. A balding man, with a gut wider than a keg, waddles forward. "Herny, you need a fifth wife like I need a wart on me eye. I challenge… I'm taking this little one for meself."

Whispers flood the hall, as Herny jumps up from his seat. "Accepted!" He yells, grinning.

The crowd shoves their way into a nearby chamber, the training hall. Huge stone disks circle the room, piled in stacks of various heights, each weighing multiple tons. Herny and Loak walk to the center of the hall, standing next to a large stone lift.

The challenger raises both his arms toward the ceiling, causing two enormous marble disks to levitate and slowly move to the center lift. Once they drift above their target, he drops his hands, causing the stones to fall with a crashing boom. Sweat drips from the man's face, and his breathing is strained from the exertion. Grunting in satisfaction, he looks at the girl and smiles a rotten smile. She shies away, looking desperately at Herny.

"You make it look so easy…" Herny says, before lazily raising one hand, bringing the lift and its load shooting to the ceiling. Gently, he lowers it back to the ground. Then turns and brings two more disks floating through the air, dropping them atop the original pair. "Your move…" He says, with a flourish and bow.

His opponent tries to lift his arms, but some force seems to keep them from rising. He strains, grunting and sweating, howling and hollering, yet the lift does little more than shake in place.

With little effort Herny raises the platform, a condescending smirk on his face.

"*Argh*, curses on you, boy." The older man spits, storming out of the training room.

Herny laughs as he puts his arm around the girl, pulling her close. She tries awkwardly to speak, but struggles to get the words out.

"I… I am excited… to help the Empire. It's such an honor, I hope I can do my part…" She shows a sudden burst of spirit. "I will give you strong sons, strong Earthmovers! I promise!"

"I am sure you shall, my darling. I'll see you tonight." He tells her, signaling for her to go. "The wives eat next door. Find my other darlings and let them know our family has grown."

As the room empties, Loak looks at Herny, then at the fully loaded lift. With an effortless move of his finger, he brings it in the air, holding it motionless above their heads. "You'd better hope I never challenge you…"

"I would never stand in your way." Herny replies, then faintly adds in a whisper. "Thanks for helping me get that up, lord knows I'd be wifeless without you."

"Anytime…" Loak answers, softly.

Relorn 4

Their riding car waves atop an elephant's back, swaying with each step the beast of burden takes. Atasio Nodovin and Councilor Quezada sleep in the lower suites of Nodovin's caravan, while the boys ride above, relaxing in the open air lounging deck. Dozens of elephants surround them, most carrying towering carriages, the rest pulling wagons full of luggage and provisions.

Reza sends arrows flying from the side of the carriage, bursting into flames as they strike the towering termite mounds littered across the open fields like gravestone monuments of some forgotten battle.

"Why did the elephant stand behind a tree?" Andrew asks, listlessly.

"Why?" Matio responds.

"To hide from a mouse." Andrew states, bored. "Why is the elephant big and gray?"

Silence.

"Because, if it was small and white it would be a mouse." He continues, talking to no one in particular.

Relorn hardly notices his friend's attempts to pass time, Eristoclese's parting words playing through his mind.

'What kind of leader will you be?'

Towering temples and expansive buildings line the shore, casting a cool shade upon the vessel as it enters the Great City. They drift past the great park, the library, and the beautiful Grand Temple of the Order. The Emperor's Alcazar stands above the river, imposing, looking down on the city below.

"I have a home in the Great City, in the Shady Quarter." McKenna says, to Ral. "I prefer not to stay in inns or rent lodging from others, so I found it necessary years ago to invest in a home away from home. You and your friend will stay with me until the Due is done."

"Thank you, senator." The boy replies.

His home lies overlooking the city, high in the West Hills, affording sweeping views of all the sights below. The senator shows his cohorts and Ral to their rooms, before heading to his own suite.

Stepping on the patio, he looks at the Alcazar standing tall and proud in the distance. That had been half the reason he chose this particular house, it is one of the only homes in the city that looks down on the Emperor's Alcazar.

That evening, he joins the rest of his party for dinner. The senators sit together on one side of the table, opposite the nobles of the River Realm. Ral and his friend speak with Vincence Viali away from the table, goblets of wine sloshing between the three.

Viali, always downing those great gold goblets. I don't think I can recall having seen him sober…

"What are you fine people discussing?" McKenna asks, as he approaches them.

"I was inviting Ral here to join us in the team melee. We need a fourth contestant, as Senator Torbus's shoulder is not better from his fall." The vintner answers, his rosy cheeks glowing red from the drink.

"What kind of man can't keep his feet on a ship?" The senator asks, with a roll of his eyes.

"He is good with a sword. I hear…" Ral's friend volunteers.

Who is this girl?

"I'm sorry, what was your name again, dear?" Senator McKenna asks.

"Her name is Satia." A voice answers from behind the group, as Senator Calisio approaches. "You own the Seaview Tavern, no?"

"Yes, senator." Satia replies.

"So, with Ral here, we have a full team." Vincence says. "Him, Orly, Darin, and myself."

"You will win for sure," McKenna laughs. "Ral was a pit fighter."

"Yes, I saw his last fight." Senator Calisio says, with a smirk. "That is a neat trick you do, with the getting cut in half and all."

"I was surprised as anyone…" The boy replies. "But it will be fun to get to participate in the melee, lower stakes than the pits."

"Don't be so sure, men have died during the melee before. The weapons may be blunted, but accidents do happen." McKenna states. "You also have to make sure you're not using your gifts during the fight. The entire team will be disqualified if you do."

"Well, the only reason I would use it is if I take a wound, so hopefully it doesn't come to that." Ral says, chuckling.

"Yes, let us hope!" The vintner exclaims, swaying as he sips his goblet. "With any luck, we shall win this year. Here's to the River Realm!"

Councilor Quezada 2

Branches brush the top of the caravan, as the elephant lumbers through the timber of the woods. The boys laugh and duck each time it steps beneath a tree limb, narrowly dodging being hit. Atasio refuses to come up from beneath, terrified by the words of the knight they had passed on the trail.

'Robberies are up as of late. Travel in groups, and only during daylight hours. A pack of wolves has been reported to be holding up travelers headed for the Great City.'

He had convinced Atasio to ignore the knight's warnings. *What was he even talking about, wolves robbing people? Ridiculous...*

So they had continued on through the night. The boys standing guard with him on the top deck, their bows strung and ready in case of attack. The rest of their traveling company from the Plateau had stopped for the night at an inn along the road through the forest.

'We mustn't stop,' Quezada had told them. *'We are supposed to meet the Emperor first thing tomorrow morning."*

In truth, it didn't matter when they arrived. He just wanted to see her… *How long has it been?* He pictures her face, but the features are blurred. He can still smell her though, like a burning hearth in winter and warm blackberry pie.

AWWOOOOOOOOOO

A howl rings from the trees, cutting though the moonless night, causing the boys to nearly jump from their skin. Reza springs up and draws his bow, the point of his arrow beginning to glow.

"Calm down, boy. You don't want to burn the forest to the ground do you? If we are fallen upon, let the others take care of it. Don't fire unless you are certain it is necessary."

Reza looks offended, but quivers his arrow anyway.

I always forget he is her nephew... They look nothing alike, aside from the tan skin.

The howl goes unanswered, as they continue marching through the woods. The sun begins to rise as the trees begin to thin, bringing the city ahead into view. Tents fill the green areas, the parks and outskirts, dotting them with a multitude of colors, bringing a vibrancy and excitement to the already beautiful city.

Why did Johaner ever move the capital from here to the Pillar? This is truly the greatest place ever built…

Their elephant meanders into the city, as the morning bells being to ring from the tops of temples and towers to signal the start of the day.

Atasio Nodovin peaks up from the carriage below. "Ah, we have arrived, finally! My legs could not stand much more of being cramped in here. Where to first?"

"To the Alcazar, we must meet the Emperor." Quezada answers.

The elephant has trouble climbing the steep hill leading to the Alcazar, and the carriage starts to tilt dangerously, threatening to slide from the elephant's back. So the group climbs the remainder of the way on foot, while attendants run to unload their luggage and bring it up to the castle.

"Son!" Jero shouts, as the group approaches the main entrance. The Emperor embraces his heir, ruffling his hair with a smile.

"It is good to see you, father." Relorn replies.

"Are you excited for the tourney? For the Due?" Jero asks. "You become a man on the morrow."

"I am very excited, father, and nervous of course." The prince pauses and looks up at Quezada. "The councilor said I must ask your permission to enter the archery contest at the tourney, would that be okay, father? Reza and Matio and Andrew will be entering."

The boys nod in agreement.

"Of course, I hear you are becoming quite the marksman. Why don't you and the boys head inside, pick out some rooms to stay in while we are here." He turns to the adults, "Atasio! So good to see you, old friend. And Councilor Quezada, you look well, the Plateau must have been kind to you."

Yes, three years away from everything. So very kind...

"Yes, it was a nice change of scenery. I must admit though, I am excited to return to the Pillar when this is over." He looks around the foyer of the Alcazar, "Where is the council?"

"We are leaving to meet them now, at the Grand Temple of the Order. They claim to have a new oracle, so I am making a trip there to see it. The council is ensuring everything is ready for my arrival. You will accompany me, no?"

"Of course, your excellency."

They travel by litter to the temple, in the heart of the city below. The building is surrounded on three sides by river, amidst weeping willows and botanical gardens. Councilor Thorne stands waiting out front, his white hair gleaming in the sun.

"All is secure, your highness." Thorne says, as they approach.

"Thank you, councilor." Jero replies, exiting the litter and heading inside the temple.

Quezada and Thorne follow him inside. The rest of the council is waiting, Te Inzu, Sage Coda Sa, Ernesto Maestas, Lanties Lingonberry and Thoo Kroonson.

"Councilor Quezada, it is nice to see you." Inzu says, smiling as she approaches him.

The words catch in his throat. "It's… It's good to see you."

An attendant leads them to into a side room. Snowy white marble benches line the white marble chamber. The ceilings towering above flaunt beautiful frescos, painted in a spectacular array of colors, contrasting sharply against their white marble canvas.

They are alone in the room, save for a single man sitting by himself across the chamber.

After a few minutes, the High Priest enters. A short, balding man, standing with his chest puffed out with pride. A cream colored kitten with chocolate paws, nose and ears rides upon his shoulder. Serving boys and attendants follow him in a cluster, their eyes locked on the floor.

"Your majesty, I hope you have not been waiting long." Without giving the Emperor a chance to reply, the priest continues speaking. "You must meet this man here, I just received word of his arrival and the peril he went through to get to us. Sir Simon! Please, if you would come here."

The solitary man stumbles across the room, his gaunt expression giving the impression of a man not far from death.

"Sir Simon was on a ship, destined to this very city, when they were attacked by pirates! I should let him tell the story, it is harrowing indeed."

"Thank you, your highness." The knight says, turning to the emperor. "We were attacked south of A'Tannia, further south than pirates are usually seen... We did not expect any trouble. They came aboard during the dead of night. Attacking while the crew slept."

"Harrowing indeed. Something must be done about these ever increasing pirate attacks, I will have my Lord Admiral look into this at once." The Emperor states, regally. "We have business inside. The Empire thanks you for your service." With that, the Emperor turns to the High Priest and asks, "Shall we?"

They walk down a passage winding beneath the ground, through the catacombs.

Why do they always keep oracles in the dreariest parts of the temple? Couldn't they prophesize just as well in a comfortable room above ground?

"This one is new…" The High Priest tells the Emperor. "Jamie, a young girl. She is most accurate in her predictions, the best we have seen in a long time."

"Better than the last, I hope." Jero replies, coldly.

"Her… She was unworthy of your time. She was gotten rid of, as you asked." The priest states, calmly.

"Good."

They enter a dimly lit chamber. Marble columns hold up a small pavilion in its center. Inside the pavilion, a beautiful young girl sits upon a silk pillow with her legs crossed. She looks up as the Emperor enters her space.

"Speak," Jero tells the girl.

"My lord." She says, respectfully lowering her head in a shallow bow.

"Tell me something." He replies, shaking his head and sneering.

"All turtles are turtles, but some are green." She smiles, mischievously.

"Tell me of the future. What greatness lies ahead?" The Emperor barks, more of a statement than a question.

She takes a deep breath and closes her eyes, then begins to rock back and forth, swaying on her pillow and chanting unintelligible phrases.

Suddenly, she stops. Frozen in place by an invisible force. Her voice deepens, crackling in a vocal fry, "Are you certain that you wish to hear?"

"Tell me!" Jero shouts, snarling at the girl.

You've never liked any prophesy before, why would you like this one? Quezada thinks back to the other oracles the Emperor had visited. All had foretold bad ends for him, and all had met bad ends of their own. *If any of these oracles are truly prophets, they would know not to give the Emperor bad tidings, wouldn't they?*

"I fear the sights I see are not pleasant, my lord." The girl tells him. "I would advise against hearing it. Prophecy gives unto reality. Makes itself true. A life of not knowing, it is much better in my opinion."

The Emperor looks to the High Priest, a flash of anger in his eyes. "Who is this girl, to question me?"

Without waiting for the priest's reply, the girl begins to speak. "Nigh draws the night of your reign. You will be your own undoing. The wisest will seal your fate. And before the end, all those you hold dear will turn their backs. No one will hear you let out your last breath, alone you will die..." The girl breaks into an inhuman laugh, throwing her head back to the ceiling.

"Kill her!" Jero screams.

Councilor Thorne steps forward, extending his arm. As he does, his hand begins to turn blue-white, and the fingers melt together, extending, replacing his forearm with a frosted sword of ice. The priest throws himself in front of the councilor, before he can swing at the girl.

"We mustn't spill blood in the temple! It would anger the Lord above." The High Priest elocutes, quickly, pushing an attendant towards her. "Tsst!" He hisses at the young acolyte, who grabs the oracle by the arm, dragging her from the room as she continues cackling. "There, he will find some alley in which to leave her body, don't worry about her evil words, my lord. All lies, I am sure of it. We will find a better oracle, for next time."

Rosemary 3

Stepping outside into the warmth of the sun, she smiles for the first time in weeks. Rosemary and her family had arrived in the Great City two days past, and she found that the change of scenery was helping her fight the melancholy that had firmly taken hold since Bastion's death.

She was scared to venture out alone, afraid of what she could accidentally do to someone. At first Rosemary was too terrified to touch anyone, for fear that she would freeze them. But so many people had bumped into her as they had made their way to the Villa du Vale, the palace where she and her parents would be staying at during the tournament, that she was fairly sure touching someone wasn't enough.

It has to be a kiss. I wonder why...

In the garden, Rosemary sees a group of girls standing in front of a fountain, circled around a young boy. As she approaches, Rosemary recognizes the oldest of the girls, Brooke Elmwood, the firstborn of Lord Elmwood's five daughters.

Those must be her sisters... Rosemary thinks, noticing the identical black hair on each of their heads. So dark, that it almost shines blue in the sun's glow.

"Do you think she's pretty?" Brooke asks, as the young boy looks around uncomfortably.

"No!" He shouts, blushing red from nose to ears.

"*AHH!*" The girls squeal, "So you think she's ugly?"

"I… No…" He tries to stammer, confusion and frustration palpable in his voice.

The youngest of the sisters purses her lips, pretending to pout, as her sisters continue to tease the boy.

"Why are you picking on him, Brooke?" Rosemary asks, approaching the group.

"He insulted Plum!" One sister shouts, pointing to the pouting girl.

He doesn't look very mean to me." Rosemary says, turning to the boy and smiling. "Run along, find your parents."

He takes off, quickly disappearing inside the villa.

"Well, aren't you just a hero?" Brooke sneers, giving Rosemary a malicious grin. "Father says that you killed Prince Bastian. Too bad no one was there to save him…"

Rosemary feels the smile on her face disappear, as tears begin welling. She turns and runs off, trying to ignore the laughter that seems to be chasing her down the street. People bump into her as she tries to brush past, making her way to the center of the city.

A large man steps out in front of her, carrying a heavy crate. She collides with him, falling hard to the rough stone ground. He begins to yell at her, causing her to start crying even harder. Trying to ignore him, she pushes herself to her feet, continuing the rest of the way at a sprint.

Fire burns in her lungs as she finally reaches the Grand Temple. Dirt and blood cover her knees, and tears sill stream down her face. Collapsing on the steps in front of the entrance, catching her breath, Rosemary looks up at the opulent temple.

As she sits, trying to regain her composure, the large doors fly open and a procession exits. A group of well-dressed people, tightly huddled around a man, his head adorned with a golden crown.

"Ignore it, my lord." She hears one of the men say. "The Emperor need not concern himself with the postulations of some ignorant girl."

The Emperor...

Rosemary stares at the group as they move past ignoring her. A moment later, the procession is gone.

Alone again, she builds up her courage before turning and stepping inside. An attendant at the front greets her, smiling kindly.

"Hello," Rosemary says, hesitantly. "I need to find someone to talk to... I wish to join the Order."

Sir Simon 2

"Your holiness." He says, as the High Priest approaches. "I heard the Emperor and his men speaking of killing the oracle. Tell me this isn't true…"

The priest smiles, leading Sir Simon through the temple. He waits to begin speaking, weaving through corridors and hallways, past prayer rooms and storehouses. They stop outside an ornately gilded door.

"Sir Simon, I don't know what type of monster you mistake me for... If I put to death every oracle that gave foreboding news to an important man, well… We would have none left."

With that he opens the golden door, revealing three girls sitting around a gently streaming fountain, gazing into the water and playing with the surface.

"Jamie." The priest says, kindly.

One of the girls looks up, smiling. Her dark hair falling past the neck of her silver gown.

"I am sorry to have made the Emperor so mad…" She states, listlessly looking into the water.

"Don't be sorry, child." The priest says. "Some men think they wish to know what their stars hold, but break when faced with the truth… Carry on."

The High Priest nods, and they turn to leave the room. As they do, the girl begins to speak again.

"Do not fret, good knight. He will be well." Jamie says, peering up from the pool.

"Who?" Sir Simon asks.

"The one you fear for." She states, calmly. "Do not try to find him… He has already been found."

Seaborne 3

Beams of sunlight crack above the horizon, reflecting blindingly across the silky sea. Captain Seaborne holds a hand up to shade his eyes, before ducking under the foredeck, heading for the sailor's quarters and brig.

Under the deck, Parrot lies drunk with his back reclined against a sack of apples, and a cup of rum lying spilled on his lap. The captured knight, Kevin, sleeps next to him, snoring loudly. His hands wrapped around a small wooden keg.

"PARROT!" The captain yells, "Why is the prisoner not in irons?"

"He uhh…" Parrot stammers.

"One of us! *SKWAAA*. One of us!" Parrot's macaw calls, landing on the knight's shoulder and bobbing its head from side to side.

"Aye, he'a gud guy. Nah gud at a booz doh." Parrot replies, groggily. "He jun us las nit."

"He joined?"

"Aye, cap'n" Parrot says, retching.

"Rise, Sir Kevin." The captain says, with a flourish.

The hungover knight struggles to sit upright. Grabbing his mouth, as he tries not to vomit.

"Parrot tells me ya have joined us. Why would a knight, sworn to the Order, join up with pirates? What mischief have ya planned? And why would ya bring poor Parrot here into you schemes?" He questions, glaring down on the man.

"No captain. I mean no mischief. I have no schemes. I swear to you!" The man drops to a knee, bowing before him.

"Then why would ya join with us? Where are ya convictions, did ya not swear yourself to the Order?"

"I did, but..." He gazes at the ground, a look of pain crossing his face. "I am a third son. I had no prospects of marriage... I tried to become a household knight, but I was never able to find anyone willing to retain me long... I joined the Order for the basest of reasons, thirst and hunger. Joining sounded better than starving, two square meals a day and a roof over my head. I couldn't have asked for more... But after hearing Parrot and the men talking last night... You are all so, free... You sail upon the sea where you like, answering to no one."

"The men here answer to me..." Seaborne says, with the authority of someone who had been a leader far longer than himself. "Ya will need to learn that fast, if ya wish to be one of us."

"Of course, captain." The knight answers, quickly.

"And I myself, answer to the Admiral. He will decide if ya become one of us or not. Well, him and the Scales... We sail now to meet them. I hope ya tell the truth about why ya wish to join us, for they shall know if ya lie."

Chion 4

The dining hall is bustling as he enters. His uncle sits with the Emperor at the head of the high table. Chion bows to the men, before sitting down in the empty seat next to his uncle and pouring himself a glass of sweet raspberry red.

"So, Chion Antissi." The Emperor begins. "Your father has sent word that he must return to the Plateau for some sort of emergency bank business... Something more important than the tourney and the Due, it would seem." He turns to the treasurer. "I apologize... It is hard for me to hide my disappointment."

"Dearest apologies, my lord. I know it must be tragically urgent if he would miss this." Chion's uncle replies. "You know my brother... Always being pulled a hundred different ways. I don't even recall the last time I saw him myself."

"It is true, your majesty," Chion adds. "I am in Panthos once every few months, when the Flying City makes its stop there. Yet it seems my father is always engaged with something. I don't know the last time I saw him either."

"Well then, the two of you shall be my guests, I insist." The Emperor states.

"We would love to, my lord. But I had my entire staff come to our family palace in the city. I am sure they would be most distraught if they prepared dinner, and there was no one present to enjoy it. Whatever would they do?" He asks, with a chuckle.

"Your brother cannot bear to grace us with his presence, and you are too good to stay with me in the Alcazar?" Emperor Jero shakes his head, the jewels in his crown shimmering in the firelight. "This is most disheartening indeed..."

"I meant no disrespect, of course. I will send word to have my servants return to the Pillar, we would love to be your guests. It will be a great honor, my lord." His uncle looks shaken, as he stammers the words.

"Good." The Emperor replies, seemingly sated with the response. "Chion, have you met my son before?"

"Only in passing, your majesty."

"Go introduce yourself. He's over there with those friends of his." The Emperor says, gesturing to the end of the table closest to the great hearth.

Their faces shine red from the wine and the heat from the fire. He recognizes Prince Relorn, the Emperor's son. Across from him is Matio Nodovin, whose father sits on the Oligarchy of Twenty with Chion's own father. He doesn't know the other two, a Firelander and Southerner, both well dressed and drinking heavily.

"Hello, friends." He says, approaching. "I am Chion Antissi."

The four boys look up at him, flashing polite smiles and nods of acknowledgment.

"Hello, Chion." Matio says, "I haven't seen you in years. Why didn't you attend the Academy?"

"I have been operating a branch of my father's bank, in the Flying City." Chion answers. "He felt that there was more to learn from experience than lectures."

Matio shrugs, pouring from a wine bottle.

"I travelled here on your father's yacht, Relorn." He adds, to the Emperor's son. "I've never been on a ship so fast before, it might move faster than the Flying City itself."

"Your father surely has a boat as fast." The Firelander says, through his goblet. Giving an exaggerated smack of his lips, as he finishes his drink. "They say he is richer than every other person in the Empire, combined."

"Have we met?" Chion asks the boy, cocking his head sideways

"Maybe…" He replies, leaning back on the rear legs of his chair, throwing his feet up on the edge of the table. "Who can keep track of all the rich boys one meets at these types of things?"

"Haha!" The other boy laughs, from across the table. "You're giving him a hard time, Reza? You're the most spoiled brat I have ever had the pleasure of meeting. You walk around with a coin purse thrice the size of mine, and my father is a king."

"A southern king, it's an empty title. Anyone with some gold or gumption can be a king these days." Reza replies, with a sarcastic grin.

"You aren't." Relorn says, grinning at the Firelander.

"Why would I want to be? The Southern Realm is so cold…" The boy retorts, pretending to shiver.

"Anyone care to join me for a smoke on the terrace?" Chion asks, already bored of their bickering.

The boys all smile and hop up, following him to the balcony outside. Reza and Andrew grab a couple of bottles of wine and bring them along, sweet red and sparkling white.

Chion lights his pipe then hands it to Reza, before taking a few steps to the edge of the terrace. The Alcazar looks over the Great City, countless temples and parks below stretch to the horizon. The lights of innumerable fires burn from infinite braziers and torches throughout the city, giving the illusion of bright daylight, even during the dark of night. The river running in front of the Grand Temple is serene, the weeping willows stretching their branches into the water, waving with the winding stream.

"Here you are." Prince Relorn says, handing Chion back the pipe, along with a bottle of red wine.

"Thanks." He says, politely. Taking a long drink before turning away from the view and rejoining the group.

"Here is to tomorrow!" Reza says, holding a bottle in the air and slurring. "Tomorrow we will be councilors. Everything will change."

"Don't get ahead of yourself," Andrew says, setting down his bottle. "You haven't been selected yet."

"Neither have you!" Reza snaps.

"Well, I am an obvious choice, I have the most powerful gifts of anyone our age in the Southern Realm, plus I am the best archer in the Empire." Andrew replies, drunkenly.

"We'll find out if that's true tomorrow…" Prince Relorn says, taking back the bottle and pipe from Chion. "Archery is the first event of the tourney, and I am going to beat you. I apologize in advance for the embarrassment you will feel at my hands."

"This will be the first of many tourneys where I defeat you. You had better get used to second place." Andrew says, laughing and patting the prince on the back.

With each drink they take, and each toast they make, their arguments grow louder and louder. A butler enters the terrace, bee lining straight towards the group. Chion can hear the man's thoughts, as loud as a holler.

'Stupid kids, people are trying to sleep... I'll shut them up!'

But as soon as the man recognizes Relorn, the son of the Emperor, he quickly turns and retreats, thinking better of his plan to scold the boys.

"I am going to turn in for the night." Chion says. "I will come watch the archery contest tomorrow, see which of you ends up winning."

With that he turns, leaving them behind. Their drunken cheers and hollers ringing through the night, noisily falling on the sleeping city below.

Tiaries 4

Sivaties Honeysuckle is an early riser. No matter what wee morning hour Tiaries tried to wake, she had yet to be able to beat him to breakfast. Every morning, as she enters the dining area of his palace, the governor of the Elven Quarter is already at his table. Drinking a piping cup of tea and snacking on fruit, elaborately cut and twisted into shapes of flowers and seashells and various sorts of abstract designs.

"Ah, Tiaries, you look lovely." The elven lord says, hardly looking away from the open wall of his open air dining room.

Across the river, the Alcazar towers above the rest of the city, almost hanging from the cliff it is built upon, casting a stretching shadow over the water and buildings beneath.

"It's a pretty view," Tiaries tells their patron.

Governor Honeysuckle is a nice enough man, Councilor Lingonberry had left her and Jaties with him when they arrived in the Great City. She had not seen the councilor since.

*He will be at the performance today tough... S*he thinks. *I will speak with him then.*

"You should go and see the tourney." Sivaties tells her. "The prince's birthday ceremony should be starting soon. You can probably still catch it if you are quick."

"I think I will." She says, with a smile. Grabbing a few pieces of fruit from the table and giving a polite curtsy, before leaving the room. She skips along the street as she heads towards the bridge that extends between the Elven Quarter and the Grand Quarter, leading to the city square, where the tourney is set to begin.

She hears trumpets ring out as she enters the square, and sees a group of men begin walking out across a large wooden stage.

That is the same stage our performance is on tonight. She thinks, anxiously.

A herald in front of the procession holds a fist up to his mouth, clearing his throat. Then he begins to speak to the mass of people congregated before the stage, countless bodies crowding into the square.

His voice rings like thunder, crashing over the audience. She cups her hands over her ears, jolted by the impossibly loud volume of his tremendous voice. The echoing of his words projects throughout the city.

"Come! Lend me your ears." He booms. "Behold, Prince Relorn. Your future Emperor!"

Cheers ring through the crowd as a handsome young man rides onto the stage, seated upon a white stallion. A bow slung over one shoulder. His mount trots to the center of the stage, then obediently halts, allowing the prince to slide off and take his position.

"Come!" The herald says. Again, as with a voice of thunder. "Behold! His Imperial Highness, Emperor Jero the Magnificent! Ruler of all that is. Lord of the Mountains, King of the Wastes, Son of Stone and Scion of the Mountain Emperors."

The Emperor enters on the back of his horse. A fiery steed, its red mane gleaming in the sun, the color of hot burning coal. Jero dismounts and walks towards the herald. He picks up a golden crown, sitting on a marble stand. Sensationally, he shows it to the crowd, before placing it upon his son's head.

Then the herald steps forward, handing the Emperor a great sword, which he takes and taps upon each of the prince's shoulders.

"Come!" Booms the herald, as the Emperor takes his position next to his son. "Behold! Lord Antissi, the Imperial Lord Treasurer, Chancellor of the Bank of the Pillar, and Vice Chancellor of the Antissi Bank."

A large man enters the stage, riding upon a black horse. He steps down, shakes the Emperor's hand, and gives a set of golden scales to the prince before bowing and taking his position.

"Come!" The voice booms, again. "Behold! High Priest Tobin, the Highest and Most Illuminated, Lord of the Grand Temple, Master of the Order, and the worldly manifestation of our Lord above."

A squat man enters. Short, square, and squinting. Riding atop a gray stallion. His pale robes glisten, as the priest smiles and scratches the head of a cream and chocolate colored kitten, perched upon his shoulder.

Attendants rush out to help him off his horse, steadying the portly man as he loses his balance and almost falls to the stage floor. Steadying himself, the priest approaches the young prince, handing him a small stack of books and scrolls. Then he bows, and backs away with a flourish of his hand.

"Your prince and future Emperor, Relorn!" The herald proclaims, taking the prince's hand and thrusting it into the air.

Roars of applause and screams erupt from the audience, and the ground shakes beneath their stamping feet.

Amidst the commotion, a man in all black armor makes his way onto the stage. His advance is met with confused looks from the men on the platform. Silence falls over the crowd, as the black knight unsheathes his weapon

"Prepare to die!" He screams, before charging. His jet black sword swinging through the sky, as he dashes towards the men on stage.

Guards rush forward from behind the side curtains, quickly moving between the man and his target. The knight cuts one down, then parries the attacks of the remaining two. He slides past them, before coming up and swinging wildly at the High Priest.

The priest jumps back, narrowly avoiding the slashing blade. Before the knight is able to swing again, one of the guards cracks the back of his helmet with a sword, sending him flying off the stage.

The audience begins to scream in fright, as the knight regains his feet. People turn to run away from the stage, trampling each other, smothering those not fast enough to move out of the way of the stampeding crowd.

Tiaries turns to run, then sprints down a side alley to avoid being consumed by the wave of yelling people rushing towards her. She keeps moving quickly, putting distance between herself and the crowd. Blocks away, she turns down an another alley, stopping for a moment to catch her breath. Hands on her knees, huffing and puffing, she feels the fire in her chest begin to subside.

As her breathing slowly returns to normal, a flashing figure cuts around the corner. The young knight in black armor runs straight into her, knocking Tiaries to the ground and tripping himself, landing atop her.

He looks into her terrified eyes, and flashes a charming grin, before clumsily getting back up. The knight's black armor clanging, as he tries to regain his footing. The yell of advancing guards rings out from down the alley.

"Please, don't tell them you saw me." He pleads. Helping her to her feet, before turning and running down an alley to the right and disappearing out of sight.

Moments later a group of guards arrive.

"Where did he go?" They yell, angrily brandishing their weapons at her.

She takes a deep breath. Then points to the left.

Jia 4

"Well, that was an exciting start to the tournament!" Jia's father exclaims, as their group walks through the city park. Meandering through the giant hedge maze, situated in the center of the gardens. The High Priest and his entourage accompanied them from the city square, feeling most comfortable in the presence of the powerful Firelanders. Her father leads the procession, as Lord Te Lau and Lord Tea Bane follow with their families, the children excitedly chirping about the upcoming competition.

"Who was that knight in the black armor?" Jia asks her father.

"I am not sure, my dear." He answers, with a shrug.

"We believe it is Alexander the Green." The High Priest says, his voice hushed to a whisper, as if sharing a secret for only them to hear. "He was the Green Knight once, the apprentice to the White Knight of the Order. When Harold the White was slain on assignment, the ministers and I decided Alexander was not yet fit to take on his predecessor's role. This outraged the boy, causing him to denounce the Order, proclaiming us all villains in some sinister plot he's concocted in his mind, and vowing to take revenge... I fear we saw his idea of vengeance today."

"So you believe he was after you, not the Emperor?" Her father asks.

"Most assuredly, I saw it in his eyes. He wants me dead... I shan't have a pleasant night's sleep as long as he is on the streets, free to make trouble." The High Priest shakes his head, "Perhaps I need to increase the presence of the Order's knights in the city. To help keep the peace and protect us from beastly men such as this... Black Knight."

"Ah, yes. These types of things would never happen in the City of Light, not on my watch." Lord Jain responds.

Jia fights to stifle a laugh as her father speaks. *Lies... These types of things happen every day on his watch.*

She slows her pace, letting her father and the members of the Order walk ahead. Te Poppy and Tea Blossom join her, their husbands trailing behind, arguing with each other as always.

"For two people who claim to hate each other, your husbands always seem to be lost in a conversation about something." Jia says, to the two Southern girls.

"It's true" Poppy replies, grinning. "Blossom and I often joke that we will wake up one morning to find that they have run away together."

Blossom tries to hold in her laughter, but ends up letting out a quick snort instead. Her face turning red as wine.

"Have you heard anything about the Due?" Jia asks, trying to sound nonchalant.

"We all assume my brother-in-law Reza will be the Fireland's selection." Poppy answers. "My husband says his brother is very gifted, and he is already friends with the prince."

"What about you?" Blossom asks, slyly, as she points to the flame flickering from atop Jia's ruby and gold tiara. "Is your power only for show? Does it just sit there looking pretty, like you would have us believe? I have heard some rumors that you're more powerful than anyone knows..."

"That makes no sense, Blossom." Poppy retorts. "If she is more powerful than anyone knows, than that means no one knows. So how could you hear rumors, if no one knows?"

"You know what I mean!" The girl shouts back, sharply.

"Yes. Yes, I do." Poppy says, giggling. "I do, I do, I do. But you are just too fun to tease."

"You two are worse than your husbands." Jia says, smirking. "And Blossom, to answer your question. No, it is not only for show... I am indeed much more powerful than anyone knows. Perhaps I'll show you sometime."

Rika 3

The master leads her through the back alleys of the Shady Quarter, down the narrow twists and descending curves. Past taverns, inns, apothecaries, butcher's shops and bustling brothels.

He'd brought a dress to her that morning. *'Wear this.'* The old man had said, *'You must look presentable. You'll be meeting the Emperor today.'*

They leave the Shady Quarter and turn onto a wide boulevard, both sides of which are lined with expansive palaces, designed in architecture from around the Empire. The house they approach is surrounded by tall trees on all sides. Oaks, maples, redleafs, and birch, all interspersed among dozens of apple trees. The cabin tucked inside the transplanted grove, looks out of place between the stately palaces around it.

The old man knocks on the great oak door, lightly. Moments later an attendant opens the entrance, ushering them inside.

"Warden Tane will be with you momentarily." The attendant says, bowing before retreating from the room.

"You're sure about this?" He asks Rika, patting her head gently with a wrinkled hand.

"Yes." She states, not looking up.

A lean man enters the room, a smile stretched across his face. "I am so glad to meet you! Warden Tane is my name, pleased to make your acquaintance." He says, cheerfully shaking each of their hands.

"Thank you, warden." The master replies. "This little one here is Rika."

"Can we see what you can do, girl?" The warden asks, bluntly. A slight look of fear falling across his face, tension visible in his furrowed brow.

She looks up at him, then closes her eyes tightly and scrunches up her face. She can smell the fear on him.

Before his eyes, Rika vanishes from sight, replaced by a tiny mouse scurrying about the floor. Then, with the blink of an eye she reappears, a mouse's tail still dangling from her rear.

The master gives the tail a flick, and it quickly disappears.

"Well, I'll be…" The warden stares at her, nonplussed.

"She has a fair mastery over it, the Emperor should be pleased." The master says. "I must be on my way. You can take it from here, no?"

"Yes, yes. Thank you." The warden says, shaking the old man's hand.

The master looks down at Rika, and whispers to her. "Chase us, the light of dawn."

She softly responds, a choked reply, addressed more to the floor than the old man. "For I am the shadow…" Warm tears gently run down her freckled cheeks.

The master turns and leaves. Not looking back as the door shuts behind him.

She stands in place gasping for breath, unable to fill her chest.

I am alone, again…

"Are you okay, child?" The warden asks, her tears making him visibly uncomfortable.

"I am… I'm fine." She replies, quickly looking away.

"Come here." He says, leading her to the kitchen. Taking a couple apples from a basket on the table, he shows them to her. "These are from the Orchard, from my favorite trees. I am sure they will be the sweetest thing you have ever tasted. Have one now, bring some more for later. You will want something more before long. The tourney will be all day, and I hear there is some play or performance afterwards."

He hands her a yellow and red striped apple, and another so green it seems to glow. Then she picks a deep red delicious from the bundle, wiping it off on her shirt before biting into the side.

Succulent juice flows from the sweet pale flesh, dribbling on her chin.

"This is the best apple I've ever had!" She exclaims, wiping away her tears.

"I am glad you like it. Let's eat and walk." He says, grabbing a gold and yellow splotched apple for himself, before they exit the building. "It is beautiful outside, such a lovely breeze. The archery competition will be starting soon. We wouldn't want to miss watching the prince compete. My son will also be in the contest, Jo. Such a good boy. He loves his apple wood bow, and he's quite the marksman. I've seen him take a small apricot from a branch at two hundred feet. This is his first tourney though... We shall see how he holds up under pressure."

She nods her head as they walk and talk, weaving through the crowded city towards the tourney grounds. They pass through the makeshift camp that the Plains Riders had constructed upon their arrival. Rhinos and Bison graze on the short grass, as people prepare food for the night's feast. Meat crackles and smokes on hot iron grills. Large disks of bread rest in ovens, baking and browning above glowing coals.

She stops, gazing in wonder as they pass a rhino steak roasting above a bonfire. The cut of meat is twice the size of Rika, larger than a full grown man.

"The Plains People sure do love to grill meat." She remarks, looking up at the warden.

"Indeed." He replies, smiling and taking in the scent of the steaks as they drip fat and seasoning into the smoldering wood chips below, sending plumes of salty smoke into the air. "And thank the Lord above, they love to share as well."

He turns to a hunched old lady, tending a grill in front of a beautifully painted tent. They exchange some words, then she takes two wooden skewers and stabs them into steak tips that sit sizzling above the open fire, giving them to Warden Tane.

He hands the lady a silver coin, but she shakes her head in refusal, flashing him a large smile. He then opens his knap sack, and hands her a few brilliantly colored apples and a handful of piquant persimmons. Her face lights up and she wraps her arms around the warden, taking him in a motherly embrace.

The meat is rich and delicious. Between the skewer and her apple, Rika has become quite full. She rubs her belly, as they take their seats in the stands that had been set out for the archery contest. Putting her feet up on the seat in front of her, she takes a moment to recline and relax before the throngs arrive.

The warden points at people as they enter the arena, telling Rika who they are and why they are important enough to merit seats so close to the action.

"Those two, the drunk looking ones, are the brothers Serent and Vincence Viali. Serent is the archer in the family, Vincence is the fighter. I've never seen either sober. I hear they have wine and oats for breakfast every day!" He remarks, with a laugh, before looking around and pointing to a tall man with closely trimmed gray stubble on his face and head, his sharp violet eyes endlessly scanning the area, like a lemur on lookout for predators. "That there is Alor Rock, the captain of the Imperial Archers. Not a man I would recommend trying to sneak up on… He isn't known for his sense of amusement."

Rika grins, then sits up straight as someone bumps into her back. Scrunching herself up, she tries to make room for the people scooting in front of her, as the crowd begins to gather in around them.

"You see those three, coming in across the way?" He asks, gesturing to two giant men standing on either side of a petite woman, barely measuring up to either of their chests. "That is Basquen Brode and his family. Basquen became the Lord Herdsman after his father's recent passing, and assumed his seat on the Oligarchy of Twenty. The beautiful little lady next to him is his wife Begonia, and that young behemoth next to her is their son Brolen."

"Those two are huge!" Rika says, astounded.

"Yes, they are large men. Brolen and his father, Basquen, the silent giant. I don't recommend asking the Lord Herdsman any questions that require lengthy replies. The poor man hasn't got a tongue. The little wife of his does all the talking."

"What?" She gasps, shocked.

"It is a terribly tragic story, not fit for ears so young." The warden says, "But who am I to tell you that you are too young. Would you like to hear?" He asks, clearly wanting to share the story.

"Yes, tell me!" She shouts.

He thinks he can scare me with a story, did they not tell him who I am?

"When Lord Basquen was a young man, many years ago, his father sent him to the Southern Realm on a cattle purchasing trip. To add head to their then dwindling heard. He stayed at an inn somewhere inside Silver Mill, with some friends and cattle drivers, waiting to finish the deal."

Silver Mill! She thinks, surprised. *That is where my first assignment was, where I made my first kill... Does he know?*

"One night, Basquen bedded the innkeep's daughter, unaware that she was a maiden. When her father found them together under the sheets, he took it as a deep insult. A cruel man... The innkeeper beat his daughter to within an inch of her life, then framed Basquen for theft, having him arrested. Unfortunately, Silver Mill's dungeon master is a cruel man as well... Before Basquen's friends could find him and gain his release, the gaoler removed his tongue and his teeth."

What? The gaoler of Silver Mill...

"When his friends finally found out what had happened to him and where he was, they informed the king of Silver Mill what had transpired. Basquen was barely hanging to life in the dungeons when he was finally freed. The innkeep was brought to justice, hung for bearing false witness. But the gaoler went un-reprimanded. The king of the city believed it would be in bad taste to punish a dungeon master for doing his job too enthusiastically. Such a shame..." The warden pauses, then finds his grin again. "Basquen married the innkeep's daughter, brought her home to the Plateau with him. She is the lady you see him with now. I hear they are as happy as any couple could be. At least there is that consolation... Begonia often jokes that handsome mutes make the best husbands."

"Do you think the same gaoler could still be working there, after all these years?" Rika asks.

"It is possible, certainly. This wasn't more than twenty years past."

I hope it was him...

"Oh look, my son!" The warden stands to get a better view, as more people enter the arena. He points out a slender young man, dressed in a beautiful green doublet and pants, streaks of red and gold and green running through his hair.

The young man waves up at them with willowy arms, smiling a wide smile just like his father's.

"The Emperor will be here soon." The warden says, excitedly searching the distance for signs of the imperial party. "Then the tourney will begin…"

Relorn 5

The boys enter the archery arena, waving off the eruption of cheers and applause that accompanies their arrival.

"They love you!" Andrew says, clapping him on the back.

"Nah, they're just cheering because we're contestants." Relorn rebuts, "They'll do it for all the others too…"

But he is quickly proven wrong, as additional contestants file into the arena and take their positions without drawing any notice from crowd.

Reza walks over to the stands, yelling up at someone in the seats. He picks up some roses scattered on the ground in front of the stand, then throws them back into the audience, eliciting cheers from the ladies before him. A moment later, he turns away from his fans and heads back to the stations with a handful of people following.

"You've all met my brother before, right? And his wife, Poppy? This here is an old family friend, Jia." Reza announces, pointing to one of the girls that followed his brother and Chion from the stands. "I'm not sure if I've had the pleasure of meeting the other two…"

"This is my friend, Tea Blossom." Poppy says, "And her little sister, Rosemary."

The family friend, Jia, has the dark sun-kissed skin and jet black hair of a Firelander, like Reza and his brother Rin. The other three girls are ghostly pale. Their light blonde hair streaked with blue and silver, in the Southern style.

"Hello, my prince." Jia says, stepping forward and offering her hand.

Relorn reaches to take it, planting a quick kiss on her soft skin. The heat radiating off of her is startlingly hot, making him quickly pull back. He has trouble looking away though, her revealing outfit showing off every twist and turn of her body. Translucent gossamer pants hardly hiding the curve of her hips.

She would be completely visible if not for a pair of lace undergarments, covering the smallest of areas between her thighs. In place of a shirt, bands of silk are elaborately wrapped around her torso and breasts, exposing slivers of bright bronze skin.

Blossom holds out her hand, drawing Relorn's attention and forcing him to finally break his stare. He takes it politely. Then the same with Reza's sister-in-law, Poppy, who blushes and giggles as she pulls her hand back.

The last girl keeps a distance between them, avoiding his gaze when he looks her way. "It is nice to meet you as well. Rosemary, right?" He asks.

"Yes, your highness. It is nice to make your acquaintance." She says, standing rigidly with her arms behind her back, cool and uninviting.

Just then, a trumpet blares. Cheers and applause begin to echo and reverberate through the tourney grounds, as a procession starts to enter from the side of the arena. The Lord Treasurer walks out and takes a seat at the raised dais in the front of the stands, shaded by a fine satin canopy.

The councilors follow him closely. Te Inzu takes her seat next to the treasurer, then Councilors Thorne and Lingonberry, Sage Coda Sa and Thoo Kroonson, Ernesto Maestas and Aloysius Quezada all sit in succession, the crowd still cheering with an overwhelmed mania.

The applause begins to wane, as High Priest Tobin takes his seat. Finally, the Emperor's herald approaches the center of the grounds. His thundering voice cries out, "Silence! All rise for his imperial highness, Emperor Jero!"

The Emperor walks out, giving way to additional applause. He stands before the dais, facing the crowds, then shouts, "May the tournament begin!"

The girls head back to their seats with Reza's brother and Chion in tow, as the contestants take their positions. Andrew, Reza and Matio surround him in the center of the arena. Other participants line up around them. Nux of the Sun and Che Hoondo of the Firelands. Alor Rock, the Captain of the Imperial Archers. Rhee Leeson, Chief of the Hill Tribe. Serent Viali, Lord of the Vineyard, sipping from his leather flask.

A dark haired young man approaches them. "Andrew…? Andrew Stein? How are you?"

"Oh lord, Jay Marsh?" Andrew laughs, embracing his friend. "What are you doing here?"

The boy touches foreheads with Andrew, then replies. "I am your competition." Giving a smile, before turning and taking an open spot next to Matio.

"Archers ready!" An announcer calls out. "Fire!"

All the contestants let arrows fly across the air, sailing towards the bullseye targets arranged neatly at the far end of the arena. Reza's arrow ignites its target, sending a flash of flame skyward. Andrew's target cracks and glistens, as a layer of hoarfrost creeps across it. Next to Matio, Jay's target also freezes, identically to Andrew's.

"You, sneaky twit!" Andrew yells, glaring at Jay.

"Sorry friend, you're so much better than me!" Jay yells back, with a grin. "I had to even out the competition… Take it as a compliment!"

The judges walk in front of the line of targets, taking measurements and comparisons.

"Te Reza is disqualified, for destroying his target!" The announcer shouts. "Advancing to round two are, Prince Relorn of the Mountain. Rhee Leeson, Chief of the Hills. Jay Marsh, Prince of the Black Marsh. Andrew Stein, Prince of Seacliff. And Alor Rock. All others, please fall back."

The rest of the contestants take a step back, leaving the five remaining archers at their stations.

"Prince Relorn!" The announcer yells, gesturing for him to shoot.

He steps forward, taking a knee, and pulls a long arrow from the hard ground beneath him. Black as pitch, and hard as diamond. He notches his bow and looses the arrow, sending it slamming into the center of the bullseye, dead on target.

"Rhee Leeson!" The announcer shouts, calling forth the next shooter.

The chief steps forward, a quick tug of his curved compound bow sends a bolt flying across the arena. Sapphire tinted sparks creep around the arrowhead, brightly tracing its path through the sky. It strikes just off center of the bullseye, the web of sparks spreading around the target and slowly dissipating into the air.

"Jay Marsh!"

Jay steps forward, shooting an arrow towards his target. A trail of blueish frost flies and whirls in the arrow's wake. Upon making contact with the center of the bullseye, his arrow shatters the target, splintering it into thousands of icy shards sent soaring through the sky like a blustering snowstorm.

"Disqualified," The announcer yells.

"What the hell?" Jay shouts, gesturing at Andrew.

"The second one's a kill shot!" Andrew yells back, with a laugh, before signaling for an attendant to replace his target with a fresh one.

"Andrew Stein!" The announcer calls.

He steps forward, loosing an arrow, then nonchalantly backs away as the projectile strikes into the center of the bullseye.

"Alor Rock!"

The archer approaches his station and draws his bow, but the string snaps as he takes aim, cracking back and slashing across his face. Alor grabs his eye, blood streaming through his fingers.

"Friar! Apothecary!" The announcer shouts. "This man needs help!"

A friar runs forward, wrapping a bandage across Alor's face, trying to stop the bleeding. Then a group of attendants come and help him out of the arena.

"Unfortunately, Alor Rock is disqualified." The announcer yells, over the boos ringing back from the audience. "Advancing to round three. Prince Relorn and Andrew Stein."

The two boys step forward.

"You have two shots each, no changing targets. Best arrow will win."

Andrew sweeps his hand forward, inviting Relorn to shoot first.

Relorn takes a deep breath, drawing his bow and taking aim. He lets one arrow fly, then a second. Both hit inside the center of the bullseye. Then he turns to Andrew, giving him a flourish and a smile.

Andrew steps forward, focusing on his target.

"He only has one shot..." Matio whispers, to no one in particular. "He'll shatter the target if he sends a second."

Andrew lets his arrow go. It flies true, landing perfectly in the center of the bullseye. He turns to the announcer and signals that he is done.

The judges walk forward, inspecting the targets. Both of Relorn's shots are inside the innermost ring, but Andrew's one arrow is perfectly dead center.

He beat me! Damn, he's good... Relorn thinks, preparing to congratulate him.

"The winner is…!" The announcer yells, pausing for effect. "Prince Relorn of the Mountain!"

The crowd erupts, chanting his name. He looks at Andrew, confused. His friend just shrugs and smiles, before stepping towards him and shaking his hand, graciously accepting defeat.

"There is no way that I beat you…" He tells Andrew, "Your shot was perfect."

"If you were a judge, would you rule against the Emperor's son?" Andrew replies, "Better get used to it. Do you think your father is ever beaten at anything?"

Without thinking, Relorn grabs Andrew's hand and raises it into the air. Then steps back, joining the applause, gesturing to his friend and shouting, "There is your winner!"

The cheers of the crowd are deafening, shaking the sprawling city that surrounds them, filling the midday air with an ear-splitting exuberance.

His father steps forward, turning to face the crowd and signaling for them to quiet. A silence falls over the audience. "Everyone, to the jousting arena!" He shouts, eliciting another bout of cheering.

People begin to file out of the stands, making their way to the next event. Relorn and his friends hang back, letting the throngs file out of the arena, separated from the crowd by a group of the

Emperor's soldiers and bodyguards. A hand grabs Relorn's shoulder, startling him and making him drop his bow.

"Calm down, kid." His Uncle Stephen says, with a smile. Pearly teeth and snow white clothing make his rosy pink cheeks look almost flushed.

He looks like mom, before ...

"How are you, uncle?" Relorn asks, embracing him.

"I am wonderful, but I think I may have dressed too heavily for the weather." He says, fanning himself off. "I'll need to lose a few layers before I don my armor."

"You're jousting?"

"I am! You'll be cheering for me, no? Your dear uncle needs all the support he can get."

"Of course! Reza's brother is jousting too. Do you know Te Rin?"

"We've met. He and his father came around the Basket to meet with your granddad, looking for someone for Rin to marry. You know how those Firelanders love setting their children up with Southerners."

A gruff voice comes from the emptying dais. "What nonsense are you filling the boy's head with?" Relorn's grandfather struggles to stand up, his girth pulling him back. "Come, help an old man up."

Relorn puts his arm around him, helping the elderly man to his feet and handing him the long silver cane he always carries. "It is good to see you, grandfather. How was your trip?"

"Fine, fine. Congratulations on your first tourney victory."

"Andrew won, there must have been some mistake with their measurements." Relorn replies, "It was good fun either way though."

"Well thank the lord you received your mother's intelligence and humility. That father of yours loves his sycophants."

"Father!" His uncle sibilates.

"Don't hush me, boy. I am the King of the Basket and you will show me my due respect."

"I meant no disrespect, father. But we are surrounded by hungry ears."

"*Humph*, curse them all. I hate this place, almost as much as that ridiculous Pillar..." His grandfather's full moon face is blood red from strain and anger, and years of drinking. "I'm sorry, I shouldn't have lost my temper. I forget myself from time to time."

"It's fine, grandfather. Travel makes us all weary..." Relorn says, rubbing the old man's back.

"Will you walk with him to the jousting grounds?" Stephen asks. "I need to get suited, and prepare for the tilt."

"Of course," Relorn replies. "Good luck!"

"Thank you, nephew." Stephen says, as he takes off through the crowd.

"So, grandfather. What can you tell me about the Due? Is the Southern Realm offering Andrew?"

"After that showing back there, I don't see how we couldn't. But Grand Marshal Barren has not consulted with any of the southern kings. He does not seem to value our input on the matter very much."

"Who else could they offer?" Relorn asks, nervously.

"I don't know. Paul Frost is too old, but not by much... Same with Stephen, praise the Lord!" He shakes his head. "There are a few I have heard of, common stock. None worth taking note of."

They enter the jousting grounds. The entrance is flanked by two large ice sculptures, shaved into the shape of stallions, casting a chill in the air as they walk past them. Relorn looks around, and sees most of their group already seated around the Emperor's dais.

"Will you come sit with us?" He asks his grandfather.

"No thank you, young man. I have a servant reserving a seat at the end of the front row, I prefer not to be squeezed between people. I find it suffocating." King Christoph turns away from his grandson, tottering to his seat.

Relorn walks up to the dais, sitting in the open chair between Reza and the Southern girl, Rosemary.

"How is the king of plenty doing?" Reza asks.

"He is well, but angry as always." Relorn responds, eyeing his grandfather.

"I'd be angry too if my wife died at sea, and my daughter..." He stops speaking, suddenly. "Sorry, I'm sure you don't want to talk about your mom."

"Its fine. It makes me mad sometimes too, but such is life... You and I will die someday as well."

Reza signals an attendant to bring them some beer. Raising his glass, he says, "Here's to our caskets! May they be made from the boards of a hundred-year-old yew, planted tomorrow..."

Relorn toasts his friend, and takes a deep drink from his mug. Looking over, he notices Rosemary staring at the ground.

"What's wrong?" He asks her.

She looks up, startled. Not saying anything.

"Sorry, I don't mean to pry," Relorn continues.

"No, I'm sorry. It's just that I am a bit... preoccupied." She says lightly, barely audible over the roar of the crowd behind them. "I am enjoying myself though, of course."

"I'm not..." He tells her, candidly.

She gives him a sideways glance. "Really? Isn't the whole tournament in your honor?"

"That's part of the problem. Everyone has been acting strange since we left the Academy. Part of me just wants to go back. Lounge on the shore, fishing for dinner. Sneak through the vines, picking grapes..."

"Why don't you?" Rosemary asks, giving him a small but reassuring smile.

"I, uh... I don't know. Is that an option?" He asks, shrugging.

"Well, I wouldn't know..." She says, breaking into a little laugh. "You're the Emperor's son. You can do whatever you want, can't you?"

"I..." He begins to stammer, before a trumpet blast thunders from a herald's horn, resonating across the jousting grounds.

His father enters amidst a grand procession, slowly winding around the jousting run. They take their seats at the center of the dais, beneath a viridian canopy.

High Priest Tobin's cat jumps off his shoulder, onto the back of the chairs. It approaches Councilor Kroonson, stalking the brilliantly dyed feathers and glistening gemstones woven into the fabric of his tunic and adorning his golden bands. The cat bats at his earring but misses, falling onto the councilor's lap, eliciting a wave of laughter from Poppy and Blossom.

His father rises from his seat at the center of the dais, and proclaims loudly to the audience. "Let the jousting begin!"

Heralds approach from either end of the tilt yard, their dressing gowns matching the colors of their own liege's pavilions. His uncle Stephen's herald is dressed in emerald and earth tones, the colors of the Basket. The challenger and his cohorts are gleaming in purple and gold.

"Entering the field, Cliff of the Canyon!" The purple swathed herald proclaims, gesturing down the tilt to a stout man trotting in on the back of a golden steed. Both the horse and rider are covered in gilded armor, enameled in purple and accented with gemstone sunflowers, amber disks surrounded by petals of topaz.

Stephen's herald waves his hands, quieting the crowd. "Ladies and gentlemen. I give you, the prince of plenty, the heir to the Basket, Stephen Pike!!!"

Cheers and stomps send vibrations through the arena, as Stephen rides around the corner. His black courser is draped in green cloth, and hung with bronze plated armor. The beast paws at the dirt and grass below, rearing up and snorting in brooding anticipation. The judge raises a white flag in the air, holding it for one dramatic moment, before bringing it down in a flutter.

Stephen's horse digs its hooves deep into the ground, as it bounds towards their foe. Sending a cascade of loam and dirt into the air, billowing and rolling behind it in a foreboding cloud, mantling across the arena. The knight in gold seems hesitant, his horse barely beginning to move as his opponent already nears a sprint.

His uncle rides with lance held high, lining up his target. Cliff brings down his golden lance. Too soon… He tries to swing it towards Stephen's shield, but overextends and hits nothing but air. Stephen brings his lance down, directly into Cliff's chest plate, splintering the weapon's wooden shaft and knocking the knight off his horse. The force of the strike breaks gemstones loose from the golden armor, sending shards of topaz aglitter, like stars shooting through the sky.

From underneath the stands, street children scamper out to snatch up the stones, their soot covered faces alight with the joy of luck. Men-at-arms quickly run out to shoo the juvenile bandits away, swinging their swords and yelling curses at the scurrying children.

Valets attend to the golden knight, assisting his awkward attempts to regain his feet. Stephen rides his horse before the stands, waving to the cheering crowd, the green enamel and emeralds affixed upon his armor shimmering brilliantly in the sun.

The score judge stands from his seat opposite the dais. "Cliff of the Canyon has been unhorsed. Stephen Pike advances."

Rosemary glances at Relorn, giving him a shy smile. "Do you think he'll win? It would be exciting, no?"

"Do you know my uncle?" He asks, giving her a curious glance.

"The Basket is not far from my home, Castle Blackburn. We have met many times, at feasts and festivals and local tourneys. My father is friends with him, as well as your grandfather. He says they are the most honorable men in the Southern Realm."

"They are, indeed." He says, looking back at his uncle prancing away to wait for his next challenger.

Next up are Sir Eric Elmwood and Victor du Mount. The du Mount family has lived in the Great City for generations. As such, when Victor's herald announces his entrance, roars and cheers explode from the city streets around them, as the citizens enthusiastically support their favorite son. Atop rooftops and balconies, hills and walls, the common people cry praise and pound their feet, sending waves of applause sweeping through the streets and engulfing the tourney grounds in vehement clangor and clamor.

Perhaps it is the support of the masses, or the home field advantage, but Victor masterfully splinters his lance on each of their first three passes, easily defeating his opponent.

Next, Cruu Bruuson rides out on an enormous brown destrier, waiting for his challenger. Blossom squeals loudly as Tea Fane takes the field, shouting cheers of encouragement to her husband.

Both contestants miss on the first two passes, eliciting boos of boredom from the onlookers. On the third pass, Fane makes contact with Cruu's torso, sending him flying from his saddle. The girls cheer, especially Blossom, who jumps up and down shouting with jubilation.

"Cruu Bruuson has been unhorsed. Tea Fane advances!"

Fane passes Te Rin on the way back to his pavilion. "Good luck!" He says, sarcastically. "If you don't lose now, I will have the pleasure of unseating you myself next round."

"Please... You can only rely on luck for so long before your lack of skill catches up with you." Rin says, smirking, as he takes his position for the next match.

Reza and Poppy shout and cheer, wishing him luck.

Across the tilt yard, Paul Frost exits his ice blue pavilion. An abnormally tall man dressed in full plate, yet walking on foot, his silver and sapphire armor clashing with each step he takes.

"I think you've lost your horse!" Rin shouts, sending a surge of laughter through the stands.

Paul smiles an icy smile, then begins to whistle. The sound echoes eerily, around and around and around.

Ahhhweeeeewhhoooooooooooooohhheeeeeeeeeee

One of the ice sculptures standing near the entrance of the arena begins to creak and crack, like a glacier lost in the summer sun. Its joints become malleable, and its musculature shimmers, flexing as if alive. It takes an uncertain step forward, like a new whelped foal, then begins to prance and dance and spin. Leaping and swirling through the air in a flurry.

It trots towards the whistle, to the amazement of the audience, kneeling at Paul's feet and allowing him to mount with ease. Rin calls over an official, gesturing at the animated sculpture with a nonplussed expression. The line judge shrugs and refers to the score judge, who turns and asks the Emperor if he will allow it. Jero looks on with fascination, promptly waving his hand in excited assent.

The contestants take position. The sight of the frosty steed sends Rin's colt bucking. He tries to calm the horse, rubbing its mane and whispering, coaxing it to relax and prepare for the pass. Once he gains control, Rin squeezes his legs, pushing the colt to a sprint. Paul whistles calmly, causing the icy horse to snort, then charge forward, sending plumes of frozen air and snow out of its nostrils, and a leaving a path of permafrost beneath its freezing hooves.

They clash, with a crash, at the center of the tilt. Paul's lance shatters into Rin's chest plate, denting the red-gold armor. Rin's lance glances of his opponent, thrown off balance by his skittish horse running off course.

"Paul Frost leads. One lance to none." A judge yells, over the crowd.

The contestants come about, preparing to charge again. This time, Rin is able to break his lance against Paul's shield, knocking his opponent back, but not dismounting him.

"Tied, one lance each!"

Relorn sees something in Reza's face, that almost looks like fear. "He's got this..." He tells his friend.

"Yeah. Definitely." Reza replies. "It's just for show, Paul is a terrible rider... Rin will dismount him this pass, just watch."

The riders face off again, rushing towards each other at top speed. Paul's lance drops slowly, but on target, catching Rin square between the eye holes of his helm and sending him flying from the back of his colt.

"Shite!" Reza curses. "Well, that's that..."

Poppy jumps up and rushes towards the field. But a man-at-arms grabs her and holds her back, while a friar pulls off Rin's facemask to ensures he's still breathing. Valets help the dismounted knight to his feet, and carry him from the field.

"Te Rin has been unhorsed. Paul Frost advances."

A standing banquet is set up for lunch. Huge turkey legs, skewered rhino, and loaves of sweetbread are stacked high on the table. Relorn holds back, waiting for the herd of humans to dissipate from around the buffet.

"Not hungry?" The voice of his father booms, from behind.

He turns to see him approaching, Councilors Thorne and Quezada flanking him like bodyguards.

"Hello, father. Enjoying the tourney?"

"Of course! Though, I will be happy to leave this place and get back to the Pillar." He sniffs the air, scrunching his nose in disgust. "The air here. I don't like it. It smells. And it's... What's the right word? Flat...? Muggy...? I don't know, but I won't miss it."

"Understandable, I already miss the sea breezes of Triali. It is hard to go from that to the suffocation of the city."

"I saw you speaking with King Christoph..." His father says, distaste palatable in his tone. "What does that fat old bear want?"

"He's my grandfather, does he have to want something?" Relorn asks, defensively. "We were just catching up. I haven't seen him in years."

"He always wants something. Insatiable, insufferable. Nothing is ever enough, no debt ever fully reconciled. You'd be better off avoiding the miser, as I do."

"Of course, father."

"I see Eristoclese didn't make it. A member of the Twenty, and your own teacher no less. I hope you don't feel slighted."

"No, no slight. He is very old, I never expected him to make the trip."

"The old fool should know his place." His father says, ignoring Relorn's reply.

"Eristoclese is by far the wisest man I've ever met." He says, stubbornly.

A flash of anger courses through his father's eyes, and his lips curl back into a twisted snarl. "His quips don't make him wise…" He hisses. "Reading the best of those who came before him, and passing it off as some genuine original wisdom. What has he ever added to the world? What has he created? The wisest…" He stops. His eyes widening, as if just having realized something.

A tall herald enters the arena, walking with rigid posture. He takes position and clears his throat, then blows his horn to call the people back to their seats for the next round.

"Round two. Victor du Mount shall face… Stephen Pike." The announcer calls.

Roars of applause erupt from the stands, while raucous calls and stomps quake the city, as the two favorites enter the arena.

Relorn hollers to his uncle through the uproar, "Get him, Stephen! Show him to his back!"

The riders rush at each other, charging down the line. Both lances miss on the first pass, the contestants cautiously testing each other, studying. They turn and charge again, Victor crushing his lance into Stephen's midsection. The blow pushes his uncle back on his saddle, but he manages to keep his grip and stay seated.

"Is he hurt?" Rosemary asks, with a gasp.

"He'll be fine!" Reza yells.

"Victor du Mount leads, one lance to none." The score judge declares.

Stephen turns his steed into position, then begins to storm across the tilt. Victor brings his lance down, but overextends, sweeping across and dropping his weapon. Stephen jams his lance into Victor's outer abdomen, sending his opponent spiraling from the side of his horse.

"Yeah!" Relorn yells, jumping up from his seat and throwing a fist in the air.

"Victor du Mount has been unhorsed. Stephen Pike advances!" An announcer calls, "Next up, Paul Frost and Tea Fane."

"Yes!" Rin yells, shaking his brother's shoulder. "Now he gets to see what it's like. This is going to be great!"

Paul's frozen stallion is still as large and foreboding as before, seemingly unaffected by the warm afternoon sun blaring down on the tourney grounds. He trots into position, a frigid air swirling around the beast and rider.

Fane takes the initiative, starting the charge. His horse is much surer of itself than Rin's had been, unphased by the moving statue of ice.

The riders lower their lances simultaneously, each bound for the other's chest. But just before they are about to make contact, the heads of their weapons strike in midair and shatter on impact.

Paul drops his lance and rides through the hit, but Fane loses his balance and slips from the back of his horse. His foot gets caught on a leather strap hanging from the saddle, pulling him like a doll along the track, until a valet runs up to cut him free.

"Oh lord, it's beautiful!" Rin yells, "Boons from above! I couldn't have asked for more!"

"Shut up! You, ass!" Blossom yells, repeatedly hitting him hard on the arm and back, as he continues to laugh hysterically.

"Tea Fane has been unhorsed. To decide the champion, Paul Frost will face, Stephen Pike!" The score judge announces.

"Drinks!" Andrew yells, from a couple seats down. A porter brings him a tray of glasses. Andrew takes a cup and holds it up, offering the others around. "Here is to a Southern champion!"

"Congratulations…" Reza sneers, "The one thing the Southern Realm is good at."

"We're good at archery too." Andrew quips, holding up his satin champion's purse.

"We will let the melee decide which realm is best!" Rin replies, toasting Andrew then taking a deep drink of cider.

Paul and Stephen canter to the ends of the tilt, then begin the pass. The icy horse charges, its hooves tearing through the soil like spades, throwing a stream of dirt behind it. As the contestants approach each other, Paul's mount twists to the left, sending its rider's lance across his opponent's front, glancing harmlessly off his armor. While Stephen's lance finds its target, driving into Paul's armor and breaking at the shaft.

"Stephen Pike leads, one lance to none." The judge shouts.

The two charge again, locked on each other. At the last moment Paul's horse jolts again, but to the right this time, sending its rider directly into Stephen's outstretched lance. With a sickening crack, the stick shatters against his stomach.

"Stephen Pike leads. Two lances to none!"

Paul starts screaming from across the field, shouting for his squire to bring a horse. His frosty mount kneels, letting him dismount. As he steps off, Paul screams at the icy stallion, shattering the mount into a million tiny dazzling pieces, casting an explosive blizzard of ice and snow over the crowd.

His squire arrives with a large white destrier in tow, offering the reigns to his liege.

Paul points at Stephen from across the field, then taps the side of his head, knowingly. The two sprint forward at the same time. Paul's lance finds its target, breaking on Stephens's chest.

"Stephen Pike leads. Two lances to one."

They begin to pass once more, Stephen's strike glancing off of Paul's armor, while Paul shatters his lance against Stephen's chest again.

"Tied, at two lances each!"

Relorn taps his foot anxiously. *Three broken lances win, this is it…*

The two riders storm down the tilt, bringing their weapons down for the strike. Paul's lance crashes into Stephen's head, catching on his eye guard and sending the helm sailing through the air.

As he leans back from the blow, Stephen's lance catches Paul low in the groin, shattering the stick and sending Paul slipping sideways off his horse.

"Paul Frost has been dismounted. Stephen Pike is the champion!" The judge yells, raising Stephen's hand in the air triumphantly.

Relorn jumps from his seat, rushing out to congratulate his uncle.

Kzhee 4

Kzhee and Rilii walk hand in hand, shouldering their way through the throngs, trying to be the first to the next arena so they won't have to fight to get good seats. Rilii's brother is competing with the melee team from the Plains, along with Taala Caalda, a master warrioress from the Great Rock, and the Herd-Chief's twin grandsons, Caruu and Ruul Caruuson.

Rilii drops Kzhee's hand, bolting forward and lunging into the last two chairs in the front row, narrowly beating a young couple about to take the seats. The couple walks away shaking their heads and whispering, as Rilii laughs in triumph.

"I am too quick!" She cheers, as he sits down next to her.

"You are indeed." He says, with a chuckle.

Rilii takes his arm in hers and tenderly leans against him, resting her head on his shoulder.

"Kzhee, do you love me?" She asks, muffledly, burying her face in his chest.

His throat tightens and his mouth begins to water. He chokes, not sure what to say.

"Ever since we were children..." He replies, in a broken whisper, "Yes."

Rilii looks up and smiles, before springing a kiss on him with lightning speed.

"Stay with me then!" She says, a cheery smile planted on her face. "Come home with me. Father will need help running the mines after Drii is selected for the Emperor's Due. You could be his apprentice... You can't stay shacked up in the Hills all your life. Come, be with me... One day, if we asked my father, I'm sure he would say yes to us being wed. Your father and he are friends, he would have to say yes... Imagine, falling asleep every night together, entwined. Lost in each other." She squeezes his hand, wiping away a tear with her sleeve.

He feels his eyes begin to well up also, but chokes the emotion back. Running his hand through her cinnamon hair, he tells her, "Yes. Yes, I will."

Vincence tilts back his wineskin, gulping down its crimson contents with one long drink. He burps loudly, throwing the skin on the ground, then continues through the entrance of the arena.

"We're about to fight, you damned drunkard!" Orly Orvani shouts, "You're going to get yourself killed!"

"I am a far supe... *Hic...* Superior fighter, when I am drunk." The vintner replies, cheerily waving to the crowd and blowing kisses of air.

Ral follows his team into the stadium, gazing at the immeasurable amount of spectators crowded around the arena and overflowing throughout the city, packing it to the brim.

I've never seen anything like this... The entire city of A'Tannia could fit inside this park.

Ral begins to feel drunk himself, as the cheers make his heart beat faster. The arena is the only place he feels at home, comfortable, listening to the audience screaming and shouting the names of their favorite contestants.

"Tristan! Tristan, we love you!"

"Nadeeeeemm!!"

"Go Stephen! Go! Go!

"Jorrun! Jorrun! Jorrun! Jorrun!"

He looks up at the stands, spotting Satia sitting in the second row with the representatives of the River Realm. She is laughing, deep in conversation with the young senator from the night before. McKenna sits next to them, peering down on the field, lost in thought.

The pulse of the crowd steadies Ral's nerves, reverberating through his muscles and tingling his extremities, as the rest of the world begins to fade from his mind.

An assortment of weapons lies near the entrance. Stepping up, Ral selects a blunted spear from the rack at the edge of the table. Vincence follows suit, grabbing a long white oak staff, caps of iron adorning either end. Darin and Orly pick swords, then embrace each other, before clasping hands with Ral and Vincence.

"Here is to our victory!" The vintner shouts, grabbing a glass of honeywine from a passing attendant and throwing it back with a gulp. Darin laughs heartily, while Orly scowls.

Across the arena a herald marches out, raising his hands in the air to indicate for the spectators to quiet.

"The grand melee shall commence." He calls out, gesturing to the teams assembling around the circular arena. "Contestants, if you receive one torso hit, or two hits to the limbs, you must leave the field immediately. The use of gifts is prohibited at all times. The entire team will be disqualified if a single member breaks this rule.

Emperor Jero stands and claps his hands sharply, signaling for the event to begin.

Ral sees the teams from the Southern Realm and the Mountains move in unison, coming together in a pincer movement upon the group from the Great City. Across the way, the Plains People spring upon the group from the Plateau, initiating combat with a war cry.

"Follow me!" Vincence shouts, rushing toward the only unengaged group, the Firelanders, standing defensively before the dais and watching the fray with their weapons ready.

Vincence had been telling the truth about fighting better while drunk. He spins and jabs, whirling his staff about like a cyclone. Two young Firelanders advance, no older than Ral, slashing with long curved swords. Vincence deflects both of their strikes effortlessly, ducking a swing from one and hitting the second in the chest plate, sending a clang ringing out from the iron cap of his weapon. Quickly, he whacks the other in the arm, spinning in a swift circle, before striking again.

"Eliminated, Fe Zanay and Lee Ryan." The nearest announcer yells.

Ral joins in the fight, jumping towards the oldest Firelander, a slim man holding a serpentine sword. The man blocks Ral's advance with a sweep of his blade, his body barely moving as his sword swings and stabs. Ral makes a defensive jump, jabbing his spear furiously from the air, nearly slashing the man's face.

Vincence and Darin are squaring off with the remaining Firelander, but he is much more skilled than the first two, easily deflecting both their blows. His heavy sword shatters Vincence's stave, forcing the vintner to back out of the action, looking for an opening to make his way to the weapon table across the arena.

Orly comes up on Ral's flank to assist, and their opponent begins to waver under the combined assault. He desperately swings at Orly, managing to hit him in the back, but Ral sees the man's torso left open and strikes him in the chest.

"Eliminated, Orly Orvani and Huo Jain."

Ral turns around to assist Vincence and Darin. The remaining opponent is a large man. Strong, yet deadly accurate with his strikes. He seems most comfortable playing defensively, letting them advance, then parrying and returning a quick strike.

Ral swings his spear at the man's head, while Darin swings low. Their opponent ducks the spear and dodges the blade, returning a cobra like strike to Darin's gut. As he does, Vincence runs up behind him, a broken end piece of his staff in hand. He slams it against the man's back plate, giving off a loud ring of clashing metal.

"Eliminated, Darin of Tarin and Jorrun Frostburn."

"Yes!" Vincence cries out, as they turn to face the melee unfolding around them.

The few remaining contestants are split in two groups. On one side, a jeweled warrior from the Plains is backed against the edge of the arena, cornered by two gigantic men, both draped in sun-bleached leather. Then, across the ring, a single contestant from each the Mountains, Southern Realm, and Great City remain, circling each other, throwing out random jabs and slashes trying to gain an upper hand.

Ral sees the two towering men from the Plateau advance on the warrior from the Plains. One of the men swings his sword, striking the cornered man's mace. As his weapon makes contact the large man appears to seize up, paralyzed in place with his back arched. The warrior swings, hitting the large man in his poorly armored chest, sending him falling to the ground gasping.

"Eliminated, Rudy Movoni."

The large man's even larger teammate screams, then furiously begins swinging in a berserker rage. The warrior from the Plains dodges the first few, then deflects a hit with his mace, momentarily stopping the man in his tracks as the metal of their weapons touch. Another quick swing, and the second man is struck on the back.

"Eliminated, Brolen Brode."

Ral and Vincence approach the now lone warrior, like cats stalking a mouse. Their opponent swings his mace around, a grin across his face. Ral rushes forward, jumping up and rapidly jabbing with his spear. Seizing the moment, Vincence sprints towards the weapon table to rearm himself.

The warrior dodges the next advance, shattering the spear with a heave of his mace. Ral rolls away from the man, just as Vincence returns and begins recklessly swinging his replacement staff. Ral finds the spear rack empty, so he grabs a sword before running back to the fight.

Their opponent strikes Vincence's staff ferociously, sending the vintner to his back, then draws his mace above his head, preparing to bring it crushing down on Vincence's chest. Ral dives into the warrior, trying to keep the strike from hitting his teammate.

As the mace makes contact with Ral, he feels a shock begin to course through his body. He stares at his arms, unable to move, watching webs and arcs of white lightning creep through him, illuminating his body and turning his skin as clear as water.

"Cheating!" A judge yells, "Drii Taliison is disqualified, the Plains forfeit!"

Murmurs creep over the crowd, as Drii exits the arena. Ral falls to the ground, choking and gasping for breath.

Vincence helps him to his feet, dusting off his back and giving a grin. They watch the fighter from the Mountains, a nimble young lady in orange silk, dancing between the other two contestants, slicing and jumping, twirling through the air like a whirlwind, then striking again.

The challenger from the Great City knocks the Southern man into her, as she spins away, sending them both falling to the ground. The man's sword hits her torso as they crash down.

"Eliminated, Ambi Boulder."

The cheers of the home crowd ring through the stadium, shaking the ground beneath their feet with a violent fervor.

"Nadeem! Nadeem! Nadeem du Ravine!"

With a gentle touch of his sword, he eliminates the Southerner, before turning to approach them.

Vincence advances, screaming at the man and swinging his stave violently. Nadeem deflects each pass of the staff with a careless swing of one of his swords, before dropping down and rolling behind Vincence. Then, lunging up, he strikes with his twin blades, hitting the vintner on both arms.

"Eliminated, Vincence Viali."

As Vincence walks off the field, Nadeem charges towards Ral, swinging and slashing with both swords, furiously pushing him back to the edge of the arena. Ral desperately tries to defend against the onslaught, but his sword is barely able to keep up with his opponent's rapid strikes.

Don't lose it, everyone is watching...

Ral dodges an aggressive attack, then slips behind Nadeem, before running for the weapon table. He grabs a small shield, then begins pacing across the arena, waiting for his opponent to come to him.

He is all that stands between you and victory... End it!

Nadeem rushes forward, sweeping both swords across his front. At the last second, Ral smashes the shield up into the blades, deflecting the strike as they whistle towards his head. The force of the blow sends Nadeem's arms flying back, momentarily exposing his torso. Ral jabs forward, hitting his opponent in the gut.

"Eliminated, Nadeem du Ravine." The judge bellows, before gesturing to Ral. "Representing the River Realm, your champion, RRAAAALLLLLL!!"

Cheers and applause explode from the stands, the loudest coming from around the senators and citizens of the River Realm. Satia runs down onto the arena, planting a kiss on his lips and patting his cheek.

Vincence grabs his arm and raises it high, eliciting additional screams from the crowd. He can hear them chanting his name.

"Ral! Ral! Ral! Ral! Ral! Ral! Ral! Ral!"

Rosemary 4

Rosemary sits next to her sister in the amphitheater, waiting for the show to start. She rubs her stomach, full from the feast they had attended after the melee. Reclining in her seat, Rosemary relaxes in the dimly lit theatre.

"I'm going to miss you so much when you go back home…" Blossom says, pouting her lip.

"I'll miss you too. But I am not going back to Blackburn. I am going to become a sister of the Order, and live here in the Grand Temple." A tear drips down her pale cheek. "At least there I won't be able to hurt anyone else…"

"Stop it!" Her sister exclaims. "You can't let one horrible moment dictate the course of your life."

"What life?" She sobs, "I am too scared to do anything! What if I kill someone else? You? Mother? Father? No one is safe with me around! I can't…"

A horn blares, and the lights in the Amphitheatre go out, signaling for the show to begin. Men and elves run about the stage, fighting. It is a play she has seen before, *The Fall of Tritan.*

Rosemary is too preoccupied to pay attention to the performance. Her stomach turning and churning, as she thinks of the next day. Her parents leaving… And her, beginning a new life as a servant of the Lord above.

The play is longer than she had remembered it being, but the final battle scene is more exciting than ever, the amazing performers drawing her attention back to the action.

Two actors duel, as a young elven girl looks on, their swords clashing with sharp clangs.

They're using real weapons… She thinks, noticing sparks fly as their blows glance off each other.

Rosemary leans forward in her seat, gazing at the flashing blades, illuminating the air each time they collide. The actor playing King Tritan ducks a sweep from his adversary's sword, but the next strike catches him in the throat.

Before Rosemary realizes what is happening, the elf's head slides off. Landing at his feet, while his body slumps down to the ground in a heap. Rosemary screams, as do a few others around the theatre.

The elf girl on stage runs towards the fallen actor, grabbing his head from the ground and placing it back on his neck. She desperately kisses his lips, tears streaming freely down her face.

As the girl kisses him, Rosemary can see the man's wound begin to heal. Winding and weaving itself back together, like roots growing and intertwining at an astounding speed. Sinew and skin creeps and crawls, closing the cut and connecting his head back to his neck.

Struggling, the actor stands up. Then, smiling for the audience, he shows off the ring of blood that remains around his throat, the only evidence of the death stroke he had been dealt.

Cheers and screams echo through the amphitheater. People stand and yell, whistling and throwing flowers. He takes the girl's hand, and together they bow.

Another elf runs on stage from the audience. Older than the actors, and impeccably dressed. "Ladies and sirs!" He says, with a bow. "Your Highness. With the hopes that it will please your most benevolent majesty. For the Emperor's Due, on behalf of the Elven States, I, Sivaties Honeysuckle, Governor of the Elven Quarter, wish to offer, Tiaries Tulip!" He yells, gesturing to the actress on stage still wiping away tears from her cheeks.

The elven girl looks up in bewilderment, her large eyes aghast, clearly unaware of the plan she was part of.

The actors push the girl, Tiaries, to the front of the stage. Rosemary can see the Emperor sitting in the first row, men whispering to him from both sides.

"Thank you, Sivaties." One of the men standing around the Emperor says, another elf. "The Emperor accepts your offer."

"That is Councilor Lingonberry." Her sister says, in a hushed tone. "He comes to visit Fane's father sometimes, always armed with delightful stories and presents. He has friends all over the Empire, everyone loves him."

Lingonberry leads the girl off the stage, to a pavilion setup behind the theatre. As they exit, a man dressed in dark green silk walks onto the stage, stopping at the center.

"With the hopes that it will please your most benevolent majesty." The man in green yells, bowing nervously. "For the Emperor's Due, on behalf of the Forest Realm, I, Tane Aru We, Warden of the Orchard, wish to offer, Rika Boro Dee!"

A tiny girl hidden behind him steps forward, apprehensively approaching the front of the stage. Taking a deep breath and puffing out her cheeks, the girl disappears before their eyes.

"Look!" Someone squeals, from the front row, pointing to a small movement scurrying on the wooden boards. "She's a mouse!"

A short man stands from his seat next to the Emperor and calls to the stage. "Thank you, Warden Tane. The Emperor accepts your offer."

Rosemary smiles at her sister, allowing herself to have some enjoyment as they watch the Due. Forgetting about her worries for a moment.

Looking up at the next man entering the stage, the smile on her face quickly fades and her stomach begins to tighten. The man, proudly striding across the platform with his chest puffed out, is Grand Marshal Barren, Prince Bastion's father. Her skin grows cold and begins tingling unbearably, as if she is being stabbed by a thousand frozen needles.

The marshal yells over the crowd, "With the hopes that it will please your most benevolent majesty. For the Emperor's Due, on behalf of the Southern Realm, I, George Barren, Grand Marshal of the South, wish to offer, Rosemary Blackburn!"

No, no, no, no, no, no! She thinks, trying not to scream. *What does this mean? I swore I would join the Order… I can't break the oath I swore hardly a day ago…*

The silent crowd looks around, waiting for her to stand. She shrinks into her seat instead, unsure of what to do.

"I think you have to go up…" Her sister says, in disbelief.

"There she is!" Someone in the crowd yells.

"Rosemary, please come here." The marshal says, not attempting to hide his malevolent grin.

She slowly stands, and begins to make her way to the stage. Her legs seem to move on their own, while she looks around, helplessly. The world begins to spin and her mouth starts to water, a gaging feeling creeps up her throat, trying to grip its way out.

She walks on stage, staring at the ground, avoiding the marshal's icy eyes.

He gestures to an attendant, who brings out a snow white bunny. Held by the scruff of its neck, its feet dangle and kick as it tries to run on air.

"Show them!" The marshal shouts.

"No, please, my lord... I can't... Please don't make me." Tears fall down her face with abandon, as she desperately pleads.

A councilor, tall and gaunt with snowy white hair, stands and speaks. "Show us what you can do, girl."

George Barren grabs the rabbit and flings it into her arms, hissing. "Now!"

Rosemary tries not to look at its eyes, as she brings it up to her face. Her lips gently touch its nose. As they do, a white-blue wave cascades over the rabbit's fur, leaving a pale icy gleam in its wake.

She jumps back, as the ice spreads towards her hands, dropping the animal on the ground with a piercing crack. Rosemary looks away as it shatters, before slowly gazing up at the marshal, a look of disgust and loathing painted upon her face.

"Thank you, Grand Marshal Barren." The white haired councilor says, "The Emperor accepts your offer."

Councilor Quezada 3

Councilor Thorne and the Southern girl walk away from the stage, towards the pavilion out back.

"She's a little weepy, no?" He asks Councilor Inzu.

"Don't be an ass." She smirks, roughly brushing his arm.

A Plainsman takes the stage, adorned in gems and precious stones. He clears his throat with a cough, before beginning to speak. "With the hopes that it will please your most benevolent majesty. For the Emperor's Due, on behalf of the Lightning Plains, I, Talii Daliison, Chief of the Cliffs, wish to offer, Rilii Taliida!"

Quezada can see that the chief's daughter looks surprised, as she rises and makes her way to the stage. Her father waves his arm, gesturing for her to go to the councilors and demonstrate.

"They must have meant to offer Drii, but thought better of it after he was caught cheating during the melee." Councilor Kroonson says, to the Emperor.

"What does she do?" Jero asks.

"I've heard she can see memories," Kroonson answers. "Or interpret dreams, something along those lines."

Jero raises his hand, stopping the girl's approach, then leans in to speak quietly with the councilors. "I have no desire to have someone around dragging up old memories, let's leave the past where it belongs. Who else is there to select from the Plains?"

"I heard from a blackbird, just the other day." Councilor Sage says. "It told me that it saw Chief Rhee's son cast a bolt of lightning, strong enough to blast through solid earth. Of course, you know birds can be hard to understand. But if what they conveyed is true, he is the most powerful lightning-bringer to be born in centuries."

"Councilor Kroonson, do you agree with this selection?" Jero asks.

"Agreed." He replies, nodding.

"Settled."

Councilor Kroonson stands and declares to the audience, for all to hear. "Thank you, Chief Talii. But the Emperor respectfully rejects your offer."

A sea of murmurs ripples through the crowd. The offering, Rilii, returns to her seat, face beat red with embarrassment. The boy in the seat next to her smiles, and puts his arm around her shoulders.

Kroonson continues, "The Emperor requests, Kzhee Rheeson."

The boy sitting next to Rilii stops smiling suddenly, upon hearing his name. He looks around, unsure of what to do. Chief Talii starts gesturing, calling him up.

Kzhee slowly stands, walking to the stage with apprehension. As he climbs the steps of the platform, the boy looks up at the chief, who responds with nothing more than an uncertain shrug.

"Please." Councilor Kroonson says, "A demonstration."

The boy looks around the amphitheater, searching for someone, before resigning to his fate. Kzhee stares at a table across the stage, a piece of scenery left from the play. He closes his eyes and seems to focus. As he does, a booming bolt of lightning cracks through the sky above, casting a bright flash of light across the theatre and sending a shockwave through the crowd. The blast reduces the table to nothing more than a handful of smoldering remnants and a billowing swirl of black smoke.

"Thank you, Kzhee. Please come with me." Kroonson says, leading the boy away.

Next, a group of men and women enter the stage in a long procession, the champion of the grand melee walking with them.

One of the men steps forward. Quezada recognizes him, Senator McKenna.

Conniving snake… Always winding and twisting words, somehow able to turn any and every terrible situation or unwinnable argument in his favor.

"With the hopes that it will please your most benevolent majesty. For the Emperor's Due, on behalf of the River Realm, I, Senator McKenna, wish to offer, Ral, the Champion of A'Tannia!"

Councilor Maestas rises from his seat, joining them on stage. "Hello cousin, good to see you." He says, shaking hands with the senator before turning to the boy. "Congratulations on your victory earlier, Ral… Is it?"

"Yes, my lord." The young man replies.

"No last name?"

"I never met my parents, my lord."

"Who raised you? Where were you born?"

"I have lived in A'Tannia my whole life. I was born a slave, Senator McKenna freed me."

"How equitable of him…" The councilor says, smirking. "Well, what is it you can do? Other than handle a sword and spear better than anyone here."

The boy takes a knife from his waistband, slowly dragging it across the palm of his hand. The wound ripples and closes behind the blade, without a drop of blood spilled. Councilor Maestas looks back at the Emperor, nodding his head and smiling.

"Thank you, Senator McKenna." Maestas says, with a smile. "The Emperor accepts your offer."

The procession exits, and Warlord Jain takes the stage, followed closely by a group of nobles from the Firelands.

The man clears his throat, looking around absently, before announcing to the audience. "With the hopes that it will please your most benevolent majesty. For the Emperor's Due, on behalf of the Firelands, I, Huo Jain, Lord of the City of Light and Warlord of the Firelands, wish to offer, Te Reza!"

The warlord steps back and waves his hand dramatically. As he does, the blaze in a nearby brazier begins to swirl and rise, forming a fiery figure. Suddenly, a smoldering bird flies from the flames, orange and purple and yellow. It takes off, soaring over the crowd.

As the flying conflagration circles above, a boy steps onto the stage. He draws a bow and takes aim at the firebird. As he holds the string taught, his arrowhead begins to glow, brighter and brighter and brighter.

Letting it loose, the arrow burns through the sky like a comet, leaving a glowing trail in its path as it soars through the night.

The projectile strikes the blazing bird, sending a huge blast through the sky, illuminating the city with a ruby glow.

Councilor Inzu stands and addresses the stage. "Thank you, Warlord Jain. But the Emperor respectfully rejects your offer."

Quezada sees Reza staring back at his aunt in disbelief, while the firelords look at each other in confusion.

Te Inzu continues. "Warlord Jain, is your daughter gifted?"

"She is, councilor. But it is little more than an accessory. A flame on her tiara…" He says, pointing to his daughter, Jia, sitting in the front row with her headpiece ablaze.

"Jia, could you?" Inzu asks, gesturing for the girl to take the stage.

She struts before the audience. Her chin held up, confidently, as she looks at her dumbfounded father with a hint of defiance burning in her eyes.

"A demonstration, if you would." Inzu requests.

Jia smiles, holding a hand out before her. The flame that burns upon her tiara abruptly flies through the air, drawn to the girl's outstretched palm.

Initially amorphous, the flame begins to swirl. As it does, the shape of a girl appears, spinning and spinning, one leg touching Jia's palm, the other tucked up in a pirouette.

The crowd sits watching, enchanted by the beautifully whirling illumination. Then, swiftly, Jia flings her hand towards the audience. As she does the flame takes flight, expanding above the onlookers. Exploding and dividing, again and again, until thousands of glowing lights fly through the air, like pixies on parade. Casting an eerie glow across the amphitheater, and mesmerizing the audience.

Breaking the enchantment with a sound, a soft whistle, Jia calls the flames back to her. The inferno blazes through the night, swirling together into a firestorm, creating a smoldering conflagration.

With an immense effort, and a fervent scream, she flings her arms forward, thrusting the flames into the air and sending a whirling column of fire blasting into the darkness and eliciting a roar of screams and laudation from the onlookers.

Jia smiles, vehemently, snapping her fingers to summon the flames back. In a flash, the firestorm ceases, and a single flame remains, dancing upon Jia's palm. It holds its hands high overhead in a merry frolic, jumping and silently cheering, as if responding to the crowd's applause.

"Thank you, Jia, please come with me." Inzu says, heading out of the theatre with the girl in tow.

Quezada remains next to the Emperor, the only councilor still in the audience. They watch the members of the Oligarchy of Twenty take the stage. Lord Treasurer Antissi joins them, taking his absent brother's place.

The lord treasurer places his hand on Atasio Nodovin's shoulder, signaling for him to make the offering.

The shipwright moves to the head of the group, announcing nervously. "With the hopes that it will please your most benevolent majesty. For the Emperor's Due, on behalf of the Windswept Plateau, I, Atasio Nodovin, member of the Oligarchy of Twenty, wish to offer, Chion Antissi!"

Quezada watches the boy stand and approach the congregation, taking a place next to his uncle.

"Lord Antissi's son?" Quezada asks the Emperor. "Why would they offer him?"

"Because I told them to." Jero states, curtly. "It is about time we reigned in Clion Antissi, and what better way than having his son? Now go accept him. I am growing bored."

Sir Simon 3

"I thought the ceremony was over, your holiness." Sir Simon says, to the High Priest. As they make their way to a lit up pavilion.

"It would be…" High Priest Tobin remarks, casually. "If that dastardly Black Knight hadn't interrupted the end of the ritual earlier."

"Oh course, your holiness. It's just… I feel I should return to my post as soon as possible. You saw what transpired with the grand marshal. Surely I must return and warm my men, the Southern Realm could be on the precipice of war."

"That situation seems to have resolved itself, by my count. The girl came to us just yesterday, asking to join the Order as a sister because she wanted to get out of the south. The grand marshal wanted to exact some type of revenge, which he feels he has done by offering her. So they both should each be happy. She gets away from the south, and he gets her out of sight and mind."

The priest pauses, "More importantly, I need you here. With the Black Knight running about the Great City wreaking havoc, I need a man like you around."

"Your holiness, how could I serve the Empire from here?" Sir Simon asks, perplexed.

"I would make you the White Knight." Tobin says, grinning. "The highest honor a knight of the Order can achieve. Your name will live on forever, glorified in the histories."

"Your holiness, I am not worthy…" He cries, falling to his knee.

"It is already done." The priest replies, kissing his fingers then touching them to Simon's bowed head. "Rise, Sir Simon the White."

"It is too much of an honor to bestow on the likes of me." Sir Simon protests. "I am not fit for the title."

"Titles mean little and less. Almost everyone in the Empire has some title or other. They think the name gives them power… But names mean nothing. It is what you do that matters. That is where true power come from. Those who take action truly rule the Empire. Take Jero for example, the leader of us all, the Emperor of the Mountains and all the streams and the valleys and the trees. Jero the Great… Jero the Magnificent..." The priest laughs, scratching the head of the kitten upon his shoulder. "Can you tell me one great or magnificent thing he has ever done?"

He defeated the barbarian uprising, did he not?" Sir Simon asks, surprised at the High Priest's candor.

"Jero never even left the Pillar during the uprising, despite what his heralds sing… His father's troops won the war under the leadership of his father-in-law Christoph, King of the Basket. Now there is true power. King Christoph feeds half of the

Empire with that *Basket* of his. He could ruin the Empire, without ever sending a single soldier to battle."

"I don't know what to say…" Simon replies, at a loss.

"I don't need you to say anything. Go, send a carrier pigeon to your men in Blackburn. Let them know what has happened. Instruct them to elect a new leader from their ranks."

"Of course, your holiness." Sir Simon says, still in shock. "I will send to them now."

Chion 5

Chion browses through the bounty of delicacies displayed across a grand banquet table in the Emperor's pavilion. The pole tent is an expansive construction, filled with every imaginable luxury. Across the table, he sees the boy from the Plains, Kzhee.

He approaches to introduce himself, offering his hand. "Hello, I am Chion Antissi. Pleased to make your acquaintance."

The Plainsman looks worried, his eyes darting around the room.

"Are you okay?" Chion asks.

"Yeah, I'll be fine. I just need to speak with my father, I haven't seen him." He answers, nervously. "My friend as well, I can't leave without talking to her…"

"Oh, don't worry. I'm sure they'll let you talk with them before we leave. I can't imagine we'll be setting sail for the Pillar in the black of night." Chion says, with a laugh, noticing the boy calm down a bit.

"You're right, I'm sorry. My name is Kzhee."

"Great to meet you!" Chion cheers, clasping his hand. "That was some crack of lightning you dropped out there, made my hair stand on end!"

"It's all still new to me. To be honest, I don't even know how they found out what I could do… Almost no one knew…"

"They must be able to tell somehow." Chion says, shrugging. "I didn't think anyone knew about me either."

"What can you do?" Kzhee asks.

Chion looks at him, wondering what to say. "I guess I can hear people's thoughts."

"Really?" Kzhee asks, excitedly. "What am I thinking right now?"

Chion shakes his head, "It doesn't really seem to work on people with gifts."

Something draws Kzhee's attention away. Chion turns to look, and sees a pretty girl slipping underneath one of the sides of the pavilion's canvas walls. Kzhee runs over to help her, and she excitedly leans up to kiss him.

"Good talking to you too…" Chion says, to no one in particular, before looking around and inspecting the other selectees.

In the back of the pavilion, he notices Prince Relorn fervorously speaking with Matio, Reza and Andrew. The Southern girl, Rosemary, sits alone in a corner, tapping her foot restlessly. Jia and Tiaries are speaking with the little girl from the Forest Realm, who sits with her feet dangling from her chair.

The melee champion, Ral, approaches the table. He grabs a glass of wine and quickly finishes it, then another.

"Hello. Ral, is it?" He asks, filling his own glass in suit and offering it up for a toast. "Chion Antissi, great to meet you!"

"Good to meet you." Ral says, toasting with his glass. "This is all unbelievable, right?"

"Yeah, I don't quite know what to make of it. I miss my house, my job." Chion sighs. "I ran my own bank. Now, I don't even know what will happen to it."

"I've been a slave my whole life, until a few weeks ago when they told me I was doing this..." Ral replies, taking a long sip from his glass.

"Well then..." Chion says, awkwardly taking another drink. "I will quit my complaining."

A few more glasses of wine, and they are clapping each other's backs like old friends.

"The way..." Chion says, slurring his words, "The way you jump up in the air and do that spear jab... Thing... How, uh, how do you do it?"

"*Hic*! I... I don't know. I just jump, and do this!" Ral drunkenly jumps in the air, violently shaking his glass in a spearing motion and spilling the contents on the dirt below.

Chion bursts into laughter, almost falling over. He holds his drink up for another toast, but is interrupted by the High Priest entering the pavilion, a little cat sitting in the curves of his elaborate crown. He is followed closely by the Emperor and his council.

Chion watches them call Relorn over. The priest takes a dagger from a ceremonial sheath, handing it to the Emperor.

What the…? What are they going to do with that?

Emperor Jero takes the knife and holds it up, letting the light run across its reflective surface. Then he quickly brings it down into the palm of his hand.

A loud clang rings out, as the blade harmlessly bounces off of his skin. Then he passes the knife to his son, who takes it nervously, his hands visibly shaking.

Relorn swings the blade, repeating his father's motion, bringing the point crashing toward his own palm. It makes contact, then slides off, the tip breaking but not leaving a mark on the prince. The councilors and priest clap their hands and pat him on the back.

The Emperor turns and begins addressing the room, "Those who have been honored with a selection, welcome. You will learn from my council. They will teach you what you need to know to help my son rule, what you need to know to become councilors yourselves. Say your goodbyes… We leave for the Pillar first thing tomorrow."

The Assassin 2

Dark air whips around him, as the dirt sinks beneath his sandaled feet. Step after step, he moves up the hill before him. The road is too conspicuous, but the hills are perfect. Clam and deserted.

He sees a soft glow beginning to grow in the distance. The ground becomes visible through the night, illuminated by the nondescript incandescence emanating from somewhere over the horizon. He trudges forward, pulling a piece of paper from his cloak and reading it once more.

The wind blows relentlessly towards him, slowing his progress.

Everything about the Plateau is pleasant, save for the incessant wind. He thinks, shielding his face from the stinging shards of sand carried by the breeze.

As he crosses the hill's summit, a city comes into focus before him. Marble columns hold up the colossal roofs of temples and palaces. Innumerable braziers and lamps burn through the city, casting a resplendent glow across the streets and lighting up the sky.

Panthos. The assassin thinks, smiling as he enters the nightless city.

Relorn 6

"What did he say?" Matio asks, as Relorn returns. "Why didn't they select us?"

"My father said it is because we are friends. He said the point of the Due is to forge new bonds, not nurture existing ones."

"Well…" Andrew starts, "I guess it is time for backup plans. What are you guys going to do?"

"The Southern Trading Company is offering anyone with the gift of fire a lordship on the Tradewind Isles, in exchange for a tour of duty." Reza says, filling and lighting a pipe he had bought from a street vendor in the city earlier that day. "From what I've heard it's an easy job, and when you retire they give you land, a castle, and servants galore. I may never be lord of Te'mont, let my older brother have that dusty old place. I will be lord of… Re'mont? Reza'mont? I'll think of a clever name, give me time."

"Well, there have been more and more pirate attacks off my family's waters." Andrew says, "I think I will take to the sea as well, join my father's armada. It'll give him some time to spend on shore with my mother."

"Maybe I'll join you!" Matio exclaims. "My father has hundreds of ships, He might give me command of some, if I ask. I could sail them down to Seacliff and join your armada. We could cruise the seas, fighting pirates and keeping the Empire safe!"

"That sounds great." Andrew says, patting his friend on the back. "Hopefully your father will go along with it, he seemed like he was going to miss having us around."

"That's true. But he was ready for me to be offered for the Due," Matio shakes his head. "No, I'm sure he'll be fine."

"You people have no trouble making new plans, huh?" Relorn says, scoffing.

"Sorry, but it's not our fault…" Andrew states. "We were all excited to be selected, but then it didn't happen. So our plans have to change. Yours remain the same however, just without us…"

"When you become Emperor, you can call us to court. Give us positions." Matio says, meekly. "But for now… What else can we do?"

"I guess… I don't know." He shakes his head. "I'm tired, I need to sleep. Will you all see me off tomorrow?"

"Of course, your highness." Reza replies, with a grin. "Go get some sleep."

Seaborne 4

Choppy waves slap against the side of his ship as it sails leeward over the sea, bouncing and bobbing with the swells. Ahead, lies home.

In the distance, Seaborne can see a great mast peaking over the horizon. Then, a titanic hull begins to come into sight. *The Flagship,* a behemoth construct rising one hundred stories from the water, drifting gently as it dwarfs the tiny island that it's anchored off of.

Thousands upon thousands of boats surround the pirate mothership. Vessels of every shape and design, forming a floating city in the middle of the ocean, interconnected by a winding maze of quays, docks, bridges and gangplanks.

"Bring us about, coxswain!" Seaborne hollers, as the helmsman maneuvers the ship into port. "New crewmates, come with me. The admiral awaits."

The men follow him as they make their way between the moored vessels, towards the side of *The Flagship*. They approach the aft, where a large wooden lift lays waiting, hovering just above the water.

"Onto the lift!" He shouts.

The platform creaks and groans, as the counterweight brings them up hundreds of feet, into a large wheelhouse above. The room is well guarded, with only one door leading out and a line of people waiting.

Andy Shipman, commodore of *The Flagship*, approaches their party. "Captain Seaborne, welcome home."

"Thank ya, Andy." He says, clasping the man's hand. "It is good to be back."

"The admiral wishes to see you and your prize officers at once."

"Of course. Give me a moment, I wish to see this one judged." Seaborne replies, pointing to Sir Kevin. "He is a knight of the Order, but he claims he wishes to join us. I am curious to see what the Scales make of it…"

"Aye, we will meet you in the admiral's audience chamber." The commodore says, spinning about and exiting with Seaborne's officers in tow.

"Let's go!" He says, pushing Kevin through the door.

Guards line the walls of a narrow hall, the room of judgment. At the end, the Scales stand behind a large wooden podium.

"What is that?" Sir Kevin asks, bewildered by the sight.

"Those are the Scales..." The captain explains, escorting him down the hall. "Lena and Christina. They can tell if ya'r lying, or scheming, or just an all-around bad person."

The Scales look up at the captain and his prisoner. Lena smiles, while Christina lets out a long sigh. The girls rise, two heads upon a single body.

"Seaborne!" Lena shouts, with a chipper smile. Waving the hand that she has control of.

"Always nice to see you..." Christina says, with an absent flick of their other hand.

"Ahh!" Lena coos, "I knew she had warm feelings for you. She never says *nice to see you*. Not to anyone!"

"Well, ya know I've nothing but the warmest of feelings for both of ya!" Seaborne says, removing his hat and bowing deeply. "I have a meeting with the admiral, could ya judge this man for me. I have my doubts about his motives, and would like to see him tried myself."

"What's going to happen?" Sir Kevin asks, fidgeting nervously.

"I can see... Your true potential. Everything you could be." Lena says, her smile fading and her face becoming deathly serious. "Christina can see, well... Let's just say, there is nothing you can hide from her."

Sir Kevin sits down, apprehensively, as the girls approach. Lena touches his shoulder with their right hand, her hand. She closes her eyes, breathing deeply. Concentrating. Letting go, her eyelids raise, and her smile widens. "He has great potential! Just like you, Seaborne."

"Let's see if your past measures up..." Christina sneers, grasping his shoulder with their left hand. She follows the same process as her sister, only much more solemnly. "Well..." She says, opening her eyes after a moment. "If that is the worst thing you've ever done... I think I can allow you to pass."

"He isn't lying about wanting to join us?" Seaborne asks.

"It would appear he is telling the truth. I can't find anything that would indicate otherwise." Christina answers, looking at a large cut on the knight's arm. With a touch of her fingers, the fresh scab begins to wrinkle and turn brittle, before falling away and revealing smooth skin beneath.

Amazement shines on Kevin's face, as Seaborne peers at him.

Hmm, so he was telling the truth...

"Parrot, ya'r in charge of Sir Kevin. Get him settled."

"Aye, cap'n." Parrot replies. The brilliantly colored bird still sits perched upon his shoulder, dozing off in the cool shade of the building.

"Thank ya, ladies." Seaborne says, giving the Scales another bow.

"Come see us soon." Lena replies, grinning.

As he waves goodbye, Seaborne can hear the man behind him being judged. Then, Christina shouts out in disgust. He turns just in time to see her whispering furiously to her sister.

Lena shakes her head angrily, and quickly touches the man on his nose. The moment her finger makes contact with him, he crumples lifeless to the ground.

Seaborne walks along the deck of the enormous ship, between the high-rising wooden structures that have been built along the sides. Homes and shops, rooms and apartments, turning the vessel into a small city.

He finds his prize officers waiting outside the admiral's chambers, ready to find out if their positions will be confirmed. If the admiral approves, they will officially become captains of the ships Seaborne had captured. If not, the ships will be added to the pirate fleet and the prize officers resume their previous commissions.

"Men, I wish ya all luck." Seaborne says, as he leads them into the chamber.

The commodore stands waiting in the room. "Was the new recruit found wanting?" He asks.

"The Scales cleared him." Seaborne replies. "My crew is attending to him and the other new men."

A door in the rear of the chamber opens, and the admiral steps into the room.

"Captain, how was your last expedition?" The silver haired man asks, taking a seat behind a desk made of weathered wood.

"Fruitful, as ya can see." Seaborne replies, gesturing to his prize officers. "We captured four ships, admiral. Here is an inventory of their cargo and a list of their crews. I present to ya the prize captains of my fleet. First Mate Goodman, Coxswain Waters, Boatswain Bradley, and Oleg the Navigator."

"Thank you, Captain. Which of their posts would you have me affirm?" The admiral asks, rifling through the accounts and dockets of the captured ships.

"If it please ya, I would affirm First Mate Goodman. He has prize officered over a dozen captured vessels in his day. I believe it is time for him to rise to captain." Seaborne answers, nodding to the first mate.

"A dozen!" The admiral exclaims. "Why haven't I already promoted you?"

"Cap'n Noft n'er sa fit, I s'pose. I n'er askt why. Aint m' place ta ques'n m' cap'n, sir." Goodman replies.

"Commendable. I suppose you are pleased to have left Captain Noft and joined Captain Seaborne?"

"Aye. I… If 'm be'n tru'ful…" He turns to Seaborne, "I tot ya was green, cap'n. I tot ya nee' ma help. Bu' I 'no 'is ol' foo' 'ere was wron' 'bout 'at."

"Well then…" The admiral replies, clearing his throat. "Upon the recommendation of your commanding officer, Captain Seaborne, I, Ishmael, Admiral of the Pirate Fleet, name you Captain Goodman. And henceforth infer upon you all the duties, responsibilities and hardships that accompany that position. Captain Seaborne will decide which of the seized ships you receive and help you fill her crew with able bodied sailors." Turning to the rest of the prize officers, the admiral adds. "You shall all receive a captain's share of the plunder, thank you for bringing these ships to port. You are relieved of your prize duties, and returned to your former stations. Men, your reward..."

Commodore Shipman hands a leather bag to each of Seaborne's men, filled to the brim with pieces of silver, stamped with the seals of the sovereigns of a hundred nations.

The Glorious Knights and Illuminated Priests of the Order of Justice, Honor, and Chivalry 2

"A bird has arrived!" Friar Philip shouts, stumbling into the tower.

"From Simon and Kevin?" Sir Joel asks.

"It looks to be, let's see what it says."

They unroll the scroll attached to the pigeon's little leg.

To Friar Philip, and Sirs Marcus and Joel

I regret to inform you that our brother,
Sir Kevin, was lost at sea. Pirates raided
our ship and have taken him captive. As
to his fate, I cannot say.

The High Priest has requested I stay in
the Great City, to serve the Order. You
must go on without me. Continue our

work, and keep the peace in the Southern
Realm.

Sir Simon the White

P.S. You have been ordered to pick a
leader from amongst yourselves, I trust
you will choose wisely.

"The White Knight…" Sir Marcus says, his jaw hanging in disbelief.

"Unbelievable…" Chimes Friar Philip.

"So, I will obviously become our new leader, agreed?" Sir Joel asks.

"We vote!" Exclaims Sir Marcus.

The men each write a name on a slip of paper, and throw them in a helmet. Friar Philip takes them out to count the vote.

"One for myself, one for Sir Joel, and one for Sir Marcus…"

"Okay…" Sir Joel says, waving his hands. "One more time. But this time, no voting for yourself."

"Fine," says Sir Marcus. "I vote for Philip."

"Thank you Marcus, I vote for you." The friar adds, with a smile.

"Well, well… Whomever shall I pick?" Sir Joel ponders, drumming the tips of his fingers together as he paces between the men.

"Just choose!" Friar Philip scolds, "There is business that needs attending to."

"Well then, Philip. I pick Sir Marcus, for he didn't rush me."

"So be it…" The friar says, "On to business. We sent a carrier pigeon to the Order's outpost in the Frozen City weeks ago, yet no reply has come. In that time, Sir Simon has managed to sail all the way to the Great City and send us back a letter."

"What would you have us do, Sir Marcus?" Sir Joel asks. "First decision as leader, don't mess it up."

The knight thinks for a moment, "We shall make for the Frozen City. Pack your horses, we leave within the hour."

Tiaries 5

"Where do you think he is?" She asks, nervously pacing along the pier.

"I haven't a clue." Her brother says, staring over the river.

"Why won't they let you on the ship?"

"I am not part of the Emperor's household. I am not on the council. I am not a newly selected councilor. I am no one." He answers, shrugging. "Why would they let me on board?"

"Well…" She says. "I am a councilor now, right? Don't they have to listen to me?"

"I don't think that's how it works…"

"Damn!" She shouts, scrunching up her face.

What's the good of having been selected, if I can't even get my brother invited onto a boat…?

"It will be fine, Tiaries." Jaties says, laughing as he puts his arm around her. "The troupe leaves for the Pillar tomorrow. I can ride with them. Everything is going to be alright."

"I know… It's just, we haven't been apart since…" She shuts her eyes, trying to fight back tears.

"I'm sure Councilor Lingonberry will tell them I can board. And if not, I always have a backup ride. We can go look for him if you like. As long as we stay around the dock, I don't want to miss them…"

"Yes!" She exclaims, smiling and grabbing his arm. "Let's take a look around. Maybe someone has seen him."

Next to the loading area, they see Ral speaking with a young lady. He hugs her, then turns and briskly walks towards them.

"Hi, Ral!" Tiaries says, giving him a smile.

"Hello. I was about to go aboard, are you two coming?" He asks, a look of stifled sadness in his eyes.

"Trying…" She replies, "They won't let my brother on. Have you seen Councilor Lingonberry? We're hoping he can sort it out."

"No, sorry. I've been with a friend all morning. She is about to leave for A'Tannia."

"Thanks anyway!" Tiaries exclaims, touching his arm. "We're going to keep looking. I'll see you inside."

Ral gives them a forced grin, then heads up the gangplank and boards the Emperor's ship.

A large gathering of men on horseback are congregated near the entrance to the docks, saying goodbye to the boy from the Plains, Kzhee. The group begins to dissipate, leaving him and a pretty girl behind. She throws her arms around him, sweetly kissing his lips.

Tiaries hears her say, faintly, "We are going to be together. I don't care what it takes…"

"Let's not bother him." Tiaries says, pulling Jaties away from the young couple. "I don't think he wants to talk…"

Across the way, the prince is speaking to his friends. The boys from the archery contest. They exchange hugs and goodbyes, before departing in separate directions.

Prince Relorn walks towards her and Jaties, heading to his father's ship.

"Good morning, your highness." She says, with a curtsy.

"Hello…" He replies, his eyes heavy and bloodshot.

"Have you seen the councilors, perchance?" She asks. "The guards won't let my brother on board. He is coming to the Pillar to be an actor, and joining the Emperor's Men. Lanties said he could come..."

"Follow me." The prince says, shrugging absently.

They grab their belongings and hurry in his wake. The guards begin to stop Jaties outside the ship, but a look from the Emperor's son causes them to back up, letting them pass.

"Thank you!" She says, throwing her arms around Relorn. He gives her a startled look, then awkwardly pats her on the back before leaving.

A steward shows her and Jaties to their own staterooms. Her room has a view of the river and a small balcony, just large enough for her to step outside and feel the gentle breeze. For the first time in days, she is relaxed.

It's going to be okay...

Each night of the voyage, they all meet in the ship's dining hall for the evening feast. The Emperor's chefs serve the best food she has ever tasted. Each meal bringing some new delicacy she had never seen before.

Tiaries had sipped beer with the performers at the carnival a few times. But on the ship, they had every beverage imaginable. She had become particularly fond of lemon wine. One of the servers made it for her, muddling in blueberries and mint leaves. Since then, she had ordered one with every meal.

She had been to the library each day looking through the volumes of books, reading stories and histories. Tiaries had been reading scripts her whole life, and loved it. But she had only ever seen a couple books before, back when she was young.

Not many people in Mr. Deepwater's carnival had kept them around. Some of the other actors weren't even literate, simply having learned the lines from watching the plays performed so many times before.

After a couple weeks of uneventful sailing, the Emperor's ship pulls into port. A small town, Boulder on the Baries, laying on the border of the Mountains and the Elven States. Outside the port, a caravan waits, ready to carry them the rest of the way to the Pillar.

They travel through the towering mountain range, a whipping breeze blowing past their traveling party, chilling her to the bone. She wraps a woolen blanket around herself, hiding in its warmth. Councilor Lingonberry takes a seat next to her on the roof of the caravan, handing her a steaming mug. Its contents smell sweet and rich.

"It's hot chocolate." He tells her, taking a sip from his own cup before pointing up to the peaks around them. "Do you see the terraces on the sides of the mountains?"

She nods, looking skyward. At the base, they seem like any other mountains. But halfway up, terraces and patios begin to wind and snake, wrapping and twisting around. Green vegetation sprouts from each level, like veins of emerald and jade weaving up the mountainside.

"Barbarians used to roam these lands, attacking settlements. So the mountain lords began building their cities high in the mountains. Each is unique, some are hollowed out with tunnels and chambers inside, protected, while others have their buildings carved into the mountainside or rising from the top." He says, pointing to a towering castle.

"Are there still barbarians here now?" She asks, nervously.

"No." He says, shaking his head. "When the Emperor's forefathers came into power, they drove them south, deep into the Wastes. They haven't been seen here for centuries."

The next day, their procession enters the valley from which the Pillar rises. It is a colossal column, reaching into the sky and breaching the clouds. A platform spirals around the edge, gently circling the outside, providing open area for housing, farms, ranches, fields and orchards. From the summit, multiple towers rise, each extravagantly colored and elaborately designed.

They approach the enormous structure. The caravan slows to a crawl, coming to a stop in front of a huge stone disk resting just inside the base of the Pillar.

Is this a lift? She thinks, shaking her head in disbelief as the caravan begins to move onto the circular platform. *There is no way this thing can be raised...*

As everything is finished being loaded on, she can feel the floor start to shake beneath them. Her jaw drops, as men situated around the edge of the circle raise their arms, somehow making the enormous stone disk begin to rise.

They pass by hundreds of levels created by the terrace that gently spirals around the outside of the Pillar. The feeling of the rising platform begins to make her nauseous, so she climbs back into the carriage and curls up in a blanket.

When they reach the summit, Tiaries looks out from the carriage window. The view takes her breath away. Mountaintops stretch beneath them, from one end of the horizon to the other. In the distance she can see the edge of the Elven States, a tiny section of green barely visible between two towering peaks.

Jaties gives her a hug, before leaving to follow an attendant to the Tower of Trade, where Councilor Lingonberry had told them the Emperor's Men live and perform. Porters begin unloading their luggage as the rest of the group is brought to the Emperor's Tower. She can hardly contain her excitement, as a valet leads her to her new home.

When the valet departs, Tiaries begins eagerly exploring her rooms. There is a large sitting area, a bedroom, a lavatory, and even a balcony. She steps outside, gazing off the patio towards the Eastern Sea shimmering far in the distance, visible through the mountain range.

She curls up in a large cushioned chair outside, drifting off to sleep.

When she opens her eyes, Tiaries sees nothing but a blinding gray haze surrounding her, suffocating... At first she panics. But then a path opens before her, as a cloud drifts listlessly by, and the evening sky breaks into view.

Tiaries stands up, feeling her way through the milky haze, entering her apartment. She picks a few purple berries out of a bowl, snacking on them as she crawls into her bed, sinking comfortably into the goose down mattress. The chill from outside slowly fades away, as the blankets swaddle her like an infant.

When Tiaries wakes, the light of morning is just starting to peek through her curtains, bathing her face with a gentle glow. She throws on some comfortable clothes, then departs for the dining hall.

Surveying the room, she sees members of court seated in little clusters, dressed in colorful robes and dining upon the most decadent of breakfasts. Ral and Chion are sitting at one of the tables towards the end of the hall, talking to Rika.

She walks up and sits with them, smiling and saying good morning. Ral gives her a nod and a hello, while Chion waves a friendly hand. Rika looks up at her with a mouth full of hotcakes, and a syrupy smile.

"Do any of you know what time training starts?" Tiaries asks.

"They said to meet here, I think we may be early." Chion answers, looking around the cavernous room.

A server stops by their table and asks Tiaries what she would like for breakfast.

She shrugs her shoulders, "What do you have?"

The server grins. "Anything you would like, my lady."

Tiaries thinks for a moment. "I am not sure. Do you have elvish toast?"

"Yes, my lady."

"With butter, and boysenberry jam?" She adds, with an elvish smile.

"Of course, my lady." He says, running off to relay her order to the chefs.

"Is this for real?" She asks the others. Her already large eyes open even wider as she gawks in disbelief.

They nod and mumble through bites of food. Ral eats sliced fruit and porridge, while Chion snacks on boiled eggs and cream sauce, resting upon slices of ham and toast. Rika's plate of hotcakes stands almost as tall her head, dripping in syrup and butter.

Rika is the first to finish, leaning against the back of her chair and patting her belly in contentment. "I hope they don't make us run…" She tells the group. "It's not *that* kind of training, right?"

"I heard we have to run the entire way around the Pillar!" Tiaries says, trying not to giggle.

"Oh please no…" Rika squeaks, letting out a burp.

"I'm just teasing, I'm sure they won't make us run." Tiaries grins, patting her on the head.

The next to join them is the girl from the Firelands, Jia. She is dressed in a tightly wrapped silk dress, exposing her shoulders and arms. An elaborate golden comb, shaped like a hibiscus, is tucked above her ear. A flame dances upon the jeweled ornament, licking her face and hair as it climbs up into the air.

How does that not burn her? Tiaries thinks in amazement, unable to look away.

Jia sits next to Ral, taking a quarter of grapefruit off his plate and flashing him a smile. She waves off the server as he approaches to take her order.

"I don't want to train on a full stomach." Jia announces to the table, nonchalantly. Keeping her gaze fixated on the door.

Kzhee and Relorn enter next, walking in together. Jia offers the prince the seat next to her, cheerfully asking him about his morning.

Rosemary is the last to join them, tightly bundled in a long armed dress. Snow white gloves cover her hands, running past the sleeves of her gown. She looks like she's been crying, the red in her eyes is accentuated even more by the pale white of her face and clothes.

Councilors Sage and Maestas enter, as the group finishes eating.

"Come with us." Sage says, leading them out of the room.

The group exits the Emperor's Tower, making their way through the lavish gardens that surround it. Flowers and plants from every realm decorate the weaving paths, fountains bubbling and gurgling around each bend. Tiaries opens her arms as they walk through the sunlight, squinting her eyes as she turns her head towards the sky, letting the warmth wash over her.

"You look like you're dancing when you walk." Chion says.

She smiles at him, then spins on her toe with a flourish. As she does, the flame on Jia's comb comes to life. It jumps off the jewelry and lands on its master's shoulder.

Tiaries looks at it, as it spins and dances. Copying her movements at first, then beginning to invent its own. She laughs and points, making the fire dance faster.

Jia holds her hand out for the burning figure to jump on. It gracefully leaps to the outstretched palm, then continues to dance.

"Can it turn into anything?" Chion asks, entranced by the flame.

"Probably." Jia replies. "Though it usually just copies what it sees."

"What would happen if it jumped on me?" He asks.

"You wouldn't want that…" She says, twirling her hand in circles, swirling the flame through the air like a ribbon trailing in the wind.

Why can't I do something amazing like that? Tiaries asks herself, gazing into the fire.

They follow the councilors off the trail and into a wooded area, filled with hundreds of different types of trees, leaves and petals of every imaginable color. They cross a small ornate bridge, reaching across a babbling brook that trickles through the woods. The councilors come to a stop in a clearing, near the edge of the Pillar.

Councilor Maestas is the first to speak, addressing the group. "We have been telling you that your training starts today, but it is not training in the traditional sense. There will be no end to your lessons, no graduation date. As long as we councilors are alive, we will continue to train you, to teach you. And in turn, we will strive to learn from you as well. Your abilities are far greater than you could ever imagine. But they are untrained, unrefined. Most people who are born with gifts never come near to what they could achieve, simply because they don't realize they can be more… You will all be more. Today we plant the seeds of your future, and you shall grow ever stronger… Each step you take, no matter how small or misplaced, brings you closer to your potential greatness."

"Thank you, Ernesto." Councilor Sage says, clapping his hands. "Let us begin! I want you each to tell us, what do you think your gift is? What do you think you are capable of?"

Jia steps past Tiaries, moving to the front of the group, fearlessly addressing the councilors. "My name is Huo Jia, and I can control fire." She snatches the flame from her shoulder and throws her hand forward, sending a fireball blasting off the side of the Pillar."

"Thank you, Jia." Councilor Sage tells the girl, grinning. "Do you need that particular flame? Is it, unique?" He asks, pointing to the burning figure standing akimbo on her hand, chin tilted up.

The flame turns away from Councilor Sage, crossing its arms as if offended by his question. Jia smirks at it, then answers. "I don't know. It's been around since I can remember. We would play in my room when I was a child. When no one was around, it would jump down from a torch and dance with me. My father never believed me, he thought I had invented an imaginary friend. Until the day came it couldn't be ignored anymore..."

Jia tosses the flame back on her shoulder, rejoining the group. Then Ral steps forward, bowing his head to the councilors.

"I am able to heal wounds I receive. It only started happening recently though..." He says, pointing at scars on his chest and back. "Before a month ago, I bled just like anyone else. But in my most recent pit fight... I was split in two. Yet somehow the wound closed itself. Since then, the same thing happens anytime I am cut."

"Can you do it without being wounded?" Councilor Maestas asks.

"I don't think so." The muscular boy says. Holding his arm in front of him, as if trying to make something happen.

"Thank you, Ral." Councilor Sage replies.

"My gifts haven't been working since we arrived," Chion volunteers. "But I used to be able to hear things in the wind. Whispers, people's thoughts..."

"Yes, people without gifts are much more susceptible to their effects." Councilor Maestas says. "Mine own abilities are much less accurate when being used on someone gifted. You will all most likely find this to hold true to some extent. For you, Chion, a good benchmark of progress will be if your abilities begin working on your fellow selectees."

Chion nods, then steps back, retreating to the shade of a large oak.

"I can turn into a mouse!" A voice squeaks, from the back of the group.

Tiaries turns to see Rika moving forward. As soon as she is standing away from everyone's feet, the girl suddenly disappears and a mouse begins scurrying through the tall grass. She reappears as quickly as she had vanished. A little girl again, only with a tail still protruding from behind her shorts.

A murmur of laughter shifts through the group. Councilor Sage clears his throat, pointing to the tail. Rika's face turns pink from embarrassment. She blinks her eyes tightly, quickly making the appendage disappear.

Relorn steps up, "I guess I'll go next." He kneels down, pushing away some grass to expose the soil below. He begins working the dirt with his fingers, sifting through it. Then he pinches a hearty clump, and pulls a perfectly formed arrow from the ground, fletching first. The sharply pointed head gleams in the sunlight, shimmering black like onyx.

"You have your family's gift as well, no?" Councilor Maestas asks.

The prince takes the arrow and slams it to his palm, but the point doesn't break his skin. Instead, it chips and slides off, as if the surface of his hand is made of stone."

"Very good," Councilor Sage nods. "Thank you, Prince Relorn."

A silence falls over the group, as those who have not gone yet look around at each other.

*Just get it over with... S*he tells herself, before stepping up.

"Hello, I am Tiaries. For those of you eyeing my ears, yes, I am an elf." She smiles and strikes a pose. "My gift is being able to bring people back to life."

Everyone looks at her, dumbstruck and jaws agape.

"Wait!" Rosemary gasps, "I accidentally froze a boy back home. The grand marshal's son, Bastion. Could you bring him back to life?"

"I'm sorry..." She tells Rosemary. "It only works for fifteen seconds after they die. Any longer and... Well, any longer and it doesn't work."

"It's ok..." The Southern girl whispers, the fleeting look of hope quickly melting from her face.

"Would you care to go next, Rosemary?" Councilor Sage asks.

"Okay... When I touch my lips to anything living, it freezes solid." She says, bitterly. "I shouldn't be here. I could hurt someone. I'm too dangerous..."

"Rosemary." Councilor Maestas says, gently. "Kzhee here thinks that he could accidentally strike someone he loves with a bolt of lightning. Ral is scared he is going to turn into a puddle of water, and that will be the end of him. Tiaries is terrified someone she loves will die, and she will be too late to help..."

What? Tiaries' stomach curls as the councilor glances at her. She tries to choke down the need to hurl. *How can he...?*

"Jia may not be afraid, but she holds herself back." The councilor continues, locking eyes with the Firelander. "You think you could lose control, don't you?"

Jia looks away, pretending not to hear him.

"See, Rosemary. If there is anywhere you *should* be, it is here." He says, smiling. "And as dangerous as you think you are, there are people around you far more so."

As if to demonstrate the point, Kzhee holds his arm out towards a yellow leaved tree nearby, its branches reaching over the stream. A slight flinch of his shoulders and chest, and a blinding strike of lightning flashes from the sky. Ripping the tree in half.

"That's what I can do..." He says, shrugging, as the tree smolders behind him, spewing smoke into the air.

For the next couple hours, the councilors speak to them about life on the Pillar. The people they will need to know, and how they are expected to behave. They take a tour, stopping by the city square, seeing the amphitheater, the library, and the grand fountain. They walk past the great lift, leading down to the ground a thousand feet below.

Councilor Sage explains how the lower castes live on the spiral circling the Pillar. That this is the only place nearby where food is grown. Not enough to feed everyone in the Pillar though, the rest has to be imported from the Southern Trading Company and the Flying City.

Next, the group stops by all the towers, learning the types of businesses and people who occupy each. All except the Tower of Earth, which they are told is off limits.

When they finish their tour, the councilors drop them off back at the dining hall.

Councilor Inzu arrives after lunch, escorting them to training grounds outside the Tower of Might.

"We will begin to work with melee weapons today. You will need to familiarize yourselves with all types of armaments, so you can be prepared for any situation." She draws a long, curved sword from a scabbard on her back, then tosses it into the air.

Out of nowhere, Councilor Quezada appears, catching the sword and swinging it at Inzu. She jumps back, grabbing a staff from a nearby stand and deflecting his strikes. Then, dropping to the ground, she sweeps the stave under his feet, tripping him.

Before Quezada can hit the ground, he vanishes. Reappearing behind Inzu and striking again. She parries the blow, then throws her arms out wide. As she does, a purple aura begins to burn around her, emanating from her skin. The staff vaporizes from her hand in a violet flash, along with her clothing, leaving behind nothing but white hot chain metal armor.

Quezada flinches away from the extreme heat radiating off her body. Dropping the sword, he vanishes again, reappearing next to the awestruck onlookers. Inzu grabs the sword, then gives a bow.

"Thank you, councilor." She says, to Quezada, before addressing the rest of them. "As you can see, in the blink of an eye your own weapon can be turned against you. Be prepared for anything. To die by one's own sword would be a cruel fate."

They each grab a practice weapon and pair up. Jia asks her to be partners, so they find an open area and begin. Years in the theatre have made her a better than average swordsmith, and she is able to deflect almost all of Jia's advances. The flame on her opponent's shoulder waves its fist, as if swinging an imaginary sword, pretending to fight along with the girls while laughing a silent laugh.

Rosemary and Rika practice with each other. Tiaries thinks it is an unfair matchup at first, until she witnesses Rika outmaneuvering the older, taller girl at every turn. Pushing her back with each advance. Rosemary keeps her chin high though, and keeps fighting, a look of determination in her eye.

Ral and Kzhee duel, but Ral wins each advance with a swing or two of his sword. Kzhee, unable to put up a fight, simply tries to deflect the furious strikes.

"Kzhee, work in with Relorn and Chion." Inzu shouts, "Ral, partner with Councilor Quezada."

The rest of them lazily practice, each eyeing the fight unfolding between Ral and Quezada. The two of them strike repeatedly. Their blunted blades bouncing and glancing off each other's, throwing splashes of glowing white sparks through the air.

Just as Ral appears to be gaining the upper hand, Quezada disappears, sending Ral's sword swinging limply through the empty air where his opponent had stood a moment earlier. Quezada appears behind him, putting his weapon to Ral's neck.

"That's a cheap trick!" Ral shouts, angrily.

"I recommend learning to use every trick at your disposal." The councilor replies, laughing as he throws down his sword. "Death discerns no difference, between honest men and cheats."

Rika 4

That night, the mouse scurries about its room, inspecting behind the chairs, tables, couch and bed. The furniture towers around the tiny rodent, as it searches for any cracks or holes that lead out of the chambers.

Near the curtain to the balcony, it finds a small hole in the mortar between a couple of stones making up the wall. Inside, the mouse runs through a hollow area, peeking through each crack it sees. There are openings to Jia and Rosemary's apartments, and upstairs a decent sized hole leads to the dining room. The mouse keeps running between the walls, up another floor, familiarizing itself with the layout of the tower.

Through a crack below, it can see the Emperor's throne. Darting through the opening, the mouse moves down the wall and into the throne room. Voices come from an antechamber across the hall. The mouse scoots along the wall, scurrying towards the noises. Squeezing under the door, it quickly moves for the shadows, staying out of sight.

"Yes, Jero. He undermined you at every opportunity. The old fool thought he was being far too clever for me to understand. You know how those pontificators think... Anyone who doesn't ramble on as they do must be a fool." Councilor Quezada says, venomously.

"That old blowhard has insulted me ever since I came into power... I have tolerated his quips and witticisms with serenity, but now he aims to corrupt my own son..." The Emperor pauses, lost in thought. "Send word to Atasio, have him deal with this."

"Of course, your highness." Quezada replies, exiting the room.

"Is there anything else?" The Emperor asks.

"I spoke with Old Man Dill, when I was in the Forest."
Councilor Lingonberry says.

"Ah, how is the elusive old fart?" The Emperor replies, "Until
you told me otherwise, I had always presumed he was a
legend... When will you take me to meet him?"

"He is famously not fond of visitors. If I try to bring anyone by,
somehow he and his home are gone. Vanished... The only time I
can see him is when I am invited, and alone."

"Next time you see him, remind him I am the Emperor, and what
an honor it would be to meet me."

"I will, your highness." Councilor Lingonberry replies, politely,
before adding. "A side note, hardly worthy of mention. There
was a young lady living with him, she looked quite a lot like the
little one on your son's council, Rika. Older than her, but very
similar. She had a little fox that followed her about... I'm sure
it's nothing, you know how youths from the Forest Realm look
alike."

Rika's stomach twists in knots, as the mouse starts to lose hold.
It darts out of the room, unable to keep control. At the throne,
she turns back into herself. Hiding under the golden seat, crying
and gasping.

Jas... I need to leave. I need to find her...

She regains her composure, then the mouse scurries into the
wall.

Thoughts fly through her head, as she paces furiously across her
bedchamber.

Lingonberry said he couldn't find him without an invitation. How could I ever find them?

If I ask him about it, he'll know I was listening...

Just wait... Calm down...

Maybe he will say something if I get him alone.

I could mention Jas... I could tell him about how she was lost, how our village was attacked...

Will he even care...?

After a sleepless night, she makes her way to the room where everyone eats. A man comes over to ask her what she will be having for breakfast. She tells him hotcakes, again, with blueberries and sweet cream. The comforting cakes relax her, calming her nerves from the night before.

Ral is the first to join her, just like yesterday. The rest flow in after, eating breakfast quickly.

When they finish their food, Councilors Sage and Kroonson take them to the edge of the Pillar, where they practice shooting targets. Attendants launch clay birds from the side, and they each take turns shooting bows. Jia and Kzhee shoot fire and lightning at theirs, hitting much more often than those using arrows.

Rika struggles to pull back the string on her bow, sending an arrow flying off randomly into the sky. Councilor Sage brings her a shorter one, with deep curves coming from each side of the handle. When she pulls it back, the wood bends easily, helping her aim. The next arrow she lets go finds it target, making her grin.

That afternoon gives way to more training, but no Lingonberry…
For what feels like weeks, they train each day, each time a
different group of councilors working with them, but never the
elf…

One evening, as she paces on her balcony, a knock comes from
the door. Councilor Sage stands on the other side, giving her a
nod. "Good evening."

"Hello, councilor." She says, "How can I help you?"

"I want to give you some one-on-one training, little Forestling.
Let's go, I'll explain."

They walk through the tower, taking the lift down to the garden.
Morning-glories curl, while the night-blooming jasmine unfurls,
wide and beautiful and thirsty for moonlight.

She follows him up a flight of decorative stairs to a wooden
pavilion, built over an artificial pond. He steps to the edge and
makes a chirping sound. A pigeon flutters down, cooing and
nodding its head at the councilor.

"Most people like you, who are able to turn into an animal, never
learn how to turn into anything more than the first one. But with
proper training, you could learn how to turn into many other
things. As long as you are willing to work."

"I can work hard!" She shouts, sending the bird fluttering.

"Good, good." He says, patting her head. With a coo, he brings
the bird back down. "Touch the pigeon… Feel it… Think of
what it would be like to have feathers, to have wings."

She imagines it. Thinking about flying, gliding, soaring. She
touches the bird, ruffling its feathers, eliciting a coo of protest.

Concentrating, she tries to turn into the pigeon, but becomes the mouse instead.

"Try from here." He says, lifting her up so her feet are on the railing, her shirt fluttering in the wind.

She attempts again, but nothing happens.

"It's a lot to expect for you to be able to do it on the first try. We will work at it." Sage says, reassuringly. "Try again, one last time."

She extends her arms, letting the wind lift them as it blows beneath her cupped hands. She focuses on the bird… On the wind… Trying with everything she has.

"Still nothing…?" The councilor asks, chuckling. "Maybe this will help!"

His arms flash forward as he shouts, pushing her from the railing. She screams, startled by his shove, and falls headfirst. In the air she thinks about the bird, picturing it flying. For a moment she almost feels her bones lighten, before the icy water slaps her face.

Loak 2

Loak sits at the dining table, listening to Herny chattering on about one of his wives. She is pregnant again, he brags. It will be his fifteenth child.

"Praise the Lord above for the nurseries. I don't think I could handle being around them when they're pregnant." Herny says, chewing on a slice of beef steak.

"I don't see why you want so many wives, if you don't even like being around them... It seems illogical." Loak says, listening more to the musicians than Herny. Their lutes and harps weeping a serene melody.

"I'll take your opinion on women when you marry for the first time. Until then, just listen to my woes and feel sorry for me." His friend says, laughing.

"You know, people outside this tower don't marry more than one person. It's strange that we do... You think it's some right that you're entitled to, some privilege for being special. I think it's them trying to put us out to stud, and I don't want to be treated as livestock." Loak pauses, then sighs. "I'm sorry, I've drank too much, ignore me..."

Herny laughs, "If this is what it's like to be chattel..." He says, gesturing to the food and drink filled table, the band playing on the stage, the attendants running about, "Then call me a stallion. I am sure there are much worse ways to live."

Loak forces a smile and a nod. "You're right, you're always right. I am glad I have you Herny, I would probably go mad without you."

"Ah, you'd be fine." His friend says, clapping him on the back before turning to listen to the band.

That night, alone in his room, Loak changes out of his deep brown cloak and tunic. The uniform of the Earthmovers. He sneaks on a bright green shirt and dark silk trousers. The style that is currently popular in the Pillar.

Once dressed and ready, he approaches a section of his wall. Touching the stone, feeling its strength. On the other side of the wall is a ventilation shaft, leading vertically throughout the height of the tower.

He moves his hand forward, and the stones gently fall back, forming a platform suspended in the shaft. Loak steps onto the makeshift lift, then lowers it slowly to the bottom of the tower.

With a sweep of his hand the exterior wall parts, the bricks moving as easily as if drawing back a curtain, exposing the night sky. A gust of air flows in and rushes up the shaft, quickly ceasing as he steps out and seals the wall behind him.

Loak saunters towards the square, taking in the evening. Young friends and lovers sing and shout, and music drifts from every open door. Laughter and lutes play across the fountain, as people toss pieces of copper and bronze into the water, coins from all over the Empire glittering beneath the rippling surface.

He walks past the library, running up the stairs and weaving between the giant columns that line the façade. The scent of aromatic smoke engulfs him, drifting by as he descends the steps in front of the building. Winding through philosophers as they sit and discuss the complexities and simplicities of life and the world, pontificating between long puffs of their elegant pipes.

Moving past the Emperor's Tower, its sprawling gardens hidden behind its vast walls, Loak continues towards the Tower of Trade. He enters through the bank, avoiding the Earthmovers working the lift in the lobby.

The grand stairway lies before him, spiraling up. He takes a deep breath, before starting to ascend, around and around and around. He is huffing heavily after ten flights, stopping to catch his breath at a nearby tavern.

A few drinks later he continues on his way. The theatre is on the twenty-ninth floor. Sweat is dripping off his forehead as he finally reaches the landing. Stepping onto a patio outside to cool off, Loak looks towards the Tower of Earth. He tries to figure out which balcony is his, counting off the floors and windows.

After regaining his composure, Loak heads back to the theatre, purchasing a ticket and entering the darkened room. Making his way up to the mezzanine, he takes his seat. Gentle music emanates from behind the curtain, as the audience waits for the show to start.

Drums begin to pound, as the curtains rise and performers run on stage. The play is called *The Pirates of Paq'uthos*. It is the story of a group of pirates who land at the legendary city, then travel across the Plains, convincing people they are the Lords of the lost city of Paq'uthos and engaging in an array of adventures. The play ends with a climactic scene, a fight on the deck of a ship, after the pirate fleet has invaded Otter Harbor. The actor playing the pirate captain is captivating, as he swings across the stage on a rope, sweeping his sword and battling with the surrounding assailants. Loak feels his smile widen, as the captain laughs and dances across the makeshift ship.

As the performers take a bow Loak begins to cheer wildly, exhilarated by the commotion of the crowd and the deafening roar of applause. He makes his way out of the theatre, stopping into a nearby pub to grab a quick bite to eat.

People all around him laugh and gossip. Parents walk about, carrying babies much too young to be out so late. The ceiling vibrates from the music of a band playing a floor above. Loak loves the sounds of the Tower of Trade, the pulse of the Pillar. All night, the taverns and pubs stay open, the noise never ceasing. It is the only place he knows of where you can get decent food or drink at any time of the day or night.

He pays his tab, then turns to leave. Near the door he sees a group sitting and laughing around a table. Loak recognizes the faces of the actors from the show earlier, the captain among them.

"Hello," Loak stammers, approaching hesitantly. "It's an honor to meet you. I loved the show tonight, you were fantastic!"

"Thank you." One of the men replies, giving a hearty chuckle. "We can never hear enough praise."

"Would you care to join us?" A girl at the far end of the table asks.

"Yes, of course!" He exclaims, taking the seat next to the captain and giving him a smile. "Hi, my name is Loak."

"I'm Jaties, the newest member of the Emperor's Men" The captain replies, removing his hat and bowing towards Loak, exposing his pointed elven ears.

"Pleasure to meet you." He tells Jaties, before introducing himself to the rest of the table.

Jaties tells him about how he came to be part of the Emperor's Men. His sister had been selected for the Emperor's Due, and he had followed her here.

"Well, you are a fantastic actor!" Loak tells him, "The Pillar is lucky to have you."

"Thanks, I already love it here. The only thing I miss is the trees. When we worked in the carnival we were surrounded by trees every day, now the best I can get are some flowers and shrubs in the sunset garden…"

"I can take you to the garden of earth sometime!" Loak quickly volunteers. "Only Earthmovers are allowed in, but if we went sometime after dark, I'm sure it would be fine."

"I'd love to!" The elf shouts, grabbing Loak's arm. "Can we go tonight?"

"Yeah…" Loak stammers, nervously. "We can go now, if you want."

They excuse themselves from the table, heading out of the tavern. One of the performers shouts after them, "Hey!" As they turn around to look at him, the actor's features warp and twist into those of an old woman. With a crooked grin, she croaks, "Don't do anything I wouldn't do…"

Laughing as they exit, Jaties begins making his way to the lift.

"Could we take the stairs?" Loak asks, pulling him towards the stairwell.

They wind their way down the steps, floor after floor. Until they reach the bottom, exhausted. The summer night outside is perfect. A warm breeze caresses the towering city, rustling through the buildings and pulling the music of the festivities together, creating a harmonic clamor beautiful to behold.

He leads Jaties to the gardens, listening to the elf talk about life in the carnival. Traveling from town to town performing, yet somehow always yearning for stability, somewhere to call home.

All he wants is a home, and all I want is to see the world. How nice would it be if we could pick our fate…?

"Sorry, I don't know why I am rambling on like this…"

"No, please go on." Loak replies, "I like listening to you…"

"Thanks," Jaties says, smiling. "I always told myself I would never be too trusting."

They enter the garden of earth, inside the walls of the Tower of Earth. The tallest trees in the entire Pillar are there, reaching up towards the tower they surround. Jaties runs his fingers along the bark of the trees as they pass. Smiling, as if reuniting with a long lost friend.

"What's wrong with being too trusting?" Loak asks.

"I've seen it have very bad consequences." Jaties answers, quickly but solemnly. "I'll tell you about it, someday. I'm having a lovely time, and would hate to ruin the mood."

"Of course." Loak stammers, "If you ever want to talk…"

"I want to talk all about you." Jaties says, grabbing the trunk of a narrow tree, holding on with one arm and swinging around, coming face to face with Loak. They almost bump into each other, laughing.

Without thinking, Loak leans forward and kisses Jaties on his lips. He pauses, feeling the breath against his mouth, waiting to see if he pulls away, scared he might storm off.

But the kiss is met with reassurance, as Jaties cups Loak's neck and pulls him in closer.

"My last trip may have proved more worthwhile than we could have ever imagined." Lanties Lingonberry says, addressing the Emperor. The morning sun glaring through the eastern windows of the throne room.

"What do you mean?" Jero asks, enticed by the announcement.

Lingonberry holds out a piece of a statue in the shape of a hand, adorned with jewels and colored diamonds.

"What is that?" Quezada asks, leaning forward.

"I believe this is the hand of a golem." The elf replies, a smug smile on his face.

"Where is it from? What do you know?" The Emperor erupts, jumping up from his throne. "Speak, elf!"

"A man said he found it, in a village on the border of the Wastes. I think I know how to get there from his description."

"Go, go at once! Take anything and everything you need. Bring all the council with you, except Thorne."

"Should we bring the children?" Quezada asks.

"What do I care? Yes, bring them. Make them useful for something." Jero says, with a wave of his hand. "Quezada, tell the rest of the council and prepare the children. Lingonberry, scour the vaults and library, the Imperial archives, find out everything you can. Also, be sure to bring an Earthmover." He stares out of the enormous windows lining the throne room, softly laughing. "A golem army…"

That afternoon, Quezada and Kroonson train the children in stave and mace combat. The Plainsman seems fairly decent with a mace, and the elf girl is a natural with the staff.

"Have you fought with staves before?" He asks her.

"We used all kinds of weapons when we put on plays." Tiaries says, cheerfully.

Quezada gives her a nod and moves on. He sees the southern girl actually putting up a fight for once, her apprehension becoming less obvious.

She has stopped her constant crying. You have to be happy for that at least...

Kroonson fights with Ral, mace against mace. The pit fighter seems to be getting the upper hand on the councilor until Kroonson lets out a gripping wave of brilliant green sparks, crawling along the boy's mace and arcing towards his feet, shocking him and causing him to drop his weapon.

"Always be prepared." Kroonson says to Ral, grabbing a drink of water from a nearby bucket.

"Always be prepared..." Ral yells back, "I feel that's what all of you say when I am about to beat you, and you have to use some trick to win."

"He is right, Ral," Quezada says to the boy. "When a man is trying to kill you, there are no rules. You have proven you are a great fighter. No one here will deny you that. But you must learn when to fight hard and when to fight smart. Now tell me, how could you have avoided him shocking you there?"

"I don't know!" Ral says, in frustration. "I guess I could have stayed farther away from him. Given myself more room to jump away."

"There you go. Now use that next time. Remember, and prevent it from happening again. Swords can't cut you, but that doesn't mean you can't be hurt."

After the lesson, Quezada brings the group together, explaining that they will be leaving for their first mission the following morning. Murmurs of excitement and apprehension move between the children. He tries to quiet the group long enough to tell them to be ready at daybreak, before turning and going his own way.

Quezada heads back to the Emperor's Tower, stopping by his chamber first. He changes clothes and washes his face, looking himself over before leaving. Then he makes his way down the hall, through the winding tunnels, knocking on a familiar door.

Inzu opens it, smiling as she invites him into her quarters. The room smells of vanilla and blackberry, accented with a hint of something smoky.

"How are you, councilor?" The beautiful woman asks, lounging back against a couch.

"Very well, councilor. I hope I find you well too."

"Indeed, why so formal?" She asks, plucking a grape from its stem.

"Jero sent me to inform the councilors to be ready to leave tomorrow. He intends to send us and the children on some expedition, to find the fabled golem army."

"Any excuse to get out of here is fine by me." She says, shaking her foot restlessly. "I so envy you and your trip to the Plateau, three years away from this place…"

"I missed it here."

"Did you?" She asks, with a grin.

"I missed you. I… I get so angry when you aren't around."

Inzu slides up from her seat, pacing across the room towards him. A narrow slit in her dress exposes her long tan leg each time she takes a step. She pushes her body against his, feeling him swell up.

"I missed you too, but you are back now. No need to bemoan the past." She whispers, pulling his shirt off and running her fingers over his chest.

He slips her dress off, letting it fall around her feet. She looks smaller without it, but her naked body is beautiful, strong. He leans down and grabs her behind, pulling her against him. She jumps up and wraps her legs around his midsection, kissing him feverously on the face and neck.

Quezada carries her across the room, then falls with her onto the bed. She moans, as he moves forward, biting his lip to keep from yelling. He looks into her eyes and sees a purple fire burning within. Her warmth emanates, surrounding him.

He holds her in his arms, firmly, while she kisses his chest and smiles. Laughing here and there, for no particular reason.

"Well, at least we will get to go on this excursion together. Those nights on the river can be so cold…" She says, pretending to shiver, as she pulls his arms tightly around her.

Whack!

Her pole strikes against the bedpost, the hit dulled by the blankets and cushions she has wrapped around the wood. Sweat drips from her forehead as she continues practicing, striking the post over and over. Dodging imaginary advances, spinning, then jabbing the dummy with her staff. Repeating and practicing the moves the councilors had shown them.

Setting the staff down and taking a quick break, she pours a glass of water and walks out onto her patio, letting the cool night air chill her sweaty body. The training grounds are visible below, empty. Yet somehow the sight motivates her. She finishes the water in a gulp, quickly returning to her training.

The next morning, she waits for their departure, sitting outside the great lift. Rika takes a seat next to her, flashing a smile and saying good morning.

Have you been to the Wastes before?" She asks the young girl.

"No, I don't think so." Rika replies, "I don't remember ever leaving my village, before..."

Councilor Lingonberry spots them, and heads their way.

"Hello, councilor!" She says, "Will we be leaving soon?"

Before he can reply, Rika interrupts. "I was just telling Rosemary about the time soldiers attacked my village, and my sister and I ran off. We got separated, I haven't seen her since... She looks like me, just a few years older. I miss her, she was so nice. Always singing and dancing, and playing with her pet fox..."

Rosemary and the councilor both look at Rika awkwardly, perplexed by her outburst.

"I am sorry to hear that..." Rosemary whispers, putting a hand on the girl's shoulder.

The councilor offers his apologies too, before quickly turning and leaving them.

"I've never heard you speak about your family before." Rosemary says, "You can tell me about it, if you want."

"No thanks." Rika replies, devoid of emotion. Glaring at the councilor as he walks around and speaks with the others.

The road to the nearest river port is long and bumpy. It seems to take longer than the trip to the Pillar had, even though it is the same route.

They travel night and day, the drivers taking shifts. Rosemary has trouble sleeping in the jostling carriage, her energy building from days of missing her practices.

One night, she joins Chion on the roof of the caravan, sharing a smoke from his pipe. She coughs and hacks, while he laughs and hands her a flask of water. Afterwards she has to stumble to her bunk, but she sleeps peacefully for the first time since they left the Pillar.

The Emperor's boat waits for them at Boulder on the Baries, ready to embark upon their arrival. Rosemary picks the same room she had been assigned the time before, a stately suite near the rear of the vessel, situated off the top deck.

There are hardly any attendants on the ship, just the essential sailors and stewards, and one of the men who operates the lifts in the towers. Though she doesn't know why he would come, as there are no lifts on the ship.

Rosemary is pleased to be able to pick out some books from the small library on board, reading to help pass the time. She is also happy to be able to resume her training, setting up a practice dummy in her suite.

One day, tired of being cooped up, she asks Rika if she would like to practice with swords. The girl shakes her head, saying that she's tired. Next, she asks Tiaries, who cheerily agrees. Rosemary had been hesitant to ask her because the elf is so good, so much more experienced. But after weeks of practice, she was beginning to feel much more comfortable handling the weapons.

They make their way to the foredeck, beginning to practice on the swaying platform. The river mist swirls around them, drifting by as the ship cuts through the water, the afternoon sun trying to fight its way through the overcast. They laugh, dancing across the deck, exchanging blows and parries, turning the ship into a scene from some adventure story.

Don't embarrass yourself... Stay focused.

Relorn approaches as Tiaries shows off a new move. Rosemary, poorly attempting to imitate the swing, almost hits the prince in his face.

"Ohh! I'm so sorry…" She says, blushing ruby red.

"No problem." He replies, laughing. "Can I join in?"

"Of course!" Tiaries responds, throwing him a sword. "You two practice with each other, while I demonstrate."

Rosemary focuses on the movements Tiaries shows them, as Relorn squares off in front of her. They start slowly, then begin to speed up as they find their rhythm.

Once they've learned a few moves Tiaries joins in the sortie, the three of them trading swings.

"Let's get her!" Rosemary says, to Relorn, cheering as they charge together, pushing Tiaries back to the ship's rail.

"I give! I give!" She shouts, giggling and tossing down her sword.

"And the students become the masters!" Relorn cheers, holding his wooden stick in the air.

"That was fun," Tiaries says. "We should do it again sometime."

"Yeah, definitely." Rosemary replies, ecstatic to have found someone to practice with.

Tiaries waves goodbye, then retreats inside, leaving Rosemary alone with the prince.

"You're getting really good." He tells her, taking a seat on a wooden bench next to the railing.

"Thank you." She says, sitting down with him, still holding her sword. "You are really good too."

"I'll never be as good as Ral, but I try… I am really good with a bow and arrow though. I could show you sometime, if you'd like, teach you some tricks." He says, blushing. The rose in his cheeks intensified by the sunset, glowing above the trees. Coral colored clouds floating in a sky of persimmon and plum.

"That would be lovely." She says, looking down at the ground nervously. "I don't have much practice with bows…"

"It's a plan then…" He stands, shivering slightly. "We should head inside for dinner. I bet they're all starting without us."

Ral 5

After a week on the river, their ship pulls into a small cove and drops anchor. Ral stands near the railing, ready to help the sailors lower the small rowboat used for going ashore. Kzhee runs up onto the deck to assist, anxious to get on land."

"I hate the water." Kzhee tells him, "I can't wait to get back on solid ground."

"What's the problem? It's just a boat." Ral replies, grinning.

The landing party heads for shore, Kzhee, Ral, Quezada and Sage. They need to procure horses for the ride inland, not having brought their own. Councilor Sage tells them how dangerous the Wastes can be, how they have to be aware of all the possible pitfalls that might be waiting for them on the trail.

"How far away are we walking?" Ral asks.

"Another hour at most." Sage assures them, moving lithely for a man so short and stout.

Kzhee moans, trudging on. While Ral keeps his eyes out for trouble, scanning the tops of the surrounding dunes and cliffs.

"Why didn't we bring horses with us?" Kzhee asks.

"There isn't enough room on the ship for enough horses for all of us," Sage answers. "Plus, on the off chance we find something, we will need the space to bring it back."

Close to two hours later, they enter a small settlement. A couple children run around, chasing after each other and squealing gleefully. The councilors lead them to the stables nearby, looking for the groom.

They rent enough horses for everyone, roping them together for the trip back to the group. Kzhee effortlessly mounts a jet black horse, grabbing the reins of the unmanned stallions to guide them back.

Ral walks up to his horse, unsure of how to get on.

Which foot do I stick in?

He struggles trying to swing his leg up over the saddle, somehow ending up facing to the horse's rear.

Kzhee starts laughing at him. "What are you doing? Have you ever ridden before?"

"No. First time. Leave me alone." He shouts, trying desperately to stay mounted.

"What's the problem? It's just a horse." Kzhee says, mocking him.

He gets himself turned around, trying to follow his companions as they ride. Struggling to keep up and fighting to keep himself in the seat, Ral slips and slides each time the horse alters its gait. Unable to use the reins to keep centered, he hugs the horse's neck instead, holding on for dear life.

After an excruciating ride, they arrive back at the cove. The ship waits peacefully anchored, resting atop the still water.

"Hello!" Kzhee yells, trying to signal the rest of the group on the ship.

"I got it." Ral says, jumping into the water, swimming out to the boat and climbing up from a dangling rope.

They unload the ship and pack the horses, preparing to make their way south into the Wastes.

"Why are we camping near the village?" Jia asks, "Wouldn't it be better to just spend the nights here on the ship?"

"It is a twelve-hour ride." Councilor Lingonberry says, "And it could take us days to find what we came for. Best to be prepared."

"You'd better learn how to survive in the wild…" Inzu laughs, tightening the pack strap on Jia's horse. "Lanties, how often do we sleep outside?"

"Often…" Lingonberry replies, absently. His attention focused on a curling map and lodestone compass.

"At least you know how to ride a horse." Ral says, to Jia, as he starts to slip off the side of his saddle.

She gives him a laugh and smiles. "Put more pressure on your feet, in the stirrups, like your trying to stand. And quit squeezing the horse with your legs, that makes it think you want to go faster."

He tries to follow the advice, but doesn't improve greatly, still struggling to keep up with the group. They ride through grassy hills, rolling at the base of the looming mountain range above.

As evening falls, the group makes camp, opting to finish the trip the following morning. Councilor Sage opens a small cask of spruce beer, passing it around as they sit by the fire listening to Lingonberry tell stories. Ral sits next to the Earthmover that accompanied them on the trip.

"Hi, name's Ral." He says, offering his hand.

"Loak, good to meet you." The Earthmover replies

"You work on the lift in the Emperor's Tower, right?"

"I do."

"I couldn't handle that." Ral says, shaking his head. "Just standing there all day."

"It's all I've ever really known." Loak replies, "I day dream a lot… Helps pass the time."

He notices Loak looking at Tiaries, casting darting glances when her head is turned.

I wonder if he likes her. She's pretty, no reason he shouldn't.

"You have a thing for elves?" Ral asks, with a grin, pointing to Tiaries.

"What!?" He says, blushing. "No, no, no. I think I know her brother. I just don't know if I should say anything."

"Yeah, I forgot that she has a brother. I don't know if I have seen him since we arrived at the Pillar." He laughs, "I don't even know if we're allowed to leave the Emperor's Tower…"

"I know how that feels." Loak says, distracted.

The next morning, they pack up and continue riding for the village. Ral has sores on his rear and legs, caused by the saddle. He winces each time the horse jolts, cursing loudly and hoping the trip is almost over.

They stop for a break, to escape the midafternoon sun, relaxing under the shade of a wide tree. The councilors speak in hushed tones, pointing in the distance. Lingonberry breaks away from the group and approaches him.

"Ral, I would like for you to accompany Councilor Sage and myself. The village is over the next hill. We will find out what we can before coming in with everyone. We don't want to be seen as a threat."

"Of course, councilor."

"Also… keep your eyes open, stay aware. It may be we need you to use your sword." Lanties stares at him, the councilor's eyes devoid of their usual kindness and warmth. "Just to be painfully clear… I am giving you permission to kill anyone who appears to pose a threat to us. We are the law."

"I understand."

The three of them gallop over the hill, then slowly work their way up the steep incline, atop which the village lies. Winding and weaving through the low mountains takes longer than anticipated, and the golden sun begins to set behind them as they reach the outskirts.

Two burley men block their path, speaking words that Ral can not quite understand. Somewhat familiar, yet foreign. Sage replies, using the same strange words the men had. After a heated exchange, and the passing of some silver, the men lead them to a tent nestled at the base of a rising peak.

Aromatic smoke drifts through the curtains as they part. Inside, a small old woman sits, huddled around a brazier, wrapped in layers of furs. She seems happy and content, throwing little balls of ice and snow into the flames before her and watching them sizzle to nothing.

Sage says some incomprehensible words, then gestures to Lingonberry. The elf pulls a stone hand out of a satchel, handing it to the smiling woman.

She begins to chatter, in words only Sage understands. Then she opens a box, pulling out a large stone head, enormous rubies laid in place of eyes. Its features muddled, as if the sculptor had not intended to convey any distinguishable emotion or personality.

His cohorts' eyes light up and they begin whispering to each other with fervor, before simultaneously falling silent.

Sage speaks to the woman, offering her a leather coin purse. Her smile widens upon peaking inside the bag and she nods to them, then draws some lines into the dirt floor of her hut. The markings seem to mean something to Lingonberry, who nods along as the woman rambles. They thank her when she finishes, turning to leave. But she suddenly stands up and stops them.

"She says we cannot leave tonight," Sage translates. "The trail down is treacherous. She says we will certainly fall to our death."

"Better to fall, than have our throats cut in our sleep." Lingonberry replies.

"Have some faith, Lanties." Sage says, grinning, "If they wanted to kill us, we'd already be dead."

That night, after eating a meal of roasted fowl and corn, the villagers beat on drums and dance. Some working themselves into a frenzy. After the dancing, an old man tells stories around the fire, Sage translates for them.

"He says there are giants living in the caves behind us," Sage explains. "Their feet quake the earth, and they eat intruders."

"Here's to finding giants." Lingonberry says, holding up his wineskin.

After the festivities are finished, a young girl shows them to a small hut. Empty except for a softly burning fire. They curl up in furs, borrowed from the villagers.

"Sleep with one eye open." Sage says, drifting asleep.

In the corner of the room, Ral can see Lingonberry laying against the back of the hut. As the elf closes his eyes his outline begins to shimmer and dissolve, slowly fading into the background, until he disappears completely into the shadows.

Kzhee 5

Night falls as they wait for their missing party members. Crickets chip about the camp and moths flutter around the fire, dancing dangerously close to the flames.

"Do we go and look for them?" Inzu asks, Councilor Maestas.

"No." He says, without hesitation.

Kzhee whispers to Relorn, "Why are they always turning to Maestas when they don't know what to do?

"That's his thing." The prince replies, taking a swig from his leather flask. "He always seems to know the best course of action."

The group sits in silence, waiting for any sign or sound from the others. Wind rustles through the tree growth around them, chilling the camp and sending a shiver through Kzhee's body.

"Did you feel that?" Rika whispers.

"What?" Kzhee asks.

"Something…"

Rika vanishes, the mouse running around where her feet had just been, quickly scurrying away from the fire. Its eyes peering through the darkness.

"Something big…" Rika says, reappearing near the edge of the camp.

Kzhee holds his finger up to his lips and points in the direction of Rika's stare. Jia and Inzu step to the front of the group. Jia's flame burns brightly, searching the night.

Inzu gestures for everyone to back up. As they do, she begins to burn with a fierce purple and white glow, illuminating the area around them with a blinding light. They all look around, but find nothing.

Rika, appearing confused, apologizes for startling the group. She sits back down, still constantly looking nervously over her shoulder.

"We should go look for them," Kroonson grunts. "It's been too long."

"Be patient…" Maestas replies, passing Kroonson a cup of beer.

The Plainsman pushes the beverage away, storming to the outskirts of the camp. Strands of greenish lightning leap from his hands, illuminating the darkness around him.

"So I take it you'll be on first watch?" Quezada yells, as Kroonson moves out of sight.

They turn in for the night, with Maestas and Kroonson on the first round of guard duty. Kzhee lays on the dirt, staring at the sky above. Too scared to sleep. He looks around at his cohorts. Jia struggles, trying desperately to get comfortable. Rika decides to sleep as the mouse, and is now curled up under a rock, close enough to the fire to stay warm. Tiaries tosses restlessly in her sleep, while Relorn and Chion slumber soundly, having passed a pipe around for hours after dinner. Loak the Earthmover looks wide awake, staring off into the night. Quezada and Inzu lie peacefully, laid out near the burning embers, seemingly more comfortable than the rest.

Kzhee feels the need to relieve himself but tries to wait for it to pass, until he cannot hold it any longer. Getting up from his furs, he makes his way into the woods, heading in the direction he had last seen Kroonson pacing.

In the dim moonlight, Kzhee is barely able to see anything. He feels his way through the trees, but quickly gives up on finding the councilor. Approaching a stump, he begins to make water, sighing with relief. As he looks up at the stars, he notices one of the nearby trees move. He pulls his pants up, startled. Then sees it beginning to move again, walking towards him and growling.

Kzhee screams, throwing his arms up to shield himself. As he does, a boom ruptures through the trees, and lightning cracks, striking the advancing monstrosity. The creature shrieks, and falls to the ground, grabbing its side in pain.

Turning and running from the thing, Kzhee sprints back to the camp and starts yelling for everyone to wake up. Inzu is the first to reach him, her skin beginning to radiate, lighting up the camp with a strong purple glow and casting eerie shadows from the trees.

"What is it?" She asks, flames raging between her hands.

"Something huge, in the woods, as big as a tree. It came at me, but I shocked it." He struggles to get the words out, shivering uncontrollably.

"Show us." Quezada says, approaching from the camp.

Kzhee takes them into the woods, to where the creature had fallen.

"What in the…" Inzu stammers, casting her fiery light over the scene.

A huge trail leads away from where the thing had fallen. The ground is ripped apart, and the nearby trees uprooted, as if something had drug a giant boulder away tearing through anything in its path.

"How could this happen?" Relorn asks, "What could do something like this?"

"Bear?" Quezada suggests.

"No…" Rika says, quietly from the back of the group. "That was way too big to be a bear."

"Get back to the fire, everyone." Maestas barks.

They re-group at the camp, everyone eyeing the surrounding forest. Unable to fall back asleep, the group sits tensely ready to fend off an attack, prepared for a fight.

Yet, as the night dwindles on, the attack never comes. The black sky gives way to deep indigo. Gradually lightening, bluer and bluer, until the first piercing rays of morning blindingly erupt over the horizon.

With the sun's light behind them, the group makes their way back to inspect the track scoured into the ground. They follow the trail, amazed by the uprooted trees and displaced boulders, thrown out of the way by whatever had run through. The tracks end abruptly, leading directly into the side of a rocky outcrop at the base of the mountains.

"So, let me get this straight…" Jia says, shaking her head. "Whatever was snooping around the camp last night is big enough to rip trees from the ground, but also nimble enough to scale the face of a cliff?"

"It would appear so." Inzu says, eyeing the mountainside above.

"Or…" Maestas ponders, knocking on the rock in front of the tracks.

"Or what? It ran into the mountain?" Inzu replies, a skeptical look in her eyes.

"Loak?" Quezada asks, "Can you move this boulder?"

The Earthmover lifts his arms, quaking the ground around them, and the large stone begins to rise into the air. As Loak casts it aside, a cave opening is revealed behind.

"Well then," Inzu says. "It looks like we have something here."

"What are you all doing?" A voice calls out from above.

Ral, Lingonberry and Sage make their way down the side of the mountain, their gear and packs nowhere to be seen.

"Where have you been!?" Quezada shouts.

"The villagers wouldn't let us make the return in the dark." Sage says, nonchalantly. "Let's grab some supplies and get back, if we don't make an early start we will be stuck up there another night."

"We have an issue down here." Quezada replies, "Something huge was lurking about the camp last night. Kzhee attacked it, but by the time we investigated, something had drug it away to this cave here."

"Did it attack anyone?" Lingonberry asks.

"No," Kzhee says. "I saw it when I was…"

"It snuck up on him while he was pissing." Maestas laughs.

"Well if it didn't hurt anyone, what does it matter? If Kzhee let it have a shock, I can't imagine it wants another," Sage says.

"What if our camp gets rifled through while we're away?" Inzu questions.

"Loak, can you close this cave?" Sage asks, pointing down the tunnel.

The Earthmover nods, waving his hands through the air and sealing the walls together deep into the opening.

"There you are." Sage says, with a grin. "Let's go."

After packing up the needed supplies and food, the group climbs up the mountainside, making their way to the settlement above. Sage and Lingonberry lead the way to an enormous cave entrance, lying behind the huts and tents.

"This is where the artifacts were found, most of the locals are too afraid to enter though. We were unable to find anyone willing to guide us, but the village elder drew a map." Lingonberry announces, leading the way into the cave.

Inside the large chamber the light quickly fades, dimmer and dimmer. Growing ever darker as they travel deeper. A whistling sound begins to emanate from a narrow passage ahead, an offshoot of the main chamber.

"The elder said the cave is a large loop. If we follow it around, we will end up back at this smaller passage here." Sage says.

They follow the larger path deep into the mountain. Inzu's fiery blaze lights their way, magnified by Jia's flame and Kroonson's creeping sparks.

The cave leads miles underground, winding through the depths. They travel deeper, navigating through a maze of rock formations hanging from the ceiling and rising from the earth.

The tunnel opens up ahead, giving way to a large cavern. The walls and ceiling are moist, dripping with liquid. Pools lay across the ground, formed from the seeping fluid.

"Over here!" Inzu shouts, calling the group to a far corner of the camber.

"What is it?" Lingonberry asks, excitedly rushing over to her.

They all look at the pool that Inzu stands above. Her burning aura casts light into the depths, showing a small opening at the bottom of the murky water.

"I'll check it." Ral says, jumping into the small pond.

Kzhee shivers as his friend jumps into the icy water, disappearing. Ral stays under for a minute, then two. No bubble or ripple to indicate life beneath the still surface. Just as Kzhee is about to say something, a shadow appears from the abyss. Those standing closest to the pool jump back in shock, as Ral emerges from the water, coughing and gasping.

"It's a..." Ral says, between coughs. "Bit of a swim... I wasn't able to see much, but there seems to be a large passage on the other side."

"Could Loak open a way for us?" Sage asks.

"It's pretty far in, and there are a few turns. I'm not sure if I would even be able to show the way from up here." Ral replies.

"We shouldn't mess with the inside of a mountain." Maestas says. "If the ceiling caves in it will be the end of us all."

"So, through the water then?" Quezada asks.

"Yeah," Inzu nods. "I will go through first with Ral, and light up the other side. Jia, you come through last, so there is light on this end.

"I... I can't go under there..." The girl stammers, looking at the flame on her shoulder.

"Leave her, there should be someone on guard anyway." Quezada says. "Someone else stay too."

"I will..." Kzhee volunteers, glaring at the turbid water with displeasure.

Better than jumping into that...

"Fine," Sage says.

"Should we leave two of the young ones alone out here? It could be dangerous…" Inzu says, apprehensively.

"Those two?" Lingonberry laughs. "I would be more worried for anything that has the misfortune of stumbling upon them…"

Chion 6

Chion takes a long draw from his pipe, filling the air with smoke as he exhales. He hands the pipe and his pouch of leaf to Jia, asking her to keep it dry, then approaches the edge of the pool. Watching Tiaries and Rika jump in and swim towards to the opening, he dives in and follows after them, Councilor Quezada on his tail.

The underwater tunnel is long and dark. The only light comes from the opening on the other side, a faint purple glow, radiating from Councilor Inzu.

His hands slide along the slimy cave wall, unable to get traction on anything. He feels something swim past him, brushing against his back. He almost sucks in water out of fright, but pushes on, trying desperately to get out of the dirty tunnel as his chest begins to burn from the lack of air. Just as the purple light begins to grow brighter, he feels his head start spinning, and the light fades to darkness.

The next thing he knows, Chion is choking and coughing, spitting out a mouthful of sour tasting water onto the cave floor.

"He'll be fine." Ral says, standing up from next to him.

"What hap…?" Chion tries to ask, spitting up water instead of words.

"You didn't make it through…" Councilor Sage says, "Ral here jumped in and pulled you out."

"Thanks." He says, to Ral. Still trying to grasp his surroundings.

"Anytime!" His friend replies, grinning and helping him to his feet.

Looking around the chamber, he sees that it is filled with pools like the last room had been. Only much, much larger. The wall behind them runs as far as he can see in either direction. Every other way stretches into emptiness. Even Inzu's light is unable to reach to distant edges of the cavern. Above, he can see quartz and other shining stones, all gleaming purple from the eerie light.

"Keep to the edge, along the wall." Lingonberry tells them.

Inzu takes a torch from her pack. It bursts into flames as she grips it with a fiery hand. She leaves it near the pool they emerged from, to serve as a marker.

They make their way deeper into the chamber, moving around the pools and ponds spotting the floor. What appears to be a small lake opens up in front of them, pressing against the cavern. In the purple glow, it almost looks like the water flows under the edge of the cave's wall.

They lose sight of the edge of the room as they walk around the lake. Inzu lights their rear, dropping torches here and there as they advance. Councilor Kroonson leads the group, sparks flying brightly from his hands, projecting a glimmering green glow ahead.

Another large pond appears to their side, forcing the group to walk along a narrow isthmus between the two bodies of water.

Chion tries hard to keep his balance, as his feet slide across the slick mossy floor. He hears a splash, as someone's foot goes into the water.

"Damn!" Relorn curses, from the back of the group. Falling as he struggles to pull his foot from the pond.

In the distance, Chion can hear something. Very soft at first, but growing louder each second. A churning, slithering sound.

"Run…" He says, softly at first. Then, as the sickening sound grows louder, he screams. "RUN!"

As they begin to sprint along the narrow way, huge beasts spring from the depths, sending showers of water flying through the air.

Chion looks back long enough to get a glimpse of the charging creatures. He can make out elongated slithering bodies, low to the ground, like large smooth lizards. Their pale skin shining with the purple and green light emanating from the councilors. Terrible jaws protrude from their large bodies, the size of crocodiles. Chion sees smooth leathery patches covering where their eyes should be. Their tongues licking the air, tasting the way to their prey.

The pool ends ahead, bringing the wall back into view. Chion hears a whisper, like air whistling through a crack in the rock. He sprints, following the sound, searching for the source. A small opening comes into view, cut into the stone. Chion darts through it, calling for the others to follow.

The creatures are right behind them, crawling across the floors and walls, and moving effortlessly along the cave ceiling above. Their jaws viciously snapping and gnashing.

Faintly, Chion can see two paths diverging ahead. He springs through the small opening to the right, just as Kroonson screams to go left. From the darkness, he sees the group run by. Quickly moving away from him, with the creatures closing in on them.

The lights disappear as soon as they pass out of sight, leaving him alone, engulfed in blinding darkness.

Relorn 7

Relorn runs at the rear of the group, trying to stay ahead of the creatures slithering and snapping behind him. They weave through the narrow stone corridor, until stumbling into an enormous cavern.

As he falls through the opening, Kroonson spins around, sending a jarring burst of sparks at the mouth of the tunnel. Most of the beasts are caught by the blast, but some manage to break through, swarming across the ceiling to avoid the creeping lightning.

Inzu fires a jet of violet and magenta flames into the cave, forcing the rest of the creatures to turn and retreat. Quezada vanishes and reappears on the ceiling, materializing next to each remaining creature and slicing with his sword until all lie dead on the ground.

"Is anyone missing?" Sage asks, brushing himself off.

"I don't see Chion." Rosemary cries, aghast. "We need to go back for him!"

"Not a chance," Kroonson says. "He finds his way back, or he gets eaten."

"What?" Rosemary shouts, a flash of anger on her face. "He's our friend. We can't leave him!"

"Chion has good hearing, and he knows we left markers." Lingonberry says, beginning to explore the chamber. "If he's smart, he'll make his way back to Jia and Kzhee."

"Maybe we should go look for him…" Relorn starts.

"I'm sorry, your highness…" Lingonberry replies, solemnly. "But, no."

Kroonson stands guard at the entrance, as they begin to make their way around the expansive cavern. This is the first room of the cave that doesn't look like it was formed naturally. The edges and ceiling are smooth and perfectly angled, as if the room had been carved from the inside. They walk for what feels like hours, coming across nothing but empty space.

"What could a room this large be for?" Rika chirps, from the front of the group.

"That is what we are looking to find out." Sage answers, enigmatically, as they travel further into the cavernous chamber.

Shapes and etchings begin to appear on the wall, stretching into the darkness. Sage investigates the drawings, seeming to understand their meaning.

"What do they say?" Relorn asks, running his hand across the markings.

"It appears to be a ledger, and an inventory of some sort." Sage replies, studying each row as they continue walking.

Relorn pushes forward to the front of the group, moving as far ahead as the light projecting off of Inzu allows.

Then, from the darkness, a huge figure appears before him. Blood red eyes shine in the dim light, as the figure towers over them. Relorn yells and dives away from the monstrosity, as Inzu sets a blast of violet and blue flames singeing through the air, engulfing the creature.

Yet no sound escapes its mouth, as the fire streams past, and the thing makes no movement. Standing still with a muted expression, impassive.

"What is it?" He asks.

"It's a golem..." Lingonberry replies, an awestruck expression glazed on his face.

Relorn walks around the gargantuan statue. In the distance, he sees more colossal figures, casting faint shadows across the cave. Approaching them, trying to get a better look, he counts six additional golems, identical to the first. As well as two that are much larger, dwarfing the others.

"Where are the rest?" Lingonberry hisses.

"There are more back here!" Relorn shouts.

"There should be thousands, legions… Sage!" Lingonberry screams, exhibiting an uncharacteristic lack of composure.

"I'm getting there!" Sage says, fervorously examining the writing on the wall. "It looks like they were all taken during the reign of Emperor Herion II, the Re-Unifier. It doesn't say anything about where they were taken to. I would assume they were used during the Bloody Years."

"What are the Bloody Years?" Tiaries asks, trying to decipher the strange etchings.

"It was an Empire-wide rebellion, hundreds of years ago. There are many legends regarding what happened, but none can be confirmed. The only things we know for certain are that the Empire fell apart during the reign of Emperor Taro IV. His granduncle Harlorn II used the situation to have Taro executed, and seize power for himself. Just after beginning a campaign to re-unify the Empire, Harlorn died as well. His son Herion II continued his father's campaign, ultimately reunifying the Empire." Sage pauses, fixated on a particular section of writing. "Herion is the last Emperor known to have used the golems. It is said he hid them after, to prevent anyone from abusing their power."

"And it appears we have chased yet another dead end." Lingonberry says, pacing along the end of the room.

"Maybe not…" Maestas replies. "Why are there still a few of them here?"

"It says the Earthmovers they brought were unable to control them all." Sage translates. "It says the most powerful Earthmover was able to control a full legion, but the next strongest was only able to move five hundred, each dropping off from there."

"Well, Loak?" Quezada asks, knocking on the leg of one of the golems. "Do they work?"

Jia sits on the floor, next to Kzhee, leaning back against a rock and flicking pebbles into the air. The bright orange flame on her shoulder sends tiny balls of fire after them, pretending to shoot from a miniature fiery sling. The flame stomps and pouts each time it misses, making Kzhee laugh.

"It's a funny little thing." He says, smiling.

"Yeah, it's a character." Jia replies, tossing another stone.

Instead of shooting a small bit of fire again, the flame erupts violently. Sending a blazing jet through the air, torching the pebble and turning it red hot. The blast lights up the chamber almost as bright as day, whilst the flame twirls in a victory dance.

"Did you hear that?" The boy asks, standing up and peering around a darkened corner.

"I didn't hear anything." She says, relaxed. "It's just your imagination."

But then Jia hears something too, like stones grinding against each other. Then gruff voices begin drifting around the bend, speaking incomprehensibly.

The flame jumps behind Jia's back, cloaking them in darkness. The sounds move closer, the ground shaking more and more with each step the disembodied voices take, until the resonance of their speech echoes monstrously loud across the cave.

Then, just as it appears the giant forms will surely stumble upon them, silence falls. They wait a minute, then Jia's flame peers around from behind her, dimly lighting their surroundings.

As it does, two gigantic faces appear before them. One is twice as tall as a normal man, the other even taller and larger, dwarfing his already giant companion. Their faces are gargantuan and disfigured, but otherwise seem to be those of men.

The larger of the two lets out a bestial roar, swinging at Kzhee. The boy throws a hand forward, attempting to shock the giant, but nothing happens.

Instinctively, Jia sweeps an arm through the air, sending a wave of roaring fire at the giants, forcing them backwards. Then she advances, shooting a column of flame at the larger creature. The conflagration consumes him, forcing a scream of agony through the cave.

The smaller of the giants jumps into the pond, disappearing. Jia stands over the edge, a firestorm spiraling around her, ready to consume anything that moves.

"My ability isn't working." Kzhee says, shaken by the attack. He stares at the burning corpse next to them, his face turning green. "That's the thing from last night..."

"Yeah, it didn't seem to like you very much..." She says, her eyes scanning the water.

Then, as they look into the depths of the pool, rocks explode around them. The shock sending them flying backwards. A roar rings out, as the remaining giant erupts from a rocky wall, knocking open a passage above the water.

The thing now stands twice as tall as it had before. Huge boulders and stones drift around its extremities, making it larger. Armoring it, and providing it with fists of stone to flail.

"What is that…?" Kzhee stumbles, trying to recover from being knocked back.

Jia doesn't respond, but swings around and unleashes a furry of fire at the huge stone creature. It throws up its arms, using the rock to absorb the flames, before screeching and charging at her.

She jumps out of the way, leaving a burning whirlwind behind to engulf the creature as it passes, eliciting a screech of pain, but not slowing its advance.

"Follow me!" She shouts at Kzhee, taking off through the newly exposed tunnel, towards the rest of the team.

The next cavern is much larger than the first, causing her to pause as they enter.

"This way!" Kzhee says, pointing to a torch in the distance burning with a purple glow.

They sprint towards the beacon with the creature quickly pursuing them, quaking the ground beneath their feet as it runs. Approach a large underground lake, they dash around it, trying not to slip on the slippery surface.

The giant slowly closes in, gaining on them as they move. Ahead, Jia hears scuffling, like something is running towards them.

Now what… She thinks, preparing to let loose a blast of flame.

Bursting into the light, she sees Chion sprinting towards them, a look of terror on his face.

"Go! Go!" Chion screams.

"No, you go!" They shout back.

Chion ducks at the last moment, sliding into the water next to them. As he does, Jia unleashes a torrent of fire ahead. The large slimy creatures pursuing him run straight into the inferno, their skin popping and sizzling as it's consumed by the blazing flames.

Kzhee grabs Chion's arm, pulling him from the lake.

"Run!" Jia yells, pushing them forward into the cave Chion had just emerged from.

"Will it be able to follow us in here?" Kzhee asks, backing away from the entrance.

"What?" Chion replies, perplexed.

Before they can answer, the stony giant bursts through the small cave opening, ripping apart the stone and rock as easily as if parting branches in a forest.

The boys scream as Jia shoves them further down the cave, forcing them to turn and run down the path. The giant crashing behind them, furiously roaring as it charges.

Loak focuses on the statue, preparing. As he waves his arms the closest golem begins to slide rigidly, dragging across the ground. He tries to make the joints move, the arms and legs swing, but he is unable to animate the stone.

"Try the others," Sage tells him.

He walks to the back of the room, to the second group of golems. He tries to move each of the remaining smaller statues, but none are able to come to life. Lastly, almost giving up hope, he tries the larger two. As he does, their ruby eyes start to glow, and life begins to course through their limbs. The largest golem slowly turns its head, coming to face Loak.

While the larger golems start to move towards him, the eyes of the rest light up and they begin to groan and creak, the rocks in their joints grinding as their arms and legs come awake. They move into position behind the larger golems, as if following their motions.

"There you go!" Sage yells, encouragingly.

"Do we try to bring them back with us?" Quezada asks.

"There must be another way out, I can't imagine thousands of these things being marched through the way we came." Lingonberry replies.

"Any ideas, Loak?" Sage asks, "Do any of these walls look like they could be opened?"

Loak lets his control of the golems slip. The light in their eyes fades, and their limbs go limp. He walks around the room, inspecting each wall.

What am I supposed to be looking for? He thinks, beginning to feel awkward beneath the stares of the councilors.

He places a hand on the wall before him, hoping to feel something, anything.

Do I try to open it? What if it's supporting the cave?

The fear of the mountain above collapsing sends his heart aflutter.

Under his fingers, Loak can feel the cave begin to shake. A slow rumble at first, giving way to a quaking roar. His hand falls as he steps away from the wall, the stone beginning to violently vibrate. Pulsating louder and stronger, until a mighty crash explodes from the wall. Rocks and debris fly across the chamber, knocking everyone back.

A deafening scream rings out from amidst the billowing cloud of dirt. As the dust settles, the form of a giant appears before them. An enormous man, surrounded by bulking armor of stone and rock, drawn to him by some invisible force.

Behind the lumbering beast, Jia, Chion and Kzhee appear from the newly exposed hole in the cavern. The giant turns to face them, rage in its eyes.

Inzu spurts purple flames at the beast, but their licks seem to annoy it more than cause any harm.

"Yeah, I already tried that!" Jia shouts, from the chasm.

The creature faces the shouting girl and charges back into the opening it had created. The second pass rips out an even larger section of the cave wall, making the mountain above begin to rumble ominously.

The beast rears up and grabs a large boulder, throwing it at Kzhee and Chion as they follow Jia out of the side passage. As the creature yanks another stone from the wall, the chamber around it begins to rattle and move.

Dust rains down as boulders become dislodged and slide away. The falling stones strike the beast, bringing it to its knees. Suddenly, the antechamber collapses, crushing the creature with a sickening crunch.

The rumbling continues into their chamber, shaking the room and showering them with falling rock. A large stone crumbles from an adjacent wall, nearly landing on Relorn. As it does, a blinding ray of morning light shoots through the exposed opening, followed by fresh air rushing in, stirring up a cyclone of dirt and rubble.

"Loak!" He hears Sage scream, over the rumble and roar around them. "Can you open that way out?"

Rocks begin to thud around him, sending echoing crashes that nearly knock him off his feet. Loak throws his hands up, trying to stop the collapsing ceiling. The rumbling around them begins to lessen, but the rest of the mountain groans in protest. He swings an arm through the air, opening the small opening to the outside, allowing everyone to begin scrambling out of the mountain.

Loak tries to make his way out after them, but the weight crushing down from above threatens to overcome him. He feels the unseen force weighing down on him, pain screaming in his back and legs, as if the entire mountain is pressing on his shoulders. Each step he takes nearly breaks him.

I'm not going to make it. He thinks, as his head begins to spin.

Then, as if from nowhere, Quezada appears. The councilor touches Loak's shoulder and together they vanish.

The feeling nearly makes him vomit, like his stomach is being pulled through the air with the rest of his body unable to keep up. Behind them, Loak sees the mountain crash down, lowering a few meters, before coming to rest on itself. He catches a last glimpse of the golems, before they are crushed to dust beneath the stone and earth.

"A fool's errand!" Inzu yells, spurting fire at the mountain in disgust. "What a waste!"

"Not so…" Lingonberry says, with a strange smile. "We know they exist. We know they can be controlled. And… We know the bulk of them are together, somewhere other than here."

"So you call this a success?" She retorts.

"Everyone is accounted for." Sage replies. "If nothing else, I would call that a success. We feared Chion was lost for certain."

The boy smiles, defiantly. "It'll take more than some slimy lizards to kill me!"

"I think we all owe Loak here a debt of gratitude." Sage says, gripping him on the shoulder. "We would all be lying dead under that mountain, if not for him."

The group sounds their appreciation, hands clapping his back. Rika runs up and throws her arms around his waist, giving him a huge smile and shouting, "Thank you!"

"What do ya see?" He asks.

"Sadness..." Christina replies, her fingers pressed to his cheek.

"Greatness…" Lena adds, gripping Seaborne's chest.

That afternoon Seaborne pages through a book, standing alone by a window in his apartments aboard *The Flagship*. He tries to focus on the words, but restlessness gets the better of him.

Placing the tome on a table, he begins to pace the room. Longing for the comfort of the captain's chambers upon his own vessel.

A knock comes from his door, a young lady informing him that the admiral sends his summons. He grabs his hat from a wooden peg and departs.

The admiral's dining hall lies at the rear of the ship. Large glass windows wrap around the room, paneled with different colored panes of glass, casting a piebald pattern across the floor.

"Hello, admiral." Seaborne says, removing his hat and bowing. "Ya sent for me?"

"I did, indeed." The admiral replies, filling his mouth with sliced mango. "Sit please, sit and eat with me."

Seaborne takes a seat across from his commander, young attendants running out to serve him a plate.

"How are you enjoying the return home?" The admiral asks.

Seaborne takes a long draw from his goblet, before replying. "It is always nice to be home, but I am ready to return to sea at any time."

Please, please send me back out! He thinks, feeling the sea calling, waves crashing against the hull.

"I know you prefer to be out there…" The admiral says, gesturing through the windows. "And I would like to send you back out, if you're ready."

"Yes, yes of course. I can be ready at a moment's notice." Seaborne says, grinning.

"You may want to hear the mission, before jumping on board. It is an unusual request."

"What's th…" He begins to ask, before a resounding crash echoes through the hall. Seaborne falls out of his chair, as plates fly off the table and attendants are thrown to the floor. He springs back to his feet, unsheathing his cutlass. "Is it an attack!?"

Admiral Ishmael begins calling commands to captains and crewmen, running for the deck at top speed. Seaborne charges after him, looking around to try and find the source of the attack.

Another blast strikes the side of the ship, slamming them both into the wall. They stumble through the doors, onto the deck. Sailors run around, screaming to each other and arming themselves.

"STARBOARD!" Commodore Shipman yells, from his position on the foredeck. "Battle stations!"

Seaborne and the admiral run up to the deck, trying to get a look off the side. Before they can see anything, a sailor shouts out. "Comin about!"

Looking where the sailor points, against the glare of the sun. Seaborne can see an enormous wake start to form on the water, trailing behind something undulating beneath the surface. The disturbance casts boats aside like toys as it passes.

Nearing *The Flagship*, a long haunting form becomes visible under the surging sea. A colossal serpent's head breaks through the surface, screeching a deafening screech, causing the sailors to cover their ears in pain. It rears back, bringing its front from the water, rising a hundred feet out of the sea.

The commodore staggers to the ship's rail, throwing his hands in the air just moments before the creature is able to crash into the hull. As he does, two enormous waterspouts rise from the sea, twisting through the air with a whirling fury. He claps his hands together, bringing the twin tornadoes crashing down into the serpent, knocking it off course and sending it plunging into the water.

"Avast!" The admiral yells, "It's coming portside. Man the scorpions! Load the harpoons!"

The crew runs across the ship, searching the sea below for the shadowy figure of the serpent. For what seems like an eternity the sea remains still as glass, reflecting the hulls of a thousand ships.

Then, in a flash, the serpent surges from the depths. Dripping fangs, the size of swords, stick out of its mouth, spread between its unhinged jaws. With a lightning fast recoil, and a fearsome strike, the beast rips a chunk of wood from the hull, sending a dozen men flying through the air and splashing into the sea below.

"Fire!" The admiral screams, pointing to the scorpioniers.

A resounding snap erupts from the ship, as all the scorpions trigger at once, sending a score of harpoons sailing towards the beast.

The serpent slams itself hard into the hull, dodging most of the projectiles and sending men sprawling across the deck.

Commodore Shipman begins to raise the waterspouts again, one after another. Bringing them up into the sky, then crashing down upon the serpent, battering it with great tidal roars.

The creature, disoriented by the tempestuous cyclones, dives back into the depths. Narrowly avoiding a second showering of harpoons.

"There's another!" A sailor calls from the crow's nest, pointing across the bay.

A second serpent roars, snapping its jaws shut on an unsuspecting ship. Screams ring out, as men jump overboard, trying to avoid the creature's savage strikes. It picks men out at random, ripping them from the sea and devouring them whole.

"My ship!" Seaborne yells, seeing the creature moving towards *The Masthead.* He takes off, sprinting to the lift, the first serpent still repeatedly slamming itself into the side of the ship, nearly knocking him to the ground with each assault. Upon reaching the lift, he screams to the attendant. "Send me down!"

"I can't, capin…" The boy stammers, terror in his eyes. "That thing'll kill ya!"

Seaborne ignores him, climbing into the lift. "Down, now!"

Without further protest, the boy pulls back a lever, sending the lift reeling into a freefall.

The serpent spins about, turning to face him, then snaps through the air in the direction of the descending lift. Seaborne can see the layers of jagged teeth, flashing as they speed towards him. Without thinking, he jumps from the wooden platform, diving towards the sea below.

The creature's ferocious teeth shred into the lift, reducing it to splinters. Seaborne watches as the shards of wood fall around him, splashing into the water.

Sinking... Sinking... He tries to swim, tries to fight for the surface. Through the murky water, Seaborne can see a shadowy movement, the serpent undulating towards him. Lengths of coiled sinewy body, wrapping and warping through the water. Terror overcomes him as he struggles for air. The light of day just a few strokes away.

He reaches up, grasping. Close, almost there. Then, just as he is about to surface, two giant yellow eyes appear before his face, and the serpent's smiling mouth begins to widen.

Seaborne summons all the strength he has, surging from the water with a mighty stroke. He grabs for the pier above, slipping as he tries to grip the wet wood and attempt to pull himself up.

Below him, the water is moving, churning. As the serpent strikes, Seaborne pulls his legs up, feeling the bottom of his feet rub across to top of the creature's head, narrowly missing being dragged under.

He yanks himself onto the dock, then starts running towards his ship. The serpent moves beneath, sending wooden boards flying into the air. Destroying the platform behind Seaborne as he sprints.

As it nearly overtakes him, another volley of harpoons comes soaring from the scorpions above. Many find their mark, imbedding in the unsuspecting creature's flank.

It screams in fury, returning its attention to the ship. As it spins around, a giant waterspout crashes down upon it. The head of the swirling column shaped like a snake.

The crashing blow of the cyclone creates a typhoon, rushing through the water towards Seaborne. Ships nearly topple in its path, closing in on the captain as he runs. Despite his efforts, the wave overtakes him, washing him roughly across the dock.

As the surging water approaches *The Masthead*, he swings his arm about, grabbing onto the figurehead secured to the front of his ship. The swell sends his vessel violently rocking through the water, but he holds tight, refusing to lighten his grip.

As the water subsides, Seaborne swings on deck. "Battle stations!" He screams, trying to organize the men as they frantically run about. "Man the scorpions! Man the catapults! Harpoons and spears ready…"

All the while, the second serpent makes its way through the ships with little resistance. Swallowing boats whole, or simply smashing their hulls and moving on.

"Prepare to engage" Seaborne yells, cutting the few remaining lines the wave hadn't snapped. "Sails down!"

The men drop the large black canvas, and with a snapping boom their sail catches a gust of wind, pulling the ship away from dock as the smaller serpent moves towards them.

"Ready!" Seaborne hollers to the men, taking his post on the foredeck. "Fire!"

Thoomp Thoomp Thoomthoomthoomp. Bolts and harpoons fly through the air, whistling towards the creature.

It screeches in writhing pain, as the shots strike its midsection.

"Shoot! Shoot!" Parrot's bird calls, fluttering above the ship.

Men on the boats around them start to join in on the assault, and projectiles begin flying from every direction.

The serpent, riddled with bolts and harpoons and spears and tridents, screams a deafening death rattle. Its eyes roll back, as it sinks into the deep.

Men cheer and shout in elation, watching the beast fade from view. But a screech from the remaining serpent sends a sobering shiver through their spines.

"Avast, bring us about!" Seaborne hollers, to the helmsman.

Their ship plunges towards the remaining beast, still embroiled in battle with *The Flagship*. The commodore's turbulent pillars of water are proving to be little more than an annoyance to the great serpent. Dozens of harpoons stick from its scales, but the wounds seem to be enraging the creature more than discouraging it.

"Fire!" Seaborne yells again, as his ship comes within range. His men let loose a direct volley, sending a peppering of projectiles into the serpent's side.

It screeches in distress, spinning about to retaliate. But, before it does, something seems to capture its attention. With a mighty roar, the creature dives into the ocean, disappearing from sight within seconds.

A suffocating silence falls over the water. No cheers of elation come from the survivors, left drifting in the bloodstained sea.

Rika 5

Each night, as they sail back to the Pillar, the mouse sneaks through the ship. Watching Lingonberry.

Rika conveniently happens to bump into him whenever he is alone. Each time, he politely pats her head then moves along, uninterested in conversing.

Tonight, after a week of being cramped up on the river, she is going to say something to make him talk to her.

The mouse darts across the floorboards, searching beneath the councilor's room. Finding nothing. Scurrying between the hollow framing, it makes its way through the bowels of the ship, peeking above every so often, searching for Lingonberry.

Above the foredeck, the mouse finds him standing and watching the boat cut through the river. Rika appears around the corner, quietly making her way towards the councilor.

"Pretty night." She remarks, meekly.

He looks at her warmly, giving a smile. "Having trouble sleeping?"

She pauses, then gently whispers. "I had a dream about my sister, a nightmare more like…" Rika looks up at him, gauging his reaction.

"Rika…" He says, looking away. Gazing at the far shore, he begins shaking his head in disappointment. "Rika, Rika, Rika… You must know, people do not like being spied upon."

Her heart sinks and her stomach turns. "What? I don't know what you mean."

"Your act may fool some, but not me. Certainly not me…" Still looking away, he lets out a long sigh. "Rika, take it from someone who knows. If you are caught sneaking around spying on people, there will be grave consequences."

"I never…" She starts to reply.

"Do not insult me!" Lingonberry quickly snaps. Then, staring at her, he begins to fade into the night.

Rika watches Councilor Lingonberry slowly shimmer, somehow becoming transparent, then disappear before her eyes.

"What?" She stammers, amazed.

"Overhearing things you shouldn't is something I have experience with as well." A disembodied voice says, barely a whisper.

The shimmer ripples through the darkness, gently reforming into the councilor.

"You have broken my trust…" He says, shaking his head again. "When you regain it, perhaps I will tell you what I know about your sister."

She nods her head, hurriedly turning to leave.

"Rika, one more thing…" He calls. "As much as I hate being spied upon, rest assured, the Emperor likes it even less. And I am afraid he does not possess my ability to forgive."

The Glorious Knights and Illuminated Priests of the Order of Justice, Honor, and Chivalry 3

Translucent spires of ice break above the horizon, reaching to the sky with a shimmering gleam. The Frozen City rises before the men as they ride, reflecting the light of the sun. Shining brighter than a star.

The men share a smile at the sight of their destination, as their horses stumble through the final stretch of tundra.

"Finally!" Sir Joel exclaims, shifting in his seat and rubbing his behind.

"Which way to the Order's outpost?" Friar Philip asks.

"I believe it is near the city square." Sir Marcus replies, turning his horse in that direction.

"Hopefully they received our carrier pigeon, I would hate for there to not be a nice meal prepared for us." Sir Joel says, hungrily rubbing his stomach.

A strong wind gusts through the steep city. The knights watch people sled down the sloped streets, some for fun, some to transverse the icy roads. Little sleighs pull trailer carriages filled with trade goods and supplies, bundles of firewood and groceries.

Up the side of the mountain upon which the city rests, a giant rope runs, drawn up by men and horses at the top of the incline. People hang onto the rope from their sleds, riding it back up the slope.

The knights meander through the city square. Snow and ice are everywhere, giving the impression of a winter wonderland. The people in the square seem to shy away from them as they pass. Some whisper in hushed tones, hiding their faces in their heavy fur cloaks and warm hoods.

"Do you get the feeling we aren't welcome here?" Sir Marcus asks, glancing about.

"I don't know..." Friar Philip says, nervously. "The people do seem to be acting peculiar."

The whisperings of one passerby catch the knight's ears. "Are those the ones that killed Prince Bastion?"

"Hurry," Sir Marcus hisses. "Make for the outpost at once."

They take off at a gallop, their horses throwing up a trail of snow, shouts and taunts following them down the street.

"They think we killed Bastion?" Sir Joel asks, angrily. "What's wrong with these fools?"

"Be calm..." Friar Philip replies. "We will speak with the Order's knights and find out what is happening."

As they round the next corner, the Order's outpost comes into view. A small icy castle, rising from the snow. Similar to their own back in Blackburn, except built from blocks of hardened ice and packed snow instead of stone and mortar.

As they ride closer, a grisly sight becomes visible. Through the billowing snow, the knights are able to make out a handful of human heads, decapitated and posted above the door of the outpost. Piles of the colorful armor of the Order lays on the snow beneath the heads, amidst piles of garbage and rotten produce.

"What is this?" Friar Philip asks, gaging and covering his face in disgust.

"We need to leave, now!" Sir Marcus yells, spinning his horse about and leading a charge towards the edge of the city.

They keep off the main roads and stay away from the square, but jeers and wicked glares still chase them as they flee. From the base of the mountain, they can hear soldiers shouting to each other, arming themselves and mounting their steeds.

"What do we do?" Sir Joel asks. "They are closing off the entrance to the city..."

"Make for the woods," Sir Marcus replies.

"Sir," Friar Philip says. "The horses won't be able to make it through the snow drifts if we leave the road."

"It's either that, or we take our chances with capture." Sir Marcus shouts.

Without further discussion, they turn and bolt into the woods. Tearing through the dense trees and loosely packed snow.

The sound of hooves beating against ice grows louder as the soldiers close in, but stops abruptly at the edge of the woods. All the knights can hear is laughter, echoing from the soldiers as they abandon their pursuit.

Tiaries 6

The breeze sweeps through her hair as they stand atop the Pillar, a cold autumn gust blowing between the lofty towers. She tries to pay attention to the lesson, but to her side Tiaries notices Jia whispering in Relorn's ear, eliciting a snicker of laughter from the prince.

"Jia!" Councilor Inzu snaps. "I just asked you a question."

"I'm sorry…" Jia replies, sweetly. "Could you repeat it?"

"I could, but I won't." The councilor says, shaking her head. "Spar with me."

Tiaries' eyes fly to Jia. The girl seems apprehensive, standing in place.

"Now!" Inzu shouts, grabbing a sword from a nearby rack and walking towards the edge of the Pillar.

Jia steps forward, slowly walking to meet Inzu at the Pillar's rim. Without picking up a weapon, Jia summons her flame between her hands. Focusing her energy, the ball of fire grows larger and larger, until, seemingly unable to control the conflagration anymore, Jia sends it hurling towards Inzu.

The councilor calmly waits for the inferno to reach her. Then, with a flash, she combusts. A scorching purple fire consumes her, before Jia's blast is able to. The orange fireball is absorbed into the rich glow that radiates from Inzu.

Before Jia is able to react, the councilor flashes across the training ring, a blur of violet, magenta and fuchsia flames. She knocks Jia to the ground, swinging her sword at the girl's throat.

The councilor stops short of slashing her, bringing the blade to a halt at Jia's beating neck vein.

"Now..." Inzu says, strikingly calm. "If you had been listening, you would have known that throwing fire at me is useless. I was asking if the same is true for you, but apparently there are other things you are more focused on."

Tiaries tries not to laugh, as Jia stands in silence. Her calm face fading from its usual rich sandy complexion, to a shade of rosy quartz.

Councilor Maestas approaches, laughing gently. "Yes, the point Councilor Inzu wishes to make is that similar abilities often have the effect of canceling each other out. You all have a natural resistance to certain elements, certain hazards, that gives each of you unique strengths. But as you have just witnessed, it also gives you weaknesses which can be exploited."

"That is why it is so important to be proficient in a variety of skills and abilities," Inzu adds. "Jia. If Ral tried to kill you right now, would you be able to stop him? He is far more skilled with a sword than you are, and I doubt your fire would have any effect on someone who can turn themselves into water."

Jia seems baffled by the question. Instead of replying she remains silent, giving little more than a shrug.

"Tiaries." Maestas says, suddenly.

What? What did I do? Her large eyes grow wider.

"What is your weakness?"

Why is he asking me? I wasn't the one not paying attention...

"I don't know…" She says, meekly. Looking up, she notices the smile returning to Jia's face.

"I'm sure you do." Maestas replies.

Tiaries chokes up, "Time…" She answers.

"Time does work against you, yes." Inzu says. "But I think he means what is your personal weakness. What can hurt you, what can you not defend against."

"Anything…" She says, with a gasp. "Everything!" The realization cutting deep.

They are all so much stronger than me… I am nothing compared to them. I can't defend myself from anything!

"Tiaries." Maestas says, reassuringly. "You are very special, and you bring something to this group that no one else does. You are our insurance, our failsafe. That is why paying attention is so important. It is true, you do have less of an ability to protect yourself. And yes, time is not your friend. But you are part of a team. As are you, Jia. You each need to find a way to work together, or you will be lost on your own. If you operate as a team, your strengths will cancel out each other's weaknesses. United, you could be unstoppable."

Later, as evening falls, Tiaries sits alone in her room, exhausted from the day. They spent the afternoon outlining everyone's weaknesses, everyone's shortcomings. At the end of the lesson they had each departed in silence, harboring what little strength and spirit they had left.

She had cried upon reaching her room, tears falling freely down her face. She wanted to go to Jaties. It has been so long since she's seen her brother, but she doesn't even know where his chambers are. Feeling more alone than she's ever felt, Tiaries curls up in her blankets, resigning to going to sleep early.

If I am asleep, I can't feel useless…

Just then, a knock comes from the door. She stands, straightening her gown and making herself presentable. When Tiaries answers the door, Rosemary stands on the other side, carrying a large canvas sack over her shoulder.

"Can I come in?" She asks.

"Of course." Tiaries replies, happily taken aback.

The Southern girl enters the room, laying her bundle down on the ground.

"What do you have there?" Tiaries asks, taking a seat on her couch. Wiping her face once more, making sure to eradicate any tears still lingering on her cheeks.

"I've been borrowing some things from the training grounds." Rosemary says, slyly, before rolling the bundle open. Inside are staves, swords, bows, bolts, even a small polearm.

"What?" Tiaries asks, gasping.

"I have felt out of place and useless since the day we arrived here." Rosemary replies. "I decided I was going to do something about it. These are my tools. Would you like to train with me?"

"Yes!" Tiaries says, almost starting to cry again. "I thought I knew what I was doing, from the training I have from the plays… But every day it becomes more obvious I have no reason to be here…"

Rosemary bursts into laughter.

"What is so funny?" She asks the snickering girl.

"You can bring people back to life!" Rosemary blurts out. "You have more reason to be here than anyone. If you never have to use your gift, great. But I am sure if anyone here could pick one person to have around in a pinch, it would be you."

Tiaries blushes and turns away, grabbing a staff from the small arsenal. "You ready?" She asks, holding the weapon outstretched.

They practice till each is covered in sweat, lungs and limbs burning. Having worked through each type of weapon in Rosemary's bag, the girls fall back into large cushioned chairs opposite her hearth.

"How is your brother?" Rosemary asks, pouring herself a glass of water from a pitcher resting on the table.

Tiaries recoils at the question, a pang of guilt in her heart. "I haven't seen him since we returned." She says, feeling a tear welling on her cheek.

"Why don't we go visit him?" Rosemary asks, bluntly.

"Are we allowed to leave?"

"I don't know, there's only one way to find out though." Rosemary says, standing up. "Let's go to the theatre, maybe there is a show tonight. Even if there isn't, maybe someone there will know where Jaties' apartments are. Either way, it'll be fun to get out."

"Okay! Let's go." Tiaries says, a wide smile forcing its way across her face.

They quickly change out of their sweaty clothes, then depart from the Emperor's Tower, heading towards the Pillar square. The night is crisp, but Tiaries' excitement warms her to the bone. Meandering through the square, the girls make their way to the Tower of Trade.

A young man calls out, yelling as they pass by the entrance of the tower, surrounded by a group of gaudily dressed comrades.

"Hello, beautiful girls! Care to come over and give us a kiss?"

Tiaries' eyes dart to Rosemary, expecting an outburst or at least a darkening of mood. Instead, she sees a smile crawl across the girl's face.

"What do you say, Tiaries, should I give him a kiss?" Rosemary asks, laughing as they enter the tower.

The central lift is bustling, full of people heading to the upper floors for the evening's entertainment. The girls crowd on, riding it to the level housing the theatre.

Bodies swarm through the lobby of the theatre, the masses being ushered through the tall arching doors into the darkened performance hall. She and Rosemary take their seats. She feels the energy of the stage, and the excitement of possibly seeing her brother.

I miss Jaties… I miss the stage… A feeling of longing creeps through her core, but quickly flees when Rosemary grips her hand. Tiaries looks at her, at her friend, and sees the excitement in her eyes. Happiness seems to flow from Rosemary.

Just a few months ago there were tears in her eyes every time I saw her. Now… It's like she's a new person.

"Does being here ever get to you?" She asks, Rosemary. "When we arrived, I was so happy. I thought I had found a home. But now, I don't know."

"It was really hard for me at first, of course. But it's been getting easier. Training at night has been helping. Helping me sleep, helping me feel more... I don't know, capable, brave." Rosemary sighs. "For a long time, after Bastion, I thought... I thought I deserved to die. But being here, it's made me feel like I have a purpose, like I can maybe do something good to make up for..." She trails off, turning her head towards the stage.

"Thank you, for being my friend." Tiaries says, with a smile. "I've always had my brother around, and now that we're apart I feel so alone... But this has been fun. I am really glad we came."

The lights fall dim, as the curtains begin to rise. Performers take their positions. The scenery is dark and foreboding, the light seeming to flood blood red across the stage.

Tiaries recognizes the script at once, they had performed it dozens of times before when she was with the carnival. The story of Rallan.

It is one of Jaties' favorite plays, he'll be in it for sure!

Her suspicions are proved correct during the next scene. She sees her brother enter the stage, playing the part of Kiago, Lord Rallan's sidekick and foil.

Tiaries cheers as he enters, patting Rosemary's hand excitedly and pointing to her sibling onstage. "There he is! There he is! Hopefully we can catch him after the show..."

The performance drags on. Tiaries knows the play word for word, yet it seems to be much longer than she remembers. As the final scene wraps up she taps Rosemary on the shoulder, pulling her from her seat and creeping towards the wings, hoping to catch her brother after the bow.

Large guards block their way. "Employees only." One grunts.

"Jaties is my brother." Tiaries says, flashing a cheeky grin. "Could you let me say hello, just ever so quickly?"

The two men gaze at her, then look at each other. With a shrug they allow her to pass, but stop Rosemary.

"It's okay, go say hi." Rosemary assures her, taking a seat in one of the quickly emptying chairs. "I'll wait."

Backstage, Tiaries scoots between the performers as they scurry about, changing from their costumes and congratulating each other on a successful engagement.

"Jaties!" She hollers, spotting her brother. Rushing through the crowd, she throws her arms around him.

"Tiaries, oh I've missed you!" Jaties exclaims, picking her up and spinning her around. "I tried to come see you, but they wouldn't let me in the Emperor's Tower."

"I'm sorry, I wanted to come sooner, but I didn't even know if we were allowed to leave. Rosemary talked me into coming tonight, and I'm so happy we did!"

"Rosemary?" He asks, looking around.

"They wouldn't let her come backstage, can you go tell them that it's okay?"

"We're all about to go grab a drink." He says, gesturing to the bustle of people about. "Meet me out front?"

"Yeah!" She replies, giving him another hug before running back to Rosemary.

Jaties and the rest of the troupe meet the girls out front. He begins introducing them to everyone, Tiaries says hello to each, shaking hands and waving.

One of the actors, Jake, turns from a man to a woman as Tiaries touches his hand. Then, quickly turns back to a man, making the girls jump in surprise, and eliciting a wave of laughter from the group.

"Ah..." Her brother says, as a familiar face approaches. "And this is Loak, we are a..." He pauses, blushing.

Loak takes Jaties hand, smiling.

"That's amazing!" Tiaries shouts, throwing her arms around Loak and her brother. "How did you meet?" She asks Loak, inquisitively.

"We met after one of his performances, before I had met you." He answers.

"Wait, you know my sister?" Jaties asks, shocked.

"Loak saved our lives, you didn't know?" She turns to Loak, "Why didn't you tell him."

The Earthmover's face turns red as he stammers, "I... I... I mean, I didn't really save your lives, it was nothing."

"It was nothing... *Pssh.*" Tiaries says, in a mocking tone. "If it wasn't for you, we would be dead. I believe that is the definition of saving someone's life."

Tiaries dramatically fills the group in on Loak's heroics, leaving out no detail. After hours of exchanging stories and catching up, the group is fairly intoxicated. Loak seems to be handling the drinks best, politely excusing himself for the evening earlier than the rest, while Rosemary begins to act foolish. Jake keeps changing his form, letting out a quip each time. Rosemary roars in laughter, finding each impression more hilarious than the last.

Jake transforms into a young boy, as a waitress walks past. "More beer, more beer!" He shouts, in a childish singsong voice, slamming little fists against the table. The waitress looks at him in confusion, before scurrying away shaking her head.

As the night progresses, their party slowly begins to dwindle. Rosemary seems to be struggling to stay awake, so Jaties offers to walk them home. He leaves them at the entrance to the Emperor's Towers, waving as they head inside.

"Shhhhh!" Rosemary says, well above a whisper. Giggling as they step off the lift onto their floor. She pulls her arm back, pretending to draw an imaginary bow and arrow, then begins creeping down the hall. *"Psst!* Follow me..."

Tiaries laughs so hard a tear rolls down her cheek, as she tiptoes down the corridor behind her friend, happily playing along.

Senator McKenna 5

"Is there any more business?" He asks, looking at the men seated around the Senate Hall.

"There is the proposed bridge to be built north of R'Athenia." Senator Torbus states.

"Where will the materials come from?" Senator Fromolio asks, "I hope not from my quarries. I haven't the stone to spare..."

"Where will the money come from?" Senator Nassius adds.

"Who would provide the workers?" Senator Calisio asks, yawning at the rear of the auditorium.

Fools, fools, fools... It's a boon from above, that I'm able to get anything accomplished around here.

"Senators, I will speak with the mason's men and see what can be done for stone and slaves. I am sure they will be most willing to assist in the building of this bridge."

A murmur of agreement falls through the hall.

"Well then, shall we call thi..."

His words are cut off by a shrill shriek, echoing from the reservoir below. The cry is followed by a crescendo of calls. Looking down, he sees the heads of various creatures breaching the murky green water. Three or four humongous serpents break the surface, and begin singing an eerie song.

"What? Have you ever seen anything like that before?" He asks, as the senators peer down to the reservoir from the patio.

"No... No, I have not." Torbus replies, shaking his head in enchanted amazement.

The group of them begin heading down the long set of stairs, leading to the reservoir below. Crowds gather around the water, onlookers pointing and gawking, shouting to one another. The senators stop a few flights from the bottom, maintaining a good view of the spectacle while still keeping a safe distance from the mounting masses.

In unison, the serpents cease their singing. A hush falls over the onlookers as well. Men, women and children waiting on held breath for the creatures to do something, anything.

The silence begins suffocating the crowd. Cries of impatience break the tension, and a group of dirty youths begin throwing stones and scraps into the reservoir, trying to initiate some type of excitement.

Then, as children hang over the inner rail and adults begin to shuffle back about their business, a tremendous crash erupts from the edge of the city. Sending a shockwave through the foundation.

He stumbles forward, nearly spilling down the stairs. Next to him, Nassius falls. A loud snap cracking from his hip, as he lands hard on his side.

Looking up, McKenna sees two teenage boys fall over the railing that surrounds the reservoir. Screams ring out from the onlookers, as the boys are violently pulled under the surface, tinting the emerald water a bloody shade of crimson and rust.

"What's happening?" Calisio cries, hiding beneath a marble table on the terrace.

He ignores the young senator's sobs, running down the stairs to get a better view. Across the city, outside the outer walls, the head of a behemoth sea serpent rises from the deep. It towers over the front of the city, dwarfing the temples and buildings below. The serpents in the reservoir beneath him begin their song again, looking like infants in comparison to the giant reaching from the sea outside, as if chicks calling for their mother hen.

McKenna runs through the city streets, weaving through panicking citizens. Mothers scream for their children. Children cry for their mothers. Chaos floods through the market, sweeping around the reservoir.

Approaching the temples on the west end of A'Tannia, he finds a stone alcove and takes shelter. Watching the serpent rise up high, showing its underbelly, McKenna can see the thick scales are riddled with arrows and bolts, harpoons and spears. Even a large silver trident hangs from beneath the creature's jowls. Remnants of some recent fight.

A shrill shriek forces him to cover his ears and cringe. Then, the serpent strikes at a temple, sending stone and marble soaring through the air. The large disembodied head of a statue flies at McKenna, crashing into the wall above, nearly crushing him as he jumps aside.

The screeching serpent throws its weight into the city's outer wall, shaking the foundation of A'Tannia and making the towering buildings built upon it tremble and sway. A second crashing blow topples some of the wooden peaks of the structures that make up the top edges of the city.

Looking around, he sees Arch-Councilor Merril climbing a rickety stairway to the top of the Sea Temple. Across the way, soldiers man the armaments and begin to launch spears and catapult stones at the swaying serpent.

The beast rears back, then quickly snaps its jaws across the platform that holds the large scorpions and catapults, sending men flying through the air.

Chirps and calls from the serpents in the reservoir almost sound like cheers for the larger beast, rooting for it as it strikes again, devouring a dozen soldiers with one sweep of its cavernous mouth.

As all appears to be lost, he hears the old arch-councilor yell from the top of the temple, throwing his hands in the air towards the sea.

As he does, the river starts to swell and a humongous wave begins to form behind him, drawing water away from around the city.

With a sweep of his arms, the arch-councilor sends the wave out to the ocean, forming a great tsunami. The serpent is pulled out to sea with the ebb of the tide, its long body scraping across the rough riverbed, leaving a trail of blood and scales in its wake.

McKenna cheers at the old man atop the temple, bent over from the exertion.

The senator sighs, looking back at the city. Devastation and death are everywhere. Screams and cries echo from around the reservoir, and wails rain from the buildings above. A smile slips across his mouth, only for a moment, as he begins to walk through the destruction.

This is it… This is my time…

The Warrior Poet

I see from golden sea, the shore of Triali

My journey ending, with the setting of the sun

He sits patiently, waiting 'neath a sweetlime tree

Eristoclese the wise, whose song is often sung

Once on shore, I nod hi, and glimpse a mist upon his eye

My dear old friend, he cries, you're a sight to behold

When was our last goodbye, did the spring sun fill the sky?

Yes, it did, is my reply, how fast time does unfold

As sunset gives to dusk, and night falls over us

My companion leads the way to the Academy

The salty scent of musk, rises from rhino tusk

A feel of ancient wisdom fills the air around me

Conversing, laughing, hours pass, like grains of sand through an hourglass

Speaking of the good, and the bad, of the beautiful, and of the sad

Remembering the years gone past, and times of peace that never last

All the things that drive men mad, to forsake the families that they had

As morning draws nigh, Eristoclese sighs, and bids me to see myself out

But when I try, I hear a sharp cry, as soldiers burst in and shout

Eristoclese, from orders on high, you have been sentenced, prepare to die

Do not beg, do not plead, we have no choice of the orders we heed

Leaping forward, I draw my sword,

Screaming at them, who is your lord?

Stand aside, they reply, this concerns not you,

We revel not, but the Emperor must have his due

They gallop on horseback, dashing through the rocky valley that surrounds the Pillar. Kzhee and Relorn are the best riders, easily pulling ahead of the group and leaving the rest of them chasing behind.

Rosemary rides upon a piebald mare, borrowed from the Emperor's stables. Next to her, Jia sits atop a black stallion, brought with her from the Firelands. Kzhee had brought his own as well, a sandy beauty named Sparks, currently outpacing Relorn and his snow white steed.

Looking back, she sees Ral struggling to keep up. Every time his horse turns or swerves, it nearly sends him flying off. Rika trots up next to him, bouncing on a yellow yearling, giving him words of encouragement and advice.

"At least he's facing the right way…" Jia says, laughing at Ral's struggles.

"You shouldn't make fun," Rosemary replies. "He's trying his best."

Jia smirks, then nods to Kzhee and Relorn. "What do you think of the prince?"

"I like everyone in the group!" She says, with a smile.

"No," Jia replies. "I mean, what do you think of him, personally…? I see the way he gets when you're around."

"I don't know what you're talking about." Rosemary says, matter-of-factly. "I like everyone the same, and I've never noticed him act strange around me."

"Okay." Jia sneers, pulling ahead to ride next to Chion as he puffs upon his pipe and blows elaborate smoke rings through the air.

Jia takes the smoking piece as he offers it, attempting to blow rings of smoke like his. Her flame dances on her shoulder and sends little balls of fire through the circular plumes, as if shooting targets.

Around midday, the group begins to head back to the Pillar, dropping their horses at the stables and taking the great lift up. Chion and Tiaries depart for the Tower of Trade, the rest of the group makes their way back to the Emperor's Tower.

Relorn approaches her as they pass through the garden, looking at the ground with a shy demeanor. "Target practice?" He asks, giving a slight shrug.

"What was that?" Rosemary asks.

"You were saying you might want to practice shooting bows. I was wondering if you wanted to now? We don't have to, if you don't want. I was just…"

"I'd love to!" She says, grinning with excitement. "I must warn you though, I'm not very good…"

"I've been shooting since I was young." He replies. "Once you get the basics down, it becomes easy."

They head back to the great lift, descending to the valley below. A small wooded area lies to the east. They casually meander towards the trees, winding with the turns and twists of the stony path, joking and sharing stories. Relorn becomes more talkative as they walk, looking less rigid and more relaxed.

When they reach the edge of the woods, Relorn strings his bow. Notching an arrow, he sends it splintering into the side of a tree. Rosemary claps excitedly, cheering for the prince.

He hands her the bow, and a quiver filled with arrows. Most are made of wood, but a few seem to be made of solid stone and rock, like the ones she had seen him pull from the ground.

Rosemary draws back the bow, listening to his pointers and adjusting accordingly. When he gives the signal, she lets loose an arrow. It flies through the air, just missing the tree she was aiming for.

"Curses!" She exclaims, stomping her foot and clenching a fist.

Relorn laughs at her outburst. "It was a good shot. Just take into account the shaft of the bow, and aim a little more to the side."

She takes another arrow from the quiver, to try again. Before notching it, she kisses the arrowhead for luck. As she does, a faint swirl of mist surrounds it. She shoots the arrow, adjusting ever so slightly to the side, and watches the projectile find its target and lodge deep into the wood.

"There you go!" Relorn shouts.

Looking at the tree, Rosemary notices a ring of frost expanding out from where her arrow had struck, creeping across the bark and limbs, freezing from the trunk down to the end of each leaf. An icy sculpture remains, lifeless.

"What?" He gawks, looking at her with astonishment.

"I don't know…" She stammers. "I've never done that before."

She tries a few more times, each shot yielding the same results.

"Isn't that something?" Relorn asks, excitedly. "See if it works when I shoot."

Rosemary kisses an arrow, then hands it to him. As he goes to notch it, the frost begins to inch across his fingers. She sees the glistening rime creeping around his hand, moving up his arm. The prince lets the arrow fly, sending it smashing into a tree. Freezing the wood, just as before.

She grabs his hand, frantically inspecting the skin. As she does, it begins to turn back to its natural tone, slowly returning to normal.

"How didn't it freeze you?" She asks, her voice shrill from fear. "I thought I killed you for sure... Oh Lord, I'm so sorry..."

"I'm made of stone." He answers, smiling and flexing his fingers and forearm. "You can't hurt me."

A feeling of relief floods over her as she throws her arms around the prince, trying not to cry.

They walk through the hills around the valley. She picks flowers while he pulls arrows from the rock, replenishing his supply.

"This is where I get the best arrows." He says, pulling one from a stony outcrop near the valley's rim.

The sun begins to set, sinking between the surrounding mountains and casting a warm glow through the sky. Rosemary sees a boulder with a seat shaped divot on top. She sits, relaxing and enjoying the sunset, while Relorn continues around her.

"What is this?" He asks, pulling an arrow from the rock beneath her.

The shaft of the arrow is made of bright blue lapis lazuli, flecked with bits of gold. The fletching is cast of brilliant sapphire, while the arrowhead is a shimmering blue diamond, sharpened to a nearly invisible point.

"It's beautiful…" She stammers, as the light of the sunset plays across its surface.

"Have it…" Relorn says, handing the arrow to her.

Rosemary takes it, then holds it to her heart, smiling. "Thank you." She says, scooting off the rock and hugging him.

As she smiles at him, the prince leans down and touches his lips to hers. For a moment, she returns his kiss, lost in his embrace. Then, suddenly, fear grips her heart. She pulls away, too scared to look up and see what has happened.

As she squeezes her eyes closed, Rosemary can hear the prince laugh. Peering up at him, she sees a layer of feathery hoarfrost clinging to the whiskers of his stubbly beard, a slight glisten of rime visible on his teeth as he grins.

"How?" She stammers.

"I told you." He says, brushing a tear from her cheek. "You can't hurt me…"

Councilor Quezada 5

Inzu lays next to him, sprawled across the bed, her soft skin held against his. He runs a finger up her leg, before gently kissing her neck.

She moans, then leans in and bites his lip. "We shouldn't..." She whispers, "It's almost time..."

"He can wait." Quezada replies, rolling her onto her back.

"Nice of you to show up..." Jero snarls, as Quezada and Inzu enter the throne room. The rest of the council already waiting to begin.

"Forgive us, your highness." He replies, giving a slight bow.

Jero ignores the apology and begins the meeting. "Sage has informed me of an unexplained occurrence in the Forest Realm. It would appear there is something, or someone, capable of causing great devastation. Many villages have been destroyed, and the people are terrified." The Emperor seems to revel in the thought, smiling a sickening smile.

"We will go to find out the cause." Sage adds, "And if all goes according to plan, we will bring back whatever is causing the destruction."

"What do you mean?" Kroonson asks, "What are we going to look for?"

Sage clears his throat, before sheepishly replying. "They say it's a dragon..."

Quezada bursts into laughter. "You want us to go investigate a dragon? A mythical flying lizard? Shall we try to find flying pigs as well?"

"I've seen men fly." Sage snaps. "Crazier things happen every day. Regardless, the reports are extensive and thorough. Hundreds of people have witnessed it. An imperial trade caravan was attacked while traveling to the Plateau, which now makes this our business."

"And I want whatever it is." Jero says, with hunger in his eyes. "Bring it to me!"

"Your highness…" Councilor Maestas adds, quickly. "I have received reports from A'Tannia. It would appear their city was attacked by an enormous sea serpent."

"They should have filled in that reservoir generations ago, maybe this will be a lesson to them." Jero replies, indifferently.

"Your Highness, with respect. The serpent attacked from outside the city. It was magnitudes larger than anything in the reservoir. The city is hurting, and it is assumed the creature survived the meager counterattack they were able to return."

This seems to get the Emperor's attention, a spark of excitement flashing in his eyes. "Fine, take Inzu with you. Boil the water if need be. Put the beast and the rest of those slimy creatures out of their misery."

"Shall we bring the children?" Sage asks.

"I do not care, I trust their training and management to all of you." Jero replies, waving the council off. "Go, bring me what I want."

The councilors depart with the exception of Thorne, who remains standing behind the Emperor as always.

"We will bring Ral and Kzhee to A'Tannia." Maestas says, as they walk towards the lift. "Ral knows the city, and I would imagine Kzhee will be the most effective weapon for attacking a creature in the water."

"Take Jia as well," Sage replies. "I don't want her burning down the Forest Realm."

"Fine," Inzu answers. "You take the rest. We'll have the A'Tannian army for support. You'll need the extra help."

"I'll go to A'Tannia as well," Quezada adds. "I never liked the Forest..."

"No," Sage says. "We need you to guard the prince."

"I have been guarding the prince for half his life." He snarls, fire flashing in his voice. "Someone else can do it."

"There is no one else can remove him from danger the way you can." Inzu says, gently touching his arm. "You should go with them."

"Why doesn't the prince come to A'Tannia as well?" He asks, not giving up.

"I have a feeling." Maestas says, almost wincing in pain. "I'm afraid the prince may not be safe in A'Tannia."

Finishing the last bite of eggs and fried potatoes on his plate, Kzhee relaxes into the back of his chair, waiting for the day's lesson to begin.

The doors slam open as Councilor Quezada enters the great hall. "Pack your things and be ready to ride, we leave this afternoon." He says, turning and exiting as fast as he had arrived.

"Where do you think we're going?" Rika squeaks.

He gives her a shrug, before signaling an attendant. "Wherever it is, I'm going to get another plate before we go. There's never anything good to eat on the road…"

After breakfast, he listlessly makes his way to the Tower of Trade. Throngs of people push past each other, as they file in and out of the large arched entrance.

"Kzhee!" Someone calls, from beyond the crowd.

Looking into the bank, situated off the side of the tower's entrance, he sees Chion waving goodbye to his uncle, the treasurer.

"What are you up to?" Chion asks, taking pace beside him.

"Grabbing some supplies before our excursion," Kzhee replies.

They enter the lift, and ride to one of the lower levels. The smoky smell of sizzling meat hits his nose as they exit the platform. Little brick shops surround the exterior of the floor, each peddling different products. Butchers throw cleavers into large beef and rhino carcasses, while others stuff ground pork into casings, stringing up sausages. Fishmongers tend to piles of trout and salmon, carefully grabbing snapping crabs and crawdads out of large glass jars. A few establishments have enormous open flame grills in front, cooking slabs of meat to draw in the hungry shoppers.

"I'm going to grab some dried buffalo. This place over here makes the best in the city. Do you want anything?" He asks Chion, ducking into one of the smaller shops.

"Yeah, grab me some honeyed beef." His friend shouts after him, distracted by a nearby cart serving steamed lobster claws.

Kzhee makes his way through the tightly packed store, surrounded by hundreds of types of smoked and dried meats. His favorite traveling food. He buys a few pounds from the kindly old proprietor, tucking it away in a leather sack.

When Kzhee steps out of the shop, Chion hands him a cracked lobster claw. Already halfway finished with his own. They head back to the lift, riding it a few levels up, before stepping off onto a floor filled with general goods stores.

"I need to grab some leaf while we're here." Chion tells him, patting his smoking pouch.

They step into a pungent shop. The smell of the place nearly knocks Kzhee back. He stares at the many selections, jars of dried plants in every color imaginable, lining the walls of the brightly illuminated store.

Chion wastes no time making his selections, buying enough to fill his pouch twice over. Kzhee can feel the smell of the shop linger on his clothes as they make their way to the opposite side of the level.

Kzhee grabs a thickly sewn sleeping skin. "I'm not going to be cold this time…" He says, to Chion, before paying the shop keep.

"Anything else?" Chion asks, moving towards the lift. "A drink for the road?"

They shuffle on the busy platform when it arrives, heading to the upper levels. Stepping off on one of the tavern floors, they make their way into a dimly lit pub.

As they enter, someone jumps behind him and pushes on his shoulders. He turns quickly, not knowing what to expect.

Kzhee's jaw drops in amazement as he realizes the figure standing in the doorway is Rilii, giving him a huge smile.

"What are you doing here?" He asks, happily surprised.

"I convinced my father to let me open up a gem shop in the Pillar, to help him expand his business." She says, running a finger down his arm. "You haven't forgotten me already, have you? I said I was going to find a way."

"I could never forget you." Kzhee says, throwing his arms around her and lifting her off the ground.

She giggles as he spins her around, gripping him tightly.

"All this time, and we are finally together!" Her excitement brims, "Can I see you tonight?"

"*Ouch…*" Chion groans.

"I'm sorry. Rilii, this is Chion. Chion, Rilii." Kzhee says, introducing his friend quickly, before continuing. "I really hate to say it, but we're leaving this afternoon... I don't know where we're going, or even how long we'll be gone for."

She stamps her foot in anger. "No! No! I say, no! I have spent my whole life waiting to be with you, and now that I am here I will not have it taken away on the very first day. No!"

Kzhee tries not to laugh. The redness in her cheeks and the furrow of her brow only making her look more beautiful.

"I am sorry." He says, taking her hands. "But we've waited this long, what is another few weeks? We will be together before you know."

She looks up at him with a glare, "I don't like it..."

He hugs her, leaning in to kiss her lips. They crinkle against his own, as she purses them in a pout of protest.

"I'll leave you two..." Chion says, smiling as he exits.

"Will it really only be a few weeks?" She asks.

"I hope so. The last time wasn't too long."

"Fine!" She exclaims, feigning a pretend smile. "Can you spare just an hour for me before you leave?"

"Of course. Where are you staying?"

"My father said that I can live in his courtly apartment, in the Emperor's Tower." She says, with a cheeky grin. "We're practically neighbors."

Seaborne had told the admiral that he didn't like the plan, but hadn't put up a fight accepting it. Now, trudging through a foot of snow in the freezing cold, he wishes he had resisted the assignment.

"Dis a pi'e o' sh…sh…sh…" Parrot shivers, trying to get his complaints out.

"It's not so bad." Kevin replies, more accustomed to the snowy tundra of the Southern Realm than his companions.

"It is bad, Parrot. Don't let him lie to ya." Seaborne stammers, through chatting teeth, wrapping his cloak tighter. "Let's get inside and get this over with. Ya remember ya lines, right?"

Parrot and Kevin nod affirmative, as they make their way into the Southern city of Seacliff. Perched high above the tempestuous ocean waves.

"Good, good. Kevin, I trust ya know how to act. Parrot though…" He says, eyeing the burly young man. "Tell them ya name, tell them that ya want to join, but offer nothing more. Only answer questions if ya must. Otherwise, I do the talking."

"Aye, cap'n"

"Remember, they are going to try to trick ya." He adds, driving the point home. "They will ask if ya have ever been a pirate. What will you say?"

The man thinks for a moment, "I te' 'em, na."

"Good." Seaborne replies, as they walk into the recruiting offices of the Southern Trading Company.

A salty recruiter approaches them as they enter. "Ahoy, good to see strong men coming in. Interested in joining are we?" The man hands them something to sign.

Seaborne reads the writing, before putting pen to parchment. One part in particular jumps out at him.

Any crewmen caught acting as thieves, mutineers, or pirates, shall duly be forced to walk the plank.

Shaking his head, the pirate captain signs the document. Then passes it to Parrot and Kevin.

"Welcome aboard men, the next rail sleigh for the Frozen City leaves this evening. You are to take it, and report to Barrenport for ship assignment." The recruiter grins, taking his seat. "Best of luck to you."

The admiral's words ring through Seaborne's head, as they wait in the cold for the rail sleigh to arrive.

'We must move the fleet to safer waters... This attack, it isn't the first. There have been others... Reports of creatures at sea destroying our ships. We've tried to keep the rumors from spreading, but it won't be long before everyone is in a panic. We need someone cunning, someone resourceful. We need you, Seaborne. We need you to find out how the Southern Trading Company is able to sail through the icy waters as they do. For we will cross the Frozen Sea. We must, to escape the terrors that dwell beneath. If not, I fear the end draws nigh for us.'

Loak 4

"I don't see what the problem is..."

"You see nothing wrong with the fact that the Emperor controls everything I do?" Loak shouts, his emotions flaring.

"I mean, you do have everything you could ever want, right?" Jaties replies, calmly changing his clothes before the evening show. "You never have any trouble coming to see me."

"I have to sneak out to see you, I am a prisoner..."

"We had to bail Jake out of the dungeons last week. I can take you there. Show you real prisoners." Jaties smirks, laying down on the bed next to him. "They don't eat filet and lobster with drawn butter, and they certainly don't sleep on feather mattresses."

"You'll never understand..." Loak sighs, rolling onto his back and gazing up at the ceiling. "They are going to make me choose a wife."

"What?"

"They gave me a list of women and said to pick, otherwise they will pick for me."

"That is ridiculous! Tell them you don't want to. They can't force you!" Jaties shouts.

"Oh, now you see the problem...? Like I said, they control everything I do. What am I supposed to say? They only care about me having as many children as possible, I can't avoid it any longer."

"It just makes no sense to me, you do your job like you're supposed to." Jaties says, standing up. "You are the strongest Earthmover they have. Isn't that enough?"

"The Pillar needs the Earthmovers. Without them, the city cannot function. They make each of them take as many wives as possible, women with gifts, in the hopes that their offspring will be born like us."

"If this place needs Earthmovers to function, doesn't that mean that you are the ones in charge? What would happen if you refused to work?"

"I don't know... Who would follow if I stopped? Every Earthmover I know loves their position, loves their life. None would risk it." He pauses, staring at the floor. "I am alone."

"You're not alone!" Jaties barks, taking a seat next to him. "What if we run?"

"What about your sister? You can't leave her."

A look of pain falls on Jaties' face. "Maybe she would come. We could try to find our mother. Tiaries has always wanted to go search for her."

"Search for your mother? What happened to her?" He asks, taking Jaties by the hand. "You don't have to tell me. I know you don't like to talk about it."

"No, it's okay." Jaties says, a tear rolling down his cheek. "To be honest, I don't even know if she's still alive. Tiaries never doubts it, but I do… My mother, she could bring people back to life, like Tiaries can. When we were young, my father met a man. A man whose father was dying. We had no money, and the man was rich. He offered a lot of gold to bring my mother to him, to save his dying father. My parents left us, saying they would be back for dinner. That was the last time we ever saw our mother."

"What happened? Did your father come back?"

"He did…" Jaties says, his voice cracking. "He returned, dead in a box."

"No…"

"Yes." Jaties says, bitterly. "Tiaries touched her lips to his. It was the first time we saw that she had a gift as well. But our father, he had been gone too long... Nothing but an empty shell came back."

"That's horrible!"

"It was… My father had to die twice." He shakes his head. "Tiaries blames herself."

"Did you… Did you have to…?"

"What? Did I kill him? No. My uncle came and put my father's body out of its misery. Then he took us to the carnival that he traveled with. He was an actor, a master of disguise, and we joined his troupe. Not long after we got settled, he left us to try to find our mother. The thought of his sister being held captive somewhere was too much to handle. We have only seen him once since then, a couple years after he left. He stopped at the carnival for one night, to let us know he was still alive and still searching… Tiaries begged for him to take us along, to help him. But he told us no, and was gone in the morning."

"I don't know what to say… My problems sound petty in comparison."

"It's in the past… Your problem is here and now, and we will face it together. Whatever may come."

"I love you…" Loak whispers, trying to swallow the tightness in his throat.

Jaties' large eyes light up, and then he smiles. "I love you too."

Chion 7

He watches the ship pull away, setting course down the river. Finding himself feeling envious of his friends aboard. Jia, Ral and Kzhee, all sitting down to enjoy dinner in warmth and comfort as they finish the trip to A'Tannia. While Chion stands on the edge of the dreary Forest Realm, made even more depressing by the gray and gloomy sky above.

The dark clouds hang heavy, beginning to pour as the group makes their way into the woods. Rika is curled up in the supply cart, hiding beneath some leathers and furs. Relorn and Rosemary ride abreast, a large blanket held over their heads. Tiaries sits atop a prancing steed, her arms outstretched, reveling in the rainfall.

"Stay close." Quezada grunts, as the towering trees envelop their group.

What little sunlight the rainy sky had provided is quickly snuffed out by the thick blanket of branches above. Chion moves his horse between Quezada and Kroonson, the constant rustling from the surrounding brush making him skittish. He takes his pipe out and begins to smoke away, trying to calm his nerves.

"We don't have to camp in the woods, do we?" He asks.

"If we don't pick up the pace, then it's possible. But most likely, no." Sage replies. "The Great Tree is a few more hours ride. Even if night falls, we'll probably press on until we arrive. It's not as if the sun makes much of a difference under this dense canopy."

Chion goes back to silently puffing his pipe, trying to ignore the terrifying sounds and movements around them. When the noises begin to grow more restless, Kroonson makes a strand of lightning arc between his hands, sending a loud crack through the woods. The sounds quiet down for a while, before slowly returning.

After hours of riding, a glowing light appears before them, dancing at the end of the trail. As they draw closer, he sees that it's a torch held up by a figure on horseback. Each step brings the figure's features more into focus. Some type of deformity seems to cover it. Quills and needles droop from the creature's skin, like a long dense coat, a million sharp points shining in the firelight.

"Who goes there?" Quezada shouts. Kroonson behind him, ready to let loose an attack.

"Hello!" A girlish voice responds, "Are you the Emperor's party?"

"We are," Sage says. "Who might you be?"

"I am Ahm An Dah." The young voice replies. "My Father is An Yan Nur, Apex of the Great Tree. He bid me guide you the remainder of the way. There have been reports of highwaymen in the area, accosting travelers."

"She looks like a porcupine…" Rika whispers, from the back of the cart.

"We hear there is some type of… Thing… Harassing people and destroying villages. Does that have anything to do with the highwaymen?" Quezada asks.

"The *thing* you speak of, is a dragon." She says, in a defiant voice. "And no, they are not related."

"A dragon?" Kroonson sneers, snorting sarcastically.

"Yes, a dragon." Ahm replies, nodding her quilled head.

She sees them the remainder of the way. The sounds of the woods cease when she joins the group, making the night almost pleasant.

"Here we are…" The girl says, as they make their way through a tight wall of undergrowth.

Before them, a gargantuan tree rises from the forest floor. Its protruding roots dwarf the redwoods around it, soaring above the surrounding forest.

"It's as big as the Pillar!" Rosemary gasps, craning her neck to try to see the top as it disappears through the canopy, reaching into the sky.

An elaborate entrance is carved into the side of the titanic tree, as large as the entrance of any city Chion had ever seen. They make their way inside. The interior is illuminated by hundreds of hanging jars, each emitting a different colored light. He takes a closer look at one of the glasses, and sees the light inside moving about, fluttering around the jar.

"Glowflies." Ahm explains, with a laugh. Noticing his bewilderment. "They're safer than torches."

Their group enters an enormous open chamber, lit up by a large hanging glass fixture, filled with thousands of the glowing bugs. Beneath it, a small man with stark white hair stands leaning on a knotted cane for support. Next to him, a strong man with wide shoulders and a bald head paces back and forth, three glowflies buzzing around his bramble crown, green and purple and orange.

"Ahm!" The old man exclaims. "Your father has been worried."

The taller man makes his way to them, a stern look on his face. "Greetings, I am glad you made it safely." He says, addressing the councilors. "I intended to send a larger escort party for you, but my advisors believed it would draw unwanted attention."

"Your daughter has been a pleasure." Sage replies, bowing his head to the apex.

"Let me show you to your rooms. Tomorrow morning, Ahm can lead you to the area where the most attacks have occurred."

Music drifts from a myriad of verandas, lining the large staircase that winds up around the outskirts of the enormous tree city. Men and women lounge about, eating dinner and socializing.

As they walk past, Chion can hear the thoughts of the people around them.

'What are they doing here?'

'Why have they come?'

'Are they going to take more of us?'

'It isn't right…'

'Hopefully the dragon takes them too.'

"I don't think these people like us…" Chion whispers, in Sage's ear.

"Just keep your head down, hopefully we won't be here more than a few nights." The councilor replies. "Let's prove this thing isn't real, so we can go home."

Tiaries 7

Tiaries rises before the sun, slowly getting up from the small comfortable bed that the apex's daughter had led her to. A soft light fills the room with magenta and azure and lime, casting just enough of a glow for her to find her clothes and get dressed.

She bumps into Ahm outside the entrance of the Great Tree, standing beneath a sod roofed stable, preparing the horses for their journey.

"Hello, Tiaries!" Ahm says, cheerfully. "You're up early."

"Always…" Tiaries replies, stepping towards a small sandy horse and running her fingers through its mane.

Looking out, she can see a clearing beyond the trees. "What is that? It looks like the forest just ends over there."

"A cliff." Ahm says, tightening a leather strap beneath a large black horse. "On a clear day you can see the Elven States from its edge. You probably have time for a look, the horses will take a while to get ready."

"Thank you!" Tiaries exclaims. "If any of my friends come down, could you let them know where I went?"

"Of course. Don't leave the path though. The Forest is dangerous, even this close to the Great Tree."

"I won't!" Tiaries chirps, skipping down the path.

The glow of the morning twilight grows slowly brighter as the sun's hidden rays creep towards the horizon. Towering trees throw darkness across the path, their shade devouring what little bit of warmth the light had brought. Tiaries shivers, as the shadows creep across her body, sending goosebumps prickling upon her skin. The cold, crisp smell of autumn tickles her nose with each breath. She breaks into a run, hoping the exertion will be warming.

The cliff appears before her, much faster than she had expected. Its precipice hardly visible against the green sea of forest behind. As she nears the edge, the trees begin to thin. Warmth floods across her skin, as the shadows dissipate. The tree line comes to a stop near the cliff, leaving a strip of grass running parallel to the ledge.

Tiaries walks along, gazing out over the vast valley below. In the distance, she sees the Shady Stream, separating the Forest Realm from the Viali Vineyard. Past that, her eyes can make out a spot of checkered colors, tucked against a curve in the Great River.

The Painted City... She thinks, with a smile.

The large trees of the Elven States are just barely visible on the other side of the river. Nothing more than a narrow band of green, nestled between the water and the sky.

Her throat tightens and her eyes begin to water, as the first beams of sun explode from above a distant mountain, shining a brilliant light on the beauty before her.

The sky is enormous! Why does it look so much larger than usual...?

The wonder of the landscape below takes her breath away. For a moment, Tiaries begins to feel lightheaded, as if she might faint. Stepping away from the ledge, she takes a deep breath, trying to stop the spinning in her head.

As the world comes back into focus, Tiaries hears something in the distance, an echoing howl weaving through the trees.

Awwoooooooooooooooooooo

A second howl joins the first, drifting from off to her right. Followed closely by a third. Dead leaves rustle and crack, not far from her. She moves away from the incoming noises, stumbling towards the cliff.

Taking a peek over the ledge, Tiaries sees nothing but shear smooth rock below. Quickly, running to a nearby tree, she grabs onto a low lying limb and pulls herself up. Then, swinging up onto a higher branch, she nestles out of sight amongst the leaves and shadows.

Not a moment after she curls into place, a clanging sound rings out from the brush. A man dressed in black plate stumbles from the bushes, tripping on a root that protrudes from the tree below. He falls hard, cursing loudly.

It's the Black Knight! Tiaries tries to stifle a gasp.

As he fights to regain to his feet, an enormous beast leaps from between the trees, knocking him ferociously to his back.

Tiaries peeks out from the leaves. Below, she sees a gigantic mastiff standing with its front paws planted firmly on the knight's chest. It lets out a booming howl, followed by a few deep yelps. Then, without warning, the large dog changes shape. In its place, a stout man in leather armor appears, holding a large halberd.

"I got him! I got him!" The man barks, excitedly.

The howls in the distance grow closer, making her spine tingle. Tiaries looks at the tree limbs around her. Just out of reach, she sees a large dead branch. Holding onto the trunk to try to steady herself, she stands up and reaches towards it.

Stretching out, she manages to get a hand onto the branch, then pulls hard, trying to break it free. With her second try it cracks, falling down on top of the man yelling below, knocking him to the ground.

Tiaries tries to grab back onto her limb, but her hand slips, sending her crashing down to the ground as well. The fall is hard, knocking the wind out of her as she lands.

"Thank you!" The knight says, pushing the man off him and getting up.

She wheezes loudly, trying to regain her breath. "Anytime…"

He helps her to her feet, then runs off the way he came. "Come on! Follow me."

Desperately, she looks around for the path back to the Great Tree. But instead, she sees a snarling wolf coming out of the woods. It takes off along the cliff, sprinting towards her. Without another thought, Tiaries turns and runs after the knight.

Unhindered by armor, she catches up with him quickly. "Where are you going?" She shouts, dodging a tree as they run.

The A'Tannians left an abandoned camp ahead. They have been raiding the villages more than usual, and were using it as a base.

"Is that why you're here?" She asks, glaring at him.

"No, I have been following the Order. They are recruiting an army... I am trying to figure out what they are raising it for."

"You are the one who tried to kill that priest, why would you do that?" Tiaries asks, considering turning and running away from both him and the wolf.

"The Order isn't what it seems... They are liars, murderers. They killed my mentor." He shouts, "High Priest Tobin is evil, and he has to be stopped."

"The Order wouldn't kill anyone for no reason. They are healers and priests, and the guardians of the weak." She says, suspiciously.

"If you don't believe me, feel free to go your own way."

She hears the snarls and howls drawing closer.

I guess I am sticking with him, for now...

Wooden structures appear before them. Makeshift buildings, pens and cages. They duck into a small shack, nearly empty except for a couple bunks and a fire pit. Crouching behind one of the bunks, he puts a finger to his lips. She squeezes in next to him, and they wait in silence.

Outside, the sound of padding footsteps approaches. Two wolves creep past the entrance, sniffing the wind, trying to pick up a scent. Behind them, a small bulldog runs up, letting out a string of yapping barks. In a flash, the bulldog changes into a short man, with a square jaw and an under bite.

"You lost him?" The short man barks.

"It sounded like we had found him. But when I got there, Ted was knocked out and alone."

"Where is that oaf now?"

The mastiff runs up, panting heavily. Its tongue hanging out of the side of its mouth, amongst an endless amount of drool.

"Right here bossth!" Ted shouts, turning into a man as he approaches. His tongue still hanging like a dog's.

"So you three let this little guy sneak into our camp, steal all our gold, and somehow get away?" The small man shouts.

Tiaries glares at the knight. He shrugs and mouths out the word, *'Thieves...'*

"Teddy was on watch duty!" One of the wolves says.

"I don't care. This is your fault too." The little man sighs, "This is worse than when you let the prince's caravan get away before the tourney. We would be retired now!"

"Sorry boss..." The wolf says, sheepishly.

"Hey, do you guys hear that?" Ted asks. His ears perking up.

"What?" The bulldog man shouts.

Tiaries grabs the knight's hand, squeezing it tightly and holding her breath.

"I don't know," Ted says. "It, uh... It kinda sounds like wings."

"Run!" One of the wolves screams out, dropping to all fours and sprinting away.

The other men follow suit, turning into their animal forms and scampering off.

"What was tha…" Tiaries begins to ask.

But her words are cut short, as a screeching wind slams into the side of their shack, splintering the wood and sending everything flying through the camp. The two of them roll through the debris, as the wind continues to rage. Looking up, Tiaries sees a great form flying across the sky. It's tremendous wings blotting out the sun.

"What is that…?" She gasps.

"Run!" The knight yells, as the shadowy figure makes its way around for another pass.

As it moves out of the sun, Tiaries can make out the creature. Its large lizard-like body is the light brown color of dead leaves, interlaced with shimmering streaks of green and yellow and orange.

"Let's go!" He shouts, grabbing her hand.

"Tiaries!" She hears someone screaming, from the woods behind them. The knight gives her a final look, then lets her hand go and runs off into the trees.

She turns and sprints the other way, towards the voice calling her name. Ahead, she sees Chion and Councilor Quezada.

"She's over here!" Chion hollers. "Where have you been?"

Ahm comes riding up behind them, followed by the rest of the group.

"Go! Run!" Tiaries yells, not slowing down as she passes them. "Dragon!"

The trees around them shake, as the beast flies overhead. Its breath raging through the woods like a violent storm. Trees fall and branches fly behind the group as they ride towards her.

As Quezada pulls by, he vanishes from the back of his horse, appearing next to her. He places a hand on her shoulder, then everything goes black. A moment later, they are both on the back of his horse, riding through the forest.

"It looks like you found what you came for!" Ahm yells, at Councilor Sage. "Now what do you propose we do?"

They ride into a clearing, and Kroonson leaps from the side of his horse. Hitting the grassy ground with a roll, then coming up to his feet in an instant.

As the dragon flies overhead, Kroonson lets out a wave of green sparks, lighting up the sky. The dragon screeches, as the electricity climbs up its leg. It rapidly ignites, and flames begin to consume the creature.

With a silent roar, the dragon vanishes amidst a storm of smoke and fire. No carcass comes crashing down, only a faint rain of ash and soot.

"What was that?" Kroonson asks. "It just burned to nothing..."

"It's not possible." Sage says, dismounting his horse and scooping up a pile of the debris from the ground.

The rest of the group looks around, dazed. The clearing has a single tree, surrounded by a large meadow and a ring of pink cherry trees and yellow leafed oaks. Everything slightly covered with a fine layer of grey ash.

"So much for a dragon…" Sage says, to their guide.

But the girl only smiles in reply, meandering through the flowers and grass.

"So, is that all?" Rika asks, "Can we go home?"

The wind begins to pick up as she speaks, sending leaves adrift in the breeze. Tiaries sees Rika's eyes widen and her mouth drop, the girl's gaze locked onto something in the distance.

Tiaries turns around, looking up at the forest canopy. The wind pulls through the trees, a tempest taking form from the leaves as it passes. She watches in disbelief as the dragon appears again. It's long pink body suspended by flapping yellow wings, perfectly blending in with the surrounding trees.

"This way!" Ahm yells, leaving her horse behind and taking off towards the lone tree standing in the clearing.

They follow her at full speed, until she slides onto her rear and disappears. As they approach the spot where she vanished, a hole appears between the knotted roots. Rika jumps in without hesitation, followed by Rosemary and Relorn.

Quezada pushes the rest of them down, before sliding after. As they land on the ground, a blast rings out above them. The root system creaks and groans, as the dragon rages.

"Let's go…" Ahm says, leading them down a tunnel branching off of the chamber. Kroonson following closely behind, sparks from his hands lighting their way with a brilliant green glow.

"I thought it died… Where did that thing come from?" Rosemary asks.

"The dragon is part of the woods, the heart of the forest." Ahm says, smirking. "The A'Tannians tried to kill it with fire arrows and burning pitch. The Order had a fire-bringer with them.... No matter what happens, it always comes back."

"Oww!" Relorn hollers. "Something just hit me!"

Tiaries looks around the dimly lit chamber, but doesn't see anything other than their group. She takes a step back, towards the tunnel wall. Then from nowhere, she feels a hand slap the back of her head. *"Ouch!"* She yelps.

"Do we run?" Relorn asks, swinging around his bow and notching an arrow.

In quick succession, something makes Ahm scream and her quills spring sharply outward. Then, behind her, Kroonson groans and chokes. Coughing up blood and sliding to the ground.

Tiaries looks up and sees the quills on Ahm's back dripping with blood, while Kroonson lays across the dirt, his chest filled with holes.

In front of Ahm, another person appears. A young girl clutching her side, groaning as she tries to pull out a large quill lodged in her stomach.

She was invisible…

Tiaries hears Kroonson give a final exhale, as the life leaves his body. Rushing forward, she pushes Chion out of the way, sliding next to the dead councilor.

She kisses him quickly, then looks at his wounds with anticipation, tightly gripping his shirt between her fingers.

After what seems like an eternal moment, Kroonson lurches up gasping for breath. Tiaries sighs, falling onto her rear in relief.

"What about me?" The girl gasps, clutching her wound. "Help, please…"

"What were you doing?" Ahm screams, "Trying to make me a murderer?"

"I'm just trying to keep her safe…" The girl says, wincing in pain.

"Who? The dragon?" Quezada asks.

"No… Not the dragon… It's just wind… My sister." She gasps, as Kroonson climbs to his feet and ruthlessly rips the quill from her side.

A stream of blood squirts from the wound, eliciting a screech of pain from the girl. As her screams echo through the tunnel, the rumbling begins to grow above them. Back the way they came, the tree covering the entrance is torn from the ground, uprooted. The dragon sticks its head into the newly formed opening, projecting a piercing roar down the pathway.

"Run!" Quezada shouts, shoving him away from the opening.

Relorn grabs Rosemary's hand, and they start running down the tunnel. Behind them, he can see Kroonson shoot a shower of sparks at the beast. Yet the jolt does nothing, save for produce a bit of steam from the dragon's snout.

"It's not real!" The wounded girl screams from the floor. "Help me, I can make it go away…"

"How?" Sage asks.

She points down the tunnel, towards Relorn and Rosemary. "There is a chamber around the next bend. Help me there and I'll show you how to stop it."

Quezada and Sage pick the girl up and they all head down the tunnel, away from the roaring dragon trying to dig its way after them. Through the winding corridor they enter a chamber. Mats are thrown on the ground, and food debris lines the edges of the room. A small fire burns, barely providing enough light to see.

The dragon's screeching grows louder as they enter the room, shaking the walls.

"Reem!" A voice squeaks, from a darkened corner.

"It's fine, Hannah." The wounded girl says. "Make it stop, please!"

"I'm trying!" The younger girl cries. "Are you okay?"

"I'll be fine, as long as you make it stop…"

The cavern begins to quake around them, as if something is crashing into the ground above.

"Reem…" The little girl says, creeping out from the corner

The wounded girl sighs and goes her body limp, the life fading from her eyes.

"No!" The little girl screams. "No! You killed her! You killed my sister!"

Dirt begins to fall from the ceiling as the thrashing and screeching magnifies. The room begins to cave in, large boulders and chunks of ground falling, threating to crush them.

"Tiaries!" Relorn yells, "It'll kill us if the sister dies!"

Tiaries springs forward, but the body disappears as she approaches the dead girl.

"What?" Tiaries asks, panicked. "Where did it go?"

"She turns invisible!" Rosemary shouts, dropping to the ground. "Feel around…"

They all begin running their hands across the ground, searching for the corpse. Suddenly, Relorn feels something with his hands.

"Here!" He shouts, his fingertips fumbling across her face, feeling for her lips. "Right there!"

Tiaries kisses the air at the end of his finger, then again, feeling around to be sure she got the lips. Suddenly, something pushes against his hand, as the invisible girl chokes and sits up.

"Wha… Wha... Wha…" Reem stutters, as her body slowly becomes visible again.

The little girl sees her sister, gasping back to life. Huge tears begin falling down her cheeks, as she rushes forward into her arms. The rumbling above ceases, while Hannah hugs her sister tightly.

"What was that?!" Rika shouts, her eyes almost as wide as Tiaries'.

"When my sister gets scared..." Reem says, stroking the girl's hair. "The dragon comes to protect her. It is made of the forest. Leaves or flowers, or whatever is around when it takes form. It isn't alive, it can't be killed. It's just leaves, blowing in the wind."

"Those were more than leaves blowing in the wind," Kroonson snarls. "Those leaves were on a mission to kill us."

"The slavers have been raiding the villages. We haven't seen our parents since the last attack. We are just trying to stay alive..." Reem says, defensively. "We were searching for food above, when we heard the dog pack coming. They're even worse than the slavers. They steal, and kill!"

"Come with us, children." Sage says, with a kind warmth. "We are the Emperor's men, nothing bad will happen to you if you are with us. No slavers, no dogs."

"Where are you going to take us?" The younger girl asks, apprehensively.

"To the Great Tree, for now." Sage replies, "It is the safest place in the Forest. Come along."

The girls agree, and begin to gather their things. Shortly after, the group makes their way back to the Great Tree, the two extra members riding along on the back of Sage and Quezada's horses.

The Apex of the Great Tree is waiting for them outside the entrance. "Ahm, daughter." He says, patting her quilled head. "Who are these two?"

She whispers into his ear.

The apex nods, approaching the girls. "I am relieved to hear we found you. We will see to your safety until your parents can be located. Ahm, please show them to a suitable suite, make sure they are comfortable."

"Yes, father." She says, leading the girls into the Great Tree.

Sage claps the apex on the back. "I told you it wasn't a real dragon!"

"That is a matter of opinion." The apex replies, grinning. "I do thank you though, it is good of you to bring them here."

"Well…" Sage says, looking guilty. "We have to bring the young one to the Pillar. Jero will want to see her."

The apex sighs, and walks among the group. "I am afraid that I cannot let them go. The dragon… It is the soul of the forest. I will not have it taken. Apologies, I am sure this is not what you want to hear."

Sage snickers, "The Emperor…"

"The Emperor may never hear of this at all…" The apex says, in a voice as light as a feather, three glowflies still fluttering around his head. "Small groups such as yours disappear each and every day in these woods. The Forest… Such a dangerous place."

"You…" Kroonson starts to say, threateningly.

"Stop!" Sage hisses. "I apologize, apex. We must have had a misunderstanding. Of course it would be best if the girls stay with you. We will tell the Emperor the situation has been resolved, no dragons..."

"I am glad to hear it." The apex replies. "I will have your supplies packed and placed next to the stables at once."

"Thank you, my lord." Sage says, bowing his head and steering his horse towards the stables. "Come!" He shouts, after the group.

What just happened? Relorn thinks, nudging his horse towards Sage. *Where are we going?*

"Not a word, anyone." Sage whispers, before Relorn can even ask. "We grab our things, and we leave."

For hours, the group rides in silence. The councilors constantly turning their heads up to the trees, eyes darting every time a branch rustles or twig breaks. They continue riding through the night, until the river appears before them, glistening in the morning sun.

Not until they find a bridge, and cross the water into the River Realm, does Sage begin to speak.

"The trees have ears..." The councilor says. "One wrong word and arrows would have fallen on us from every direction."

"Do we tell Jero?" Quezada asks.

"Let's charter a ship to the Great City." Sage says, gesturing to the trees along the riverbed. "We may be out of the Forest, but we are not out of the woods... There will be plenty of time to talk later."

They find a ship outside the Vineyard, and sail to the river city of Manti. From there, it is a short journey on horseback to the Great City.

"Look!" Rosemary says, pointing up and squeezing his hand. "The Flying City is docked here."

Relorn looks up above the Great City, at the floating disk in the sky and the enormous balloon suspending it.

"Perfect timing!" Sage shouts, "Let's catch a lift home."

They make their way through the streets, heading towards the park at the city's center. From there a hot air balloon lifts them up to the Flying City, taking two trips to bring up their entire party and all their gear.

Chion chatters excitedly, as they ride up with the second group. "This is perfect! I own two buildings full of suites. We will ride in style the whole way back to the Pillar. I wonder how the bank is…"

Once on board, they drop the horses off at the stables. The councilors stay in the Imperial Residence, a luxurious townhouse in the center of the Flying City. The rest of the group takes up rooms in Chion's building, a nice set of apartments above a quiet tavern.

As Relorn gets comfortable in his room, Rosemary slips in.

"Tired?" She asks, sliding under the covers next to him.

"Exhausted…" Relorn says, as she curls up and lays her head gingerly against his shoulder.

He rubs his hand along her arm, feeling her warmth. With a smile, he closes his eyes.

When he opens them again, the morning sun shines through his window. Rosemary is sprawled across him, her face peacefully resting on his chest. He wraps his arms around her, holding her tightly.

"Good morning." Rosemary says, as she wakes. Stretching and twisting the knots out of her back, before kissing him and smiling.

They spend the entire day in bed, talking and laughing, wrapped in each other.

As the sun begins to set, both of their stomachs start rumbling. They make their way downstairs to the tavern below. Chion and Rika relax at the bar, laughing about something, while Sage, Quezada and Tiaries sit at a nearby table, hungrily devouring the plates of food before them.

As he and Rosemary go to take a seat next to Rika, a voice calls out from across the tavern.

"Relorn! Hey, Relorn!"

Looking around, he sees Matio hop up from a booth against the wall, excitedly making his way towards them.

"How are you!?" Matio asks, throwing his arms around his friend. "What are you doing here?"

"We're on our way back to the Pillar," Relorn says. "What about you?"

Matio falls quiet, the excitement in his voice quickly fading. "I, uhh…" He pauses, looking at the others sitting at the bar. "Hello, Chion."

"Hello, Matio. Good to see you."

Matio nods in response, then turns back to Relorn. "Could we talk outside?" He asks.

"Yeah, of course..."

They head out front, Matio fumbling with a pouch of leaf.

"How long have you been smoking?" Relorn asks.

"For a bit now." Matio says, lighting his pipe from the flame of a nearby lamp. "Things have been... Well, it's been rough."

"What happened?"

Matio takes a deep breath, then exhales. The fog drifting from his mouth moves across the air, as the Flying City sails through the night sky.

"Relorn... Your father, he... Well, I mean, my father I guess... Well not him, but, you know... His men..."

"Spit it out, Matio." He says, shivering in the cold wind. Gazing back at his friends inside the warm inviting tavern. Rosemary turns her head towards the door, giving him a smile.

"Relorn..." Matio says, with a deep sigh. "Eristoclese is dead... They killed him..."

He is the first to jump off the ship, as they pull into the vast wooden harbor built around A'Tannia.

"Ral!" Councilor Maestas yells. "We're staying in the Imperial suites. You know how to get there?"

"A few floors above the Senate Hall." Ral yells back.

"Good, we'll see you there."

Running through the city, he stops at the pits to watch two young fighters in one of the side arenas. Each time one of them lunges with an advance, he finds himself instinctively dodging invisible blows, as if he is a participant in the fight.

Turning from the gladiators, he makes his way through the winding paths and alleys leading through A'Tannia's upper levels. A moment later, he is standing outside Satia's tavern. Stepping inside the dimly lit place he finds her tending bar on the fourth floor, leaning on the end of the counter with her chin resting on her palm, gazing out the open wall at the city below.

A warm breeze blows in, as he sits across from her.

She turns to take his order, but her eyes light up when she sees his face.

"Ral!" Satia shouts, jumping onto the bar and spinning around onto his lap. "I've missed you! What brings you back?"

"We are looking into the serpent that attacked the city." He says, his arms around her waist.

"Well, hopefully it is a long stay." She says, smirking. "The attack was something terrible. Can't say it was bad for business though… People seem to be drinking more than ever."

"I can imagine."

Satia looks across the bar as a few men enter. Ral notices one of the senators from the trip to the tourney. They approach, taking a seat next to him.

"Hello, Satia. Do you think you will be busy tonight?" The senator asks.

She looks at him, then coolly replies, "The bar will probably be busy, yes. It has been a lot lately. I won't be around to see however. My friend is here visiting." With a large grin, she gestures towards Ral.

The senator turns his eyes at him. "Oh yes, good to see you. Paul, was it?"

"Ral…" He says, shaking the senator's hand.

"Ah, right. I am Senator Calisio. Good to see you again." With that, he turns and leaves. His men following close behind.

"That was strange…" Ral says, raising an eyebrow.

"He's been hanging around ever since the trip. Who knows what these people want. I just pour the drinks and smile." Satia says, flashing a large grin to demonstrate the point.

"Such a pretty smile." He says, in a mocking tone. Gently pinching a dimpled cheek.

"Take me upstairs." She purrs, running her nails along his back. "It has been far too long…"

The Glorious Knights and Illuminated Priests of the Order of Justice, Honor, and Chivalry 4

It had been over a week since they entered the woods surrounding the Frozen City. The horses had died quickly, unable to move through the waist high drifts of snow. After days without food, they found themselves regretting not having eaten the horses as they fell. In the moment it had seemed wrong, but now the hunger was becoming unbearable.

The three of them crawl along over the surface, trying to sprawl out to keep from sinking into the loose snow.

"I think this might be the end…" Sir Joel sighs, rolling onto his back.

"No, keep going." Friar Philip says, "When things seem darkest is when the lord above shines his light."

"Sure," Sir Marcus replies. "I don't know how much darker it could get. Let's see that light!"

"Stay strong." The friar says, pulling himself across the snow. "If we keep following the sunsets, we will get out eventually."

"Or we'll starve…" Sir Joel says, with a groan.

"Or freeze," Sir Marcus adds.

"Freeze?" Friar Philip asks, "I am burning up! I have no layers left to shed."

It had been days since they abandoned their armor, finding that it was making travelling across the snow too difficult. At this point they were down to their soaking wet underclothes, which seemed to alternate between uncomfortably clinging to them with sweat, then painfully freezing to their skin.

"Keep your faith men, and we shall be delivered." The friar shouts, to himself more than anyone.

As they slowly make it to the top of the hill before them, the valley ahead comes into view. Beyond the woods, standing between the knights and the way home, lie thousands upon thousands of tents. The camp of an enormous army.

"They are going to take Blackburn..." Sir Marcus says, shaking his head.

Friar Philip lets out a sob. "This is it, the darkest... Starvation and death behind us, capture and death before us..."

Sir Joel begins to laugh. Lightly at first, then quickly becoming a roar. "Just keep our faith, huh?"

His laughter shifts the snow beneath them, causing the group to slide forward down the slope.

"Oh no!" Friar Philip yells, grabbing for a branch or rock, anything to stop their momentum.

The snow around them starts to give way faster, bringing them speeding down the side of the hill in a miniature avalanche. Trees fly past like brown and green blurs, as they slide and twist down the mountainside.

"This is it!" Sir Joel yells, "It was nice knowing you two!"

The snow piles into a ball, and the men begin to roll inside. Spinning over and over as it tumbles.

AHHHHHHHH! The men scream, as their snowball slams into ground below, splitting apart and sending a shower of snow through the air.

Friar Philip looks up, dusting the snow off of his face. In front of them lies a small tent, three overflowing bowls of stew set before it. He smiles at the knights, struggling to rise next to him, then shouts, "I told you!" Before collapsing back into the snow.

They huddle around the fire, and greedily devour the warm stew.

"What are you soldiers still doing stuffing your faces?" A man barks, as he passes by. "It's time to break down camp. We leave for Blackburn within the hour!"

Seaborne 7

The rail sleigh flies along its track, throwing snow up from beneath the runners as they speed towards Barrenport.

"Look!" Seaborne says, pointing out the window at the towering castle of ice visible from their car. "What is that place?"

"The Frozen City," Kevin answers. "That means we are nearly in Barrenport. The two cities are so near they might as well be the same place."

As they draw closer to their destination, a trail of soldiers comes into view aside the tracks. Legions of footmen, pike men, archers and knights, all moving away from the city.

"I wonder where all these men are marching…" Kevin remarks.

"Not our business," Seaborne replies. "Focus on the task at hand."

"Aye, cap'n." Parrot says.

"I know them!" Kevin shouts, pointing at a group of three men marching among the soldiers. "They're the knights of the Order from Blackburn. What are they doing marching with Barren soldiers?"

"Cap'n say ta focus, dum dum." Parrot snickers, at the knight. The bird on his shoulder chiming in. *'Dum Dum, Dum Dum.'*

Seaborne breaks into laughter, as the bird continues taunting Kevin. "Alright, enough joking. Hush that bird up, we're slowing down. It's time to get ready."

The pirates file off of the sleigh car as it comes to a stop outside Barrenport. Following the other new recruits as they form a line, the recruiter leading them into town. The group stops outside a large meeting hall.

"Inside you will describe your talents and experience. Then, the shipmasters will assign you to a job and vessel." The recruiter shouts, as he opens the door and leads them inside.

A roaring fire warms the hall, its pungent smoke hanging low in the room. They are led to a long bench, where they all take a seat waiting for their turn to be assigned.

"What happens if we get assigned to different ships?" Kevin asks.

"I hadn't considered that," Seaborne answers. "Let me go first. If they ask ya any questions, just, well... Just act like Parrot."

"Aye, cap'n." Parrot says.

"Aye, cap'n." Kevin adds, smirking.

When he is called up, Seaborne approaches briskly and takes a seat.

"Name?"

"Lucky's the name." Seaborne answers, wearing a wide smile.

"Skills?"

"First rate chef, sir. I can turn gruel into gold. I have two men with me, together we have sailed around the world thrice, or so about."

The man looks up, measuring Seaborne with his eyes. "Two men, you say?"

"Aye, my assistant chef and a cabin boy. Neither is smart enough to make it on their own, sad to say. I've taken it on meself to see to their care. If we could all be assigned together, I'd be forever in ya debt."

"*Cascade* needs a chef and cabin boy. Take your men to the table at the end of the room there, and report to Captain Heenson."

"Thank ya, sir."

As they sit waiting for an audience with their new captain, Seaborne listens to a hushed conversation at the table behind them.

"With Bastion gone, and my dear wife passed, I want to bring my firstborn home. My illegitimate daughter. You remember her mother, the beauty I met before father died? Back when we were young…"

"Do you know where she is?"

"No, dear brother. I sent her and her mother away after I married. For my wife's sake. I haven't heard from either since. But you… You can find her. I know you can."

"My contacts do run deep," The voice says, with a boom of laughter.

"Thank you, brother."

"I see your men march on Blackburn. It is sooner than we had planned."

"It must be done. Do not worry though, it will be a decisive victory. I expect to return home within the month."

"I couldn't care less whether or not you're victorious. When the Emperor hears that the Imperial Admiral's brother has defied a direct order, and declared war on a peaceful neighbor, I will be called a traitor."

"Are you not a traitor?"

"Regardless, we didn't need him to find out this soon."

"Are you scared he'll tell everyone your little secret?"

"Don't worry about that, he has more to lose from the truth than me. People would say he's insane, more often than they already do."

"Then it's time to prepare."

"I control the Imperial Navy. My preparations are more than complete. The only worry we have is on land. You must hold up your end."

"Without Blackburn, what ally…"

"Next!" Captain Heenson shouts, calling them up the table.

"Name and station?" The captain barks.

"Lucky, sir. Chef. These fine men are Nate and Iago. Chef's assistant and cabin boy, respectively.

"Welcome aboard men, those two behind you are heading to the ship now, have them show you on board."

They thank the captain and follow after the men, out through the door and towards the port below.

"Lucky's the name." He says, introducing himself to their new shipmates.

"Te Reza." The taller one says, extending his hand. "This here is Jay Marsh."

"Pleased to make ya acquaintance." He replies, taking the young man's hand.

Councilor Quezada 6

"He stands next to the outer rail of the Flying City, watching as it slowly pulls next to the Tower of Trade. The moment it comes within range, men drop a gangplank to bridge the flying ship and the tower. They rush across and affix enormous steel chains to large bollards on the edge of the docking platform.

Making his way to the gangplank, Quezada makes sure to be one of the first off the ship.

I must get to Jero, before the whispers do...

Rushing down the lift and through the square, he hurries to the Emperor's Tower. Loak greets him inside, but Quezada ignores his pleasantries. All the possible outcomes of the next few minutes run rampant through his mind.

Quezada throws open the doors to the throne room, stepping into a meeting already in progress. Lingonberry stands next to the Emperor, his eyes cast at the ground. Thorne watches silently from the corner, while Jero laughs with maniacal energy.

What is this?

"Quezada, friend." Jero says, after realizing their conversation has been interrupted. "The news Lanties brings… It is wonderful!"

Wonderful enough to cushion the news I must deliver?

"What news, your highness?" Quezada asks, bowing his head.

"Lanties has found them! Legions upon legions." He breaks into a fit of laughter again, like a child just having opened an unimaginable gift. "Lanties, tell him…"

Lingonberry looks at him, a hint of dread hidden behind the gleam of his large eyes. "I was successful in finding the golem armies. They are lain underneath an abandoned ruin, north of Seacliff, deep in the Wastes."

"Impossible…"

"It's true, Lanties saw them with his own eyes!" Jero gasps, between bursts of laughter. "Oh this changes everything, don't you see!"

"Of course, my lord." Quezada says, pausing for a moment. "Your highness, I bring news as well."

"What? What is it, my friend?" Jero says, intently gazing out the gigantic windows of the throne room.

"Eristoclese is dead my lord, Atasio Nodovin's men stormed his rooms at the Academy and killed him."

"Of course, of course." Jero replies, "Who knew it would have taken so long?"

"My lord, someone saw it happen, we are unsure who it was. But the Oligarchy of Twenty have found out what occurred. They have seized Nodovin's businesses, his wealth, and his entire fleet. His mercenaries have all but abandoned him, and he is now under house arrest. Troops are stationed outside his home, not allowing anything in or out. His son, Matio, is here to plead for help on his behalf.

"What a stupid man. How could he let himself get in this predicament?" Jero sneers, "He got himself into it, he can get himself out of it."

"Of course, my lord." Quezada says, unsure if he should continue or not.

"Is that all, Aloysius?" Lingonberry asks, knowingly.

"Your highness, the Twenty have proclaimed that the Plateau is no longer part of the Empire. They have cut all ties with us." He looks away quickly, avoiding the Emperor's piercing gaze. All remnants of the man's cheerfulness are gone, replaced by a murderous look on his face.

The door opens behind him. Sage and Kroonson enter the room, solemnly joining the assembly.

"Is anyone of importance from the Plateau still in the Pillar?" Jero asks, surprisingly calm.

"The Lord Treasurer Antissi," Lingonberry answers. "And Clint Pollent's…"

"Pollent is a member of the Twenty!" Jero interrupts.

"Yes, my lord. He is not here, his son is." Lingonberry finishes.

Jero's eyes light up with that news. "Bring him, and Antissi."

Thorne clears his throat, "We have Aloysius Quezada, as well."

"What are you saying, bastard?" Quezada snaps.

"Exactly what I said." Thorne replies, coolly. "You are from the Plateau, no?"

"Thorne," Jero interjects. "Quezada is our friend. He would never betray me."

Thorne nods, smiling at Quezada with an icy grin.

"Kroonson," Jero barks. "Bring me Lord Antissi. Quezada, find the Marble Master's son. And Sage… Bring me the boy, Lord Antissi's nephew. He may need to pay for his father's insolence."

They all nod their agreement, and exit the room. Quezada asks, Sage and Kroonson, "Do either of you know what Pollent's son can do?"

"No clue," Sage replies. "But I do know that his father can fly..."

Quezada shakes his head, then breaks away from the group. He makes his way through the training grounds, and enters the Tower of Might. Quickly, he finds Alor Rock eating his lunch in a dining hall with the rest of the Imperial Archers.

"Alor, I need you and a few archers to accompany me on an arrest. Bring your best shots, he may be able to fly..."

The commander smiles, his one eye not covered by a patch lighting up. He grabs his bow, signaling to a handful of men to follow.

The party heads to the Tower of Trade, filing onto a lift and riding it to one of the uppermost levels. Loud music plays from inside an enormous establishment, occupying almost the entire floor. Two large men stand blocking the entrance, each taller and wider than the door.

Quezada briskly approaches them. "I am here on the Emperor's orders. We are looking for Chase Pollent. Can I come in?"

"No." One of the men grunts, turning away from him in a display of indifference.

"No, what?" Quezada asks. "No, he isn't here? No, I can't come in?"

"No."

Quezada nods his head and turns back to Alor and his archers. "Wait out here, if someone comes flying out, feather them... Try not to kill him though."

Then he vanishes in the blink of an eye, reappearing inside the establishment. Looking at the large tavern around him, Quezada sees multiple stages throughout the room. On the one nearest to him, a man leans his head back dramatically. Then, with a flourish, he takes a burning sword and swallows it, until nothing but the hilt is visible.

Across from him, a woman dances seductively. He notices that with each swing of her hair and hips, the girl's skin changes color. Not from beige to brown, or anything human, but brilliant yellow to orange, then red. With deep purple eyes she glances his way, and with blue lips she blows him a kiss. Then with a green twist, she looks away.

Walking up a circular flight of stairs, he enters a small loft. A heavy haze hangs in the air, as attendants move about the room handing patrons elaborately carved pipes and terribly pungent leaf to smoke.

In a large leather chair, at the end of the room, sits a young man. A smile and look of contentment rest on his face, as he reclines into the overstuffed seat.

Quezada slides into the seat next to him, clearing his throat gently. "Chase?"

The man slowly leans forward, meeting his gaze. "To what do I owe the honor?" He asks, offering a beautiful amber and emerald pipe to Quezada.

He shakes his head no, then whispers. "The Emperor wishes a word. If you could come with me."

"What an honor." Chase says, shaking his head. "But I am afraid I have an appointment this afternoon, that I cannot reschedule. Tomorrow morning, perhaps?"

"He insists. You must come now." Quezada stands, gesturing for the man to follow him. "It would be best if you came willingly, and not in shackles."

Chase laughs at the words, shaking his head again. "No, with all due respect, I will not be coming with you." Then, with a sudden burst of energy, he springs from the chair and swings his arm through the air.

Quezada feels an incredible force strike him square in the chest. The air rushes from his lungs as he finds himself sailing across the room. Just before crashing into the wall, he vanishes, appearing directly behind Chase. He pulls a dagger from his belt and holds it to the man's throat. "Stop, now!"

With a flex of his shoulders, he sends Quezada flying through the air again. The knife flies from his grasping fingers, straight into Chase's outstretched hand.

"Run, tell your Emperor that I will not be able to respond to his summons." With another swing of his arms, he sends Quezada flying out of the loft and down towards the tavern below.

Before crashing into a table full of patrons, Quezada disappears, then softly lands on the floor across the room. Getting up and dusting himself off, he moves between his target and the door. "Alor!" He yells, towards the entrance.

Looking back, he sees the doormen backing into the room, an archer's bow trained on each on their heads. Alor enters, as they move out of the way, drawing his bow.

A commotion erupts from the loft above, as tables levitate into the air and fly across the room towards him. Quezada disappears, just as a large oak table comes splintering down where he had been standing.

Chase jumps down, slowing to a stop before hitting the ground. With a swing of his arm, he sends Quezada soaring again, towards a heavy stone wall.

Vanishing just in time to avoid the hit, he appears between Chase and Alor's bow. An arrow slices through his arm, sending a surge of pain through the limb. He disappears again, a second arrow narrowly missing his heart.

Chase listlessly waves his hand, and the arrows switch direction, sailing back at Alor and his men. Then, he throws his whole body forward, generating a great force, sending tables and chairs and people flying indiscriminately across the room.

Quezada lets the invisible blast carry him through the front door. Then quickly, he jumps to the side of the outer wall. A man screams and soars through the door, as Chase makes his exit. Quezada appears behind him suddenly, grabbing the knife from his hands and trying to run it into his gut. The point of the blade breaks without even hitting Chase's skin, as if an invisible barrier surrounds him.

With a swing of his arms, Chase sends him crashing into the lift shaft. Quezada tries to spin through the air, as he falls down the opening, and sees the lift rising quickly towards him. He tries to vanish, but as he does, a blast rains down on him from above.

Chase drops down, sending him flying into the lift below. He attempts to vanish on impact, but the effort is only half successful, and he finds himself falling hard into a group of passengers.

As the men he lands on begin to yell and hit him, Chase lands by his side. Raising his arms, he sends him flying up into the air, then crashing back into the ground.

"Had enough?" Chase asks, preparing to lift his arms again.

Before he is thrown, Quezada vanishes, then reappears on a passing level. He stumbles past a carpenter's shop, grabbing a thick wooden post. A moment later, he reappears on the lift, the post already swinging through the air. The blow lands on Chase's head, knocking him to the ground.

"Yeah," Quezada says. "I've had enough."

He waits at the bottom of the lift shaft, until Alor and his man catch up. They begin carrying the man back to the Emperor's Tower, passing the edge of the Pillar as they make their way to the entrance.

As they near the ledge, Chase's eyes open. "Thanks for the ride!"

The man flexes outwards, easily destroying his restraints. A gesture of his hand sends the men around him flying backwards. Landing softly, he bows to Quezada and waves, before turning and jumping off the edge of the Pillar.

Quezada curses, then runs forward and leaps off after him. His head begins to spin as he plummets down to the valley floor, thousands of feet below, rising towards him at an alarming pace. Looking around, he sees Chase shooting headfirst in a full dive.

Appearing behind him, he grabs on and vanishes, taking the man with him. Then reappears next to the edge of the Pillar, slamming him into it with full force.

Chase grunts, then quickly throws his arms out, pushing himself away from the wall. Spinning in the air, he sends Quezada slamming into the edge with a flick of his wrist, then pulls him back and sends him into it again.

Quezada disappears just before he hits the second time, appearing behind Chase and throwing his arm around his neck, choking him.

As the ground races towards them, Chase holds his hands out, pulling them away from each other. As he does, an invisible force grips Quezada's wrists, pulling them away with impossible strength. Turning around, Chase sends one final blow his way, sending him speeding towards the ground.

He closes his eyes, preparing to hit the hard earth. Before crashing, he manages to vanish once more, reappearing a couple feet above the ground. He lands with a thud, groaning and clutching his side. Pain shoots through his limbs, worse than anything he has ever felt. Every bit of his skin is covered in cuts and gashes. He tries to stand, but falls forward.

Looking up, he sees Chase, slowing down as he falls, coming to a gentle stop on his feet. With a lift of his finger, the man pulls Quezada across the grass and dirt. He screams from the excruciating pain, like lightning coursing through his limbs.

Pulling forth the last of his strength, he vanishes, appearing next to Chase and swinging hard at his face. But with the lifting of his palm, Chase freezes him in place.

He tries to vanish, but nothing happens.

Chase chuckles, making Quezada's arms and legs stretch out, like a prisoner chained to a dungeon wall. "I didn't want to have to do this to you. We are brothers, no? Both men of the Plateau." He walks around Quezada, patting him on the back gently. "I am sorry, you know?"

"If you're going to kill me, just do it." Quezada chokes out, barely able to open his mouth.

"Kill you?" The man laughs. "Never! Not only will I not be killing you, I extend you an invitation... Come home. We will be waiting with open arms."

"What?"

Without another word, Chase throws a fist into the air, as if throwing a rock towards the sun. As he does, Quezada begins to fly, sailing high up into the air. As he reaches the upper edge of the Pillar, the force holding him in place releases, allowing him to vanish and appear gently on the path outside the Emperor's Tower.

Trying to ignore the blinding pain of each step, he walks inside. His mind racing.

Chion 8

'Chion... Chion, over here.'

He hears his uncle's voice, as clear as if he was standing next to him, but the man is nowhere in sight. Looking around the lobby of the Tower of Trade, he spots his uncle standing outside his bank, gesturing to come inside.

Chion makes his way into the marble building, then up a flight of stairs to his uncle's office.

"Matio Nodovin was in the Flying City." He tells his uncle. "He says the Plateau has left the Empire."

"It is true, I fear. We must leave before word reaches Jero. Go, pack quickly. I have made arrangements with the Captain of the Flying City, they will shortly be making an unannounced departure."

"Yes, uncle." He says, quickly leaving the bank and making his way to his chambers.

Tearing through his rooms, Chion throws a bag together. Packing some clothes and riding leathers, and a large knife. Pulling a cushion off a chair, he fishes through the stuffing until he a finds a large velvet sack. He opens it quickly, revealing a large amount of gold, interspersed with rubies and emeralds and diamonds. Adding it to his bag, he runs out of the room.

Outside the Tower of Trade, he notices a group of guards. Ducking around them, he looks into the bank from the tower lobby. Inside, he sees Councilor Kroonson leading his uncle out of the building.

What do I do? He thinks, desperately. *I can't leave him...*

Unable to come up with anything, he begins following them out of the tower and through the square. As they head back to the Emperor's Tower, Chion hears a commotion from outside the entrance. A few of the guards run towards the edge of the Pillar, shaking their heads in disbelief.

"They jumped!" He hears one of them say.

In the excitement of men peeking over the edge, he seizes the moment and runs up to his uncle. All the guards have left, leaving Kroonson and him alone. Grabbing a loose brick from the path below, Chion hits the councilor hard in the back of the head, sending him crumpling to the ground.

"Come on!" He shouts, at his uncle. "Let's get out of here."

As they turn to run away, Councilor Sage walks around a corner, placing himself between them and their only route of escape.

"Chion." The councilor says, shaking his head. "Why would you hit Kroonson like that? Do you know you could have seriously hurt him?"

"I didn't do it!" Chion lies, "He was already like that when we walked up, something is going on over there, I think someone jumped off the edge."

A large black raven lands on Sage's shoulder, clicking its beak next to his ear.

"I'm afraid the bird says otherwise." He grins, before yelling. "Guards!"

Men come around the corner, marching towards them with weapons drawn. He and his uncle begin to take a step back, before a rustling makes them turn. The last thing Chion sees is a flash of green light, then his body seizes, and everything goes black.

He wakes up sitting on a hard wooden bench, with a splitting pain in his head and his hands chained together. Looking around, he sees Rika, Rosemary, Tiaries and Relorn sitting across from him, their chairs against the wall. He can see the worry on their faces. The girls stare at him, their eyes welling, while Relorn looks away, averting his gaze.

"How do you answer for your treasons, Lord Treasurer?" Emperor Jero shouts, at Chion's uncle.

"I have committed no treasons, your highness. I swear to you." His uncle pleads, knelt before the Emperor, his hands chained behind his back.

"Then why were you fleeing? Why attack my councilor?"

"My lord, we were scared. The traitors, back in the Plateau…
We have nothing to do with them. We are loyal to you, always."

"Your loyalties lie with the gold in your vaults, you know
nothing else."

"I would never betray you, I swear my lord."

"Your brother has betrayed me. Are you telling me, you would
take my side over his? I think not…" Jero shakes his head.
Looking back at Councilor Thorne, he makes a gesture and turns
away.

As Thorne steps forward, Chion's uncle stumbles to his feet,
running for the door. "Someone, save us! I can give you
anything!"

While his uncle runs, Chion sees Kroonson let out a stream of
sparks, freezing him in place and making his back arch and
contort in the air.

Thorne walks towards him, as he collapses to the floor. The
councilor's arm begins to extend, turning into a long icy blade.
Thorne grabs ahold of his uncle's hair, pulling his head up and
exposing his neck.

'I'm sorry…' He hears his uncle think, as Thorne swings his
arm.

Chion turns away, but the sound of his uncle's head hitting the
floor screams through his mind, the loudest sound he's ever
heard.

Staring at the door, unwilling to look back at his uncle, tears
begin welling beneath his eyes. He painfully tries to choke them

back, but it's no use. Through his mounting sobs, he hardly notices the door open and Councilor Quezada limp into the room, covered in blood and bruises.

Across the way, out of the corner of his eye, Chion sees Lingonberry begin to shimmer and fade. Disappearing from sight, as the rest of the room stares morbidly at his uncle's corpse. A moment later, Rika, noticing the councilor's departure, turns into the mouse and scampers out of the chamber.

"The son too!" Jero yells, "We must be sure his father gets our message."

Kroonson grabs Chion, throwing him down before the Emperor.

"Father…" Relorn says, barely above a whisper.

"Shut up!" The Emperor screams, turning to Thorne. "Do it!"

Thorne swings the icy appendage, still covered in his uncle's blood. Chion closes his eyes, waiting for the blow to land.

Yet, instead of a sharp pain across his neck, he feels someone pull him backwards. Looking up, Chion sees Quezada grabbing the collar of his shirt. A moment later, he feels his stomach churn as they vanish, reappearing at the door. He nearly vomits from the displacement, but before he can, they disappear again.

Each time Quezada vanishes, they reappear further away from the throne room. Pulling him towards a balcony, Quezada makes them materialize in midair, falling above the city square. Then, a gut-wrenching moment later, he looks around to find them standing in his uncle's bank. The doors are locked and employees gone, obviously having left after the treasurer's arrest.

"The vault," Quezada grunts. "Open it."

"Can't you just appear inside it?"

"So I can form around some shelf? Get cut in half? End up with my insides filled with gold?" He shouts, "Open the vault!"

Jumping over the marble counter, Chion takes the key to his own vault from a pocket sewn into his pants. *Let's hope it works…* He thinks, slipping the key into the elaborate locking mechanism.

With a few twists and clinks, the lock begins to turn. With some help from Quezada, they pull the tremendous door open.

Inside the vault, beneath a set of stairs, lies a cavernous chamber, filled with millions and millions of pieces of gold and silver. Quezada's jaw drops, as he surveys the room.

"What is this?" He stammers, "I never dreamed…"

"All the good it'll do." Chion shouts, "Will it get us out of here?"

"Possibly…" Quezada says, looking back outside the vault. "Fill up your pockets with all you can carry, we need enough to get somewhere safe."

"What are you doing?" Chion asks, as he runs and begins to fill his pockets.

"You'll see…" Quezada says, scooping armfuls of gold into his shirt, then vanishing.

A moment later, he reappears without the gold. Filling up his shirt again, then disappearing.

Chion hears screams from the square outside. Running to a window, he looks out and sees a panicked scene. People shove and claw at each other, fighting over gold showering down from the sky.

Appearing beside him, Quezada grabs his hand, and then they are off again. Outside the bank, Quezada yells over the screaming crowd. "The vault is open!"

A flood of people rushes towards the tower, just as Chion and Quezada slip past and make their way for the great lift.

Once they are safely outside the Pillar, Chion looks up at the councilor. "Why?" He asks.

Looking back, Quezada shakes his head and lets out a sigh. "Money is what wins wars… And I know who controls all the wealth in the Empire. Jero thinks he rules everything, but it is an illusion. A portrait, painted by your father's gold. Killing your uncle shattered that illusion, as our Emperor will soon find out."

Jia 6

Jia paces back and forth, across the floor of her room, like a tigress locked in a narrow cage. Her flame burns listlessly, waving behind the cover of its ornate lamp.

"Quit being moody!" She shouts, at the flame, but it gives no discernable reply.

A knock at the door draws her attention from the glowing colors of the lamp. She answers, to find Te Inzu waiting outside.

"Come, we are going to meet with the senators." The councilor tells her, before turning away and knocking on Kzhee's door across the hall.

Jia looks back at the lamp. "Let's go!" She calls, but still nothing. Taking a step towards it, she nearly screams when the flame jumps out at her from a torch above the desk. It lands on her shoulder, in the form of a girl, silently laughing and pointing at Jia's startled face.

She angrily throws the flame to the ground, but it lands nimbly and springs right back onto her other shoulder, smiling up at her with a childish grin. Jia looks over at the still burning lamp. "You tricked me!" She hisses, indignantly. "If you ever do that again, I'll throw you into the river myself!"

Her and Kzhee follow Inzu, through the imperial suites, making their way down to the Senate Hall. Ral waits for them outside, tossing an apple in the air and grinning.

"You look cheery." Jia says, as Ral falls in with them.

"You look irritated." He replies, offering her an apple from his pocket.

She takes the fruit and sinks her teeth into it, viciously, tearing a large chunk off and trying to chew her frustration away.

They step into the Senate Hall, a grand room, its ornate ceiling supported by large gilded columns. Jia glances around, unimpressed, before taking another bite of the apple.

Councilor Maestas is already in attendance, speaking with the senators in an annoyed tone.

"Where is my cousin, Senator McKenna?" Maestas yells, at the lounging senators.

"He has gone to raise troops." One man calls, from an upper row.

"To help keep A'Tannia safe." Another bumbles, a fat man seated near the front.

"Not like the Emperor will do anything to help us, we must take matters into our own hands." A stout shouldered man hollers.

"You all seem to be spouting mindless rubbish, do you not see us here now?" Inzu says, to the audience.

"The Emperor will do nothing to help us." A man repeats.

"No, we must protect ourselves." Another adds.

"We'll accomplish nothing here…" Maestas says, walking past them and exiting the hall.

"What do we do?" Inzu asks, in a hushed voice.

"We wait for my cousin to return." Maestas answers. "These men... They are all sheep, and he is their shepherd."

Rika 6

After having pursued Councilor Lingonberry as he fled the throne room, the mouse lost his trail somewhere near the lift. Its nose is good, but the scent keeps sending it in circles.

Thinking quickly, it scampers down through the Emperor's Tower. Once safely past the guards and outside the entrance, the mouse darts into a bush. Rika steps out, brushing off her clothes. She makes her way through the square, ducking into the Tower of Trade. Catching the lift and riding it up to the landing paddock, she ducks behind a crate, turning back into the mouse and scurrying toward the gangplank leading to the Flying City. The mouse sticks its nose up, surveying the air, but the councilor's scent is nowhere to be found.

He must not have come through yet... She thinks, figuring the Flying City would be his best means of escaping the Pillar. If that is even what he intends to do.

Having no other ideas, she finds a hiding place and resolves to wait.

After a few minutes, the mouse's ears catch the sound of frenzied screams, drifting up from the base of the tower. The market and stalls around her begin to clear out, as people push and fight their way towards the lift and stairs.

Where are they all running? She doesn't follow the crowd, letting them go their own way. *If he tries to sneak onto the Flying City, now would be the best time.*

A moment later, as the last of the bystanders clear off of the platform, a group of men march into view. She looks up to see Emperor Jero, Councilors Thorne and Kroonson standing behind him. A score of archers following closely.

"Where is the captain?" Jero shouts, to the guards standing across the gangplank.

The men murmur amongst themselves, before one of them nods and runs off. A couple minutes later, a tall handsome man comes walking briskly towards the edge of the Flying City.

"Emperor, to what do I owe the honor?" The captain hollers, leaning over the outer rail.

"You won't come down to greet me? Where are your manners?" Jero shouts back.

"In all my years of life, I have never stepped off of this city." He says, with a laugh. "Today will not be the first time."

"I am sending guards aboard your ship. We are taking anyone from the Plateau and holding them here." Jero sneers, "Just until we can figure out what is going on, of course."

"You will send no guard aboard this city, and you will remove no passenger. You have no authority here."

"I have no authority!?" Jero screams "I will send your city crashing to the ground. I will raze the wreckage. I will destroy you!"

"Ports!" The captain yells. As he does, small square doors begin opening around the edge of the Flying City, one after another. He signals to the men attending them, "Sixty-four, fifty-seven through fifty-three, FIRE!"

Large metal tubes stick out from the openings on either side of the gangplank. With a resounding roar, flashes of fire explode from the protruding weapons. A solitary shot to the left shatters the thick steel chain tethering the city to the edge of the tower. The rest of the firing broadsides the tower itself, above the Emperor and his men. They jump out of the way, barely missing a shower of large stones and mortar.

Before the archers can regain their feet, the Flying City veers away, quickly sailing out of the range of their arrows.

The Emperor screams and throws his hands in the air. "How much incompetence can I be expected to handle?"

The words barely leave his mouth, when a messenger runs towards them.

"My lord, the bank's vault was opened. The citizens are sacking the city square. People are looting, stealing. It is mayhem, your highness."

"Call the city guards, tell them to kill anyone found looting."

"Yes, your highness."

The mouse runs past them, ducking back into the tower. Risking the trip through the turmoil in the square, Rika makes her way back to Lingonberry's apartments in the Emperor's Tower.

She rummages through his room, looking for any hint indicating where he might have disappeared to. Pulling back the tapestry hanging across his wall, she sees a wooden door, sunken into the stone. Pushing on it, the iron hinges creak and the door swings open.

Through the opening, a stairwell spirals down. Rika steps into the passage. As she lets the tapestry fall, the light goes out, leaving her in suffocating blackness. The mouse has no trouble seeing though, as it bounds down the steps one by one, emerging in an open chamber.

Rika looks around at the shelves and cases piled full of books and scrolls, potions and poultices. She pushes aside a pile of parchment, exposing what appears to be a human skull.

"Hello, Rika." A voice calls out.

She jumps, startled. Then turns to survey her surroundings. A subtle shimmer, floating in the corner of the room begins to become visible.

"I think you can help me, Rika. If you do…" Councilor Lingonberry says, taking form before her eyes. "Then I will tell you where your sister is."

Loak 5

Each day had crept by slowly since the citizens of the Pillar sacked their own city, and the masses were beginning to grow hungry. Loak and his fellow Earthmovers still had plenty to eat, safely hidden high in the Tower of Earth. But looking out at the city below, it was clear the common people were taking the brunt of the punishment.

Loak turns away from the window, taking a seat in the throne room and waiting his turn, while the Emperor speaks with Councilor Sage.

"Have the fleets been raised?" Jero asks, pacing before the window.

"No, my lord." Sage answers, "Seacliff has replied that they can't spare the ships to help. A'Tannia says that they *can* spare the ships, but the senators have voted against it."

"Traitors, all of them…" Jero says, shaking his head in disgust. "What of Barrenport, my Imperial Fleet? Barren's ships are all that matter. The Southern Trading Company could sail against every armada in the Empire and come out unscathed!"

"Lord Barren has not sent a reply, your highness. But the last two scheduled shipments of food have not arrived from the Company."

"Damn him… How much food is left in the Pillar? In the Mountains?"

"Things look bleak, my lord." Sage replies, "The stores of food were not unloaded from the Flying City before its departure. The shipments from the Southern Trading Company have ceased. And since the looting of Antissi's bank, the entirety of the city's food supply now lies in the hands of a very small number of people. Gold and silver have become worthless. The masses are beginning to starve... We must consider letting people leave the Pillar, stopping the great lift has only caused the situation to become worse."

"No one leaves!" The Emperor screams, "Not before these rogue realms are dealt with."

"It will be nearly impossible to mount an offensive against the Plateau by land. The cliffs surround it on all sides. An invasion by sea, offloading at Triali, that is the only way. But without ships…"

"I intend to use the golems. The rest of the realms will come in line, once they see the destruction brought on by the stone horde."

"Without Lanties, can we even find them again?" Sage protests.

"He left his maps, I have them here. Do these mean anything to you?"

Sage looks over the parchments, scanning the maps and notes. "Yes, I believe I can find them again."

"Good," Jero says. "Loak, come here."

Loak gets up from his seat, bowing his head as he approaches the Emperor. "My lord, you grace me with your summons."

Jero waves his hand, dismissing the pleasantries. "I have an important mission for you, Loak. If you succeed, you will return as a hero of the Empire."

"What is the mission, my lord?" Loak asks, nervous to hear the reply.

"You will go south with Councilor Sage, and assume control of the golem legions. Take them north, to A'Tannia and lay siege to the city. Bring them to their knees! March the golems through the river if need be, rip the foundation out from beneath them."

His heart drops upon hearing the Emperor's command. *He would make a murderer of me?*

"Sage," Jero continues, "Pick a few more Earthmovers. A helper for Loak, and a couple more to take a separate force south to teach Seacliff what happens when they do not follow their Emperor's orders. If Lord Barren has still not given his reply after Seacliff falls, we will sweep across the Southern Realm and remove the rebel lords."

"Yes, your highness. Which group shall I go with?" The councilor asks.

"Go ahead of Loak to A'Tannia, retrieve Maestas and Inzu before the siege begins. Bring them back here at once."

"Of course, my lord." Sage turns to leave, gesturing for Loak to follow.

Loak bows his head to the Emperor, then follows Sage out of the throne room.

"I have business to attend to." Sage tells him, once they are on the lift. "Pick a few Earthmovers to come with us. Also, please go to the Tower of Might and select a couple battalions of soldiers to support the golems."

"Of course, councilor. When must we be ready to leave?"

"Have the troops prepared by midday tomorrow."

"Councilor…" Loak stammers, "I've never led troops before."

"Neither have I…" Sage replies. "They come with commanders and generals. You just point, they'll fill in the blanks."

Loak looks at the councilor with confusion, but the short man simply nods his head and excuses himself.

Later that evening, Loak sneaks out of his chambers, making his way to Jaties' room in the Tower of Trade. He tosses him a bundle of food, then closes the door.

"My hero!" Jaties shouts, unwrapping the package and biting into a hunk of roast lamb. "I would have starved by now, if not for you."

"I'd never let you starve, my love." Loak says, taking a seat on the bed, his stare cast towards the floor. "I have to talk to you."

Jaties looks up at him, his large elven eyes glistening in the light of the fire. "What do we have to talk about? Please don't be something bad. I don't know if I can take much more…"

"Emperor Jero asked me to go to the Wastes and retrieve an army of golems, then use them to destroy A'Tannia."

"What!?" Jaties cries, "You can't!"

"I don't know what to do…" Loak says, "I have to select troops tomorrow to accompany us. If I disobey the Emperor's orders, they will be the same troops that end my life."

"They're just letting you pick who comes along?" Jaties asks, "Can I come?"

"Jero and the councilors seemed preoccupied with everything going on. It was like I was just a side note," Loak replies. "Would you really leave the Pillar?"

"It's been days since we have put on a performance, not enough people can afford tickets. The city is running out of stuff to eat. Would you leave me here to die?"

"No." Loak stammers, "I only meant… Never mind. Of course I want you to come with me."

"Good!" Jaties says, smiling between bites of food. "Because I think I have an idea."

They depart the next day for the Wastes. Herny insists on being one of the Earthmovers brought along. In addition, Loak selects Gen and Nal, brothers he had known for years. Good men. Loak figured they would be the two least likely to start a massacre, should they managed to take Seacliff.

The voyage is long and tedious. Each day he thanks the Lord above that Jaties had decided to accompany him, unable to imagine how terrible the journey would be alone. Their friend Jake had chosen to come along as well, disguised as a soldier and bunking with the troops.

Their ship reaches its destination, just after the first days of winter arrive. The few trees that spot the Wastes are grey and bare of leaves, their limbs knotted and twisted like bony hands grasping from the ground.

Sage leads them through the dreary morning fog, up through the hills that run along the shore. Their destination is a day's ride from the ocean, nestled away in a hidden gorge. Enormous ruins, that span the entire valley, extending up the edges of the surrounding hills and mountains.

Leading them into the ruins, Sage pauses to read the sheets of parchment he had brought along. The notes and maps.

"This way, I think…" The councilor says, heading down a narrow path.

Hours later, Loak begins to grow tired. "Can we wait back at camp while you search?" He asks, Sage.

"Ah, but I have almost found it." Sage replies, time after time. "It'll be just another moment, I swear."

The rest of the day goes by, and the sun begins setting in the sky, leaving them searching the ruins in the dark. It is only on accident that they finally find the chamber, when a soldier slides into the hidden entrance as they pass in front of a collapsed temple.

They climb down into the chamber, their torches casting a faint glow across the enormous room. But the cavern extends beyond where the light can reach. Loak gazes out in disbelief at the huge stone statues before him, arranged neatly in rows, lined up into the distance as far as his eyes can see.

"So, how do we move them out?" Sage asks, with a grin.

Loak walks to the far end of the chamber, mesmerized by the sheer number of golems filling the room. He finally makes his way to the rear of the chamber, stopping to survey the back wall.

With a wave of his hands the wall melts away, sinking into the sand. The starry sky outside shines in on them through the wide opening. Loak turns and lets out a whistle, calling the others to the exit.

Waiting for them to make their way towards him, Loak closes his eyes. He feels himself inside the stone giants, and feels their power coursing back through him. With nothing more than a thought, the golems begin to move towards the door, marching in formation.

"You can control them all!?" Sage shouts, struggling for breath as he comes running up. "How is that possible?"

"I don't know." He says, to the councilor. "It feels effortless. I think about them marching, and they start to move."

"Fascinating," Sage gasps. "You are truly remarkable."

Loak leads the golems in a line, filing out of the ruins, back to the camp at the base of the hills. Herny is waiting with Nal and Gen, as the group enters the encampment. Their jaws drop upon seeing the stone giants marching towards them.

"How are you doing that?" Herny asks, in disbelief.

"I don't know how to explain it. Just try to imagine what they see, try to look out through them." Loak replies, releasing control of the golems.

Herny tries first, and after a few attempts is able to make a small cluster of them move. Nal and Gen join in, and soon each of them is able to make a few hundred move at a time.

Nal and Gen begin moving the full amount they are able to keep under their control into formation, pointing south, towards Seacliff.

"You aren't leaving tonight?" Loak asks them, as they begin chatting out of earshot.

"Yes, we are." Nal replies, "You should as well. If we are seen marching by day, we will lose the element of surprise."

"And what a surprise it will be!" Gen says, laughing and patting one of the golems on its massive leg.

Nal and Gen depart shortly, with a fraction of the troops and about five hundred golems each. Sage said he counted nearly ten thousand total, thanking the Lord above that Loak had come and been able to move them all.

"Well." Jaties says, walking up through the tents. "Them leaving tonight complicates things."

"It does. But if we act quickly we may be able to catch them in time."

"Let's move then." Jaties replies, turning towards the center of camp.

They make their way to where the soldiers are eating, not far from Councilor Sage's own pavilion. Loak looks around at the troops. Each of them has the light olive complexion of someone born in the River Realm. He hoped Jaties' plan would work, needed it to work. If not, he might very well be meeting his end. Jaties squeezes his hand, then lets it go as Loak climbs onto a crate stacked next to the fire.

"Men!" Loak shouts, "Hear me! Emperor Jero has ordered us to lay siege to A'Tannia."

A murmur rustles through the ranks, as the men hear their assignment for the first time.

"After it lies in ruin, he wants us to raze the River Realm. To crush its villages beneath our feet. To use you as a tool of destruction."

He can feel the energy building in the crowd, the soldiers whispering to one another. The idea of attacking the land that many of them call home seems to sour their resolve.

Jaties' plan is working! He thinks, as the men's whispers grow quickly into a fervor of dissent.

Choosing the right moment, Loak yells over the muttering roar beginning to consume the crowd. "Well I say, NO! No, we will not be a tool of his destruction. No, we will not cut down our own countrymen over the squabbling of some lords, that sit safe in some tower! No, we will not be used!"

"No! No! No!" The men chant, raising their fists in the air and cheering him on.

"What are you doing!?" Sage yells, roused from his tent by the commotion.

"We are saying, NO!" Loak shouts, at the councilor.

Sage turns to run from the camp, not even wearing shoes on his feet.

"Stop him!" Loak calls out.

A group of men step in front of the councilor, blocking his escape.

"No, please! I will do anything… I can be of use, I swear!" Sage quivers in the dirt, as soldiers stand above him with their swords drawn. "Please, don't kill me…"

"Kill you?" Loak asks, shocked. "The whole reason I am doing this is because I don't want to kill anyone. Can't you see that?"

"Okay," Sage replies. "Then take me with you. There is nothing for me back at the Pillar. I won't run, I swear to you."

"You can swear all you will. I am still leaving guards to watch you."

"Well within your right," Sage replies. Then, looking at the soldiers and swords around him, he asks meekly, "If it's all right, can I go back to bed now? It has been a long day…"

"I am afraid not…" Loak says, shaking his head. "Men! Clear out the camp, we are going after the others."

They break camp quickly and begin marching south, leaving the golems behind to be able to move faster through the night.

Herny pulls up next to him as they move, raising his eyebrow as he begins to speak. "So… What was that back there?"

"I'm sorry. I wanted to tell you, but I thought you would be safer if you didn't know."

"Well, yes." Herny replies, "I am safer. But what about my wives and children back home?"

"I'm sorry, but what was I supposed to say? Things would have looked strange if you brought along your five wives and countless children."

Herny shrugs. "Yeah, I can't deny that. But it still would have been nice to know…"

"You're right, and I will do everything I can to get them out of there. As soon as we stop these two from annihilating one of the biggest cities in the South."

"Okay, thank you." Herny says, gently clapping Loak's back.

The sun is rising in the sky, when they come over the last hill before Seacliff. Moving past the precipice and down a windy path, a large ledge opens up before them.

Loak looks off the edge, down at the stretches of land between them and their destination. In the distance, he can see Seacliff, nestled high above the ocean. He can also make out the columns of golems beginning to march away, as the last of the city's great towers crashes into the sea below.

"We're too late…"

Quezada 7

They stand at the base of the Plateau, looking up. The giant platform used to reach the top had been cut free, severing the Plateau from the realms around it.

"How do we get up?" Chion asks, "Can you do your thing, blink us up there?"

"Not us and the horses both." He says, begrudgingly. With the amount of gold they are carrying, he knows getting new horses will be easy. But something about leaving these ones behind, after having just paid for them, doesn't sit well with him.

"We'll buy new ones up top. Come on, we're almost there." The boy says, seeming to complain more and more the closer they get to their destination.

"Fine." Quezada growls, leading them along the bottom of the cliff until he finds a low lying section. Taking the boy's shoulder in his hand, the two of them appear a moment later on the upper edge of the cliff, inches away from the ledge.

"Cut it close enough?" Chion asks, rolling his eyes.

"Complain enough!?" Quezada shouts, moving away from the ledge.

"Do I complain enough? Do I complain enough!?" Chion begins yelling. "I was taken away from my perfect job, my beautiful apartment, and made to live in some dreary tower. Sent out on fool's errands, where I continuously come within inches of death. All the while, my father is nowhere to be heard of. Has that never occurred to you? He didn't come to the tourney. He hasn't been to the Pillar. My uncle is the closest thing I've had to a parent, and I watched him be murdered before my very eyes. So, YES! I think I complain the perfect amount!"

"Let's go." Quezada says, ignoring Chion's outburst and turning to walk in the direction of the town in the distance.

They march along with the soldiers from the Frozen City, hidden in plain sight. Pushing onwards towards Blackburn, through the heavily falling snow. The onset of winter slows their progress, as the ever increasing fresh power makes each day's trudge more difficult than the last.

"When should we break away?" Sir Joel asks, in a whisper.

"Tonight," Sir Marcus answers. "They will set up camp outside the city. When they do, we will slip away."

"We must make for Castle Blackburn as soon as possible, to warn the king before Barren can make his move." Friar Philip says, wheezing and winded from the long day's march.

The sun hangs low in the sky, as the troops reach the outskirts of Blackburn, providing just enough light for the soldiers to hastily set up camp. The three of them string up their tent, and wait patiently for the troops to begin dinner.

The area around them begins to clear out when the dinner bell rings. As soon as they are alone, the knights scurry out of the camp and begin the trek to Castle Blackburn.

As the stars begin to fade into the early morning twilight, the knights enter the city. They quickly move through the snowy streets, making their way up towards the castle.

Sir Marcus bangs on the outer door with a heavy fist. "Open the gate! We must see the king at once!"

Guards raise the gate and allow the men in, but stop them before they can enter the keep.

"What is your business here, knight?" A guard asks, lowering a large two sided axe in their path.

"The grand marshal!" Friar Philip shouts, "He is camped outside the city with a large host. They plan to attack at daybreak!"

The soldiers begin to murmur and move about. "Follow me," The head guard says, ushering the knights into the castle's great hall.

Minutes later, King Birch makes his way into the room, trying to stifle a yawn as he rubs the sleep from his eyes.

"What is this about?" The king asks, gesturing for the knights to have a seat.

"My lord, the marshal and his troops are preparing an attack." Sir Marcus says, nervously glancing out a nearby window. "You must get ready for battle."

"What?" The regent asks, confused. "Why would George attack me?"

"We do not know my lord." Sir Joel stammers, "They killed the Order's knights stationed in the Frozen Palace. Their heads are hanging above the streets, for all to see."

"It is true," Friar Philip adds. "It would appear he has declared war on the Order itself."

"He is mad…" The king says, shaking his head.

"What defenses can you raise before morning?" Sir Marcus asks, impatiently.

"I don't know." The king ponders, "Maybe a thousand men."

Sir Joel gasps. "Your highness, the marshal rides with more than thirty thousand!"

"Lord help us…" Friar Philip prays, falling to his knees.

The knights follow the king outside, as he moves around the castle raising his troops. The bells in the city begin to ring, calling the common folk to fall back inside the outer walls of the castle.

The courtyard becomes congested with women and children. Soldiers and farmers alike run to take up arms in defense of the keep.

From over the hills, far to the east, drums begin to boom. The call of a war horn echoes across the tundra, as the marshal's men march into sight. Hushed whispers fall across the castle, as the full force slowly becomes visible.

Sir Marcus looks to his companions, "Men! It has been a pleasure."

"To you as well!" The friar replies, bowing his head.

The screams and jeers of the advancing army become audible as the soldiers draw closer. A baby cries loudly against its mother's chest, the only sound coming from inside the castle walls.

Friar Philip continues to pray. "Lord above, see us through. Shine down your loving light. Help them know, what they do. And see us through the night."

The marching army moves into the city, winding up towards the castle. The pounding of the drums vibrates through the stone walls, pulsing like a beating heart. The soldiers behind the portcullis prepare to defend, as the men along the ramparts hoist up barrels of boiling pitch and oil. Archers notch their bows, gazing out at the overwhelming force approaching below.

"Charge!" A commander yells, sending the attacking force into a sprint. They move a large wooden ram into place outside the portcullis, and begin laying blows against the gate.

The defenders drop barrels of boiling oil from the top of the wall, sending patches of attackers running and screaming. But for each man that falls, two more rush forward to take his place. Metal creaks, as the gate begins to give way, bending beneath the crushing blows of the ram.

"This is it!" Sir Marcus calls, drawing his sword. "For the Order!"

Charging forward, he screams, as the gate comes crumbling down. Men begin pushing into the courtyard, yelling and swinging wildly. The defenders fight desperately, trying to hold the marshal's troops from overtaking the castle.

As the defenders start to become overwhelmed, the ground around them begins to rumble and quake. The advancing troops slow their attack, and look in disbelief, as a chorus of trumpets erupts from the hills to the north.

Sir Marcus runs up a flight of stairs, to the top of the outer wall. Looking out, beyond the marshal's army and over the sloping hills, he sees countless men riding across the horizon in perfect formation. Each mounted on a charging steed, and fully armored in the bright regalia of the Order. Their banners fly through the blazing sky, flooding forth like a cascading sea, the sweet song of their trumpets rising higher and higher.

"Boons from above!" Friar Philip cheers, falling back to his knees.

"Look!" Sir Joel says, pointing to the head of the incoming legions. "Is that…?"

Sir Simon 4

Sir Simon rides at the head of the main column, his shimmering white armor gleaming brighter than the snow in the morning sun. The knights around him have come from all corners of the Empire, pouring forth at High Priest Tobin's summoning.

Looking down at the battle below, Sir Simon sees the marshal's army breaking through the castle's front gate. He urges his horse forward, tearing down the hill at full speed.

"For the Order!" He cries, as the mounted knights crash headfirst into the confused army below.

"For the Order!" The knights around him call, breaking their lances into the waiting shields of their foe and swinging their swords as they pass.

The marshal's troops are completely unprepared for the Order's surprise attack. The men break quickly, abandoning their position and turning in retreat. The defenders inside the castle push forward, clearing out the soldiers who were able to break through the gate.

The High Priest approaches the scene, stroking the chocolate colored ears of the kitten perched on his shoulder. "Kill him…" He says, calmly, as the soldiers drag Grand Marshal Barren and throw him at the priest's feet. "And kill all his men." He adds, pointing towards the marshal's fleeing soldiers.

"Aye, my lord." A knight replies, as they ride towards the retreating troops.

"What are you doing?" Simon asks, sharply. "Since when does the Order cut down retreating soldiers?"

"It must be done," Tobin sighs. "Shall we let them run off and regroup, mount a counterattack?"

"We could take them prisoner. This is murder!"

As Sir Simon screams, the marshal's head is severed with one clean swipe, falling to the ground as his body crumples.

"They are the murderers." Tobin says, "They killed our knights. Probably drug them from their beds as they slept. And you would take them prisoner…? Look around, do you see any crops growing? What do you propose to feed these prisoners?"

"I don't know, my lord." Sir Simon stammers, "But this seems wrong."

"Do not make me regret promoting you to the White Knight, and do not forget, there are many others who would love the position." Tobin hisses. His eyes narrowing to slits, as the kitten playfully bats at his ear lobe.

Chion 9

They ride into Panthos, and immediately make their way to his father's establishment. The first and largest branch of the Antissi family banks.

A beautiful woman stands inside the front entrance, greeting them as they enter. "Hello, honored customers. How may we assist you today?"

"I am not a customer." Chion says, removing his dusty coat.

"Are you interested in becoming one?" She asks, the smile never fading from her face. "I am afraid only customers may enter the establishment."

"I am Chion Antissi, son of Clion Antissi. I need to see my father."

Unflinching, the woman nearly purrs her reply. "I would imagine that Lord Antissi's son would know that his father has been away on business for months. Now, if you would please see yourselves out."

He looks at Quezada, confusion on his face. "Let's try his home, I guess. I can't think of where else he would be."

They make their way to the outskirts of town, winding through the vine covered hills of the wine country. As they approach the enormous front gate of his father's estate, Chion waves to a soldier on guard.

"Hello, my lord." The soldier replies, "Welcome home."

The guards uncross their spears, allowing him and Quezada to enter the grounds. The house is set back far into the property, surrounded by sprawling gardens, manicured orchards, and rows and rows of grape vines.

"Ridiculous..." Quezada mutters, as they pass by a gigantic fountain cast of solid gold.

The main house is a palace, standing atop a hill, overlooking the beautiful surrounding landscape. Walking up to the front door, Chion notices an attendant rushing out to meet them.

"My lord, welcome home. We did not expect you."

"I am looking for my father, where is he?" Chion asks.

"My lord." The attendant replies, an inquisitive look upon his face. "The Lord Chancellor has not been to this property in quite some time."

"Where is he?" Chion asks, growing frustrated.

"I'm sure I don't know." The attendant answers, "Your father owns many properties, as you are aware."

"Fine then," Chion says. "Prepare rooms for me and my guest, and have dinner arranged."

"Of course, my lord." The attendant replies, returning to the palace.

"At least we have somewhere to stay." He says, to Quezada. Shrugging his shoulders and loading his pipe.

The next morning, Chion wakes up in his oversized feather bed, wrapped in silk sheets and blankets. He dresses himself in clothes from his youth, now two sizes too small for him. Large double doors lead from his chambers to the gardens. He opens them, letting in the cool morning breeze.

Outside, he sees Quezada relaxing in a hot spring nestled in the garden. An attendant brings him a drink, then clears away a devoured setting of food.

"Good morning, my lord." The attendant says, with a smile. "Will you take breakfast outside?"

"No, thank you." Chion replies, dismissing the man.

"No?" Quezada asks. "It is delicious…"

"I grew up here, I know the food is good. Do you not care that we can't find my father?"

"Honestly, no. I don't care." Quezada answers, taking a drink from his glass. "I am going to stay right here. The water is great, and Jero most likely has every assassin in the Empire out there looking for us. The last thing we need to do is draw attention." He takes another drink, then smacks his lips. "So have some breakfast and get comfortable, we could be here for a while."

"No. I am going into Panthos, to the Hall of the Twenty. My father is the chancellor, the head of the oligarchs. Someone there has to know where he is. He can't have just disappeared."

"Do what you want…" Quezada says, sliding deeper into the water. "When they catch you, don't tell them I'm here."

Chion picks a stallion from the stables and rides into town. The streets are bustling, yet pleasant, as he makes his way towards the heart of the city. The Hall of the Twenty is a large temple, where the leaders of the Plateau meet to govern their realm.

Pulling up in front of the hall, Chion dismounts and makes his way inside. The building seems nearly empty, disheartening him as he winds through the corridors looking for someone he recognizes.

He sticks his head into the assembly room, but it is dark and silent. The oligarch's private chambers are locked when he tries the door.

Chion asks an attendant, lazily sweeping a nearby corridor. "I am looking for Lord Antissi. Do you know where he is?"

A shake of the head is his only reply, as the attendant continues to sweep in silence.

"No... Are any of the Twenty here?"

The attendant quietly shakes his head again, before giving his work a contented look of approval and turning to leave the room.

Chion gestures rudely as the man walks away, then returns the way he came, making his way back outside.

He notices a tavern across the street, so he stops inside to have a drink. Hoping to find someone who might know where the oligarchs had disappeared to.

The tavern is immaculately clean, and luxuriously furnished, standard for the area. He sits in the corner, surveying the room from a chair almost as large as a couch. A server promptly arrives to take his order, then leaves to go pour him a drink. When the server returns, Chion casually asks him about the oligarchs.

"They have been away for a long while." The server answers.

Looking up at him, Chion hears the man thinking, *'Not that I miss them. How is it that the richest men in the city somehow leave the worst tips?'*

"Do you know where they have gone?" He asks, the server.

"No. No, I don't." The man says. "Though, I heard… Sorry… I shouldn't say."

Focusing, Chion listens to the man's thoughts again, fishing for what he wants to know. *'They say those cowards are hiding, waiting in safety to see if the Emperor attacks us or not.'*

"No," Chion replies. "You shouldn't say."

The sound of breaking glass crashes from across the tavern, drawing the server away. Looking up, Chion sees a burly doorman throwing a skinny patron out the front door. A young man he recognizes follows behind, finishing his drink before exiting as well.

Chion leaves some coins on the table, more than enough for his unfinished drink. Outside he sees the young men making their way down the street. One of them stumbles, while the other tries to keep him standing.

Is that…? He runs to catch up with them. "Matio?"

Matio looks at him, his eyes glazed over. "Chion! So nice… *Hic…* Nice to see you. Do you remember Andrew?" Matio gestures drunkenly to his companion.

"Of course, good to see you again." Chion says, extending his hand.

Andrew looks at the hand, like one would a snake ready to strike. "Good to see me?" He glares in disgust, before beginning to scream. "GOOD TO SEE ME!? Your friend, Jero, destroyed Seacliff! He destroyed my home! My parents... Lord, my parents... They took refuge in Seacliff's central tower, waiting in horror while huge stone monstrosities ripped the foundation out from under them. They sent the tower into the ocean. Men, women, children... My parents... All dead! And you have the nerve to tell me, 'Good to see you?'"

Chion shakes his head. "I had no idea, I'm so sorry... Jero tried to kill Councilor Quezada and I, after he killed my uncle. We have been on the run for over a month, fleeing from the Pillar and making our way here."

"Where is your father?" Matio asks, growing angry. "He ordered his men to guard my father's home, made him a prisoner!"

"I don't know where he is, or what is happening." Chion says, sighing. "I have been trying to find out where he is, but no one seems to know."

"I don't care about them anymore." Andrew says, hatred swimming in his voice. "I am going to end this myself."

In a flash, Andrew swings the bow from his back, and sends a barrage of arrows flying at a nearby statue. The marblework, a gargantuan depiction of Emperor Jero, shatters as the arrows strike.

"How far away can you hit a target from?" Chion asks, amazed by the crumbled stone before him.

Andrew shrugs. "Sixty yards, maybe more with no wind."

Chion nods his head and grins, as an idea begins to take form. "I can get you within sixty yards, but there is definitely going to be wind…"

Senator McKenna 5

He stands on the floor of the Senate Hall, tired and sore from his travels. It has been less than an hour since his return to the city, but this meeting could not wait. There is too much that needs to be done.

"You would have us make you the supreme commander of the A'Tannian Army?" A wrinkly old senator asks, from the back of the room.

McKenna stares at the man, before continuing his speech. "It is time now for strength and unity. If we need to take the army to war, there must be one voice leading it. We cannot squabble and cast a vote every time a choice must be made. We would never win a single battle."

"I just don't see why it must be *you,* that leads them." The old man adds, crossing his arms defiantly.

"The troops are outside, Senator Nassius, awaiting my command. Perhaps you should ask them who their leader is. Who it was that brought them together from all the corners of our realm." He laughs, "Why are we wasting time discussing this? Let us vote."

"The vote must be unanimous." Senator Torbus grunts, from the front of the room.

"That is fine." McKenna replies, smirking. "All in favor?"

"AYE!" The word reverberates through the room, as nearly every man votes for the measure.

"Against?" He asks.

"NAY!" Senator Nassius calls, alone.

Why did he have to make this difficult? Such a frail old man... He gazes at Senator Nassius. "We are going to vote again. This time, *everyone* will vote aye."

The old man's eyes glaze over, as he hears the words, his stare becoming vacant.

"All in favor?"

"Aye." The senators mutter, unanimously.

"You all may leave." McKenna tells the audience. "Except you, Nassius. I would like a word."

Senator Nassius limps to the front of the auditorium, watching the men file out past him. When they are alone, McKenna puts his hand on the old man's shoulder.

"Why must you make things so difficult for me? Every time I try to do something, there you are... Like a thorn in my side. I wanted you all to see what needs to be done, I didn't want to have to force it..." McKenna rubs the sides of his forehead, sighing. "Your apartment is high in the city, is it not?"

"It is," Nassius answers. Staring forward, as if mesmerized.

"Good. Leave here, go home… Speak to no one." McKenna turns, looking out over the city. "When you get there, I want you to throw yourself from the balcony."

The old man's eyes widen in horror, as his lips betray him. "As you command…"

Seaborne 8

The crew loads crates onto the ship, goods destined for the Tradewind Isles. Kevin and Parrot drop a cask of wine in the cargo hold. Cracking open the top when no one is looking, they slurp the blood red liquid from cupped hands.

"Knock it off," Seaborne scolds. "Ya'r gonna get us flogged."

A cough echoes from around the corner, as Reza approaches. The young man smirks, as he sees the sailors' red hands.

"My kind of men!" Reza says, pulling a melon from a nearby box and cracking it in half. He scrapes out the insides, eating a few bites and throwing the rest to the floor, then dips the rind into the cask like a cup. "Cheers!" He says to the men, before taking a long drink.

"They call ya an Icebreaker, what is that?" Seaborne asks, trying to get the information the admiral had sent him to retrieve.

"It's my job…" Reza sighs, "And I detest talking about work. If you want to know what the Icebreakers do, just wait for us to set sail. I'll show you myself."

Damn, Seaborne thinks. He had hoped to find out the Company's secret before setting sail, not knowing when they would have a chance to escape once at sea.

"Don't leave me in suspense…" Seaborne continues, prodding the point. "Tell me now, show me later."

Reza hands him the other half of the fruit. "Have a drink with me, then maybe we'll go up top."

Seaborne fills the rind and knocks it against Reza's, then finishes it in a single gulp. A few drinks later, and Reza is leading him up the stairs to show him how the Sothern Trading Company clears ice from their ship's paths.

As they come topside, Seaborne hears screams in the distance. Shielding his eyes from the bright midday sun, he sees people running into the city. As they draw nearer, their pursuers come into view. An enormous army, charging into Barrenport on horseback.

"That armor…" Kevin gasps. "It's the arms of the Order."

Bells ring out through the city, as men scramble out of taverns and brothels and rush for their ships. A few guards attempt to mount a defense, but they are struck down by lances, swords, flails and morning stars. Causing the rest of the city watch to turn and retreat.

Within minutes, the large host of knights have taken the city. He looks at the men running about the ship, dropping the sails and pulling out into the cove.

Seaborne shakes his head, peering around at the hundreds of ships setting sail simultaneously. Fleeing to the sea.

Heavy morning raindrops pound rhythmically on the roof of
Satia's apartment. Ral lies next to her, stroking the small of her
back as she sleeps. Feeling the warmth of her skin against his
fingers.

She rolls over, giving a girlish groan, stretching out across him
and rubbing the sleep from her eyes.

"I have to go." He says, leaning in to kiss her forehead. "The
others are waiting for me."

"No." She protests, wrapping her legs around his waist and
squeezing tightly. "It's still dark outside! I won't let you go."

"Those are clouds…" He says, with a grin, playfully trying to
push her off. "The sun is hiding up there somewhere."

"Fine…" She says, relaxing her hold and rolling onto her back.
"Leave me then."

He looks at her, laying seductively next to him. Then, fighting
the urge to lean in, he gets out of her bed and starts to dress.

Satia pouts, and turns over. "Well, I am going back to bed. It's
going to be yet another long night."

"Sleep well." He says, kissing her head as he leaves. "I'll be
back tonight."

He makes his way out of her apartment, down through the tavern
below. Opening the front door, he finds two heavily muscled
men waiting in the rain outside.

"The bar is closed." He tells the men, pushing his way past them. Standing to their rear is the man who had sat next to Ral at the bar on his first day back, Senator Calisio.

"Hello." The young senator says, with a smile wide enough to show each of his teeth.

"Good to see you." Ral replies, curtly. "I would love to stay and chat, but the councilors are waiting for me."

"Let them wait, I have a few questions for you." The senator replies, as one of the men places a large hand on Ral's shoulder, holding him in place.

"Your owner was a man named Bentino, no?" Calisio asks.

"Yes, before I was freed." Ral replies, in a growling voice.

"Could you tell us where you were last night?" The senator continues.

Ral looks back at the tavern, "I was here."

"Likely story." The senator says, still smiling. "So you mean to tell me you didn't kill Bentino last night, then throw his body into the reservoir?"

"What!?" Ral shouts. "Bentino is dead?"

"Don't act surprised. We have multiple witnesses who say they saw you do it." The senator sneers.

"No, I was here." Ral shouts. "Ask Satia, she knows."

"Hmm, I am sure the senate will care about the testimony of a girl like, *her...*"

"What does that mean?" Ral asks, his anger beginning to seethe.

The man holding his shoulder replies, "It means they don't care what some streetwalker has to say."

Upon hearing the reply, Ral spins around and lands a punch on the large man's jaw. Sending him crumpling to the ground. He then ducks a blow from the other guard, and pushes forward with his shoulder, sending the man falling to the level below.

"Guards!" The senator shouts, bringing a group of men running around the corner, cutting off Ral's path. "He's resisting arrest, take him!"

Ral tries to charge through the guards, knocking one man down and hitting another in the stomach, causing him to double over. Jumping over a railing, Ral makes a run for it. At the bottom of the steps, a large herd of soldiers cuts him off. Behind him, the first group catches up, blocking off his retreat.

The man he had hit in the jaw comes walking up, holding his face. "That hurt! You… Ass!" The guard screams, as he punches Ral in the chin with a heavy hand.

Falling to the ground, Ral hears the senator whisper in his ear, as the world around him fades in and out.

"She crawled into my bed… No more than a night after you were gone."

With that, Ral blacks out.

Coming to, he finds his arms and legs tied to a solid marble chair in the corner of the Senate Hall. He struggles against the bindings, trying to loosen them.

"Calm down, young man." A senator calls, from above. "Please state your name."

"I am Ral!" He shouts, at the handful of men before him. "If you don't let me go at once, the council..."

"The council no longer has authority here." Senator Calisio announces. "We have left the Empire. You will suffer the consequences of your actions, just like anyone else. No hiding behind the Emperor, like a coward."

"Take off these ropes, then call me coward!" Ral yells.

"There will be none of that." The man closest to him replies. "Bring in the witness."

A scraggly man is pushed into the room, new clothing draped across his filthy body. He walks forward, standing in front of the audience, refusing to look at Ral.

"Tell us what you saw." A senator says, from the front of the room.

"I saw him." The man replies, gesturing back at Ral. "I saw him cut the fat man and push him in the water."

"You are sure it was him?" Another man asks. "Take a look at his face, before you condemn him."

The man looks back at Ral quickly, before turning to Senator Calisio. "Yes, I am sure. It was him."

Calisio grins, as the man leaves the room. "I say we vote now, who finds him guilty?"

"Stop!" Ral shouts, desperately looking around the room for any friendly face "Where is McKenna? He will speak for me, I know it."

"Senator McKenna is raising additional troops." A man calls, from the back of the hall. "To defend us against your Emperor and his armies!"

"Guilty?" Calisio asks, again.

"Aye!" The senators answer.

"Ral…" Calisio says, signaling a group of guards. "We hereby sentence you to death."

Loak 6

"Tell me where they are going next." Loak says, to the councilor kneeling before him.

"The Basket," Sage answers. "The King of the Basket is the father of Jero's late wife. The army and golems are to rest there and resupply, before making the push towards the Frozen City. Jero wants to punish the Barren brothers for not answering his call."

"Then we will make haste for the Basket," Loak replies. "Try to intercept them before any more people are killed."

"Will the King of the Basket raise his armies against us?" Jaties asks, the councilor.

"I am not sure…" Sage replies.

"Why wouldn't he help his own son-in-law?" Jaties presses.

"There are rumors… Reasons why he might not be inclined to help the Emperor," Sage begins. "When Jero was young, it was actually his older brother, Jeron, who was meant to be the next Emperor. A rebellion broke out in the Wastes, and the King of the Basket requested the help of Jero's father, Emperor Johaner, in quelling the barbarian uprising. The King sent his wife and daughter to the Pillar, while he stayed behind to continue the war. The Queen of the Basket proposed that their daughter marry Prince Jeron, after the fighting was finished. The proposal was accepted, and they departed for the Basket to put down the revolt, leaving the daughter behind to wait until after the fighting. During the trip south their ship was destroyed, attacked by pirates. There were no survivors. Jero's father and brother died, and the King of the Basket lost his wife."

"We've all heard the story," Loak replies. "Would that really keep the king from providing support?"

Sage shrugs his shoulders, "That alone, maybe not. But it isn't the end. Jero became Emperor at only seventeen. He refused to help with the uprising unless the king honored the marriage arrangements. Christoph agreed, and Jero married his daughter soon after the war was won. Yet, only a couple years passed before his daughter fell down a set of stairs in the Emperor's Tower, not long after the birth of Prince Relorn. From that day forward, the King of the Basket has become more and more angry, more suspicious." Sage laughs, "To hear the king tell the story, you would think Jero singlehandedly sunk the ship carrying his entire family, then shoved his own wife down the stairs after the birth of their son."

"That might make him reconsider helping…" Jaties says, looking at Loak.

Loak nods his head, "Let's move. Have the men tie our supplies to the golem's backs, we will make them carry everything. It will save time and speed up the march."

One of his commanders gives a nod, the leaves to rally the men.

Loak turns to Jaties, "What if we arrive too late again?"

"All you can do it try, it is more than a lot of men would." Jaties replies, taking Loak's hand. "If we miss them, then we will continue to push on until they are stopped."

The march is long, made lengthier by the icy terrain and constant snowfall. Loak practices using his gift and controlling the golems simultaneously, smoothing hills and casting aside boulders that stand in their way. After a week of constant travel, their columns approach the edge of a seemingly endless valley. An expansive stretch of lush greenery, cut into the tundra.

"The Basket." Sage says, walking to the ledge and peering off. "It is an anomaly, something about the winds and valley walls keeps the Basket warm all year. This is the only place in the Southern Realm where crops will grow."

They begin walking along the length of the cliff, continuing their march, until an encampment becomes visible in the distance.

Loak asks Jake to sneak into the camp, then begins moving the troops into position. Preparing their defenses for a possible attack. It isn't long before Jake returns, breathing heavily from the run back.

"You have to see this…" Jake says, with a huff. "Come on."

They make their way to a nearby hill, looking over the encampment. Loak's stomach turns as he sees the scene below. The soldiers from the Pillar lie strewn about, dead. Blood staining the snow, pooling and melting the ice. Peering towards the center of the camp, Loak can make out Gen and Nal, their dead bodies riddled with arrows, wine goblets in their hands.

"What happened here?" Jaties asks, shaking his head in disbelief. "Who would have done this?"

Jake points to a group of workers in the distance, diligently breaking the golems into pieces with large hammers and chisels. A heavy man with a cane walks around them, laughing heartily.

"That's the king." Sage says, pointing. "I can't believe this... I questioned whether or not he would help Jero, but this is a declaration of war."

"Do you think he means to join with the Barrens?" Loak asks.

"I couldn't say." The councilor replies. "It may be revenge for Seacliff, King Stein was his friend after all. It may be his way of avenging his wife and daughter. You're welcome to go ask him."

Loak shakes his head. "No, I don't think I would like to meet that man."

With a wave of his hand, the golems in the encampment come to life, turning to attention. The men breaking them apart jump up screaming, and run off at top speed.

The king and his guards back up in confusion. Quickly deciding against a fight, they begin to flee as well.

"Our business here is done." Loak says.

He turns and walks away from the valley, the golems marching closely behind.

Kzhee 7

"Where is he…?" Kzhee moans, leaning lazily against the wall.

"It's time to go, with or without him." Maestas says, making his way out of their chambers.

Kzhee follows the councilor, Inzu and Jia in tow. They head through the city, towards the ferries that connect A'Tannia to the mainland.

"Where are we going?" Jia asks, the flame on her shoulder squirming at the sight of the reservoir in front of them.

"My cousin returned to the city, but has already left again. We need to catch up with him, and find out what is happening. I have a feeling we shouldn't return to the Pillar now." Maestas answers.

"You know I trust your intuition," Inzu says. "If you say we stay, then we shall stay."

A commotion breaks out ahead of them, spreading quickly around the reservoir. People scream and cheer as a crowd begins to form.

"What is this?" Kzhee asks, looking at the scene playing out across the water.

The mass of people parts to make way for a group of men being pushed towards the railing. As the crowd moves away, Kzhee can see that Ral is among the men being shoved towards the reservoir.

"What are they doing to him?" Kzhee asks, the sound of fear thick in his voice.

"They're going to throw him in!" Jia screams, taking off at full speed towards the crowd.

They follow closely behind her, trying to get to Ral in time. Soldiers push one of the men off the edge. He screams as he falls, splashing into the calm green water. Something swims towards him, just beneath the waterline. With a ferocious snap, the top side of an enormous set of jaws breaks above the water, then comes crashing down on top of the struggling man.

Another prisoner is thrown from the edge, just as Jia disappears into the crowd. His cries ring up from the reservoir, but are quickly drowned out by screams above. Kzhee looks up in time to see a large blast of fire exploding into the sky. The crowd begins to break apart, people running from the expanding flames.

Amidst the confusion, and the roar of the fleeing spectators, Kzhee notices a guard shoving Ral towards the ledge. Jia's flames fly through the air, but she is too far away from the railing to help in time.

Kzhee throws his hands out towards the guard. As he does, a blast of lightning cracks from the sky, striking the man dead. Ral looks at the guard's corpse with confusion, then jumps out of the way as a herd of people stampede towards him, fleeing from Jia and the raging firestorm swirling around her.

A barrage of arrows rains down from a balcony above, streaking towards Jia. She screams as they nearly strike her, but they are burned away as Inzu sends a wave of purple flames barreling towards the projectiles. Burning them out of the air, and sending molten arrowheads splashing to the ground.

"Run!" Maestas yells, as a group of soldiers sprints towards them, spears outstretched.

They run through the streets, away from the reservoir. Inzu pulls a knife out of her waistband, and cuts the ropes binding Ral's wrists together.

Soldiers begin closing in around them, as they near the edge of the city. "We have to jump!" Inzu yells, hopping off the outer ledge and plunging towards the fast moving river that surrounds A'Tannia.

"I can't do it…" He hears Jia cry, as Maestas and Ral dive off after Inzu.

"Yes, you can!" Kzhee yells, tackling her and sending both of them tumbling into the freezing water below.

Rosemary 7

A loud bang startles Rosemary, as a guard throws the door open and steps inside.

"You are to come with me, now." He says, sternly, escorting her from the room.

"Where are we going?" She asks, worried.

He throws open the door to Tiaries' room, then shouts. "The Emperor wants to see you, at once."

A group of guards wait for them at the lift, escorting the girls up to the throne room. Shuffling into the chamber, she sees Relorn standing in front of his father. A look of fear in his eyes, as the Emperor screams at him furiously.

"There are the traitors!" Jero screeches, as he takes notice of the girls. "Come to pay for their crimes."

"They didn't do anything," Relorn protests. "Please…"

"Her brother," Jero hisses, through clenched teeth, pointing at Tiaries. "He and the Earthmover have taken control of my golems! The Southern Realm has turned its back on the Empire as well. These two will pay for the crimes committed against me!"

"Father…"

"Kill them!" The Emperor screams, spit flying from his mouth.

Councilor Thorne steps forward, his arm slowly extending into a blade of ice, stretching towards the floor. He swings wildly, sending the razor sharp edge whistling towards Rosemary's neck.

"No!" Relorn yells, stepping in the blade's path.

Throne's arm cracks into Relorn's shoulder, shattering as it strikes against the prince's stone skin. The councilor cries out in pain, dropping to the floor and clutching his wrist.

"How dare you!" The Emperor yells, pointing a finger at his son and shaking with fury. "How dare you! Who do you think you are? No one will stand in my way, especially not my own son! I killed my father and brother to take the throne. I killed your mother, when she threatened to leave. What makes you think I won't kill you too!?"

Relorn stares at his father, a look of confusion on his face. "You… What…?"

Tiaries whispers, in Rosemary's ear, "Run!"

The two of them turn to flee, rushing for the door.

"Guards!" Jero yells, "Seize them! Kroonson, take these two to the dungeon. My son as well... Make him watch while you kill them, slowly..."

Soldiers step in their path, cutting them off from the door. Councilor Kroonson walks up behind them, a ball of lightning crackling and pulsating in his hand, webs of green sparks crawling up and down his arm.

"Move." Kroonson says, pushing the three of them forward, a group of guards surrounding them as they make their way to the dungeons.

Approaching the lift, they hear screams and a loud crash coming from behind them.

"Go!" The councilor grunts at the guards accompanying them, sending them back to investigate.

When the guards leave them alone, waiting for the lift to arrive, Tiaries begins speaking to Kroonson. Disgust overflowing in her voice.

"I should have let you die..." Tiaries says, staring him in the eye with an icy hatred. "I told myself, 'He might be mean, but he doesn't deserve to die.' And then I saved you. If I had known who you really were, I would have left you there... I would have made the Empire better for everyone."

Kroonson stares at her as the lift pulls up, ignoring the Earthmover when he asks which floor they are heading to.

"Leave..." He says, quietly. "Leave the Pillar, and don't return."

The councilor turns, and begins to walk away. As he does, Rosemary sees a small blur out of the corner of her eye. In an instant, Rika appears before Kroonson, driving a dagger beneath his ribs.

"Run!" Rika says, before turning back into a mouse and darting away.

"What was that!?" Rosemary shouts, "He was letting us go!"

She and Relorn turn to Tiaries, and watch her coldly stare at the dying man.

"Are you going to let him die?" Relorn asks, as Kroonson gasps out his final breath.

Chion 10

He watches the Pillar come into view, as the Flying City sails through the sky. An attendant fills a hot air balloon on the launch pad, a large pouch of Chion's gold jingling in his pocket as he works.

"We only have one shot at this." Chion says, to Andrew. "You sure you're ready?"

Andrew nods, stepping into the basket below the balloon. Chion follows him, the attendant cutting them loose as the Pillar approaches. They begin drifting through the air, slowly floating towards the Emperor's Tower, high above the top of the Pillar.

"What happens if we fail?" Andrew asks.

"We are in a lot of trouble…"

"What happens if we succeed?"

"We are in a lot of trouble…"

Drifting across the back side of the Emperor's Tower, the huge windows of the throne room become visible.

"Now or never…" He says, to Andrew, pulling a fist sized stone from the floor of the basket.

Andrew nods, picking one up as well. "Now!" He calls, and they throw the stones at the large window.

"Damn!" Chion curses, as his stone bounces off the wall below the window.

Andrew's however, finds its mark. Shattering the large sheet of glass. In the distance, Chion sees Emperor Jero step towards the now open window and look out in confusion. Andrew unslings his bow, as the tower begins to move further away.

"Do it!" Chion says, tensely, as the wind picks up and the window begins to shrink in the distance.

"The wind…" Andrew says, "I don't know if I can."

"Do it!" Chion yells, gripping the rail of the basket.

With a few quick pulls of the string, a volley of arrows set sail towards the tower. Quickly disappearing from sight.

"Did you hit him?" Chion asks, squinting and shielding his eyes from the sun, trying to watch the arrows.

"I don't know… I need two arrows to hit him. The first will only freeze his skin, I don't know if that will be enough." Andrew looks around, as the wind picks up and begins pushing them east towards the ocean. "How do we land this thing?"

"Hmm, I forgot to ask…" Chion says, fidgeting with the flame beneath the balloon. "It has to quit burning eventually right?"

Andrew shrugs, as the balloon crosses over the beach and starts drifting out to sea.

Rika 7

The mouse darts through the walls of the tower, heading for the throne room, Lingonberry's words swimming through it head as it runs.

'I know who you were, before the Emperor's Due. Little assassin girl… Jero must be stopped. I have been planning his fall for many years, but it is understandably hard to kill a man made of stone.'

'If I do it, you'll tell me where my sister is?' She had asked, the councilor.

'I will take you to her myself…'

After weeks of careful planning, she finally felt ready for her task. Stabbing Councilor Kroonson had been an impulse, but she couldn't let him hurt Rosemary and the others.

A cry rings out from the throne room, as she peeks around the scene. The Emperor's throne is tipped on its side, dead and dying men lay around it. Councilor Thorne swings madly, as guards charge towards him from all directions.

"Why, Jero?" The councilor screams. "I have always been loyal."

"The oracle…" Jero yells. "She said you would all turn on me! I am stopping you, before you have a chance."

"I would never!" Thorne calls, cutting down two soldiers approaching from his rear. "You are letting the traitors win!"

"Kill him! Kill him, now!" Jero screams, as the guards begin to overwhelm Thorne, forcing him to retreat from the chamber in a bloody swirl of blades.

As the soldiers pour from the room, pursuing Thorne down the hall, Rika sees her chance. She begins to creep up behind the Emperor, as he makes his way to gaze out the window. A thick purple poison dripping from her blade.

A drop in the mouth, or two in the eye. She thinks, moving silently towards him.

Just then, the window shatters before them, broken by a rock sailing through the opening. Jero bends over to pick up the stone, then looks out at something drifting away in the distance.

As he peers out the window, an arrow strikes him in the shoulder, causing the Emperor to scream out in pain.

"What is this? Guards!" Jero yells, before a second shot hits his stomach.

Rika watches as a crack forms across the Emperor's midsection, splintering through his skin. A third strike hits him, an arrow in the chest, shattering his body in a flurry of ice and bone.

Guards rush into the room, as Rika stands above the remnants of the Emperor.

"It's the mouse girl... She killed the Emperor!" A guard yells.

They rush towards her, weapons swinging.

She turns into the mouse, trying to make for the hole in the wall, but the metal greaves of the soldiers come crashing down around her, standing between her and her escape.

As the men close in, backing the mouse against the window, Rika appears and looks around desperately. Unable to find a way to run, she turns and leaps out the window, soldiers screaming as she plunges. The wind flies past as she falls towards the valley floor.

She squeezes her eyes shut, as the ground races towards her, feeling the air rush beneath her arms.

Jas... She thinks, imagining her sister's laugh.

When she opens her eyes, Rika sees the ground moving quickly below her. But, instead of falling, she is flying. Soaring above the rocky valley floor. The wings of a pigeon, where her arms had just been.

"The Emperor is dead!" He hears a guard yelling, as a group of men run past them.

"What...?" Relorn stammers, his body frozen in place.

Rosemary takes his hand, looking at him worriedly. "Are you okay?"

He looks at her, unsure of what to say. Turning silently, he leaves Rosemary and Tiaries standing in the hall, Kroonson stumbling to his feet next to them.

He's dead... The prince thinks, a strange numbness flooding through his body, as he stumbles towards the throne room. *What does that mean?*

Entering the chamber, he sees dead guards littering the area around the door. At the back, near the window, his father lies dead. Scattered in a dozen pieces across the floor.

Relorn feels nothing, as he picks the crown up from amidst his father's remains. Hearing a gasp, he turns and sees Rosemary walk in. She covers her face with her hands, turning from the carnage.

He walks to her, putting his arm around her shoulders. "Let's go. It's over."

As they leave the room, the Emperor's herald rushes up to him.

"Your highness." The herald says, bowing his head. "The people await you."

He leads Relorn to a balcony, overlooking the city square. Silence falls over the crowd below, as Relorn steps out above them. The prince fumbles with the crown in his hand, bringing it up and placing it on his head.

The herald announces, in his thunderous voice. "All hail, Emperor Relorn! Ruler of all that is, Lord of the Mountains, King of the Wastes, Son of Stone and Scion of the Mountain Emperors!"

Relorn looks out at his subjects, as the deafening thunder of cheers and applause cascades through the Pillar. He can hear their cries and screams, rising up through the air as if on wings.

"Long live the Emperor!"

"Long live Relorn!"

The Assassin 3

He sits, waiting in a damp chamber, spinning a golden coin on the table. A door opens, and the master enters.

"It has been a while." The old man says, taking a seat across from him. "When was the last I saw you?"

"Just before the tourney, master. I was waylaid in my return."

"The Empire is a much different place then it was before the tourney. It is strange to think what changes a year can bring..." The master smiles, placing a very full bag of gold on the table. "I was glad to hear of your success. This is for your troubles."

The assassin takes the bag, feeling the weight of a fortune in his hand. "If you have heard of the death, you must know I didn't take the life."

The master ponders. "Does a man's soul lie on the shoulders of he who takes it? Or with he who orders it taken?"

"Both, I suppose." The assassin shrugs, "I need some time away. I have personal business to attend to, things I've been putting off."

"Of course, of course. Though... I did think of you when we accepted this one." The master places a sheet of parchment before him. "But feel free to say no. There are plenty of others who will gladly take it."

The assassin looks at the contract, his large eyes widening even more as he sees the name of the target.

"Shall I find someone else?" The master asks.

"No." He answers, "Consider it done."

Proof

Made in the USA
Charleston, SC
03 April 2016